Praise for

LAST BREATH

D0957115

continued . . .

"I'm seriously at a loss for words to describe to you how good this book is. It has everything you could ask for. There's tons of action and suspense. But somehow there are tons of sweet and sexy moments in this and it just all works together so well. If I ever have to be rescued by a man—I hope it's someone as dreamy as Daniel. . . . I cannot stress enough how much I think you should read this series and particularly this book. It's one of a kind and you won't regret it." —*All Romance Reviews*

Praise for the novels of
New York Times bestselling author
Jessica Clare

"Blazing hot." —*USA Today*

"Sexy." —*Smexy Books*

"Sizzling! Jessica Clare gets everything right in this erotic and sexy romance . . . You need to read this book!" —*Romance Junkies*

Praise for the novels of
USA Today bestselling author
Jen Frederick

"Sexy and sinful." —*New York Times* bestselling author Katy Evans

"I love these strong characters." —*Sizzling Pages Romance Reviews*

"Wonderful . . . I wholly recommend you read it."
—*Nocturnal Book Reviews*

LAST
BREATH

Jessica Clare
Jen Frederick

BERKLEY BOOKS, NEW YORK

THE BERKLEY PUBLISHING GROUP
Published by the Penguin Group
Penguin Group (USA) LLC
375 Hudson Street, New York, New York 10014

USA • Canada • UK • Ireland • Australia • New Zealand • India • South Africa • China

penguin.com

A Penguin Random House Company

LAST BREATH

ISBN: 978-0-425-28151-2

PUBLISHING HISTORY
Pear Tree Publishing eBook edition / March 2014
Berkley trade paperback edition / March 2015

PRINTED IN THE UNITED STATES OF AMERICA

10 9 8 7 6 5 4 3 2 1

Cover design by Meljean Brook.
Interior text design by Kelly Lipovich.

To D. S. Linney and Heather,

thank you for your beta reads and

spot-on advice at improving this book.

To Meljean Brook, for being an amazing

author, designer, and friend.

REGAN

I never really knew what misery was until the day I was kidnapped and sold for being in the wrong place at the wrong time. Two months later, I'm at a brothel in Rio when I meet Daniel Hays. He says he's here to save me, but can I trust him? All I know of him is that he's tough, sardonic, and has a tendency to solve every dispute with his gun. Yet he's the only safe thing in my world, and I know it's wrong to fall in love with him, but I can't seem to help myself. He says he'll protect me until his last breath, but I don't know if I should believe him or even if I can.

DANIEL

For the last eighteen months, I've had one goal: to find my kidnapped sister. I've left the army, turned paid hit man, and have befriended criminals all across the globe. In every brothel I raid or every human trafficking truck I stop, her face is the one I'm desperate to see. In Rio, I find Regan Porter, bruised but not broken and still sane despite her weeks in hell. I should leave her behind or send her home, because the last thing either of us needs is to get involved. But with every passing minute, I find I can't let her go.

CHAPTER ONE

REGAN

The man above me pushes into me with a grunt, his weight heavy on my back. I stare at the wall and think of zombies and play a mental alphabet game. I'm a horror movie aficionado, but I can't recall if there are any zombie movies that begin with the letter *A*. *Attack of the Living Dead*, maybe? It's a probable title, but I might be making it up.

The man fucking me squeezes my ass and bites out something in a foreign language. Portuguese, maybe. I ignore him and mentally continue sorting through my list of zombie movies. There's *Dawn of the Dead*, of course. *Night of the Living Dead*. *Shaun of the Dead*. *Land of the Dead*. But I can't think of a single movie that begins with *A*. *Arrival of the Dead*? *Anarchy of the Dead*? Surely someone's had a movie called *Arrival of the Dead*, haven't they? Pretty sure there's a *Return of the Living Dead* out there, so if they're returning, they have to arrive at some point. Right?

Someone should really get on to the whole *A* title thing. I shift my hands on the floor, thinking. Okay, now I can't think of anything with the letter *B*, either. Jeez. I suck at this game.

The customer squeezes my hips painfully, drawing my attention back to him. "*Cadela*," he snarls out, smacking my skin hard enough to sting as he drives into me again. He's deliberately trying to hurt me, but in the last few weeks, I've become amazingly good at tuning men out.

At least from this angle. When they shove their rubber-covered dicks into my mouth, it's harder to push the world out and keep my mental narrative running. That's usually why I bite. Most have learned not to stick their dick in the American girl's mouth because she's a biter, but occasionally, I have to remind them.

The man shoots an angry stream of words at the back of my head and pulls on my hair, but I still ignore him because I know it will piss him off. The men that buy my time want a girl that struggles. One that weeps and cries. Pussy is a dime a dozen in Rio, or so I am told by the brothel madam, but fucking a captive American girl that will fight you and weep? That is something special, and they pay extra for that.

And because they do pay extra, I do my best to ignore them, even when they're hurting me.

He saws into me, slamming his body into mine so roughly I tumble to the thin, dirty mattress that has been my home for the last few weeks—ever since I went to sleep in Russia and woke up here in Rio, nursing a hangover from shitty roofies. Now my owners speak Portuguese instead of Russian, but they still chain my ankle to the wall so I can't escape.

Some things don't change.

Grimly, I press my cheek to the mattress and let him pound into me, ignoring the hand tangled in my hair that pulls a little too hard. He wants me to cry and weep and beg for mercy, so I won't give him the satisfaction. I go back to my mental game instead. Where was I? *B*? Oh wait, *Bride of Re-Animator*. That's a *B* movie for sure. I move on to *C*. *C* is an easy one. *Children of the Living Dead*. *D* is easy, too—

The man pulls out of me and drags me up by my hair, shouting at me now. He wants my attention, and I'm not giving it to him. When he pulls me up to his face, screaming, I give him a thin, pained smile and shoot him the bird. *Fuck you*, I think. *You're not getting tears from me.*

I cried a lot in the beginning. I never understood what was happening, really. What I had done to somehow get kidnapped and sold like I was nothing.

All I knew was that I'd driven my roommate Daisy to work one afternoon and I'd settled down to study. I'd borrowed her phone because mine was lost, and I had it on me. Daisy was supposed to call me when she was ready to leave work.

An hour after I dropped her off, two men had showed up at the door. Two tall, frightening strangers in suits with cold eyes. One was blond and enormous, and the other one was slim and ugly. They both had thick Eastern European accents, and I immediately regretted opening the apartment door. By then, it was too late. They'd forced themselves into the apartment, bound and gagged me, and then dragged me into their car. Thirty minutes later, we went to the gas station where Daisy worked and they grabbed her, too.

Later, I was told that Daisy's boyfriend was mixed up with the wrong people, and that was why she had been taken.

Me? I had been taken because I had Daisy's phone . . . and because I had a pretty mouth.

Daisy and I were hauled onto a private plane, and before long, I was dragged in the back and raped by the ugly one. Yury. I fought him a little, but he drugged me into a stupor. I guess he didn't care if his girls struggled or not.

That was about all I remembered. Then, two days later, I came out of the drugged stupor and realized that I was sore all over from Yury's attentions. I was in a small hotel room, and I was alone with one of Yury's new friends, who also raped me.

I loathed myself for letting him do such horrible things to me. I wasn't a virgin, but I wasn't all that experienced when it came to sex. I'd had sex with my boyfriend, Mike, but no one else. Now here I was, having sex with two men against my will.

Yury never came back. His friend did, though. And after he raped me again, he put a bag over my head, shoved me into a car, and drugged me. It seemed that I had been stolen twice now. Once from the States and now this man was stealing me from my original kidnappers. The shit just kept piling on around here.

The next thing I knew, I'd woken up in a Russian brothel, chained to a wall.

I was terrified, not only for myself, but for poor Daisy, too, who was utterly sheltered and innocent. She was somewhere out there, likely living through the same hell that I was. She could be dead, even.

In the beginning, I told myself that someone would find us. That Regan Porter, all-American college student from Minnesota, couldn't fall off the face of the earth and not have someone looking for her. Not the girl who once thought her biggest fear was driving into a deer in the middle of the night.

Finding me and Daisy would take time, I told myself. The police were bound to come looking for a pair of American girls that vanished, weren't they? My boyfriend Mike wouldn't give up on me. Neither would my family and friends.

So I clung to hope.

I cried all the time the first week in the brothel, and I hoped. I cried every time a man touched me; each rape felt like it was the first one. I cried every night, biting down on my knuckles to stifle my sobs. And I fought back when they touched me because if I gave in, it wasn't rape, right?

I stopped crying once I realized two things.

I realized no one would be coming. No Daisy. No Mike. No one. They left me here to rot. I had vanished and no one would find me, ever.

I realized, too, that the men that paid to fuck me? They liked it when I cried and fought. They got off on that just as much as they got off on shoving their dicks inside me.

After that, I learned to mask my emotions a bit more. I learned to mentally shut out what men were doing to my body, protecting my mind. They could have my body all they wanted, but that would be all I would give them. So I distracted myself. I rewrote horror movies in my head. I recast roles of my favorite films, switching out actors and actresses and replaying scenarios in my mind. I made up games, like the alphabet one, naming films I had seen and characters from B movies.

I did everything I could to distance myself from what was happening to my body.

Eventually, it wasn't so bad. I guess. If I didn't pay attention, I wouldn't remember faces. Wouldn't remember men slapping me in the face and yelling for me to put up more of a struggle. I almost forgot that my ankle was chained to a beam in the wall and that I was a prisoner. I lived inside my head.

And I don't let myself think about the men. They are nothing to me.

If they like fighters, I don't give them a reason to be rough. The new Regan won't fight. Won't even pay attention.

Sometimes, though, they are tougher to tune out. Like now.

The man grabs my hair and drags me to my knees, yelling obscenities in my face. He slaps me across the mouth, and I taste blood.

I want to claw his eyes out, but he'd like that too much. He wants me to fight. I am always at a disadvantage when it comes to these men. If I fought, I'd end up with my cheek pressed to the wall as they raped me harder than before. Fighting is never the answer.

Usually.

The man leans in, his face ugly and lined from too much time in the sun. His brows are thick, and he smells sweaty. "You," he says in halting English. "Eat my dick."

"Didn't they tell you?" I say. "I bite." And I click my teeth. I'd bitten two men before they got the idea and started warning clients. "Your loss."

The man gives me an ugly grin and reaches behind him. He pulls a gun out, cocks the hammer, and holds it to my temple.

My breath hisses out of my lungs in terror.

He's not supposed to have a gun in here. He's not supposed to have a gun, and I'm not supposed to get damaged by the customers. Of course, it's a bit too late for anyone to argue.

"You scared now?" he asks. "Eat my dick. No bite. I paid good money." And he pushes the gun against my temple, harder. His hand twists in my hair and drags my face downward.

I still want to live. The tears I hate pool in my eyes and stream down my cheeks. "Please don't kill me."

His smile grows broader, and he directs my face toward his condom-sheathed dick again.

I don't fight.

After he is gone, I vomit the contents of my stomach into my piss bucket and curl up on my mattress, staring at the wall and crying. I always cry after they leave. It's my release. I try to think of zombie movies—I never got past *D* earlier—but my mind is in shock at the moment. The gun flashes through my mind, and I swallow hard, thinking of the click of the hammer.

Swallowing reminds me of his taste, the mix of sweat and latex that seems burned in the back of my mind, and I lunge for my bucket again.

Someone comes to the door a few minutes after I finish puking for a second time. A knock and then the door cracks open. "Regan?"

It is one of the workers here. Alma. She's nice to me. I sit upright, pushing my hair out of my face. "Hi."

She looks around anxiously, then smooths her gray maid's uniform. She wears it every day, and it, along with her nervous demeanor, tells me that she only works here in a cleaning capacity. "Senhor Gomes sent me. He says you will see a very special friend of his after you clean up."

"Oh goody," I say in a flat voice. I know what that means. It's the man that I see even in my nightmares.

I don't know his name, but I first saw him in Russia. I'd been at the brothel for a few weeks and was still working on tuning out my "clients" when I'd met Mr. Freeze.

Mr. Freeze was different.

At first, I was excited to see him when he came in the room. He looked American and, better yet, spoke with a nasally accent I attributed to New England. If he was American, he was here to save me, right? The fact that he was pale, ice-blond, and remote-seeming didn't bug me. Nor did the fact that he was wearing such an expensive suit and was followed by a rather frightening body-guard with a massive form and hooded eyes. I didn't care who he was hanging around with as long as he got me out of here.

He'd entered my room, a flicker of interest in his eyes as he regarded me from my place huddled in the corner. "Stand up so I can look at you."

My heart had sunk all over again. Those weren't the words of a man who was here to save me.

So I'd ignored him. Scared or not, I wasn't performing tricks for any man.

It had been a mistake. The bruiser had immediately charged forward, grabbing me by my hair and hauling me to my feet. I'd screamed, but no one came running to see what was wrong. No one cared what happened to me when Freeze had me.

I soon learned that no one approached Mr. Freeze. Everyone was terrified of him.

He dragged on plastic surgical gloves and then proceeded to examine me like a racehorse. As his bodyguard held me upright, his hand moved down my legs, checked my thighs, my pussy, my ribs, and my breasts. And then he made me open my mouth. To my surprise, he pulled out a flashlight and examined my teeth.

"Are these your real teeth?" he asked me. "Do you brush twice a day? And shower?"

"Fuck off."

He slapped my face and grabbed my chin, careless of the blood dribbling from my split lip. "Answer me."

I didn't answer. I tried to bite him instead.

He slapped me again, and this time it left me reeling. "Answer me. Do they shave you or have you had laser treatments?" He lifted my arm and examined my armpit, then bent to study my pubic hair again. "Natural blonde. That's good."

It was like I wasn't a real person to him. I was a doll he was checking out to purchase. Or a car. "You want to kick my tires before you take my ass around the block?"

He pulled back and gave me a look so cold that I knew immediately that I'd made a mistake. Now I was dead.

It had been a good run . . . for a while anyhow.

But Freeze only looked at his bodyguard and nodded, and the man released me. I sank to the floor and wrapped my arms around my body, waiting for the inevitable rape.

It didn't come. Freeze and his guard talked for a long minute in Russian, the words sounding strange in his mouth, though I noticed that no one dared to correct his pronunciation. Then the bodyguard left, and Mr. Freeze stared at me with those cold eyes, watching me.

The Russian housemother came into the room a few minutes later with the bodyguard, and she was clearly nervous.

"This one," Mr. Freeze said in English. "I like her. I will take her."

"Fuck you," I spat from my corner of the room. He wasn't here to save me at all. He was here to fucking groom me. What an *asshole*.

"Very well," the housemother said. "You know her price."

"It is a rather high price for one that bites," he said in a chilling voice. "She nearly took off my finger."

The housemother stopped in place, and then she shot me a killing look. I was going to be punished, I knew it.

"You know how I like my girls," he told her. They're still speaking in English, which means he wants me to hear this. "Clean and broken. This one is not clean, nor is she broken."

"We will keep her clean."

"And?" He waited.

"I know where we can send her," the housemother said quickly. "Give Senhor Gomes a month and he will have her gentle as a kitten."

"A month," he agreed. "Until then, I want you to have her brush her teeth three times a day. Vitamin supplements with her food. Bathe her daily and make sure someone shaves her twice a week. No hitting her in the face. Condoms for every client. And no drugs. Not even if she asks for them."

The housemother nodded.

Mr. Freeze got back to his feet and left the room. "I will return to check on her."

I figured out after that night that Freeze had a blonde fetish of some kind and he liked me. Lucky, lucky me.

He returned once more while I was in Russia, checking my teeth and body and *tsk*ing when I tried to bite the fingers he put in my mouth.

The next week, though, everything changed. After three weeks in the brothel in Russia, men came after me with needles full of drugs and a sack they shoved over my face. I'd been terrified, thinking that I'd outlived my usefulness as everyone's favorite captive American pussy, and now they were going to kill me.

I'd fought, but they'd drugged me before I knew what was happening.

When I woke up, I was in my current room, my ankle chain locked to a new wall, and a dirty mattress in the corner for me. The room was no bigger than a walk-in closet, with a cracked tile floor that slanted toward a drain at the far end of the room and a nice corner bucket for me to shit and piss in. An industrial-sized box of condoms was set at the foot of the bed. There were cracks in the ceiling and no windows. I hadn't seen the sun in weeks. I wondered if I'd ever see it again.

My new owners had given me clothing, though—an American flag string bikini covered in beads and itchy sequins. And they talked loudly in a different language. By listening at my door, I figured out that I was now in Rio de Janeiro.

And the Rio brothel was run by Senhor Gomes. I remembered that name—Freeze had mentioned it.

Being Freeze's new little plaything had apparently gotten me sent here to Rio. But captive blond American pussy was as hot in Rio, and neither Gomes nor Freeze cared who fucked me as long as they didn't mess me up.

Freeze has visited me once while I've been in Rio. I bit and fought and spit in his face. It was like he didn't notice, though. He simply watched me with those cold eyes, checked my teeth, insisted that they wax my eyebrows into shape, and left.

He'd wait for me to be broken.

The customers in Rio are no different than the Russian customers. They like to rough a fighter up. They like to hit and smack around a girl before they fuck her. I'm sure there are nice men out in the world that just want to screw and cuddle, but that's not who come to the whorehouse of Senhor Gomes. They're here because they like to be rough with girls, and I'm here because Freeze wants to break me. But I'm not broken yet.

I sit upright, and Alma comes to me with a towel and a shower cap. We've fallen into habit already, and I move to the corner of the room, above the drain and as far as the chain will let me go. Today isn't shaving day, so I pull my hair into the shower cap and she turns on a water hose that is connected to the sink in the room. She hoses me down like an animal, and I feel a little more of my humanity die with this ritual.

Paying customers don't want to touch a dirty whore. Everyone uses condoms, not just because Freeze says so, but because they don't want to catch anything I might have. Fuckers.

Once my awful shower is done, I towel off, trying to ignore the fact that the towel smells like someone else's perfume. I don't want to think about how many other whores have used it before me. I let down my hair, and she hands me my American flag bikini again. It's faded and grimy, but I never get to wear it for long.

Then, I'm given a travel toothbrush and toothpaste, and I brush my teeth obligingly, then spit into the grate. Ironic that now I get to spit instead of swallow.

Alma gives me an apologetic smile and grabs the towel, refolds it, and leaves the room quietly.

I curl up on the mattress, hugging my legs to my chest, and wait. There will be another man soon enough, and then Freeze, so I enjoy the moment of silence while I can. My lip hurts, a bit puffy from where the last man hit me, and I touch it with my fingertips, wincing.

Then, I lay my head back against the wall, thinking. My mind is filled with the gun and the man I was forced to service, and my stomach roils uncomfortably again. I swallow hard and force myself to think of zombie movies, instead. *E.* I don't know what movies begin with *E*. This one will require some thought. Maybe something with *Enemy* in the title.

I ponder this for minutes, staring at nothing, when there is a knock at the door again. I get to my feet automatically. God, I hope it's not the man with the gun again. I don't think I could stomach seeing him twice in one night.

But when the door opens, it's not Freeze.

The man that steps in is unexpected. He's accompanied by Senhor Gomes, the master, a man I have only seen once but hear about all the time. Gomes looked me over when I arrived, and then left, as if I were an uninteresting piece of property.

The man with him is tall, good-looking, and wears a casual suit. He's got nice brown hair, sharp eyes, and I can tell immediately from the cast of his features that he's American.

What the *fuck*. Not again. Not another American jackass. It doesn't matter if he's American—he's here to rape me like all the others before him. Except this time? I'll know all the nasty, shitty words he yells into my ear.

And later, when he's done with me and leaves, I'll feel even dirtier because he's only made things worse.

He looks me over, his gaze sliding to my star-spangled bikini, and I can't help myself. "What's the matter," I ask, "international pussy not good enough for you?"

CHAPTER TWO

DANIEL

She's a biter. That the warning given when I point to the blonde with the glazed green eyes in Senhor Gomes's book of whores. He shakes his head and says that he has access to dozens of others that are better and all willing to engage in whatever perverse activity I want. He brags that there isn't a sick sex act I can think of that Gomes can't fulfill. I like home cooking, I tell him. A Texan in Rio sees a lot of beautiful Brazilian women, but sometimes you want a little star-spangled banner in the rotation.

He nods as if this makes sense to him, but I think it's the money that I'm flashing that he understands. We walk up to the second floor and down a narrow hall toward the back, a windowless part of this brick-and-metal building. I can't call it a home or even a brothel. It's a dingy place where men with deep perversions but shallow wallets can get their rocks off.

I don't want to have sex here, I've explained to Gomes. I have a thing against hellholes and having sex in them. I wave around a lot of cash, and Gomes nods and asks no more questions.

We're a strange parade—Gomes, me, and some house mom trailing behind. He stops at the second-to-last door and removes a key.

I've seen pictures of Regan Porter before, and not in Gomes's look book, but nothing prepares me for her full-fledged, magazine-quality beauty. She hasn't been eating well; her delicate bones are beginning to look sharp in places—at her shoulders, ribs, and hips. But there's no denying her breathtaking looks. Her blond hair is damp, and small strands stick to her perfect skull. Her oval face, with its pink cheekbones and lush lips, and eyebrows that look like wings, stands out like a piece of fine china at a flea market. Though she's thin, there's a delicious curviness in the slope of her side as it dips into the waist and flares back out to form a cuppable roundness at the hip. And those endlessly long legs.

Shit. I close my eyes and swallow. No decent man would be standing here thinking about those legs wrapped around his waist. But then again, I'm not decent. I'm no longer army sniper, Special Forces Daniel Hays who may have once been lauded as a hero for killing insurgents in Afghanistan. Now I'm Daniel Hays, mercenary who kills people for money and spends all his spare time in brothels and flesh dens like this one. Decency is a word I don't even know the meaning of anymore.

It's been too long since I've had a woman. That's my only excuse. That and I'm becoming the monster that I'm hunting. I focus on the bruises on her knees that are scraped red and raw from time on the floor and the manacle around her ankle. Any feelings of arousal are jettisoned by the obvious signs of abuse.

Glancing sharply at Gomes, I wonder how he's come to possess a beauty like Regan Porter. Gomes is a small-time flesh peddler, stuck up here in the slums, with a house full of females—half of which are missing their teeth or are too old or too broken.

He usually gets what the market calls secondhand goods, the girls that no other house wants. But Regan Porter is gorgeous, and while she looks a little run-down, she's still model beautiful with big pink lips and wide green eyes.

"Nice tits." I smirk for Gomes's sake, and her shudder of disgust only feeds into my growing belief that I'm as dirty as the flesh trader beside me. The dark edges of the world that I now inhabit are seeping into my skin like an oil slick covering an ocean. I shouldn't want to touch her. And if I have to fuck her in front of Gomes to get her out of here—I don't even let myself finish that thought.

There's still life in her eyes. If she's biting and spitting out acerbic insults, there's spirit left in her, and I don't want to be the one to snuff out that last flame. Her eyes convey her hate, and if she had a knife, I'd be sliced from my throat to my belly. I stare back, not because she's fucking beautiful, but because she's still standing. I'm not sure I would've been as strong. I don't know if she sees my admiration or whether she can only interpret varying degrees of lust and degradation, but she sees something. An invisible string spools out between us, and her eyes widen when it hits her like an electrical shock.

For months I've swum in a pool of blood and death and ugly deeds, and to hold on to my sanity and maybe my soul, I've told myself that saving these doves balances the scale. For every life I take, if I save one then it's all a wash in the end. Don't think it's tallied that way at St. Peter's gate, but that's the lie I tell myself so

I can sleep at night and look at myself in the mirror the next day. Regan Porter will either be part of my attempt at salvation or the bloody stone that etches out the words *He Failed* on my headstone.

"She looks like a live one," I say to Gomes, playing up my role as the asshole merc who's just been paid for some godforsaken deed and needs to plow his victory lap into some unwilling broad.

He squints at Regan, tallying up her worth. She's valuable now because I'm willing to pay so much for her, and Gomes doesn't really understand why. "Twenty-five thousand could buy you a harem. Her pussy isn't lined with gold. Let me hook you up with someone different," Gomes whines.

Don't know why he wants to hold on to her so bad, but I can see that he's torn between wanting my money and wanting to keep Regan in the whorehouse.

"I prefer to eat domestic," I say. Gomes doesn't really expect a response, or at least he shouldn't. Buying and selling human flesh requires some discretion, even here in Brazil, where prostitution is legal but houses like these aren't. Gomes and I stare at each other while the bangles on the dirty American flag bikini tinkle in the background. *Don't draw attention to yourself*, I silently command the girl.

The urge to beat Gomes until his own mama won't recognize him washes over me in a red, violent haze. My fist in his mouth, the heel of my boot crushing his dick, would be phenomenal. I've been in and out of these houses of horror for the last eighteen months looking for my sister. She went on her first and only spring break trip and never came back. I was in Delta Force, playing sniper, when I got the news. I arrived home to find my mother distraught and my dad . . . fuck, I'll never forget the look on his face. Dad was a hardened rancher who'd held on to his family legacy by the repeated sacrifice of his blood to the land. He'd seen shit and done shit, but the loss of his baby girl had hollowed him out. His eyes looked empty as if the news had sucked his insides dry.

I stayed one night and in the early morning hours of the next day, he walked me out to my truck and told me not to come home until I'd found her. And I haven't found her and I haven't been home. There won't be anything to go back to unless I bring her home.

In the months since my sister was kidnapped from Cancun, I've rescued hundreds of girls either in the sex trade or headed for sale. They've been grateful, traumatized, and tearful. I've never once encountered a mouthy one. Not until Regan. She looks like she might bite off my hand if I try to reach for her.

It took me nearly two months to find her after she was sold from Russia. And that snaps me back. Killing Gomes in a black rage isn't going to keep Regan safe or help me find my sister.

Gesturing toward Regan, I try to get him to speed up this transaction. "We're done talking now. Get me a coat for her. I can't take her outside in that getup. Shit."

Gomes leans out the door and yells to someone to get Regan a coat. "*Depressa! Vai-me buscar um casaco.*"

I cross my arms, looking like I'm seconds away from walking on this deal, when really I have my fingers close to the guns inside my coat. I could shoot Gomes right now, and I kind of want to, but hasty decisions like that would only hurt my situation. I learned that early on. You can kill a Gomes, but a dozen others like him will rise up from the sewer like an army of rats. If you want to stop something like this, you have to find the source of the rats and cut off the damn head and then cauterize it. But I'll be back for Gomes. I won't be able to sleep at night until I know the only hole he's plundering is the asshole of a demon in the underworld.

The house mom appears at the door and hands Gomes a tissue-thin jacket that won't even cover the tops of Regan's thighs. I rip the thing out of Gomes's hands. He's not touching her again.

"Let's go, sweet cheeks," I command, snapping my fingers toward Regan. She lets out a low, feral growl. I want to laugh in Gomes's face at this—that she's withstood his treatment—but I can't let any approval for her show. Gomes gives a jerk of his head and the house mom scuttles over to unlock the chains around Regan's ankle. As the iron falls away, I see that the skin is scabbed all over. I'm surprised it's not infected. Suddenly the contents of my stomach are at the back of my mouth, and I scrub my hand over my lips to disguise my reaction. I want to throw a blanket over her, shoot everyone, and carry her away.

This is such a goddamn travesty. My tone is sharp and angry. "Put this on." I throw it to her and she catches it almost reflexively, but she's slow as molasses putting on the coat, as if she's weighing whether I'm worse than the devil she knows. Gomes motions for the house mom to hurry Regan up, but I put up a hand to stay the house mom's actions. Regan doesn't want to be touched by anyone. You can read that aversion in every line of her body, which is why I threw the coat to her. I don't need a fight from her. And truthfully I feel sorry for her. God, she is barely a woman—around the same age as my sister, who was twenty when she was taken. Regan is twenty-two or so, Nick had told me. Nick, who sent me here to retrieve her.

"I don't got all day." I point to my wristwatch. It's a reward,

I've told people, for killing some family who had the nerve to tell me no. Half the time a badass reputation gets you out of tight spots better than two guns and a dozen magazines. Although I'd take those, too. I glance over and Regan is still taking her sweet time. "You can either stay here chained to a wall or come with me."

It's no kind of alternative, but I'm banking on the fact that she's currently thinking about a million ways she can escape me once she's outside of this place. She gives a little nod, not really to me, but acknowledging some decision she's made in her mind. I step out and walk away, pretending like I don't care for a minute if she follows. Gomes doesn't move but instead exchanges sharp words with the house mom in Portuguese, thinking, I guess, that I won't understand him. But I do. The ability to pick up different languages and quickly is almost a requirement of being part of Delta Force, and I've spent time in both Portugal and Brazil.

"*Faz com que ela veste o casaco!*" says Gomes, ordering the house mom to help Regan put on the jacket.

"*Eu não posso. Ela vai me arranhar,*" the house mom responds. The house mom refuses, fearing that Regan will scratch her. Regan's a terror even chained to the wall. Her fierceness is metal as fuck, and that almost cranks my chain as much as her legs. Some of the girls I've taken from these places are so broken that they don't see anything but their abuse anymore. Some fall back into the business, working on their own or as part of someone's stable, because they can't function normally. Although what the hell is normal, I have no goddamn idea anymore.

A shuffling sound occurs behind me, and I pause. The steps are light, so they don't belong to Gomes or the heavier house mom.

"You aren't going to like owning me," Regan hisses quietly at my back. If I really were an angry john with a taste for home, I'd backhand her, but my response isn't one of anger but of resignation. I want to shake some fucking sense into her and beg her to make it easier for both of us for one hot second. Instead I grunt because deep down, part of me wants to show her how wrong she is. In different circumstances, if we were alone in a dark corner of some bar back home, I'd back her right up to the wall and tell her that not only would she like being owned by me, but she'd fucking beg for it.

But we're not alone. She's not some college girl slumming it in a hole-in-the-wall outside of Fort Benning, so I don't back her into a corner. I don't slip my leg between her golden thighs, and I don't start sucking on the tender skin at the base of her neck. I don't even turn around to look at her, and I guess this makes her even angrier. "I bite and I don't cry and I'll vomit and pee all over you."

Jesus Hermione Christ. This girl has balls of freaking steel. "Can't wait, baby doll," I say, trotting sideways down the narrow stairs. And for all her threats, Regan is close behind me. I can hear Gomes and the house mom making up the end. I can see the front door and our potential freedom beyond.

"You still want this whore?" Gomes calls out. "I have so many others. This one's too much trouble for you."

I laugh, a sour sound so Gomes knows I'm not really amused. "You took my money, Gomes. I'm not into international pussy, so I'm taking this girl and you're going to be happy with the quarter I dropped for her."

We're at the front door now, and Regan has stopped hissing insults at me because she's stunned into silence by the prospect of escape. "How long you think you will keep her?"

Turning to face Gomes, I place my hand on the door. Down here in the entrance, it's actually more dangerous. Gomes has guards at the door, inside and out. He's having trouble processing that I don't want to fuck in his little shithouse.

"You think I'm paying a quarter for her and that I'm going to just trot her back after an evening?" From Gomes's frown, it's clear that he thinks she is coming back tomorrow. I shake my head. For the money that I've given him, he should've assumed that Regan would be fucked until she's dead. "She'll be back when I'm good and ready to return her. I didn't pay that kind of coin for one night."

"What will you do with her?"

"What do you care?" I ask impatiently. Regan is shivering beneath the jacket, the bangles beating a faster rhythm. Her feet are probably cold on the red clay tiles. Outside she'll be warmer, though, and as soon as we're out of the favelas I'll get her some shoes.

Gomes looks a little ill. "I need her back."

I shake my head. "You let me worry about the disposal of this one. You should worry about the fact you've been spreading the tales about your wares into some dangerous places. Places where *Polícia Federal* might have to take notice. Don't be a shithead and ruin it for the rest of us." *And by the rest of us, I mean you, asswipe.*

I look at the two hired muscles standing inside the front room, which serves as Gomes's office and showroom. It's got a deep red carpet that has stains all over it. I don't know whether it's come or blood, but I'm glad I was wearing shoes when I made that transaction with Gomes thirty minutes earlier. With my hand on the doorknob, I give everyone a leveling gaze. "We're done here."

Gomes looks at his goons and then at me. There's something about me Gomes doesn't like, or maybe it's because he thinks he's losing a valuable piece of property. Second thoughts are all over his face, and I ruck up my suit coat on the side so I can have ready access to my gun, just in case. The goons move toward the door of Gomes's front room and the tension becomes heavier, like dense smog descending over the slums. I calculate my next course of action. Gomes does not look armed. He's wearing a thin cotton Panama shirt and linen pants, wrinkled and splattered with liquid around the ankles. The cotton would reveal any hidden guns at his waist or back. He could have an ankle piece, but I'm a good enough shot that he'd be dead by the time he bent over. I dismiss the house mom. The two muscled guys are my only worries. The entryway is narrow, like the stairs, and we are packed into the foyer like little sardines in a tin can. If a firefight breaks out here, we are all toast. I know Regan doesn't want to be touched, but I need to signal her, somehow, to get behind me.

"I worry about you in the favela," Gomes says. He waves his hand and one of the goons steps forward. "Ricardo will escort you out, to be sure that you get back to your hotel safely."

Or he'll shoot me in the back and take your blond American prize back to the stable. No, not happening, but I'm anxious to get out of the house. Ricardo can be taken down once we are outside. No doubt there are several other thugs along the way that Ricardo intends to meet up with, but we have way better odds outside.

"Whatever," I answer and then throw open the door, hard. It hits Ricardo in the nose and he curses. Behind me I hear a muffled snort. *Good girl*, I think, and then I walk outside with Regan close on my heels.

CHAPTER **THREE**

REGAN

I can't tell if I'm happy or numb with panic. For the first time in almost two months, the horrible, horrible chain is off my ankle. I've been given a coat to wear. It's not warm, but it covers the ridiculous bikini and makes me feel almost human. We're heading outside. I should be ecstatic.

But I can't quite shake the feeling that I'm in bigger trouble than before. They never let me out of my room. Never. The fact that they've unchained me and are letting me walk out with this smooth-talking American who sticks out like a sore thumb can mean only one thing:

He's bought me.

And that could be very, very bad. No one wants a whore for longer than a night. I glance over my shoulder at Augustina, the housemother, and Senhor Gomes, but they look mildly unhappy. I see fear flickering on Augustina's face, and that panicky tightness returns to my stomach.

This man is worse than the place I have just left. I know this. I am starting to suspect, that from the look Augustina's wearing, I am a dead woman walking. I swallow hard. I've longed for freedom, but never to the point that I wanted to die. I want to live. Always.

The American continues to spit rapid-fire Portuguese at Senhor Gomes, and they argue over something as we go down the stairs. I walk, ignoring the fact that the floor is cold on my bare feet and I'm barely dressed. What is going to happen to me now that I have been sold again?

Nothing good, I am sure.

If I want to live, I need to escape this man. I need to get away from everyone—Gomes, Augustina, this new American in the suit. Somehow I need to get away and run. Run until I find someone that will take me to the closest American embassy.

Gomes says something else, and Ricardo steps forward, a big bruiser who works at the brothel. I've had to service him before, and I hate his guts. He isn't coming with us, is he? But it appears like exactly that; he follows us closely. The American asshole doesn't look pleased, either. He slams the front door of the brothel open and smacks Ricardo right in the nose.

I can't help it. I snort with a stifled laugh. I like seeing these jerks get hurt. It soothes my soul. I'd scratch all their eyes out if I could.

The American turns to me and raises an eyebrow, and I give him a challenging look. "Are you going to kill me?"

He glances at the others standing close nearby. They are listening to every word he says to me. "Not today," he says.

That's not reassuring.

I cross my arms tighter across my chest. "Where are we going?" I don't step through the front door even though I can see the dirty street outside, and every instinct screams for me to bolt out of there and make a break for it.

"It's a great little place I like to call Shut the Hell Up and Quit Asking Questions. Now, come on." He gestures at the wide-open door. There's a hard tone in his voice. "Stay close to me. You won't like it if I have to chase you."

Ominous words, but I'm not scared of him. What's the worst that could happen? I get stuck here sucking the dicks of strangers? End up in a shallow grave? I feel as if I'm out of choices as it is. You can't really threaten someone with nothing to lose. An hour ago, I would have feared for my life, but if I go with this man, I've lost it anyhow. The scared looks Augustina shoots in my direction are real. She thinks I am already dead.

I need to do something. The open door, so close, is a challenge I can't resist. I take a few steps out, following the man in the suit. He's tall and clean-cut. I'd find him handsome enough if he wasn't here in a Brazilian brothel purchasing me. Since he is, he's clearly a deviant.

As soon as I step outside of the front door, a barrage of sensations hit me. The streets are narrow, a tight cluster of haphazard slums. The night air is cool and crisp and carries a hint of garbage. But I feel a breeze ruffling my hair and nearly choke on tears. I am outside. Escape and freedom are so close that I can feel them in my grasp. I tremble all over, my toes curling on the dirty, cracked pavement lined with trash.

"You cold, sweetheart?" The American puts a big hand on my shoulders, urging me on. At the end of the street, I see a taxi waiting, and he gives me a little push toward it.

I stumble forward, my legs stiff, and jerk away from his hand, whirling around. "Don't touch me."

As I turn, I see that Ricardo is moving ahead, too, and his hand is in his jacket. But the American has obviously used me as a distraction. Before I fully realize what is happening, the American's hand is already on his gun and it's pointed at Ricardo's forehead.

"Nope," says the American quietly, his intense focus on Ricardo's face. "Don't even think about it unless you want your brains on the pavement. Drop it on the ground."

I freeze in place, watching the men. The first thought that flashes through my mind is that if I had a gun, I'd have all the power. A gun can make a person do anything, by waving it around. And I'm so tired of being on the other end of the gun. One day, I'm going to be the one holding the weapon, and someone else is going to weep and beg for me not to hurt them. And I'll think about it.

I'll have to be quicker to get the drop, though. The American man is so speedy with that gun, so deadly. He moved faster than I could imagine.

I'm so dead if I go with him.

Ricardo slowly reaches into his pocket and lets his gun fall to the ground, gaze on the gun barrel pointed between his eyes. As I watch, the American stoops to grab it, does something with the gun, and the entire magazine of bullets drops to the ground. Two more swift motions and the barrel is separated so the entire thing looks like a dissected animal in pieces on the pavement. Just like that, Ricardo has been disabled.

I stare for a moment, and then I run. I bolt like all the devils in the world are at my feet. Not toward the taxi and where the

American wants me to go—down the street, into the slums them-selves. The houses here are narrow and tight, and the streets equally so. I will lose myself in the maze, get away from both brothel and American psycho. When it's safe, I'll emerge.

I dart down an alley, my bare feet slapping on the broken con-crete of the street. "Hey!" the American calls after me. "Wait!"

I don't wait. I'm not stupid. I turn down a trash-strewn alley and slam away, running like I never have before. *I'm free*, my brain calls with every beat of my feet on the pavement. *I'm free. I'm free.*

Steely arms grab me at the waist, hauling me aside so roughly that my entire body flails, and a man's arm slams the breath out of my lungs. I choke and gasp as a big, sweaty-smelling man presses my body against his, his hand moving to my neck and pinning me against him. I start to fight. A moment later, there is a gun pressed to my forehead.

It's not the American. It's someone new.

Two guns to my head in one night. If I were in a horror movie, I'd be screaming at the screen at how stupid the heroine is. A laugh chokes from my throat and ends up as a sob.

The man holding me strokes a hand down my throat in a way that makes my stomach revolt. He murmurs something in Portu-guese, and then says something to a friend that emerges from the nearby shadows. I catch the word *Gomes* in their foreign chatter. These men work for the brothel. They are retrieving me.

I'm not free after all.

A loud pop sounds in my ears. Behind me, the man slumps and falls to the ground. A second pop, and I turn. His friend falls to the ground, too. I blink in shock, chest heaving as I try to pull air back into my lungs.

The American strides forward from the far end of the alley and gives me an irritated look as he reloads his gun, a long, skinny barrel-looking thing on the end of it. A silencer, perhaps. "I guess I should thank you for flushing them out, but all I really want to do is choke that skinny neck of yours. Can we quit with the bullshit and get out of here, already? As much as I love the atmosphere of the favelas and all, I'm tired, dirty, and hungry, and I'd really like to call it a night. So can we do that, please?" His voice is laden with sarcasm. "Or did you have any other blind alleys you wanted to charge down, half-naked and barefoot?"

I stare blankly at him for a moment, and then I shake my head. "I-I'm good, thanks."

"Any other genius plans for escape?" he asks, pulling the silencer off his gun and tucking it back into his jacket. "Because I'd really prefer not to spend all night chasing your ass, Regan."

A bitchy retort rises to my lips, and then I snap it back as I realize—"How . . . how did you know my name?"

"I know a lot about you. What, you think I like trolling the slums of Rio de Janeiro for blondes because I can't get laid?" He gestures back to where I came from. "Come on. The meter's running." The man reaches for me again.

I sidle away so he can't touch me, tugging the coat closer. I look at the two dead men at my feet. I should feel something for them, right? Some sort of horror that they died right in front of me? That this man shot at them while I stood here? But all I can think is that they were this close to dragging me back to the brothel.

And this man knows my name. He was looking for me. My heart thuds in my chest. Once. Twice.

Maybe I'm not forgotten after all.

"Who are you?" I ask as I step over the lifeless body of one man.

"Call me Daniel."

DANIEL

Regan is looking at me like I'm going to kill her or, worse, take her to someplace that will make Gomes's brothel look like Disneyland. Not that I blame her. If I were in her shoes I'd be running in the other direction, too. She doesn't know jack about me other than the shit I spouted off in front of Gomes, which was essentially that I was taking her to my hotel room where I'd pound her so hard that there wouldn't be anything left but a corpse. She's unlikely to believe that the only place I'm taking her is to the U.S. Embassy, so rather than waste time arguing with her, I start walking. Actions over words and all that.

The taxi is likely long gone and even if it isn't, bringing Regan back into Gomes's reach isn't an option. He's too interested in her return. Why he's having second thoughts about selling her for the night doesn't add up for me. It's not like Regan's the only blonde in a hundred-mile radius. I'm not even convinced she's the only star-spangled pussy around. She's damn pretty though, and maybe if I were a half-rate, back-alley brothel owner, I'd think a girl like this could elevate my reputation among the expats who like a taste of home. But I'm not paid to think about why. I'm paid to do.

I've located Regan after running around Russia like a fool, freezing my nuts off until the head of the Petrovich *Bratva*, a powerful Russian criminal family, learned that she had been shipped down here. By accident, Vasily Petrovich told me. That's some kind of accident. Vasily had stashed her in a Petrovich house, only someone stole her from there and sold her to some rich dude in Rio. Then when I arrived in Rio, she wasn't with the rich dude but was in Gomes's place. Another week wasted. I just need to get her to the embassy, and then I am on to the important part of my task: finding my sister. Vasily gave me a tip in exchange for retrieving Regan that there was a stream of blond girls from the United States being funneled down to some guy in Rio. One of those blondes might be my sister.

Petrovich should've known I'd come for Regan anyway since Nick was kind of a friend and Regan was his girl's best friend, but instead he gave me two pieces of information. I'm supposed to be looking for some hacker that Vasily wants called the Emperor, but his little task will be put on the back burner until I find my sister.

Wary of me, Regan walks a half step behind. Or rather, I let that distance between us exist. She's more afraid of bogeymen jumping out of the houses or back alleys than she is of me right now, but that could change at any moment. Fear is a good thing. It makes you sharp and aware. Complacency makes you dead.

"How do you know my name?" she repeats.

"Ask me no questions and I'll tell you no lies," I quip.

She curls her lip at me, telegraphing disdain for my humor. But I'm not telling her anything. Who knows what she will tell the folks at the U.S Consulate? If she's smart, she'll tell them everything—including how a tall guy with a black suit and big black guns killed two Brazilians in the slums—and then I can add the U.S. military to the number of people who want to see me captured or dead. The list is long and varied, but I'm still alive and most who've encountered me are not.

Fighting the urge to stare at her is more challenging than I expected. As we walk down the hill, several boys make hooting calls that cause her to flinch and drive her closer to me. I take her in surreptitiously. Only the lights from the homes and the occasional streetlight illuminate our path. The dirt and poverty looks more like quaintness than squalor. And Regan Porter looks like the shiniest rock in the diamond mine. I can't fucking take my eyes off her.

Maybe she's been sent to me as karmic punishment. You can look but don't touch. Or worse, you shouldn't even be looking.

Despite all that she's gone through, Regan is magnetic. Her blond hair has dried in a cloud around her face, and neither the dirt nor the trauma can disguise the oval perfection, high cheekbones, and full lips. My hand rises of its own volition to tuck a few strands of hair behind her pretty, pale little ear. She jerks back from me, wide-eyed, nostrils flaring like a scared wild mustang I've brought in to tame.

And then my dick takes over and my thoughts go on an inappropriate detour thinking about all that pale pinkness riding me and that long blond hair brushing my bare chest. And those plump lips making a perfect circle for my—oh fuck. I am such a fucking asshole. Clenching my hand, I force myself to back off. *Time and place*, Daniel, *time and fucking place*.

"Hurry the fuck up," I bark out. She flinches, and that helps to suppress my ill-conceived desires. I'm not into chicks who don't want me and particularly not those who are scared of me.

But I'm not the only one drawn to her. I should've asked for a paper bag to place over her head, but you'd still see those long legs, the sexy indent of her waist and the thrust of her tits against the tissue-thin coat. It's a good thing the night air is warm because between the swimsuit and the napkin that we're calling a coat, she doesn't have much protection from the elements. I can't even take off my suit coat because I have a brace of guns underneath, but I can do something about her lack of shoes.

Her feet are dirty from both Gomes's place and the unpaved roads. I hadn't expected her to run through the favela. I figured I'd hustle her into the taxi, drop her off at the embassy, and be done with it.

But now we're walking in the back alleys, drawing all kind of unwanted attention, and I can't stop thinking about those tender feet being eaten up by the dirt and stones. Stopping abruptly, I swing around to face her. She makes a small sound, like a wounded animal. I wonder what she thinks I'm going to do out here, throw her down and mount her? Heaving a frustrated sigh, I kneel down to unlace one shoe and pull off my silk dress sock. Shoving my foot back into the rich leather of my shoe, I repeat the action on the other side. Raising one knee, I gesture for her to lift her foot up. "I'm going to brush the bottom of your foot off, okay?" I ask, patting my knee so she knows to rest her foot against my leg. Peering up at her, I can see her big green eyes wide with wonder. Or suspicion. "Look, doll face, I don't have some weird sock fetish."

Her lips are trembling and her eyes are beginning to water. Oh shit. She's going to start crying, and I don't need that. Holy fuck do I not need that. So I pull out the asshole because I sense that she'll snarl back at the asshole but weep at a nice guy. "I'm tired of hearing you snivel while we walk, but if you're going to sit there and cry, I can put it back on."

Just as I suspect, the steel rod returns and she's rigid again. She lifts her foot, pressing two fingers against my suited shoulder. And despite the suit coat, dress shirt, and beater underneath I can still feel the heat, and it's burning a path from the shoulder right down to my groin. I hate myself. I really fucking hate myself.

It gets worse when she lifts her high-arched foot to place it gently on the edge of my knee. My finger itches to trace the curve and fondle the delicate skin behind her ankle bone. My whole body feels on fire. I deserve her disgust, because her back isn't the only thing that is turning stiff as a steel rod. There are so many things I like doing on my knees between a pretty girl's thighs. Things I haven't done in a long, long time.

Carefully I brush off the dirt and pebbles from her foot. I take the time to run a finger, a quick one, between each toe. This ankle has no marks around it but I do a quick once-over around her lower legs before pulling the socks on. From my pocket I pull out a zip tie that I normally would use for restraints and pull it around her calf to hold the sock up. Above me I hear a gasp of breath, and her fingers press into my shoulder. For a moment, I think she's going to take flight, but I don't look up. Not once. Because if I do, I'll have to look at her soft thighs, the hidden V between her legs, her breasts, and by the time I get to her face she'll see the lust in my gaze and have a good reason to run away. So I keep my gaze on her feet.

"Just a way to tighten the socks around your ankles," I explain. When she doesn't move, I take this as assent and tighten the zip tie.

She switches feet without a prompt. This ankle has the scab marks. I inspect the wound. It looks old, sore but not infected. Regan's pretty lucky. From my position I notice handprints on her thighs and any arousal I once felt dies off quick. This girl's been so abused, and what little humanity I have left aches for her. I'm going to kill the man who put those marks on her. Before I leave Rio, I'm hunting him down and cutting off his dick and feeding it to him, one inch at a time. I'll take pictures and send them to Regan.

I hurry up with my cleaning of her foot and slip on the sock, securing it with another zip tie. I sneak a look at her and she's looking half pissed off and half ashamed. I want it to be all pissed. She's got nothing to be ashamed of. "You've got a pretty rocking body, Regan."

"Fuck you," she says. "I'll kill you with your own gun before you get to lay a finger on me."

We both know that she'd never be able to disarm me, but I nod as if her threat has real teeth. "I'll never touch you unless you give me the okay." It's not something I'm making up for her sake. Eighteen months in and out of brothels like Gomes's have made me never want to have sex outside of a relationship where I could be certain that the person I'm having sex with wants it a hundred percent. And given that the last eighteen months have been spent hunting and rescuing and killing people . . . well, the only relief my dick has seen is Rosie Palm. Maybe that's why I've got hard-dick disease around Regan.

"Likely story," she scoffs, and the ease at which she insults me tells me that she's more comfortable with me than she knows or may be willing to acknowledge. It tells me she'll follow me without much hesitation, so we head off, me in my shoes and Regan wearing my socks. It's not ideal, but my shoes would be boats on her, and I don't think she's ready to be carried.

"You ever been to Rio before?" I ask as we wend our way

down the hill. I figure from the increasing noise that we can find a taxi soon.

"No." Then after a short pause she asks with incredulity, "Are you trying to make small talk with me?"

"Would you rather tell me how long you were with Gomes?"

She's silent, so I take that as a no. When we arrive on a main drag, I'm able to hail a taxi and hold the door open for Regan. She hesitates and looks around, weighing her chances of survival in the favela. I shift slightly and pull back my jacket so she can see the butt of one of my guns. She closes her eyes in resignation and climbs in. Smart girl. She's going to be one of those who make it. Many don't. Their time in captivity fucks them up so bad that they fall back into the trade either because their families won't take them in, they need to fund their newly acquired drug habit, or they don't have any other place to go. That's another shitty lesson I learned early on. I'm going to hold tight to this memory so that I can pull the gun away from my head the next time I see one of my failures.

"U.S. Embassy," I bark at the driver and then settle back, resting one hand on the butt of my gun, scanning the streets for trouble as we take off. There isn't anyone behind us, but the sense of wrongness is still dogging me.

A hand grabs at my arm and I twist around to look at Regan, who's only inches from my body. Oh shit. The closeness is generating some warm feelings in my lower body. I wish my conscience had more control over my goddamn body. I clear my throat. "What is it?"

"You're taking me to the embassy?" Regan's voice is high and tremulous, either on the verge of tears or laughter. I nod cautiously. Please don't let it be tears.

She gasps and then covers her mouth. Water begins coursing down her face, and she throws herself at me. "Thank you. Thank you," she repeats, and I feel her soft cheek rub against my stubble-filled one. Vaguely I wonder if I'm scratching her with my facial hair, but mostly I'm wondering where I should put my hands when her supermodel body is pressed against me. Her tits are burning a hole in my chest, and over her shoulder I can see her fine ass waving in the air. I catch the cabdriver looking in his rearview mirror, and I push Regan aside. He doesn't need to see her ass.

"Look at her again and you're a dead man," I bark at the cab-driver. His eyes drop immediately to the road but I hear him muttering in Portuguese that if I didn't want him to look at her ass then I should make sure she wears more clothes.

"Don't like touching a dirty whore?" Regan says bitterly.

Her words don't really register at first, and then I realize she was offended that I pushed her away. I run one frustrated hand through my hair. "A guy like me would be pretty damn lucky to be permitted to touch you."

She snorts. "Nice talk. Doesn't really match your actions."

I can't believe this. She was afraid to wear my socks, but now she's mad I'm not mauling her. I guess I should be happy she's still fiery after all she went through. Gives me hope that she'll go home and live a good life. Although from the sounds of it she needed a new boyfriend. Nick, formerly known as "feared hit man Nikolai Andrushko" and the guy who sent me to find Regan, told me that she had an asshole of a boyfriend. One who didn't even know she stroked herself off while he snored beside her. Per Nick, Regan's boyfriend couldn't give his girl an orgasm if Dr. Ruth were in bed with them giving him step-by-step instructions. At least that was my interpretation of Nick's dour statement that the boyfriend deserved a bullet in the head for failing to pleasure his woman.

To my way of thinking, men who can't give orgasms to their women don't need to be shot, but they don't deserve goddesses like Regan in their beds, either. They should be celibate, lest some cranky Russian hit man goes around putting them into eternal sleep. Fortunately for the dickless wonders of the world who don't care about a woman's pleasure, Nick's too busy boning Regan's best friend back home in Minneapolis to be concerned about killing men who are bad in bed.

"Neither of us is ready for any action." I raise my arm and sniff. "Jesus, I'm ripe. I need a fucking shower." I'm dead tired, and despite the completely wrong thoughts running around my head of Regan nude and spread out like a feast at Thanksgiving, I'm too tired to do anything but sleep. I've been up for about seventy-two hours straight and need some rest before I fall over.

"You're quite the metrosexual, aren't you?" She raises a foot toward me and wiggles her toes. The movement is provocative. My eyes arrow right down the black-silk-clad foot toward her inner thigh, and in the dim light of the taxi there are enticing shadows cast by the valley between her legs. The hide-and-seek nature of the shifting light begs me to reach down and explore . . . I force myself to turn away once again.

"I like nice things. Sue me."

"Why didn't you tell me you were taking me to the embassy?" She nudges me in the knee with her foot. Does she realize how flirtatious she is being? I mean, she's fucking touching me with her foot. That's intimate shit right there. It's a good thing I'm wearing a suit coat. Jesus Hermione Christ.

"Would you have believed me?" I say evenly. Her foot drops away, and I swallow a groan with a heroic effort. *Good job, Daniel.* I give myself a little pat on the back. She has no idea what she's doing because she's thinking about freedom and escape and the good ol' U.S. of A. I'm the dirtbag having dirty thoughts about a girl who I've just hauled away from a whorehouse where she was chained to the wall. And because I can't be nice to her, I snap back, "You wouldn't have fucking believed me."

"Yeah, I guess." Her attention is distracted and I see we've drawn up to the embassy.

"We're here," I say with relief, but she makes no effort to get out. "This is it." I wave my hand out the window. "Consulado Geral dos Estados Unidos."

CHAPTER **FOUR**

REGAN

Hope flares in my heart at the sight of the embassy. I am free. I am steps away from going home. Soon, all of this will be a bad memory and I can return to my previous life. Then, I want to laugh at the thought. I am a scholarship student; all of my grades will be torpedoed by my absence. I'll have to figure something out. Maybe Mike will let me move in with him.

If he can stand to touch me after what I've been through. If he hasn't already moved on and found another girlfriend after my absence. I like to think he's waiting for me, but Mike has never been particularly emotional. I cling to him more than he clings to me. I have no illusions about our relationship.

I stare at the embassy through the dirty taxi window. Once I step out of this car, everything goes back to normal. I'll return to the normal world, a slightly dirtier version of the girl who left it. For some reason, that scares me.

"There you go," Daniel says at my side, voice dry with amusement. "I told you I'd take you to the embassy, and there it is. Don't act so excited."

I look over at him, hiding my uncertainty. "Thank you," I say, hugging my jacket closer. "You don't know what this means to me."

"I can guess."

I give him a faint smile, and I think for a moment that he's a good-looking guy. I don't know what he's doing in Rio in whorehouses, but he's saved me. Impulsively, I lean in and kiss his cheek, feeling the stubble under my lips. I want to recoil immediately at the touch, but I know it's the right thing to do. He likes my touch. His sarcastic gaze softens as he looks at me and he nods. "You stay safe, okay?"

"Okay," I breathe, and turn to the window again, my hand on the door. I can do this. I'll introduce myself as Regan Porter. I'm an American who was taken from my home country, and a nice stranger rescued me from a brothel, and I'd really, really like to go home.

I tighten my grip on the handle and look out the window.

The breath dies in my throat.

There at the front of the embassy is the big bruiser. Mr. Freeze's bodyguard. It's dark outside, but he's standing near the door, and I recognize that bald head and big shoulders. If it was light outside, I'd see those awful, hooded eyes.

He knows I'm gone. Someone's called and let Mr. Freeze know that his favorite dentally perfect whore has flown the coop without his permission. I know as soon as I enter that embassy, I'll be right back at the whorehouse.

I tremble, and then hate myself for it. He hasn't seen the taxi yet. He doesn't know that I'm here. I think for a minute and then turn back to Daniel, the nice-looking American man that has somehow, for some reason, tried to help me escape. I turn to him and give him a faint smile. "Can I ask a question?"

"Shoot."

His words remind me that Daniel is carrying guns. He killed two men tonight that tried to take me back to the brothel. Whoever he is, he's not with Freeze. That automatically makes him safer. "Who sent you?" I asked this earlier and he'd danced around the question.

He gives me a serious look, then glances at the cabdriver, as if to point out that this isn't a safe place to talk. Then he looks me over again. "Mutual friend."

I don't know who he means. I can't think of a single person who would know a killer who hangs out in Rio brothels. I glance up at the embassy doors again. The bruiser is gone, but I know I saw him. I know he's there, waiting for me.

I look over at Daniel again. He's trying not to look at my legs. Trying, and failing. He's clearly attracted to me. I've seen appreciation flash across his face a few times, quickly hidden. He's trying not to be, but it's hard for him.

If he's attracted to me, I can use that. Sex means nothing to me now. Whatever intimacy it might have meant before has been beaten out of me. I can have sex with this man. I can use him to keep me safe from Freeze. This man killed two men tonight. He's dangerous.

"You said you won't touch me unless I want you to," I whisper in a low voice and then bite my lip in a deliberate manner. I notice his gaze flicks there, to my mouth. He's definitely attracted. "Is that true?"

"I'm not a monster, sweetheart," he tells me, and looks almost insulted at the question.

I slide a little closer to him in the car, and my fingers touch the front of his jacket. "Then . . . can I stay with you?"

Daniel looks surprised at my suggestion. No, shocked. His brows draw down, and he flicks a glance at the embassy. "You can't stay with me. This is as far as I go. I'm dropping you off here. I have other work in Rio. Come on." He reaches over my lap for the door handle. "They'll be good to you in the embassy. You don't have to worry."

I press my body closer to his, letting the fear I feel tremble through me. It's not faked; I'm terrified that if I get out of the car, I'm heading right back to the brothel. "Please, Daniel. Please let me stay with you for just a bit longer." And I cling to the front of his jacket and look as helpless and lost as I can. When he still looks doubtful, I try a different tactic. "I don't want to go there looking like this."

He examines my outfit; his eyes narrow as he considers me, then glances out the door. He leans in close. "You scared of something, sweetheart?"

I nod, my eyes wide and pleading. I don't want to say it aloud because the taxi driver is watching us in his rearview mirror. For all I know, he works for Mr. Freeze, too. If the bruiser can be at the embassy waiting for me, no one is safe.

Except maybe Daniel.

Daniel, who has guns on him. Maybe I can take one of them while he sleeps. Maybe I can seduce him into giving me one or showing me how to shoot them. But I need more answers from him. I want to know who sent him, so I can know if I'm truly safe or if I've jumped into more danger.

But Daniel is the devil I know at the moment, and he can't be as bad as Mr. Freeze. He hasn't looked at my teeth once, after all.

Daniel seems to consider my frightened snuggling. It's hard for me to do because I don't want a man touching me, but I fight back my bile and continue to try and look helpless and innocent. I paw at the front of his jacket. "I . . . can we go to a nice hotel room somewhere? I'd really like a bath and some real clothes. Then maybe we can go to the embassy tomorrow morning, okay? Once I feel human again."

But my mind is already whirling with new plans, new options. The embassy isn't safe. I need some other way to get out of this country. Once I figure out how Daniel knows who I am, maybe I can use that.

"All right," Daniel says reluctantly, then wearily scrubs a hand down his face. "Shit. Fine. One night, and then we're going back to the embassy. I have a schedule I have to keep."

"One night," I agree with relief and force myself to hug him, pressing my breasts against him.

I'm going to use this man.

I'm going to flirt with him, and seduce him, and suck his cock if I have to. Whatever it takes to get him to take me with him and keep me safe. If he's willing to shoot men for me, he's a better bet than anyone else I have available at the moment.

I refuse to be abandoned again.

DANIEL

I know better. I really do. I should push open the door and haul Regan's fine ass up to the embassy. There have got to be people inside who can handle this situation better than me. I'm bound to fuck something up. Hell, I can't even stop looking at her legs like some goddamn pervert. First thing I'm going to do when we get to the apartment is start knocking my head against the floor tile, in hopes that some sense is pounded into my head.

But she looks damn scared, and so I give in to her pleading even though I'm on my last fumes and I need some serious sleep so I can move on to my next goal—finding my sister—and then find the hacker Petrovich's got a hard-on for.

Weirdly all three roads—Regan, my sister, and the hacker—led straight to Rio. It might be due to the increase in economy Brazil has seen due to the impending World Cup and Olympic Games or the rise in overall global prominence. More money means more dickheads willing to spend it on illegal things. The banking industry here is becoming huge, as is the biofuel market. It makes some kind of weird sense that there's a corresponding rise in the demand for female flesh. It's not a puzzle for me to figure out. I'm a weapon. Point me and I'll shoot.

When I learned that Naomi might be here, I entertained the idea that she was the hacker. Naomi's smarter than half the continent. Running a deep web ring would be something she could do in her sleep. But she's so smart that I have to believe she would have found some way to contact me. I've never used an alias, wanting the word to get around that Daniel Hays was looking for his sister. But she's never once sent me an email or a text or even a smoke signal.

Letting Regan stay the night with me isn't going to delay my hunt, because I'm in desperate need of sleep. Maybe she's embarrassed about how she looks in her tiny coat and even tinier bikini. I'll take her back to my temporary residence and fix her up. We'll both sleep, and in the morning she'll be begging me to return her to the U.S. diplomats. I can keep my hands off of her.

"Avenida Nossa Senhora de Copacabana." I tell the driver to take us to an address down by the beach. He gives me a quick nod and we take off again. The trip from the embassy takes less than fifteen minutes and it's a beautiful drive along the Guanabara Bay. The pavement and the high-rise hotels give way and for a few minutes we drive along the bay, where seawaters pelt the rocks. In the distance, Sugarloaf Mountain rises like a stone torpedo.

Regan has her face glued to the window. "What is that?" she asks, pointing to the mountain.

"It's Sugarloaf Mountain. When the Portuguese were transporting sugar from Brazil to Europe, they'd press the sugar cane into these cone-shaped molds called sugarloaves, and one day, I guess, someone said, 'Hey that bump in the sky looks like a sugarloaf.' The Portuguese name is Pão de Açúcar." I found myself leaning close to her, almost whispering the native name in her ear. Another Portuguese phrase comes to mind. *Eu quero te abraçar agora.* I want to touch you.

I force myself back against the seat. The taxi drivers smirks at me.

"*A mulher e a sardinha querem-se da mais pequenina,*" he mutters merrily. He's lucky he's driving and that Regan doesn't speak Portuguese.

"What'd he say?"

"That the cable cars are packed like sardines," I lie. He really said that women and sardines should always be small, which I guess is a reference to Regan's tight ass he saw waving in his mirror, but I'm not telling her that. Trying to distract her, I point to the wires running from the mainland to the mountain. "There's the cars that take you to the top of Sugarloaf."

"Huh."

I can't tell if she's intrigued or whether she can't wait to get the hell out of here. I'm guessing the latter. I have the taxi driver pull over on the corner. He doesn't need to know where we are staying. I wish it were *Carnaval* because Regan in her spangly bikini wouldn't look out of place during the festival. But as it is, she's going to draw attention in her black socks secured by zip ties, the thin tan jacket covering the swimsuit. Nothing to do but brazen it out.

"There's no hotel here," she notes with worry. The buildings along Avenida Nossa Senhora de Copacabana are nothing like the favela. Here we are on level ground and it looks like any other metropolitan area near a beach. Touristy and a tiny bit run-down. Rather than hotels, I always stay in these apartments, which are run by individuals who are trying to avoid government regulations and extra taxes. These folks aren't running to spill to anyone who their guests are. Pay them in cash and they are even more thrilled to pretend like the place stood empty for the entire time you were there.

"Walk like you own the place," I mutter under my breath as I lead her past two large apartment complexes and down an alley to a three-story thin building that houses three flats. Mine is the top one.

Regan sucks it all up and walks like a queen, head held high as if black socks, no shoes, and jackets are all the rage. If anyone is looking it's because she's fucking amazing. Can I hope that my sister will be like this? For so long I've worried that when I found her she'd be a shell, addicted to drugs, strung out, and barely functioning. But Regan's nothing like that. She's mouthy and straight backed and clear eyed. I like her, more than I should.

No one says anything to us, and we're inside the one-bedroom flat before much more time passes.

"You live here?" She wanders in and looks around. It's a tiny place. One tiny kitchen, one living room with a partial view of the bay, and one tiny bedroom with one queen-sized bed. She skitters away from the bedroom.

"Rent," I answer. I open the door to the bathroom, which contains a shower and a normal-sized toilet. Some things can't be small for me. I point to my one extra set of towels provided by the owner of the house. "Feel free to clean up."

She nods and disappears. The water runs for a long time. So long that I'm able to shrug off my jacket, pull out my guns, discard my shoes. During the time the water is running nonstop and steam is starting to seep out from underneath the bathroom door, I'm trying to keep busy, to drum out the image of Regan completely naked inside the shower, running her hands down her gorgeous body, over the firm breasts she pressed against me earlier, and down between her legs. I'm cleaning a second gun by the time she pokes her head out the door. I'm surprised we had that much hot water.

"What?" I ask her, and it comes out more sharply than I intend because I need to turn off my desire for her. Her head inches back so all I can see are her eyes between the frame and the edge of the doorway. It's not her fault I'm a dick with no self-control. "Sorry." Standing up, I gesture toward her. "Need anything?"

"You got more than this towel for me?" she asks.

Okay, I should've thought of that. "Sure." Inside the bedroom I rifle through my pack. I have a few white dress shirts, beater tanks, dress slacks, and cotton pants. I pull out a beater tank and a dress shirt. It'll hang down to her thighs. Maybe later I can run outside and get her something from one of the shops along the beach. They'll have at least a sundress.

"This is all I got." I hand her the things, making sure I don't look at her. When she takes them from me, her hand brushes mine, and that tentative accidental contact sends an electrical current down my spine. Stiffening, I quickly snatch my hand away, but this only causes her to seem offended. I barely withdraw my fingers fast enough to avoid getting a crush injury when she slams the door shut.

In the kitchen, I heat up some sauce while putting water to boil. I like to eat in if I can. You're never more vulnerable than when you're eating, shitting, and sleeping. Or been kept in sexual slavery for two months. I pause. No, Regan's not vulnerable. That's what makes her so attractive. In the months I've been searching for my sister, I've seen hundreds, maybe thousands, of girls and none of them has been able to walk out with pride and fire like Regan Porter. The thing that draws me to her isn't just her looks, it's her attitude. I *admire* her. She's a rarity. And I decide then and there I'm going to do everything possible to make sure she's returned safely to the bosom of her family, because sometimes the good guys have to win one in order for there to be enough fight left in the white hats.

I've got the food plated and ready for her when she finally opens the door. Her long blond hair is turbaned in a towel, and the white shirt hangs open over the beater. I think I can see the shadow of more intimate places, and I force my gaze up to her face.

She looks speculatively at me, as if she's a customer at the butcher's shop, counting and weighing what kind of cut of meat I am. *I'm the part you leave behind, honey. I'm old, chewy, and about as tasty as a leather shoe.*

"Come eat." I gesture to the table, shoving aside my gun parts. My primary weapon is a Ruger SR45, and it's the one I cleaned first. I've got it lying on a chair next to the table. Easy to grab and shoot if necessary.

"Milk?" she asks, with raised eyebrows. "Are we five?"

"No. I'm twenty-seven, but I still need it." I pull out a chair for her and she sits down. I wonder if she's wearing underwear and curse mentally. Of course not; I didn't give her any. "Do you need anything, uh, downstairs?"

"Like French bread?" she asks.

French bread? Is that a special term for a woman's pussy? I gape at her, and she flushes under my scrutiny. It takes a superhuman effort on my part not to allow my gaze to drop to her chest to follow that rush of blood and see how much of her body turns rosy.

With her eyes cast downward, she gestures toward the food. "Sorry I asked. This is fine. I don't need any bread."

Oops. I guess maybe she took *downstairs* to mean me literally going downstairs to find more food. I try to be more direct. "I meant, do you need any underwear? I forgot to give you some. I don't have boxers. I'm more of a briefs man myself." When I wore any. This causes Regan to turn beet red.

"No, I'm fine." She shifts uncomfortably on the chair, which tells me she's not fine at all. I don't want to leave her by herself, but I need to get her some clothes.

"Eat. I'll be right back," I say and turn toward the door.

"No," she jumps up, her hip catching the table and knocking it over. Sauce, noodles, and milk go flying. "Oh shit!" she cries, and then suddenly the warrior princess breaks down. She crumples to the floor and begins to sob, huge, wracking cries that sound like she's being torn apart. My promise to not touch her until she gives me permission dissolves like sugar in water and before I know it, I've scooped her up in my arms and am carrying her over to the sofa. I try to set her down but she clings to me, and I take that as consent of an unspoken kind.

Settling into the corner, I hold her body as she trembles and quakes against me. There's a storm inside of her, and I don't know how long it's going to take to die down, but as I cradle her in my lap I realize that the world could burn up and I wouldn't let her go. Not at this moment. Not until she doesn't need me anymore, because I can't remember the last time I felt this good. Maybe I never have.

CHAPTER **FIVE**

REGAN

I've totall lost my shit.

I thought I was holding together pretty well. That I'd buried everything so deep inside that nothing could affect me anymore. Guess I was wrong because the longer things seem normal, the more frayed my nerves get.

Daniel has taken me to a nice apartment. Not great by American standards, but cleaner than the brothel, and private. It's only me and him, and I immediately think he's going to pounce on me as soon as we get inside. That's okay; I'm ready for that and I'm fine with having sex with this man as long as it gets me to safety. Pleasing one man in bed would be child's play after what I've been through.

But Daniel is . . . nice. He lets me shower in his bathroom and gives me clean clothes to wear. Nothing slutty, just clothes of his own. It's clear that he wasn't intending to bring me back with him, which lends credence to his story about taking me to the embassy. This man, this nice man, meant what he said. He was really going to drop me off at the embassy and go on with his life. He wasn't going to use me for sex even if he was attracted to me.

And this confuses me. My new reality is that men want a quick fuck. I don't know how to deal with people that are nice for the sake of being nice. Not anymore. I dress in the clothes he's given me and sit down to eat the food he's made. And I'm bitchy. I can't help it. Hiding behind a shitty attitude is all I've got anymore.

But he's trying to make me comfortable. He's not looking at my body, even though it's clearly outlined in the thin undershirt I'm wearing without a bra or panties underneath. He's even made me dinner and poured a glass of milk. And he starts to leave to get me clothing. Or bread. Something.

"Eat. I'll be right back," he says.

My mind flips out. I'm being abandoned again. I want to scream, but I jerk to my feet instead, and spill everything. My plate shatters at my feet, and it looks like I feel, all broken and piecemeal.

And I lose my shit.

I start crying uncontrollably. Everything feels like it's crashing on me at once. Tonight I escaped the brothel, but now the embassy is lost to me. Freedom was so close and yanked away again. And this man is trying to be nice to me, but he wants to fuck me. I don't know what to think anymore.

So I sob.

Like a hero in some fairy tale, Daniel grabs me in his arms and carries me to the couch. This only makes me cry harder because if he threw me down and started fucking me, I'd expect that. I'd know how to handle that. But he's petting my hair and whispering soothing things to me.

And I. Cannot. Deal.

Great, wracking sobs escape my body. My hands curl in his shirt and I lean against him, crying my heart out. I'm so scared and lost. And even though this man is holding me, I feel completely and utterly alone.

"Sweetheart, don't cry," he murmurs as he strokes my hair. "It's going to be okay. We'll take you back to the embassy in the morning, and you'll be on a plane home in a few days. I promise."

His mention of the embassy only makes me cry harder. If I go there, Mr. Freeze will find me. He'll check my teeth, order me "gentled" for a bit longer, and when I'm totally broken . . . what then? I have visions of him sculpting me into the perfect woman he wants . . . and then, I don't know, pulling my skin off and wearing it as a hood. He may want a blow job from a pretty slave girl, but I no longer have optimism as a fallback.

My hands slide around Daniel, and I hug him as he strokes my back. It occurs to me that I'm practically in his lap. I want to pull away and take another shower, but a different thought flickers in my mind; this time, when I press my cheek against his neck, it's to hide the fact that my tears are drying up.

Daniel has weapons.

I move my hands to his waist, still weeping and sniffing, and delicately try to feel for his gun. There's one taken apart on the table nearby, but Daniel seems like the type that would have one at the ready at all times. He must have another one on him. It's become my goal to find it.

So I sniffle and burrow against him, noticing the tent rising at the front of his pants. He's trying to be comforting, but his body is responding all the same. I pretend not to notice it, even as I let my breast brush against his chest. "I'm sorry," I say in a wobbly voice. "I don't know what's wrong with me."

He gives a brief chuckle. "You kidding me?" His fingers stroke my damp cheek and I do my best not to recoil from his touch. All touches seem to lead to rough, horrible sex lately. "You've been through hell and came out the other side. I think you're allowed a cry-fest. Try not to slobber on me too much."

I like Daniel's humor. A watery laugh escapes my throat, even as my hand grazes something hard tucked into his belt that can only be a gun. Yes!

Before I can grab it from him, though, his hand covers mine, preventing me. "Cry all you want, sweetheart, but the weapons stay with me."

I jerk away from him, wiping my eyes. The time for cuddling is past. "You have to give me credit for trying."

Daniel laughs again and shakes his head in admiration. "I do." He gets to his feet, adjusts himself surreptitiously, and then gestures at the kitchen. "I'll clean that up, and then I'll head out and grab you a change of clothes . . ."

"No!" I yelp again, and I grab at his trousers. The old panic returns, and I don't care that I'm clinging to the front of his pants and my mouth is pretty much level with his crotch. I look up at him, pleading. "Don't leave. I don't want to be left. I don't need new clothes. These are fine." Shit. I'm babbling, but I can't help myself. "Give me a pair of pants and I'll be fine. I promise."

He stares down at me for a long moment, and then scrubs a hand over his face and nods. "Okay. You can borrow some of my stuff and we'll go in the morning. Together."

Relief courses through me. "Yes. That sounds good. Thank you."

Even though I protest, Daniel won't let me help him clean up in the kitchen. Instead, he gets me another plate of food and another glass of milk, and makes me sit on the sofa and eat every bite while he sweeps up glass and mops the floor. He chats the entire time, too. It's clear Daniel doesn't like silence much. He talks about the weather, and how different food is here in Brazil, and the upcoming World Cup. They're harmless, simple topics—like a conversation you might have with a cabdriver. I listen but don't offer additional commentary. I haven't seen most of Brazil, after all. I've been chained in a whorehouse.

But I like to hear talking other than "open your mouth, slut," so I appreciate it. His normal conversation makes me feel a little more normal, too.

When I yawn and curl up on the end of the sofa, all food eaten, he pauses and comes to my side. "Come on. Time for bed."

I stiffen but get to my feet. Here it is. Here's where I have to pay to earn my keep. "I'm ready."

We head to the bedroom, and the pasta I ate feels like lead in my stomach. I can do this. I can.

Daniel moves ahead of me and pulls down the blankets on one side of the bed. "The windows are nailed shut, so I wouldn't recommend escaping through them. Plus, this neighborhood is kind of shit. Again, wouldn't recommend escape."

He offers me a pillow and I clutch it to my chest, waiting. Is this for my knees? So I don't get more bruises while I service him? "All right."

Then he walks past me, back to the door of the bedroom. "I'll be in the living room. If you get scared or need anything, you shout. Okay?"

And then he closes the door.

He doesn't want sex with me after all. At least, not tonight. He's giving me this bedroom. I'm shocked . . . and then my mind starts racing. I can push the bed against the door and barricade myself in. Or there's a heavy, scratched-up bureau against one wall that I could use to barricade the door if the bed is too bulky. I can wall myself into this room and be completely, utterly safe.

But . . . what if he tries to go out again?

What if he leaves me?

The familiar panic surges, and I'm close to throwing up the food I've eaten. I yank the door back open and run into the living room, startling him. He'd sat back down to work on cleaning his guns but stands up.

"What's wrong?"

I can't explain the sheer relief I feel at the sight of him. I wring my hands and try to think of a probable excuse as to why I don't want him in the bedroom with me . . . but I don't want him out of my sight, either. "I . . . um, I'm scared."

"Of the dark?" he teases, all smiles again. "You want a night-light?"

"Very funny, asshole," I say, but I'm cracking a faint smile myself. I glance over at the couch. "Can I . . . um, can I sleep here?" I point at it.

Now he looks confused. "You want me to sleep in the bed and you on the couch?"

"No," I yelp out quickly, thinking. If he's in the bed, he's in the other room. "I . . . uh, I want to be in the same room as you. Not the bedroom," I add, ". . . here. Where it's safe."

Where I can see you.

He digests this and then nods. "Sure. Get your blanket. I'm going to be up for a while anyhow."

I race back to his room, snatch the blanket out of the bed so I don't have to spend longer than a moment with him out of sight, and then wrap it around me, heading back to the living room. Daniel watches me as I return, his face impassive, but soon returns to cleaning his guns.

I relax a bit more now. We're not in the bedroom, and as I lie down on the couch, I face the table so I can watch him work. So I can keep an eye on him. I pull the blanket tight around me and curl up. It's soft. It's the softest thing I've felt since I was taken, and I immediately feel like weeping again at the small luxury.

Tomorrow I will figure out some way to make Daniel keep me at his side. I can't go to the embassy. I can't chance it. I'll have to figure out some other way to get home.

I watch Daniel work until I fall asleep, exhausted.

CHAPTER SIX

DANIEL

She looks fragile. For the first time since I've taken her out of the whorehouse, she looks like I can break her. I prefer the feisty, sarcastic girl. This teary-eyed victim scares the hell out of me. None of my past dealings have prepared me for her. *What the hell were you going to do with your sister?* a little voice mocks. I had hoped to find my sister, take her home, and let the land, the horses, and our mom heal her. But as I look at Regan's sleeping form, tense and protective when most people are completely lax, I realize what a dumbass idea that was. It's going to take more than sitting on the porch and drinking sweet tea for a few weeks to recover, and Regan is only a few hours out of her imprisonment and torture. Even trained soldiers need time to recover, and Regan didn't have any training. When I was part of Special

Forces, we all went through training on surviving capture and torture, which basically meant being captured and tortured.

A group of older soldiers would kidnap you and take you to a solitary cell. They'd place a wet towel on your face and leave you there. At first, you feel like the towel is nothing. You can survive a towel. But an hour or so of being immobilized, sucking in the wet fabric with every breath and then having more water poured over your mouth and nose and into your ears while you vomit into your mouth and then swallow it back—all the while choking on the fabric, puke, and water—is hell. Then when you are about to pass out or you think you'll die, the towel is ripped away and you're stuck in a room where fluorescent lights flicker off and on while random noises are piped in, sometimes for what seems hours at a time and others randomly. After that you listen to your friends call out from the next room while they seem to be tortured or raped and they are calling out your name, begging you to help them, save them, rescue them. But you can't do anything.

Oftentimes the soldiers trying to get into the Special Forces fail these mental tests, not the physical ones. Lots of people can swim, run, and carry a rucksack weighing a hundred and fifty pounds for twenty-six miles. Not many can survive mental torture and not come out of it a deadweight victim.

I don't know what Regan has endured and I don't like envisioning it. But I'm guessing that Regan's suffered more than any Special Forces soldier ever has, and she's not catatonic. So what if she broke down? That shit's normal. I couldn't barely say more than two words when I finished my psychological training. Unlike Regan, though, I was alone in the shower of my apartment when I had my mental vacation, and the next day I could pretend that it was nothing when everyone was patting me on the back for graduating and buying me drinks. A few of the old-timers, though, passed me a drink and gave me a knowing look that said my bravado was a thin front. So yeah, Regan's little torrential outburst was nothing but normal. I hope she knew that. Getting her back to the consulate and on her way to the good U. S. of A. would make a helluva difference.

The first thing we need to get her up and on her feet are real clothes and shoes. It is tempting to leave right now. Rio is like Vegas—open all hours of the night. But if she were to wake up and find I wasn't there? That seems like a bad idea. I'd deal with the clothes thing in the morning. I kick off my boots, pull off my T-shirt, and settle into the hard-backed chair for some much-needed shut-eye. My last thought is there's a damned good bed not getting used tonight.

"You can't leave." Regan's voice is tinged with desperation that she is valiantly trying to swallow back. I pretend like I don't notice that she's huddled onto the edge of the sofa, as far away from me as she can get while still maintaining two eyes on me at all times. It's like she wants to see me there and feels safer that I'm around but can't really be sure I'm not going to hurt her like she's been hurt the last couple months.

I inject as much gentleness as I can into my voice and hold out a hand—not for her to touch, but to show her I mean her no harm. It's worked with horses in the past and it's not like I have any better ideas. "I can't take you downstairs. You stand out too much, and we need to keep a low profile until we can take you back to the consulate."

She nods, but I'm not sure if I'm getting through to her. I swipe a hand down my face. Hating to leave her but having no choice, I look around. How can I make her feel safe? My eyes fall on one of the guns I have disassembled on the table. A weapon. She'd been feeling me up yesterday after her storm of tears, searching for a weapon. For a quick moment, I'd thought she was caressing me and I had to fight back a completely inappropriate boner brought on by her soft body and her need for comfort, not to mention her slim fingers running up and down my abdomen and around the waistband of my pants. "Have you ever shot a gun before?"

"No." The word is quavering and soft. I go over to the table and reassemble my Ruger. It's not a good gun for a beginner. A Glock would be better, but I don't like those and, more importantly, I don't have one with me. This piece will have to do.

I carry it over and hand it to her butt first. Her hands curl around the stock and her finger is immediately on the trigger.

"Nuh-uh, uh." I pull her trigger finger out and rest it along the barrel. "Only put your finger on the trigger when you're going to pull it," I instruct. This time her nod is matched by some understanding in her eyes.

"See the switch here? It's the safety." I slide her thumb along the safety, making her push it up and down. "Up, and the safety is engaged. Down, it's not." I wait for her acknowledgment and watch her flip the switch a couple of times. I take her other hand and pull back on the barrel. "Your chamber is loaded. The gun is hot. You disengage the safety and wrap both hands around the stock." I pull her left hand off and fold it around her right hand. "The SR45 has a soft recoil, but it's still going to kick, which makes you point upward. Always bring your gun back down when you shoot, or you'll only hit the ceiling."

"Pull back the chamber, disengage the safety. Got it." She

rubs her index finger almost lovingly along the side of the barrel and my junk starts swelling again. Shaking my head at my own dumb response, I redouble my efforts to concentrate on showing Regan the rudimentary steps of using a handgun.

I pull the gun from her hands, but she won't release her grip. I tug on it and then promise, "I'll give it back. Just a minute." Reluctantly, she lets the weapon slide out of her hands. Pulling back on the slide, I release the bullet we've chambered and then press the magazine release. It drops into my hand and I push the bullet back in. Checking to make sure the safety is still on, I hand her back the gun and then walk out fifteen paces, which puts me right in the kitchen about ten feet from the door. "Wait until your intruder is right here and then shoot. Anything farther away and you're bound to miss."

She scowls at me. "Because I'm a girl?"

"Because you haven't shot a gun before. Doesn't matter if you're a girl or a guy," I correct. "I'm going to run out and get you some clothes and shoes and a case and . . ." I wave my hand toward her body. "Other stuff. When I come back, I'll say my name. If I think you're in danger, I'll say 'Honey, I'm home' and that's your signal to run to the bedroom, grab my pack, and climb out onto the fire escape. Instead of going down, go up to the roof and wait there."

"I thought you said the windows were nailed shut." She scowls at me.

"I lied."

"And if you don't come?" A fearful look creeps into her eyes.

I crouch down so we're both eye level. "I'm coming back for you, Regan. I won't leave you until you're safe. I promise."

"Why?"

It's an easy question and there are easy answers if I trusted her to keep her mouth shut, but it's not just my life that is on the line. It's Nick and his girl Daisy, who happens to be Regan's best friend. I don't know what story they want me to tell her, so until I can make contact with them, I have to keep my mouth shut. But I don't want to leave her hanging.

"Because you're too important not to save." I know it's the truth the minute I say it. I'm not going to let her be hurt again, not on my watch, not while I'm still breathing. Because I'm a stupid piss, I lean in even closer and I give her a soft kiss on her temple. The air around us grows thick with tension. I know what the tension is on my side because I can feel my pants getting too tight. Her tension is fear based. I stand swiftly, feeling something like embarrassment, and pull up my pants to check my service revolver strapped around my ankle.

"Why can't I have that gun?" she asks. "It looks like it would be easier to shoot."

"Nope." I shake my head. "This baby only has a .22 and your big-girl gun is a .45. You can shoot a lot bigger holes with a .45."

Shrugging on a loose-fitting linen top over my beater tank to cover the two knives I have strapped to my sides, I turn to face Regan. She's pointing the goddamn gun at me. "You aiming to shoot me, sugar?"

"What?" She looks confused and a little distressed.

"Then don't point the gun at me." I point to the ceiling. "You only point the gun at a target, so ceiling or floor unless I've done something to piss you off so much that nothing short of a bullet is going to clear the air."

She flushes but lowers the gun.

"Good girl." I pull open the door. "What's our code?"

"Your name is safety. 'Honey, I'm home' is danger."

"Good girl," I repeat and close the door behind me. The door's thin and I can hear a muffled sob and then a deep breath. Then . . . nothing. Good girl, indeed.

I run downstairs, not wanting to be gone too long. The drumbeat in my blood says that Regan needs me back soon, soon, soon.

Once on the street, I head for Copacabana Palace Hotel. While there are dozens of small stalls along the beach, I figure it will be easier to get everything I need from one place. But first . . . I duck down the closest alley I find and then wait three heartbeats. When my tail, a dark-haired male in his late twenties with pockmarks and loud boots, pauses at the mouth of the alley, I reach out and grab his windpipe. His hands come up to claw at my fingers, but my grip doesn't abate. With a fierce jerk, I pull him into the narrow passage between the two cement structures. It's easy to swing his head back against the wall, and though he might outweigh me by a good twenty pounds, I'm far stronger than him and at least four inches taller. My forearm keeps him from breathing for thirty seconds. When he's turning blue and his breath is noisy and labored, I ease off slightly.

"Why does Gomes want her back so bad?"

He spits in my direction. Gross. This is why I hate close-up contact. All the fucking fluids like blood, piss, spit, and vomit can cover you like spray from a shaken soda can. Maybe he doesn't speak English. I ask him, "*Falas Inglês?*"

He presses his lips together in a universal nonverbal refusal to answer, so I reapply my forearm to prevent a bunch of spit in my face again. "I don't care if you speak English or not, because if you don't give me a good answer, you're going to die here."

"*Engasga na minha porra!*" he gasps out, telling me that I should choke on his come.

"No, thank you. I prefer eating pussy to drinking some stranger's come."

"That *puta* does not belong to you," he finally says, showing that he does speak English just fine.

"Who does she belong to?"

Gomes's man struggles ineffectually against me. I lift him higher until he can barely reach the ground. The muscles in my right arm are shaking, and I know I'll have to put an end to this soon.

"*Não é da sua conta.*"

None of my business? Is he fucking kidding me? "Since you're following me and trying to kill me, it kind of is my business."

He tries to swing his head forward to head butt me, but the forearm against his windpipe prevents such movement. An evil grin spreads across his face, and I know what he's going to say even before it comes out of his mouth. "That whore loved every minute of my cock inside her."

My left fist smashes his mouth in, and I feel the gratifying crush of jawbone under my hand. Blood sprays out of his mouth onto my shirt. It's linen. Blood is fucking hard to get out of linen. There's no Tide Stain Stick for Assassins at the supermarket. Playtime is over.

With a swift upward jerk of my knee, I introduce his balls and cock to his kidney. "Guess you won't be using that anymore." I release him to fall to the ground at my feet, moaning out of his broken mouth. Deciding the world can do without one more rapist, I twist his head to break his neck with one swift motion.

My shirt is covered with his blood and spit. Crap. Can't go into the hotel like this. At one of the street vendors, I buy the first shirt I can find. It's bright blue and can be seen for five miles in the dark, but it's better than the fluid-splattered cotton I've left in the alley shrouding the dead man.

The whole thing has only taken about five minutes, and I'm at the hotel in no time.

My visit to the hotel shop takes longer than I'd hoped. They want me to make decisions about color and fabric. Patterns or solids. I don't care and I'd venture to guess that Regan doesn't, either. After about fifteen minutes of nonsense, I buy everything they recommend. I pay for the load of clothes and shoes and underwear and other female stuff in cash and no one blinks. It could be because I'm a stupid North American tourist or it could be that crime is so common that no one cares if my money is clean or dirty so long as it is negotiable currency.

I take my three shopping bags and hurry back to Regan. My watch says I've been gone an hour. It feels like two days. As I approach the door I hear the chamber on the Ruger being pulled back. "Daniel here," I say while knocking and then move to the side in case she shoots through the door.

Inside there are some muffled sounds and then a curse. Finally she says with resignation, "Come in. I've got the gun pointed at the ceiling because I don't know how to do the fancy thing with the bullets."

Disengaging the lock, I go in low in case there is anyone else with Regan, but it's only her. She has a funny look on her face, but it's indecipherable to me.

"Something happen to your shirt?" She gestures toward my shirt. Not wanting to tell her that Gomes has sent yet another man after us, I shrug. "I like blue, what can I say?" Holding up the three bags, I ask, "Trade?"

She sets the gun down on the floor in front of the sofa, barrel pointing toward the wall. Smart girl. She picks up stuff fast. I like that I don't have to repeat anything with her. She knows and goes.

"What's all that?" Her head jerks toward the bags.

Setting them down on the table where I cleaned my guns, I pick up the abandoned Ruger off the floor. "Stuff for you. Clothes, shoes, shit," I reply absently as I shake out the bullet and then eject the magazine. Once everything is back together, I go into the bedroom and pull on a nylon holster vest and stick my two Rugers inside the breast pockets.

When I get back into the living room, Regan is sifting through all the stuff. The near-sleepless night and early morning excursion is hitting me. I stretch out on the sofa and watch her as she unpacks the bags.

"This is a lot of stuff."

"Figured you can tell the consulate that you lost all of your luggage but a carry-on. Not sure how long it will take you to get them to ship you back, so I got you a bunch of stuff. There's a carry-on for all that shit in one of the bags."

Regan looks pissed at something, but I decide that I'm too tired to care. The adrenaline spike from my fight outside is fading fast. I've been hunting for her for weeks now and getting into Gomes's whorehouse wasn't easy. I figure that killing the last scout bought us a little time. I need some shut-eye if I'm going to do Regan any good, because I can't think right now. I'm too fucking tired.

"I'm going to take a quick refresher and then we'll talk about taking you back to the consulate." My eyelids are heavy, and I allow them to drift shut. "By the way," I say sleepily, "there are biscuits in the refrigerator. They're for breakfast."

CHAPTER **SEVEN**

REGAN

I don't give a shit about the breakfast he's left for me. I can't possibly eat, not when he says he's going to take me back to the consulate. That can't happen, and I need to act.

My mind is whirling a million miles a minute as Daniel relaxes on the couch and pulls the blanket over himself. He looks exhausted, and part of me feels a little bad that he's clearly been run ragged looking for me. The panicky part of me doesn't care, though, and it's screaming in the back of my mind. It wants me to run over to him, shake him awake, and force him to protect me from the world.

Sad how quickly Daniel has become the only safe thing in my life. Pretty sure there's something fucked up about that.

The clothes he's picked out are garish, in bright, touristy grandma-ish patterns that I would have laughed at back before all of this. Now, I touch the soft fabric of a cotton sundress and appreciate that it'll cover all of my body. There are bras and panties here, too, and some boho-looking leather sandals. They don't match the clothing, so it's clear he was trying to find me something practical for my feet. Nice thought.

I pull out a bra and underwear, frowning at the sight of them. These are not granny-like in the slightest. These are a bit slutty. The fabric of the bra and matching panties are sheer and clearly meant for romance and not practicality. I shoot Daniel a suspicious look, but his eyes are closed and his face is relaxed as he sleeps.

Or pretends to.

I consider the lingerie. Did he buy this with an ulterior motive in mind? Or was this the only thing he could find? I don't know the answer, but I don't trust men anymore, so I suspect the worst. It confirms that Daniel wants me. As long as I can use it against him, I'm fine with that.

I watch his sleeping face as I slide the panties under my clothing and tug them on. They're a little tight across the ass, but I don't care if I have a plumber's crack. They're clean. That's all that matters. I don't leave the room to put on the bra, either; I slide my arms under my current clothing and work the clasp around my back, watching Daniel as he sleeps. I should go to the other room and change, but I don't want to.

The thought of leaving the room kind of freaks me out. It's like, if I leave, he'll vanish and I'll be alone all over again. So I stay, switching out my clothing piece by piece, pulling off tags as I do so. Daniel sleeps through all of this.

When I'm dressed, I sit down at the kitchen table and try not to panic. I'm clothed now. I'm clean and I'm clothed. I should be feeling human now, more relaxed. Instead, I'm shaking with fear, my mind whirling and chaotic. When Daniel wakes up, he's going to take me back to the consulate. If he takes me back to the consulate, Mr. Freeze is going to find me and I'm going to end up right back where I started. If I tell Daniel, though, will he care? He's made it clear that he's ready for me to be out of his hair, and I only made things worse by falling to pieces last night. I could kick myself for having a sniveling sob-fest last night, because I think it scared him.

Think, Regan, think.

I drum my fingers on the table, and my gaze rests on his light-weight blazer on a hook by the table. I bite my lip, look over at Daniel, and when I see he's still sleeping, I get up and approach his jacket. I search his pockets, curious to see what I'll find. Condoms? Bullets? Knives?

I find a wad of Brazilian dollars, a vial of some sort of white powder that looks kind of dangerous, and a cheap flip phone. A burner. All righty, that's interesting. I flip it open quietly and hit the down arrow, looking for messages.

He's got several, all from unlisted phone numbers. I read the most recent one.

Understand R. is retrieved. Need status update on Emperor.

Another from the same number sends me into a panic.

R. is not en route to US. Report back. I grow impatient.

My heart thumps erratically in my chest. Fuck fuck fuck. It's clear that Daniel is on a retrieval mission for me. He's supposed to be done with me, and someone's unhappy he's not. Damn it. I bet I'm not his only pickup. He's going to dump me at the consulate and be on his merry way unless I do something.

I gingerly snap the phone shut again, thinking. I don't have a lot of options. I could take Daniel's gun and escape on my own with the cash he has—but an American woman alone? I don't feel safe. Plus, I can't get very far because I don't have a passport or ID on me. Going to the consulate would take care of that, except for obvious reasons. If Daniel is rescuing American girls from brothels and thinks nothing of shooting men and walking away, he's got better connections than I do.

I think about the texts. And I think about Freeze. Daniel is good with a gun. I need to stay with him.

I *need* to.

I know what I must do. I swallow hard and close my eyes, bracing myself. *You can do this, Regan. He's another john.* I've had plenty of those since I was captured, and most blur into a faceless blend of rapists. What's one more meaningless fuck, right? My stomach is queasy at the thought, though. Daniel has been nothing but kind to me. It feels wrong to use him.

And yet, I know he wants me. I've seen the way he looks at me. It's clear he thinks I'm pretty—and off-limits. Time to make myself no longer off-limits for him. If I'm his favorite fuck toy, he'll keep me at his side and protect me.

I pull my new soft sundress off over my head and carefully fold it on the table. I fluff my hair and lick my lips, then pinch my cheeks to give them a bit of healthy color. I need to look sexy, needy with desire, and, above all, like I want it. Like I'll die if I don't get his cock in the next few minutes.

I can do this.

I give my nipples a hard little twist to make them point, even though the last thing I'm feeling right now is desire. More like dread. He's going to know that as soon as he touches me and feels how dry I am. I think for a moment and then gather saliva in my mouth. When I have plenty, I coat my fingers and shove them into my panties to make myself wet. That'll have to do. By the time he gets there, I'll have him so hot and bothered that he won't notice . . . or won't care. Most men don't care.

I quietly approach Daniel. He's still sleeping, his breathing regular. His arms have fallen forward, no longer holding the blanket to his body, so I peel it back carefully, letting it pool at his feet. He's wearing a belt and trousers. All right. I'll have to rub him, get him good and aroused first, and then unbuckle him.

I kneel next to him and reach for his cock before hesitating. I need to make sure this goes smoothly. I stand up and tug my panties off, even though my mind screams for me to put them back on because panties are safe. Then I sit down and lightly place my hand on his chest, watching his face.

He stirs, but he doesn't wake.

Gently, I rub my hand along his length, feeling it harden. A twinge of worry creeps over me because Daniel's flaccid length is still pretty impressive. That's going to hurt, but nothing to be done about it now. I cup my hand and continue to stroke it up and down his cock, as it grows and hardens under my ministrations.

He mumbles something and reaches for his cock, eyes closed—and finds my hand there. His fist closes around my wrist but he doesn't move. His eyes snap open, and he gives me a vague, confused look. ". . . the fuck?" he mumbles, trying to sit up.

I lean in and press my mouth to his parted one, letting my

tongue graze his lips. My hand remains on his cock and I push a hand on his shoulder, trying to force him back down on the couch. "I have a problem, Daniel," I say in my sexiest voice as I keep rubbing his cock. I press my tits against his arm, too, and his girth swells thicker in my grip.

Suddenly the fog clears from his eyes. He jackknifes upright and tosses me aside, sending me reeling. "What the fuck are you doing?" he roars.

The realization of what I was just about to do—what I was doing—hits me. I've tried to use this man like everyone has used me. Like he was nothing.

Like he was just a body part.

Like *I* was just a body part.

I'm stricken with horror and I can't pretend any longer. I struggle to my feet. "I'm sorry," I manage to say at his forbidding stance, fists on hips, glaring at me like an angry god. "I think breakfast isn't sitting well."

I stumble away and barely make it to the bathroom before I puke everywhere.

CHAPTER **EIGHT**

DANIEL

I dream often. Too much. Usually my dreams are about my sister, Naomi. I'm with her on vacation, and sometimes I save her from the kidnapping. But most of the time I'm left standing on the beach as the waves come up and take her out to sea, and I swim and I swim and call out her name but she never responds. When I try to turn toward the shore, my dad is standing there with my mother prostrate at his feet, so I turn around and dive back into the ocean. When I wake up, I'm gasping for breath.

Other times I dream of my missions when I was a sniper in Delta Force, lying in a ghillie suit in the sand with my spotter next to me. I'm shooting people regardless of their sex or age, like I'm in an arcade. I don't know from my position who they are—and for my own sanity don't want to know. I only know they are a danger to my brothers, and I'm to kill them before they harm any members of my unit. After these dreams I wake up holding my breath, waiting to pull the trigger.

This dream is so different than all my other nighttime movies. In this dream Regan is telling me that the only way I can save her is to have sex with her. No doubt this dream is going to end as badly as all my other dreams, but I can't figure out whether fucking her is swimming toward the shore or back into the ocean. She keeps saying that this will make it all right for her—that she'll be healed by my dick. There's something about it that I know is wrong, but the press of her body against mine drowns out all those concerns. It's a pretty fucking good dream, and then . . . I wake up and realize it's not a goddamn dream. That the fucked-up chick is stroking my cock, but her eyes are dead, and I'm not into drilling corpses.

I stuff my stupid-ass hard cock into my pants and zip up. Even though I'm pissed as hell at her, I get her a glass of water.

Inside the bathroom I see Regan leaning over the toilet, her bare ass resting on her heels. She's not just gagging. She's crying and trying to retch out every ounce of her body. I kind of want to start vomiting right beside her. Half of me wants to scream at her until my throat is raw and the other half stupidly wants to pick her up and soothe her tears.

"Here's a glass of water. We need to talk."

She doesn't acknowledge me. Her shoulders are heaving and every breath is labored. I place the glass on the sink, and my hand hovers over her head. Apparently the side that wants to comfort her is winning out. That's probably my dick talking, so I clench my fingers into a fist and back out, closing the door quietly behind me.

The sounds of her sobs and dry heaves are muffled but still

audible. Each reverberation of her grief is like a fucking needle into my skin. I grab my burner phone from the counter. She must have looked through it, because it was in my jacket pocket. This morning I was dead tired from flying from Seattle to Russia down to Rio in three days followed by three more days of looking for Regan at Gomes's. I've had only a handful of hours of sleep, and this morning, after disposing of Gomes's thug and buying Regan some clothes, I thought I could give in and rest a moment. We'd have a few hours before Gomes's dead man would have to check in.

I'd thought that I'd have time to sleep. I needed a few hours, but apparently my body and mind had shut down so completely I couldn't tell what was going on. But what the fuck was she trying to seduce me into doing anyway? I let anger at Regan, at the whole goddamn situation, burn away my guilt. She had no business trying to have sex with me. I've been nothing but good to her.

Fuck. Me. Sideways.

Climbing out onto the fire escape, I dial up Petrovich because if I don't check in, the motherfucker will keep texting me. And that pretty much ruins the purpose of the fucking burner phone.

"I'm working, and if I have to stop every goddamn second to tell you that I'm taking a shit, then you're not going to see any results."

"You sound angered, Daniel." Petrovich's nearly accentless voice tumbles down the phone lines.

"Not angered. Irritated. Do you know what that is in Russian?"

"Yes. I went to Oxford, do you not remember?"

"I could give two shits where you went to college. Just fucking stop texting me." I wish I could pace, but the fire escape is about four feet by four feet. There's barely enough room to take one step.

"I should come," he muses.

"Sure, come on down. This place definitely needs more Russians. You aren't going to look out of place at all," I say.

Petrovich grunts. "The Emperor. Remember, he must be captured but not harmed. You must do everything possible to keep him out of harm's way."

"Yeah, I know." I sigh and lean against the iron railing. My previous anger is draining away. Regan's fucked up. Of course she's going to do stupid shit. I just need more patience. It's what I would want for my sister. "Who is this Emperor person anyway?"

There's a pause as if he's trying to weigh whether I'm worthy of the information, but I know far more about Vasily than makes him comfortable. I know enough to blackmail him. Why he wants the Emperor is no big deal when it comes to the fact that he had his uncle, the former head of the *Bratva*, murdered.

"You know of the Emperor's Palace?"

"Yeah, it's the place where I get most of my commissions." And the light dawns. "You want the person who created this underground network. Not for the money. You don't need it."

He's silent, unwilling to give me more information, but it is all so clear to me now.

"You must want to hack into something that is unhackable, and you think the Emperor can do it," I guess, but I know I'm right.

"Yes," he snarls, confirming it all. "The person who can create a network that facilitates the trade of guns, drugs, everything and not get caught? I want him."

"My sister could do it," I told him. "Not that I'd let you get your dirty hands on her."

"Find me the Emperor. It's what I've paid you for." He hangs up, and I let the empty static buzz in my ear for a minute. Find the Emperor. Find my sister. Well, to do all that I needed to shed some baggage. Regan needs to get going before the two of us do each other in. I key in another number to help that process along.

"*Da*." Nick's harsh Ukrainian accent is a welcome relief from the soft romantic tones of the Portuguese language. I can't handle soft right now.

"Your girl is a basket case," I tell him.

"Regan does not belong to me. She is not mine. I have only one."

Nick is so goddamn literal. Usually it makes me laugh but not now. "Put Daisy on the phone."

"*Nyet*."

"Yes, put your goddamn girlfriend on the phone or I'm walking away from Regan right now."

There's a shuffling in the background and a grunt from Nick. "Hello?" Daisy sounds breathless but happy. A little of my anger leaks away. I can't ruin her happiness. Daisy's been through too much, and I know she's crushed with guilt. If it weren't for Daisy, Regan would never have been kidnapped. If Daisy hadn't been a virgin, Regan wouldn't have been raped. I can't tell her what is going on here.

"Daisy, sweetheart, that dour Ukrainian keeping you happy? You know I'm more than willing to come to your rescue?" I try to inject some false cheeriness into my voice.

She giggles. "Nah, I love my dour Ukrainian. You're too laid-back for me. I like them morose and uptight."

Boy, she has Nick pegged perfectly. "You've never had a Texan. Once you have a taste of big sky country, you can't go back."

"I thought big sky country referred to Montana."

"We're so awesome that all the best slogans are used to describe us. Montana's a copycat and they know it. Plus, their motto is used to describe why they get away with copulating with cattle. No one around to see."

"That's really gross, Daniel."

"I know. It's why I don't visit there." The small talk is actually wearing on me, so I get down to business. "It's good news. I've got Regan."

When Daisy begins to cry, I want to crush the phone in my fingers. I've had it up to here with the tears. I can't take one more woman sobbing, even if she is happy. But Daisy's tears aren't cries of relief. I can hear the guilt and sorrow and pain in them. "Did you hear me? We're safe," I bark into the receiver with more force than I intend.

"Do not raise your voice to her or it will be the last thing you say," I hear Nick threaten.

"Yeah, yeah." At this point, I'd welcome being put out of my misery. I stick my head back into the bedroom, but I don't hear any sounds from Regan. Hesitantly I climb through the window and into the apartment again. It sounds like dead silence. Shit, did she hurt herself? "Gotta run," I say and throw down the phone. In less than five seconds I'm at the bathroom door, but it's open and the bathroom is empty. A light cough sounds behind me and I spin around, gun in hand. It's Regan, sitting on the corner of the sofa, her hands upraised. I flick the safety on and stick the gun back into my tactical vest.

"You look like shit," I say because I'm at a complete loss for words. My throat aches from holding back all the shouting I want to do. Before she can respond, the phone rings. Nick and Daisy. "Get another bottle of water and drink it all down. But slowly. You're going to be seriously dehydrated."

Her eyes dart toward the bedroom where my phone is ringing. Ignoring the incessant rings, I stomp over to the refrigerator and pull out another bottle of water. *Patience*, I counsel myself. This girl has been through hell and she needs some patience. Treat her as you would your sister.

With another deep breath, I gather my tattered self-control and give her a gritty, barely there smile and hand her the bottle. The phone has stopped ringing, but then it starts again.

"You better get that." Her voice sounds like someone has scratched it with sandpaper. It's rough and gravelly and sexy as fuck.

"Yeah." I make no move to answer the phone, though. After two rings, the voicemail kicks in and a beep lets me know I have a waiting message.

"I'm sorry about this morning," she whispers, and then she looks down at her hands that are busy peeling the label off the bottle.

My first instinct is to say it's no big deal, but it's a big fucking huge deal so I'm not going to try to sweep it under the sofa like it's nothing. "I've got to make a phone call, but then you and I are going to talk. You're going to tell my why Gomes keeps coming after you. You're going to tell me why you won't let me take you to the embassy. Then we're going to talk about this morning."

She nods again and takes a sip of water, looking at me with wet, huge eyes over the plastic container. Looking as if I'm going to drop her off on the side of the road. Rubbing my forehead, I try to find some patience.

"I'm not going to hurt you, Regan. And I don't want you to use me to hurt you." I stroke a finger alongside of the back of her hand, and when she doesn't flinch I squeeze it. "I'm on your side, no matter what. But I can't fucking help you if you don't allow me to know what's going on. I spent weeks looking for you, and I'm telling you right now that I'd rather be dead than allow anything bad to happen to you. So plan on talking when this is all over."

This causes her to give another little watery gasp, so I back off. I can't handle another crying bout this morning. My nerves are shot, and I'm sitting on the knife's edge of insanity with no sleep, a shit ton of guilt, and the worry of Gomes's men coming and tracking us down. I wasn't lying when I told Regan that I'd die before I let harm come to her again. I don't want to hear those broken sounds from her. Not ever again.

Inside the bedroom, I pick up the phone and see that Nick's called me three more times. I step out onto the fire escape again and pull down the window. This is not a conversation Regan needs to hear. Not yet.

"Is Regan okay?" Daisy answers before the first ring completes its cycle.

"She looks okay. I haven't taken her to a doctor or anything." I figured someone at the embassy would take care of that.

"She can go to one when she's back in Minneapolis," Daisy muses. "Why isn't she at the embassy? I thought the plan was to get her and then take her to the embassy."

"Thanks, Daniel, for saving my best friend when you had nothing to do with her kidnapping," I say a bit sarcastically.

When my harsh words are met with silence, I feel like a dick. "Look, sorry. It's been a tough few days. I took her to the embassy, but she wouldn't get out of the taxi. Rather than go through a big production by carrying her nearly bare-assed through the front doors, I brought her with me."

"How will you get her home, then?"

"I'm taking her over today, but here's the deal: she's scared of me and she doesn't trust me, so how much do you want me to tell her?"

"Everything."

"Everything? That Nick's a former Russian hit man and that she was kidnapped because they didn't know which girl he was boning?"

"Yes, all of that," Daisy says flatly. "Or I'll tell her. Put her on the phone."

"Fine."

I climb back in and hand the phone over to Regan. "It's for you."

She looks at me like there's a snake that will crawl through the earpiece and bite her, but after a moment she reaches out and takes the phone from me.

"Hello?" she asks tentatively.

CHAPTER **NINE**

REGAN

"Oh my god, Regan. It's so good to hear your voice."

I'm startled to hear her on the other end. "D-Daisy?" She's the last person I expected. My mind is still back on the sofa, where I more or less tried to rape Daniel.

Oh my God. I've become just like those assholes that used me. I feel so revolting, so unclean. I swallow back bile and try to concentrate on the phone.

"It's me." Daisy's sweet, tearful voice makes me feel worse. My roomie, innocent Daisy, is the one that sent Daniel? I don't understand. Daisy wouldn't know someone that ran red lights, much less a man that kills people and frequents brothels.

I look over at Daniel, confused. His tired face is lined with anger and hard as he crosses his arms and watches me talk on the phone. He's pissed. No, he's beyond pissed. Trying to fuck him was a bad call, and now he's going to ditch me and that Mr. Freeze guy will be there to scoop me up.

"Thank God," Daisy is babbling in my ear. "Are you okay? Are you hurt? Talk to me."

I don't know what to say. "I'm okay." All my war wounds are on the inside. Physically? I'm dandy. "I'm just . . . confused."

Daniel grunts and pulls another phone out of his pocket, another burner. How many does this man have? He starts texting, and his gaze flicks to me. "Tell her to start at the beginning."

I lick my lips—they still taste like bile—and speak, "Daniel says to start at the beginning."

"Okay." She exhales loudly, as if steeling herself. "You know Nick? The Ukrainian guy I've been dating?"

"Yes." I haven't met him personally but I've seen him a few times in the hallway of the apartment building, and innocent Daisy is head over heels for the guy.

"He's a hit man. Or he was. He's giving it up for me."

I'm not entirely sure I heard her right. "He's what?"

"A hit man. An assassin. He used to kill people for a living." It's so strange to hear those words come from innocent Daisy's voice, but she's not apologetic about it. She accepts it. "Someone killed his mentor, and Nick was hunting him down. That's why he was in Minneapolis. Well, that and another job. It's a little complicated." She's rushing through the words as if they're not important. "Nick was being chased by the Russian Mafia—the *Bratva*. And . . . remember when you had my cell phone? They thought you were me. They were going to take me to force Nick to do their bidding. And I think they kept you because . . ." She hesitates. "You're pretty."

I swallow hard, memories flashing forward. Of a scary, hulking blond man showing up at the apartment with the ugly Yury. Yury pushing a needle into my arm, drugging me. Yury ripping my clothing off—

I shake my head to clear it of the horrible memories, but they lurk at the edges of my mind, waiting for a weak moment. *They kept you because you're pretty.*

"I . . ." I try to think of what to ask. I'm revolted, and yet I have questions. "How did you get away?"

"Nick saved me," she says, and I can hear the love in her voice, and the affectionate murmur of a man's response nearby. "We tried to find you, but . . ." Her voice wobbles.

Resentment flares in my gut. I try to bury it, but it's difficult. I keep silent, lest I say something I regret.

"They sold you off to someone," Daisy continues. "And then people kept coming after Nick, so we had to go into hiding. We sent Daniel to find you."

Daniel, who I've treated like shit. Who I've used, who I've done nothing but cry around. I give him another wary look. "He's a hit man, too?"

"Yes. He's one of Nick's friends."

"Okay."

"O-okay? Don't you have more questions?" She sounds confused, like she's pictured this conversation in her mind a million times and it's not going the way she wants it to.

"No," I say flatly. "I'm good." And I hand the phone back to Daniel.

He cocks an eyebrow, giving me an odd look. Then he takes the phone back, gets to his feet, and stands again. His voice is low. "Daisy, sweetheart, why don't you put Nikolai back on the phone?" A moment later, he switches to a foreign language and begins to spit words out. I don't catch most of it but I hear *Gomes* and *Regan* intermixed with what must be Russian. Or Ukrainian. I don't know either one. He's talking about me, and in another language deliberately so I can't pick up what they're saying.

I clasp my hands together and stare down at them in my lap. I'm trying not to, but the truth is I'm burning with bitterness at my conversation with Daisy. It sounds like while I was sold into a brothel, she was running back to the United States with her boyfriend in tow, the very same boyfriend that got us into this mess.

And because they couldn't be bothered, I was left behind for someone else to find.

I'm sure that's not the full story, of course. If I were rational, it'd make sense to me. But I'm not rational anymore. I'm a freak show who tries to fuck men—even when they don't want it—and who cries at the drop of the hat.

They kept you because you're pretty.

My fingers curl, and I fight the urge to claw my own eyes out, to mark myself up until I'm no longer "pretty" enough to be a whore. Although the way that Daniel looks at me after I tried . . . well, after what happened maybe no one will want me anyway.

I bet if Daisy had been sold into a brothel, she'd have been retrieved right away. Her dangerous Ukrainian boyfriend would have seen to that. But my boyfriend is Mike. Mike didn't come for me. No one did.

Until Daniel. And I've been awful to him.

As if he knows my thoughts have veered in his direction again, Daniel turns around, barks a quick word into the phone, and then closes it with a snap. It's clear he's still seething, but he doesn't want to lash out at me.

"Sorry," I murmur, my voice thick. "I know I'm a head case."

He gives me an exasperated look and then heads for the kitchen. As I watch, he grabs a bottle of some sort of liquor and two glasses. He heads back to the living room, sits on the other end of the sofa, puts the glasses on the end table, and begins to pour two drinks. "Regan, you've been through hell in ways I can't even imagine. No one's expecting you to be shitting daisies right now. But you and I have to work together to get you out of here, okay? I need to know what's going on so I can save both of our asses."

I watch him for a moment and then offer something that's not quite an apology. "I panicked earlier. That's why I . . . tried to seduce you. I thought you were going to send me away. I thought you'd like it. I've seen you looking at me. And I saw the panties you bought me." Tears pool in my eyes, and I swipe them away. "I'm sorry. I'm so sorry. I wasn't thinking. I was just . . . desperate. I didn't know what to do. So I just . . . acted. Now I'm as bad as the men at the brothel." Snot's running out of my nose and I'm a mess, but I don't know what to do to make things better. I tried to fix things and I just made them so much worse.

Daniel leaves the room and comes back a moment later with a roll of toilet paper, which he hands to me. I blow my nose and wipe my eyes obediently.

"Yeah." He shakes his head. "You fucked up. Not gonna lie, I'm more than a little pissed about the situation. Listen,"—he hands me a glass of the clear alcohol—"truth is I think you're gorgeous, okay? But I'm not that big of a dick. I wouldn't touch you because I know what you've been through. You're safe with me. I bought you girly panties because that was what they were selling at the store I was at and I didn't want to leave you alone for any longer than necessary. I'm sorry if I sent you the wrong signal. I'm not here to fuck you, okay? I'm here to save your ass." He downs his drink and lifts the glass in a toast. "However fine it might be."

A reluctant half smile touches my mouth. I glance down at my drink and sniff it. It smells . . . strange. "What is this?"

"Local drink of choice. Cachaça,"—he says it like *ka-shah-sah*—"kinda like rum, kinda not."

"So why are we drinking?"

"Because I sure as shit need a drink after this morning," he says, pouring himself another one. "And you need to relax. Now, bottoms up."

I shrug. He's right. I do need to relax. I feel like I've been in panic mode for the last twenty-four hours. I tilt the glass back and down its contents. At first it tastes a bit like rum, then it explodes into something totally different, and I cough. My throat is raw from all the puking I've been doing. "Whoa."

"Yeah, it's something else." He refills my glass with another shot of the cachaça. "Now, drink that and then we'll talk."

I suck down the next shot of the cachaça, and the alcoholic burn begins to float through my limbs. Normally it would take more than two shots to get me plastered, but I've got an empty stomach and the alcohol is strong. I hold my glass out for another shot, and Daniel obliges.

"So," he asks, "we feeling better now?"

"Better," I agree. And I am a little better. "Thank you."

"How come you didn't want to talk to Daisy?"

I give him a skeptical look. "So the plan is to get me drunk and quiz me?"

"Bingo," he says, filling my glass again.

I down the newest shot and I'm definitely feeling floaty and relaxed. I notice Daniel has been holding the same full glass while I've been pounding them away. Sneaky man. A thought occurs to me and I stiffen. "You're not getting me drunk so—"

Daniel's eyes widen. "Christ, no. That fantasy's a little ruined for me at the moment with that whole you-jumping-me-and-then-puking thing."

I wince. "Bad call."

"Yep," he says flatly.

"Ugh. That was rapey of me."

"Eh. It makes sense, in a fucked-up sort of way. You're desperate." He refills my glass before I can ask. "When you're desperate, you do crazy shit. Been there."

I muse on his words, languid now that the alcohol is doing its magic. So sex with me was a fantasy, huh? If only he knew. "Probably for the best that the sex fantasy is ruined," I confide to him. "I don't know if you noticed, but I have a few issues."

He snorts. "Darlin', you are the poster child for issues."

I giggle at that, unable to help myself. I should be insulted, but he's right. I'm all fucked up in the head, and I acknowledge it. Then I sigh, looking down at my glass. "At least it's just sex I'm messed up about. It's not like I'm missing out."

"Do tell."

I peer over at him and am reminded he's rather good-looking. He's got that all-American-boy thing going for him. I'd have totally crushed on him if I'd had a class with him back at college. "It's not like it was great before, you know? Never had an orgasm with a guy. Pretty sure it's bullshit."

Daniel groans. "You are positively killing me here, Regan."

"Why?"

He shakes his head. "Change of subject. Why were you short with Daisy?"

I lick the rim of my glass since he's not refilling it. Maybe I should stay drunk for the next month. "Because I didn't want to be mean to her."

"Why would you be mean to her?"

"Because she got away," I whisper. "She got away and left me. Everyone left me." I swallow hard and put my glass down. Then I look at Daniel. "You're not going to leave me, are you?"

"I'm not, sweetheart. You have my word on that." He looks at me thoughtfully and then downs his drink. "But you need to tell me why you won't go to the embassy. What's there that scares you?"

"I saw a man," I whisper. "Mr. Freeze's bodyguard."

"Mr. Freeze? Arnold Schwarzenegger? Like . . . from the shitty Batman movies?"

I shake my head and rub my arms, as if chilled. I'm not warm and toasty from the alcohol anymore. "The blond guy. The scary one. He buys girls. He bought me. He sent me to Rio to be 'broken in.' They can be as rough with me as they want, as long as they don't mess up my face, wear condoms, and make sure I brush my teeth."

"Your . . . teeth? Wear condoms?"

I rub a finger over my front teeth thoughtfully. "I think he has a hygiene fetish. He'd come and visit me at the brothel. Wouldn't fuck me. Just put on plastic gloves before he touched me and looked me over. Asked them if they shaved me. Everything." I shiver. "He scares me."

"Maybe he's a germophobe."

I shake my head, remembering the bodyguard that was with him. "Everyone's scared of him. Even Senhor Gomes."

"So some rich guy has a fixation on you. Sends you to Gomes for what? Training? I guess that explains the use of condoms and good hygiene and why Gomes wants you back." He doesn't look happy with this news. "And you said you saw him at the embassy?"

"His bodyguard." I shiver again, unable to help myself, and I realize for the first time that I'm sitting on the couch in nothing but my bra. Whoops.

Daniel notices my shivering and pulls the blanket around me, tucking it around me like he would a child. "Good to know. I'll make a few calls and see if I can find out what's going on. And then we're going to have to move."

"Move?" I blink at him, still drunk from the cachaça. "Why?"

"Because they're going to know we're in the area once they find out I killed Gomes's little scout." He says it so casually, like someone would comment on the weather. "We're safe for now, but tonight we need to move on."

I hug the blanket closer. "And you'll take me with you?"

"I'm afraid you're all mine until we figure out what the deal is." He rubs his neck and looks agitated, but not at me. "It's a goddamn mess, isn't it?"

"Can I get a gun?"

He gives me a speculative look. "Do you promise to stop crying?"

"I will, if you get me a gun. Then I'll shoot you if I get upset."

For some reason, this makes him laugh. "I think we can manage that."

CHAPTER **TEN**

DANIEL

Regan still looks on the verge of tears. I miss the army because there's only a short range of emotions that are acceptable in there, particularly within Delta Force. Mostly it's cocksure bravado and weary acceptance. Regan's feelings are hard for me to process because introspection is not encouraged in the army. I spent eight years suffocating my feelings so I could become an efficient killing machine. It was great training for being a hired assassin outside the military but had shit-all to do with helping wounded girls.

There's no question in my mind that her sticking to me is going to mess her up more, but I didn't bust my ass finding this girl to let her be stolen again. Taking a stab in the dark at what's really got her worked up—and not in a good way—I tell her, "They would've come and searched for you, but Nick's supposed to be dead. He can't be running around down here in Rio because if his name leaks then he's on the run again, along with Daisy. Plus Nick's a shitty people person. He'd never have been able to get you out of Gomes's place without a huge gunfight."

I don't know why I'm explaining this to her. Nick's not a friend at all. He's an acquaintance. If pressed, I'd say he was a colleague. Part of the fraternal order of the Fucked-Up Guys Who Can't Function Without a Gun. I'd watched him for a while because I was always looking for connections—anyone I could find that might lead me to my sister. And Nick had worked with scum since he was a kid. He'd been a paid hit man working on his own since the age of fifteen. He looked his age of twenty-five, but his eyes told you he'd seen and done hellacious things that men the age of eighty wouldn't come close to dreaming up in their worst nightmares. And I wasn't wrong to hook my wagon to Nick, because helping him off a Russian Mafia boss gave me my first good lead in a long time. A blonde taken from Cancun turned up in an auction in Rio eighteen months ago and then disappeared, sold through the same channels that Regan had been funneled through. Boom. Two birds. One fucking heavy stone from me.

I've got Regan, and now I need to find my sister. As Regan's face loses its pinched, hurt look, the tension knot at the back of my neck releases. She's not going to cry. I pour her another drink because the worst feeling after being drunk is the cessation of liquor. And if there's anyone who needs the little peace that the brown bottle can bring, it's Regan.

"So they didn't leave me?" she asks in a stronger voice, the tremors all but gone.

"Nah, they sent me. Trust me. I'm far better looking and a better shot. Not to mention a helluva lot funnier. You'd rather have me, wouldn't you?" I flex for her, and she chuckles like I intend.

"I guess so. I mean, I like Daisy, and it sounds stupid after all that I've been through that being abandoned by her hurts worse."

"Sugar, you're allowed to feel any damn way you want." *Just don't cry, because your tears hurt worse than a knife wound to the gut.*

She nods slowly, as if she's trying to rearrange her internal feelings toward Daisy. I guess betrayal by someone close is worse than constant abuse from strangers?

Her head is starting to bob now. Lightweight. I could drink the whole bottle and feel nothing. It's my party trick. I can drink nearly anyone under the table. Vasily Petrovich—the newly installed head of the Petrovich mob family—and I had a contest when we were waiting for Nick to show up so we could go kill Vasily's uncle. He swore no westerner could drink as much as a Russian. I kept up and Petrovich deemed me suitable to retrieve his hacker. Shit, why is everyone in Rio? I shake my head.

So helping Regan fell to me because Nick Anders is not a hit man. He's an art student. It's hard to kill the head of the *Bratva* and come out alive, which is why Nikolai Andrushko is dead, killed by Vasily in retribution for his uncle's death. From the ashes rose Nick Anders, a quiet, brooding American. So no, Nick can't be running around the slums looking for blond girls from the U.S. when he's supposed to be dead, and Daisy . . . well, there isn't anyone less suited for doing the rescue of her best friend.

"You sleepy?" I ask gently. She nods. "I'm going to pick you up and carry you to the bedroom." The up-and-down motion of her head could be consent or it could be that she's too drunk to hold her head up. I pick her up, and she doesn't protest. Instead, she snuggles into me, her soft cheek pressing against the skin exposed by my unbuttoned shirt and beater tank. "We're going to need to take you to a doctor and make sure you're okay on the inside."

She ignores this and instead proceeds to rub the tip of her nose into the hollow of my neck, and I tremble like a goddamn preteen. I need to rub one out. It's just a desperate backlog of sperm. "You smell good," she murmurs. Man, I had no idea that spot on my neck is such a sensitive place on my body. Picking up the pace, I stride over and drop her onto the bed. She bounces a little and the mattress squeaks, but she doesn't appear fazed.

The shopping bags are not completely unpacked, so I dump everything out on the table and start rolling up the items into the new bag I bought her. But as my hand brushes over the lace and satin of the bras and panties the sales associate had picked out, I pause. It's sexy stuff, but I didn't understand the leap in logic from the nice fabric to *I better fuck Daniel before he leaves me.* We don't have time to stop and get new stuff. Hopefully, Regan will put this out of her mind, or we are both in for a bad time.

I stuff the rest of the purchases into the bag and set it on top of the table. Shrugging into the tactical vest, I gather up all my shit and set my packed bag next to Regan's. Two guns are shoved into my vest along with a full case of ammo.

Taking one of the chairs, I stick it under the handle of the apartment door. After rechecking all the windows to make sure they're locked, I lay down beside Regan. It's hot inside the apartment with all the windows and doors closed, but better to be hot and safe than cool and open for anyone to climb in.

My phone buzzes and I pull it out. It's a text from Pereya, a contact I made who supplies bad people—and good ones, too, I suppose—with everything from medical supplies to guns. He does a booming repeat business.

Informant in Morro dos Macacos. Futbol field. Dawn.

Isn't that fucking great? I will have to take Regan into one of the most dangerous favelas in order to gather some intel. I'm betting if I take her over to the Palace she'd run away, no matter that it's the nicest hotel in all of Rio. And the soccer field? Last I heard there were circular burn marks all over those fields because the drug gangs liked to place their torture victims inside a ring of tires, douse them with gasoline, and burn them alive.

But if what Regan says about the embassy is true, I can't take her back there. The revelation that one of the embassy guards is working for some human trafficker shouldn't surprise me but it does. I doubt he's a marine, though. A lot of embassies hire contractors—most of them former military—and they're supposed to pass a deep background investigation, but the government often cheaps out on the firms running the background check; and, hell, fake backgrounds are easy to concoct if you've got enough money, and one thing traffickers don't seem to lack is a ton of coin.

My phone beeps again, this time with a message from Vasily.

All roads lead to Rio. I'm coming. Find him. -V

Even better. I force myself to loosen my grip so I don't crack the plastic clamshell. A new Russian Mafia boss in search of a computer-hacking genius is coming to Rio. We should hole up in one of the favelas and have a shootout until the last man—I look over at Regan—or woman is standing. Keeping her with me wasn't the plan. I was going to locate her, drop her at the embassy, and then find my sister. But now our destinies are bound. Fate, karma, whatever shitty fucking overlord above who shines his paltry light down on us has put us together. So be it. We're going to go in together and get out together.

I text my contact in Morro dos Macacos.

Thanks. Will need some supplies. USD cash?

USD OK.

And then because she needs it, I text back.

Need female doc to run some tests. Blood work.

No problem.

Nothing is a problem for Pereya.

Tomorrow I'll get more ammunition, have Regan checked out, go see an informant, find Vasily's hacker, save my sister, and get the hell out of South America. Right now, though, I need some fucking shut-eye or I'll be completely worthless. I allow myself to doze off, one hand on the grip of my Ruger. Anyone comes in and I'll blow their head off. At this point, I wouldn't even care if it is Vasily.

Scratching sounds in the exterior room wake me up. In her sleep, Regan has cuddled up close to me. Her long, naked leg is thrown over mine. I'm amazed I didn't wake up when she got close. My body responds to the closeness of hers, and I grow semi-hard in an instant. Fuck. Ain't got time for that now.

I disentangle from her and roll off the bed, pulling Regan with me to the edge. With one hand over her mouth, I shake her a bit with my other and then slide my palm down her side to press her legs into the bed. Predictably, when she wakes, she's violently furious at being held down.

"Regan, it's Daniel," I hiss. "There's someone outside. I'll let you go, but you have to be silent. Nod if you understand."

It takes her a few seconds, but then she nods. The minute I release her, she curls into a fetal ball. "No worries," I tell her. "But crawl into the bathtub."

She shakes her head, slides off the bed, and hunkers down behind me. Her fingers tuck into a strap on the back of my vest. I'm guessing my promises to return aren't something she puts a lot of faith in. "I'll let you stay, but you can't hold on to me." I'll be hampered in hand-to-hand combat if she's holding on to me.

Crouched low to the floor, I creep to the entry. Once I'm situated with Regan behind me, I reach for the knob and release it. The door swings open and the scuffling in the outside room ceases. A second later, the drywall above our heads explodes. Plaster debris rains down as shots are peppered along the wall.

"Bathroom. Now," I command. This time Regan doesn't hesitate. She jumps up and races to the bathroom as I shoot twice to the right and roll across the open doorway. Then I hear a crash as the intruder stumbles into a table. I smile maliciously to myself. Shoot first and you give away your location, asshole. Creeping out on my belly, with a Ruger in one hand and knife in the other, I see a black shoe. I aim my Ruger two feet higher and when a loud, high-pitched squeal is released, I know I've hit a kneecap. I follow it with another shot, this time slightly to the right. When a thud reverberates, I know I've hit my mark on the shoulder. People are predictable. You shoot the leg and they bend over to grab their wound. It'd be easy to have made a head-shot kill, but I wanted this asswipe alive.

Still crouching, I move farther into the room and switch on my laser sight. The little red dot never fails to scare the piss out of people and, if the pain is too much, he has something to focus on. I'm a giver. My target is on the ground, writhing and moving his hands from his shoulder to his knee as if unsure which wound he should try to compress first. It won't matter. Once he answers a few questions, I'll make sure he doesn't have to worry about either injury. A quick glance around the interior shows that the room is empty. The window near the sofa is open, and a rope is dangling down. He must've come alone, because anyone else would have rappelled down to save this guy once the gunshots went off. Despite the suppressor, there's no good disguise for the supersonic boom that a bullet makes when fired, not to mention the screaming he made when I popped his kneecap. That's a painful injury.

I walk over and pick up his gun, tucking it into my vest. As I walk to the window, I step on his wounded shoulder, which makes him sob out in pain. Reaching out, I tug at the rope. There's no return resistance, which means it's passively secured. The rope comes tumbling down with a few flicks of my wrist, and I haul it inside. No sense in advertising a break-in.

"Senhor Gomes really likes this girl, huh?" I say, winding the rope into a loop and then tucking it into a bag. "Regan," I call, "need an ID, please." Maybe she'll recognize him. I sure as hell don't.

Regan comes tiptoeing out.

"Just as far as the doorway." This asshole isn't in any shape to attack a kitten, but I want to be extra sure that Regan's out of harm's way. Kneeling behind the intruder, I lift up his head by the hair and jerk him into a sitting position. "You know this guy?"

A cry of anger flies out of her, and she rushes toward the both of us. His hands are outstretched as if to repel her attack, but rage powers her straight through and she kicks him in the gut, causing him to crumple over. Another kick hits his knee, and he starts babbling in Portuguese for me to make the devil woman stop. I guess she does know this guy.

Reluctantly, I put a stop to the action, although it was kind of amusing in a dark way.

"Okay, Regan, I need to ask this asshole some questions, so you need to dial it back."

She restrains herself, huffing and puffing. There's blood on her leg, probably from her inadvertent kick to the gun wound on the intruder's knee.

"Better go wash that off. No telling what he's got in his body."

She looks down at her body and then shudders. With a short nod, she spins and heads into the bathroom. When I hear the water running, I pull the guy into the remaining chair, forcing his legs into a bent position, and zip tie his hands to each side.

"*Ai meu Deus do Céu!*" he pleads. I can't work up any sympathy for this rapist.

"Nope. No god is helping you today." I tap his knee again, and he starts blubbering. While he cries, I examine his gun.

"What is it?" Regan is back. In the moonlight, her legs are exposed and shiny from the water, and if I'm staring at them, no doubt our intruder is.

"It's an African Vektor SP-1. A nice piece not usually carried by someone from the slums. Most of those guys either have their AR47s or *arma improvisadas* makeshift weapons with pipe and a firing pin." I heft the gun. "This one, though, shows he's part of a well-funded, well-armed gang." I turn to her. "Go put some pants on."

She flushes but hurries over to the bag and pulls out a pair of linen pants. I realize as she's tugging them on, right in front of both of us, that she's scared shitless. She's not letting me out of her sight. Running to the bathroom was an extreme act of bravery and trust on her part. She needs a reward and a security blanket.

I flip the Vektor around and offer her the grip. "Here, have a souvenir of your time in Rio. It's a 9 millimeter with a short recoil. Not a bad gun for you. Chambers thirteen, but I think he's wasted about seven of those."

Turning back to our captive, I spin the chair around. "Here's how it's going to go. You're going to tell us what your objective was, and then I'm going to make all the pain go away. Okay?"

He nods.

"I know that Gomes wants my girl back, but that's not happening, so start talking. Oh, and in English for the lady, *por favor.*"

"Gomes sends me to retrieve girl. Kill you."

"Then what?"

He shrugs a little and then winces when it pains his shoulder. "Nothing."

"You on staff or for hire?"

"For hire," he says, and a glint appears in his eyes. Maybe he thinks he's going to be able to bargain his way out of here.

"Got any questions for him, Regan?"

"Does he like eating his own dick? Because that's what should happen to him."

"Do you?" I ask him.

"She's a whore. I can get you dozens more, better than her," the man says to me in Portuguese.

"He's trying to sell me on the idea that there are other girls I can get if I give you up," I translate for Regan. Then I say, "In English, dickwad." I kick him in the shin, and he cries out and shakes the chair, trying to escape the pain. "Want to kick him?" I ask Regan.

"Yes," she says emphatically. She wants to do more than kick him.

"Hold on." I pull out the chair that I'd used to secure the front door, and break off the leg. "Use this. Don't want you to have to shower again."

She holds the chair leg like a bat and hits him, not across the knee like I thought she would, but across the face. Once, twice. I catch her on the next downswing and she fights me for a minute, panting like a wild dog until, I guess, reason finally dawns on her. "Yeah, we want to keep him conscious enough to answer a few more questions," I say.

Turning back to our intruder, I see he's nearly passed out. "Sugar, run to the kitchen and get me a pan full of water and toss it in his face. He needs to wake up." I figure these tasks will help her stay focused. When she returns from the kitchen, her breathing is under control and she doesn't even hit him with the pan. He sputters awake.

"She doesn't like you much, and I don't want anyone else but her. I mean, come on, where am I gonna find someone who swings a chair leg like Babe Ruth?"

He doesn't get the reference or he's out of it, because he stares at me blankly. "The fact that you're a hired guy kind of bothers me, because Gomes isn't the type to hire out. He's stingy. And even if he wasn't, he doesn't have the kind of coin to maintain a little army full of mercenaries like you. Who hired you?"

The intruder doesn't respond, simply looks away. He's obviously had some training, and it's kicking in now because he decides that's all the information I'm getting.

"Should I hit him again?" Regan asks eagerly.

"Nah. I think he's too scared of your Mr. Freeze to give any more information, and we gotta get going."

She looks disappointed.

"You got anything in the bedroom? Why don't you do a sweep and make sure we're not leaving anything behind?"

She sets down the pan and the wooden stick with some reluctance but heads into the bedroom.

Once I see she's out of eyesight, I turn and shoot the motherfucker in the head. Twice. The sound of the gunshots brings Regan racing into the living room. "What did you do?"

"Put him out of his misery."

The dismay showing on her face makes my insides shrivel a bit. Of course having sex with her is only fantasyland for me, because there's no way this diamond wants my black hands on her. I strip the guy down and take everything out of his pockets, including a bag full of bullets, a knife strapped to his leg, and a thick white vellum card with my address on it. I run my hands along the hems of his pants and shirt, searching for any hidden pockets or secrets but find none. Dropping the clothes in the tub, I soak the entire pile with alcohol and then light it up.

"Why are you burning his clothes? Haven't you left clues all over this place? You aren't even wearing gloves." She raises her hands. "Neither am I. Oh my God, am I going to jail for this?"

"No, you aren't because no one knows you're here, sweetheart. And I don't care if anyone knows I'm here. I just want our late-night friend to be a little harder to identify."

In the living room, I toss a sheet over the dead man, as if the white cloth can somehow hide my sins. But all the bad deeds I've done have marked me with permanent ink. My soul is tattooed over with the faces of everyone I've killed. I like to tell myself that they're all righteous kills. But the truth is that from the first life you take, you become a different person. And guys like me don't deserve a woman like Regan, no matter how much I might want her. On that depressing thought, I grab both our bags. "Let's go. We need to find a new base, and then we've got an appointment in Morro dos Macacos."

CHAPTER ELEVEN

REGAN

"The way I see it, baby doll, we have three big issues," Daniel tells me as he hands a wad of cash to the taxi driver that drops us in the middle of a disgusting slum and speeds away.

I'm sure the nickname is to distract me from the fact that we've been dumped in the middle of hell. I still fall for the bait. "Baby doll? Are you for real?"

"Oh, I'm real." He gives me a roguish grin and winks at me. "One hundred percent prime specimen."

I roll my eyes and shoulder my backpack. Daniel's been needling me ever since we left the apartment. I know he's doing it on purpose. It's obvious. Normally he's understanding and gives me space, but right now he nudges me with his elbow and calls me names like "sugar pie" and "baby doll." I guess he figures if I'm riled up and want to choke him, I won't flip out and go into another crying jag.

He's right, too. I have to admit that I'm still freaked out. I'm trying to hold it together, but tonight Daniel executed a man in the middle of his living room. I turned my back for two minutes, and *boom! Boom!* The man was shot twice in the head. Daniel didn't even blink.

I hated the man, but I'm still shocked to my core. This is the third man that has died in the last two days, each effortlessly dispatched by Daniel, who makes it look as if he hasn't broken a sweat. He's a dangerous man behind all of his laughing grins and teasing names.

Weirdly enough, though, I trust him. If someone had to die, I believe it. I don't think Daniel would kill anyone frivolously. He's had lots of opportunities, especially when he saved me, but he tried talking his way in first. The gun is the last course of action.

That he's had to pull out his gun so many times the last few nights tells me how much shit we're in.

Daniel eyes the graffiti-decorated slums of Morro dos Macacos. "Home sweet shithole," he says. "Stick close to me, baby doll. This is one place we do not want to get separated."

"Enough with the 'baby doll,'" I tell him but move a little closer. His arm goes around my waist, dragging me against him, and I'm about to protest until I see a few men lurking in the shadows nearby. All right, if I need to hang off of Daniel to make things look good, I will.

"So, where are we going?" I ask in my sultriest, sexiest voice. I try to give Daniel a heated glance in the hopes that it looks like we're heading for a midnight rendezvous. I'm hoping no one stops to ask why the hell we'd be doing that here.

Daniel must've guessed the reason for my new attitude because he flashes me an appreciative look. His hand is still at my waist, but I know it's resting on the gun he tucked under my shirt earlier. "I told you. It's a surprise . . . but you've gotta be good."

We pass by the men lurking in the shadows, and I do my best not to tense up. I play along instead, and trail a hand down the front of Daniel's shirt. "Oh, I can be really good to you, baby." Strangely enough, the urge to vomit at his touch is gone. I guess I got it all out of my system earlier.

"Damn," Daniel says hoarsely, and I want to laugh at his expression. He looks as if the pretending's getting a little too real for him. But I keep rubbing my hand on his chest, looking like a devoted, slutty girlfriend who can't wait to get him home.

We pass by the men without incident, and Daniel's arm loosens around my waist a few minutes later—a sign that the danger has passed, but our charade needs to continue. We walk a few blocks in the slums, which Daniel tells me are called favelas. They're concrete cinderblock and rickety wooden houses all held together by garbage and spray-painted graffiti, and they pile on top of one another like cockroaches. I'm sure the rest of Brazil is pretty, but so far, all I've seen are slums.

"So," I ask him as we walk, "you never did tell me the three problems?"

"Hmm?" He brushes a hand over mine absently, then pulls away as if remembering that I don't like to be touched. Again, I'm surprised Daniel's not setting off my puke trigger. Maybe our ugly little interlude this morning was cathartic, like a boil that needed to be lanced. It's a gross mental image, but those are all I've got lately. "Oh, yeah. Three problems. One is that your sweet little ass has no papers. Two is that we can't go to the embassy to get those papers for obvious reasons. And three is that pissant

Gomes keeps pulling more guys out of the woodwork to go after you. Mr. Freeze wants you back, and bad."

"I don't know why. I'm no one special."

"Baby love, you are all kinds of special."

"You are the worst at coming up with pet names."

"It's a talent of mine." He grins at me and then gestures down the street. "There we go."

"There we go, what?" I stare at the building and try not to panic. It honestly reminds me of the brothel. It's a narrow, three-story redbrick building. The windows have strings of laundry hanging out of them, and a nest of wires overhead shows the building has electricity. "Not in there, surely?"

"'Fraid so," Daniel says casually. "We're going to hide under their noses for a few days. I'm going to pull a few connections, see what I can find out, and a partner is heading this way."

He doesn't look afraid of the shitty building, so I swallow my fear and let him lead me onward. I have a gun tucked into my pants, and I'm going to use every bullet before I let anyone drag me back into the brothel again.

We approach the building, and there's music blasting from a nearby apartment. The door is wide open, and people are lounging inside the grimy hallway. I'm pretty sure someone is shooting up in the corner. It smells like piss, shit, and, of all things, wet dog. Daniel walks in with a smile and heads for the nearest man. "Pereya," he asks, and from the tone of his voice, it's a demand to see someone, not a question.

The man studies Daniel, his clean-cut looks, and glances at me. I sidle closer to Daniel, in case. Then he holds his hand out.

Daniel says something friendly in Portuguese, but he brushes his jacket back as he does so, revealing his gun. "Get me Pereya," he says again. "Now."

The man nods and disappears into the building.

A few moments later, another man comes out, all smiles. He's wearing a Manchester United jersey, despite the fact that it's a British team, and a baseball cap. He has a scraggly goatee that's so long it's been braided, and he grins at Daniel and throws a hand up. "My man."

"Pereya. How's it going?" They exchange an intricate hand-shake as if they were bosom buddies.

"Can't complain, can't complain. Got your stuff inside." Pereya looks me up and down. "Sweet little honey."

"She's mine," Daniel says casually, as if I'm not my own person. I want to protest, but Daniel's arrogance brings safety, so I'll let him take the lead. He's leaned closer to Pereya, asking, "The doc, too?"

Pereya nods, touches the side of his nose with his thumb, and glances around.

"Yep," Daniel says to the unspoken question.

"Come on, then." He gestures to a couple of the men loitering in the doorway, and they shuffle outside. Bodyguards, perhaps. Pereya looks at Daniel and nods his head, acknowledging a back room.

Daniel grabs my hand and begins to head back, but Pereya shakes his head. "Just you, Hays. No chickies."

Panic swirls, but Daniel gives my hand a squeeze and pulls me closer. He clearly doesn't like that idea, either. "You didn't hear me, Pereya. I said she's mine. She's staying at my side. You got a problem with that?"

Pereya considers me and mutters something in Portuguese, then shrugs and leads us to the back room.

It's surprisingly clean, the back room. There's no windows, and the only light is a bare lightbulb that flickers overhead. Pereya lets us into the room, shuts the door behind us all, and then pulls a ring of keys out of his pocket. There's a short wooden table in one corner of the room, and Pereya heads there. He drags it over to the side, revealing a trap door with a padlock on it, unlocks it, and flips it up. Under the floor, there are two military crates, also padlocked. He hops down into the crawlspace and opens the first crate. "What's the order of the day, Hays?"

"I'm thinking a GPS tracker if you have one. Couple of semi-automatics. More bullets. Maybe a nice grenade for shits and giggles."

Pereya grunts and unlocks the case, revealing a veritable armory stored in the boxes. My eyes widen. Did we come here to get more guns? How many more do we need? Pereya digs through the stack of arms and pulls out another handgun. He offers it to Daniel, who inspects it with a clinical air.

The room's quiet. Oppressively so. I lick my lips, nervous as Pereya drags gun after gun out of the case, along with boxes of bullets and cartridges.

Daniel looks over at me. "You want anything, baby doll?"

"For you to stop calling me baby doll," I say in a sweet voice. Then I add, "Maybe a couple of knives." I want to be armed to the teeth.

"You heard the lady," Daniel says, and I catch a drawl in his voice. Southern, or that's part of his act, too. "Got any knives?"

Pereya pulls out a couple of small knives in leather sheaths. "For your girlfriend. She can slide them in her boots." He gives my ugly sandals a skeptical look.

"You got boots for her?" Daniel asks.

"Size seven," I offer hopefully. I like the idea of getting boots and filling them with weapons. "Maybe some jeans, too. Size two."

"I'll see what I can find," Pereya says, tossing stuff into a pile at Daniel's feet. "Give me until the morning."

"Doc?" Daniel asks again.

"Soon," Pereya answers.

"We also need a place to stay tonight," Daniel says, pulling out a wad of money from his pocket and peeling bills off. "Though I think it goes without saying that no one saw us here."

Pereya gives us a skeptical look, then shrugs again, as if he doesn't care. "Got a room upstairs. I can toss my old lady out of it for the night, but it'll cost ya."

"Not a problem," Daniel says smoothly, flipping more money out of his stash for Pereya.

I look around at this room. No windows. Only one door. And we're close to the front of the building. I point at the floor. "We want this room."

Pereya looks at me like I'm crazy. "Ain't no bed in here, chickie."

"Bring us blankets and pillows," I tell him. "I like this room." It's true—I wouldn't feel safe upstairs in a room full of windows. In this place, we can barricade ourselves for the night . . . and we're close to the exit if we need to escape.

Daniel's giving me a half smile, as if he's wondering what I'm thinking, but he doesn't argue. He looks over at Pereya, pulls out a few more bills and then offers them to the man. "Think you can set us up for the night?"

Pereya takes the money without even looking at the amount. He simply pockets it and begins to put his guns carefully back into their cases, locks them, and then shuts the trap door and padlocks it. "Be back in a bit with your bedding," he tells us, leaving me and Daniel in the room.

When Pereya returns he brings an older woman with kind eyes. She's carrying a black bag.

"Hello, I'm—"

Daniel cuts her off. "No names."

Pressing her lips together, she nods and opens the bag. "I'm going to take blood and urine samples. I can have your results back in an hour."

I don't know if I'm relieved or terrified to see the doctor. Both, I suppose. I'm afraid of what she'll find swimming in my system after all the "clients" I've had. But . . . I also want to know. So I let her examine me thoroughly, not flinching when her touch becomes as invasive as any client's. She asks me personal questions without judgment on her face and takes blood and urine. Daniel's there the whole time, at my insistence. I don't think I'd be comfortable with a stranger touching me if he wasn't there. He keeps his face averted out of respect for me, though.

Then the doctor leaves to run tests, and I sit in the room, waiting, my arms wrapped around my torso as if I can hug out the fear tumbling through my body.

The call comes back quickly. Daniel listens, speaks a few words into the phone, and then hangs up. "All clear," he tells me.

I want to collapse with relief. "Nothing?"

"Nothing. No STDs; no bun in the oven. You're right as rain."

I stare at him. Right as rain? I didn't catch anything, but that doesn't mean I'll ever be "right" again. Still, I'm relieved beyond words that I'm not a walking stick of hepatitis. Small blessing, I suppose, that Freeze was such a hygiene freak.

"I told you that they used condoms. Even when I blew them."

"Can't believe Gomes sold you. What a stupid, greedy fuck. If I don't get to him, Mr. Freeze will." He sounds disgusted, as if he can't believe the stupidity.

I slide to the floor, my knees feeling weak. I'm sitting close to a load of weapons at Daniel's feet, and he's casually picking through them as I watch. I glance around the room once more. "You sure this place is safe?"

"Not at all," Daniel says. "But the devil you know, and all that."

I know how that feels. "Good point."

Daniel stuffs a few of the new guns into both of our bags. "So why do you like this room?"

"Two things: no windows and close to the front door."

He grunts, not looking at me as he organizes his new stash of weapons. "So you'd rather be close to the front door than have a bed?"

"The way I look at it, everyone here is dangerous," I say. "If I was in a zombie apocalypse and I wanted to be safe, I'd pick a room with no windows and close to the ground floor. You don't want to be upstairs in case of an emergency."

Then he looks at me, and his gaze is amused. "Zombie . . . apocalypse?"

"Yeah," I say. "So? I like horror movies. They're underappreciated gems of filmography."

Daniel shakes his head, grinning. He doesn't say anything else because Pereya has returned with a sulky woman in tow. They give us several pillows, a few blankets, and some questionable-looking sheets. Doesn't matter to me. I've slept on worse recently. I take them from her and begin to make a bed in the corner of our little fortress room while Daniel and Pereya talk for a moment more. A bag of junk food and some sodas are exchanged.

Then, the door closes behind us, and Daniel throws the lock and pushes the squat wooden table in front of the door to make a clumsy barricade. He returns to my side and sits next to me on the makeshift pallet.

He nudges me with his elbow. "I wasn't giving you shit back there," he says. "It's actually pretty smart to suggest we stay here. I was surprised, is all."

I nudge him back with my elbow, a shadow of my playful old self returning at his compliment. "When in doubt, look to the zombie apocalypse."

Daniel chuckles, and it turns into a yawn. I suddenly remember how tired he was before I started getting crazy on him. He's exhausted, and I need him healthy and on his feet in case we have to mow down any other bad guys, get into gunfights, or whatever assassins do. "Why don't you sleep?"

"I can take watch," Daniel says. "I sleep light anyhow."

"I can watch, too," I tell him. "I have guns. And a knife. And apparently a grenade for shits and giggles." I elbow him again playfully.

"You think you could shoot someone if they came through that door, sweetheart?" No more "baby doll" now. Daniel's done teasing me into irritation. I can hear the exhaustion in his voice.

"Sure," I say blithely and pat one of the dirty pillows, inviting him to lay his head down there. "I'll pretend that whoever comes through has been infected with a virus that turns them into a brains-eating monster."

Still, he hesitates, clearly torn.

"There's a crack under the door," I say, pointing at it. It's about an inch high. "I'm going to be watching that all night anyhow. And I'll scream 'Zombies!' if I think there's any trouble. All right?"

He rubs his face slowly, his eyes hollow. "All right. But if you get tired, wake me up."

"Get some sleep," I tell him. Strangely, being bossy to him is making me feel a bit more like my old self, too. Give a girl an ounce of power and all that. But I pat the bed again. "I'll even tuck you in."

"How can I resist that?" Daniel says and climbs into the bed fully dressed. Within two minutes, he's asleep, despite the constant noise outside. There are people talking and walking around upstairs, and I tense at every creak of the boards. Daniel went to sleep with his hand on his gun, so I'm guessing he still doesn't feel a hundred percent safe. But he's got to sleep at some point.

I take my sandals off and pick up my gun, making sure the safety is on. Then I creep toward the door and lie down flat so I can watch through the crack underneath.

CHAPTER **TWELVE**

DANIEL

When I wake up four hours later, I have a raging boner and an armful of warm woman. Regan has once again rolled over and plastered herself all over me. It'd be nice if it's because she wants me, but her subconscious is probably screaming for her to hold on tight to the buoy in the water. *I've got something to hold on to, sweetheart*, my sleepy, subconscious self mumbles. Just like earlier, I slide out from under her, but this time she stirs and grips me harder, her knee sliding up my legs to rest under my balls, which are straining toward her flesh. *A little rub, Danny boy*, they beg.

I can't give my package the good slap that it needs, and I'm a little afraid that if I even come close to touching it, my wood won't go down until I find some place to jack off. Lusting after this girl is thirty kinds of wrong. If she had any idea about the thoughts that ran around in my monkey brain, she'd bash me across the face with the chair leg. And I'd let her.

Because I can't stop thinking about how her plush lips form a perfect O when she's thinking—or how her legs seem to be endless acres of smooth flesh. When we walked up the steep path to Pereya's, my gaze wandered to her ass, the firm globes pressing against the fabric of the knit skirt as she climbed. I finally took the lead because I wasn't going to be able to walk if I kept looking at her.

The puzzle of Mr. Freeze concerns me. He obviously wants Regan back, and Gomes was a greedy fuck for letting her out of his sight. Even for twenty-five grand. Sick people get fixated on things sometimes with no good explanation for it. In her late stages of Alzheimer's, my Grandma would only drink out of a certain plastic cup. She'd throw a fit if someone offered her some other container. Apparently Regan was that plastic cup to Gomes's rich patron.

Thinking about Regan being mistreated by Gomes and his pals is as deflating as a pin in a balloon, but I'm grateful. The last thing I need is for Regan to encounter the rod in my pants and then look at me for the rest of our time together like I'm one breath away from throwing her down. The last of my erection wanes away, and I'm left feeling awkward and anxious. Twin emotions I haven't experienced since I was fourteen and about to take Marybeth's virginity in the back of my dad's Ford pickup. Even then I was more excited than anything.

I pull back her fingers that are wrapped around my waist, and she whimpers in her sleep. "Hey, sweetheart," I say. This only causes her to snuggle closer, putting her nose and soft cheek in that angle between my shoulder and neck, fitting perfectly, as if I was made for her. And that erection I thought I'd killed off comes raging back. From a fucking nose rub. I swear to God, the minute I am done here, I'm going to find a willing woman at a bar in Dallas, and we are going to fuck until I'm so raw my dick is red for a week.

Needing her off of me, I use the nickname she hates the most and inject as much asshole into it as I can. "Baby doll, I'm all for a morning fondle, but I prefer the hand to the knee." Then I lightly slap her butt for emphasis. She jumps off me like a cat doused in water.

"What was that all about?" she asks, brushing hair out of her eyes with one hand and rubbing the spot on her ass where I slapped her with the other.

My hand tingles from the contact with her butt. It wants to make contact again. I want to make contact with every part of her. Turning around I bend over to gather the blankets, using the housekeeping as an excuse to hide my erection. "Just waking you up, baby doll, and letting you know that I'm all up for a romp around the floor here, but I hope you don't mind being on top. Ever since Afghanistan my knees are for shit."

My back's to her so I can't see her face, but I assume she's seething. At least she's awake.

"Why do you say stuff like that?" she asks in a quiet voice which, shit, is not what I was going for. Now I'm feeling bad on top of crappy.

Holding the thin pillows and bedding in front of me, I face her. There's a look of speculation in her eyes as if she's trying to decode me. "I was concerned you might jack my manly bits into my throat, so I wanted to make sure we had a clean separation."

"Nice." Her nose—the one that fits perfectly into my neck—wrinkles up. I'm rank. Maybe I should've let her sniff me more, because that would be enough to send any girl into a fit. I've got dirt, blood, and who knows what other bodily fluids from two dead men on my clothes, and I haven't showered in . . . I count back. Three fucking days.

If I were with my team, we would've joked about the smell, saying that if you aren't riper than a rotten peach, then you haven't been outside the wire long enough. I've gotten soft in the years since I've been out. Sleeping in a "ranger grave" is common enough during deployment that blankets and pillows should be a luxury, but the services of hired assassin pay pretty well and I've gotten used to feather beds and down comforters, not to mention hot showers.

I lay the bundle onto the wooden table and then stare down at Regan. My tired mouth speaks before my filter can catch up. "You are really fucking beautiful, you know?"

I'm grateful but surprised when she shakes her head and laughs disbelievingly. "You know my boyfriend Mike said I looked like a colt. All legs, no torso."

"Shit-for-brains-Mike? The one who couldn't give you an orgasm? You actually listen to what he says?"

Regan's face falls. "I should've never told you that. You think I'm a weirdo."

Leaning against the table, I shake my head in disbelief. "You're the weirdo because he can't give you an orgasm?" I don't even tell her about the other stuff I know, like how he'd sleep through her masturbating right next to him. And how he hasn't called, not even once, to find out where she is. Nick told me that he'd considered shooting Mike because he was taking up space in the universe that could have been given over to someone who actually gave a shit.

"No, because I told you all the stuff and . . ." She waves towards my crotch. "Other stuff."

I don't need for her to notice my other stuff, because it's swelling in hopes that she pays real close attention to it. I need to get her out of sight and out of mind before I start telling her that I'm not going to be a tool that she uses to get off. What I'd like to say is that the next time my touches are going to be personal, and when she gets wet, it'll be because of my up-close attentions.

Worried that she's a distraction to me, I cast around for a place to stash her. In Morro dos Macacos everyone is armed—from the residents to the police force that regularly marches through trying to clean up the slums so that Rio is respectable for the world stage. Regan could easily get hit by a stray bullet, which to my way of thinking would render this whole escapade worth about a Benjamin ripped in half. Meaning, less than nothing.

Mentally I check off the things we have to do. First, we need identification and passports for Regan or she is never leaving Rio. Second, we need to get to the airport and send Regan home. Third, I need to find the hacker. Fourth, I need to find my sister, and then the Hays siblings get on their own plane and return to their ranch and never, ever leave it again. But before all that I need to hustle up to the hill and meet my informant, the one that Pereya found that might have information about Naomi.

Running an agitated hand through my hair, I order her, "Stay here. Be right back."

Upstairs, I find Pereya sleeping like an innocent next to his wife. My knife hand itches, and I place my palm against my ankle so I can feel the outline of the sheath against my hand. Pereya has sold me ammunition and given me a place to stay. I don't need to threaten him with a knife across the throat. Not yet at least.

I give him a few alternating taps on the side of his face, and when I see his eyes pop open I cover his mouth. When the warm saliva and tongue hits my palm, I wonder why I don't wear gloves more often. Resisting the urge to pull my hand away, I whisper in his ear, "Need one more thing from you before I leave."

Pereya nods and I release him, swiping my hand across the fabric of my pants. A wet wipe will be in order as soon as Pereya gives up a source. "I need to know of a good paper maker."

"Lots of them in the favela, but none that are good. You'll have to go to Ipanema. See a *mermão* by the name of Luiz Soto. He can hook you up." Pereya holds out his hand, and I slip him another hundred. It's an expensive tip.

"So about the girl," I begin to say, but he holds up his hands.

"No way." He makes a shooing gesture with his fingers. "She needs to go. Take her down to Copa. No trouble there. There's *os homi* by the Rio."

"Pereya, I can't leave Regan at the Rio by herself even if there is a police station next door. Let me leave her here." I pull out more bills and start flicking through the stack. "How much?"

"How much for what?" Regan says behind me. I turn and the expression on her face says I've betrayed her.

"I'm not leaving you behind," I say, but my words are belied by my fat wad of cash. I feel more exposed here than if I were a john on a street corner with my pants around my ankles and the police headlights shining on the glossy wet of my dick that was polished by the mouth of the street vendor. *Officer, I was not soliciting. I was taking a piss and my dick fell into this young lady's mouth. All a misunderstanding.*

The stricken look on her face says that I've struck a blow deep, harder than the guy I capped in the apartment we'd left. Cursing, I take her arm and drag her down the stairs, pretending to gain a little privacy. Pitching my voice low so that I can at least make it difficult for Pereya to hear our business, I tell her my plan. "We need to get papers, and out there,"—I gesture over my shoulder toward the street—"you're more likely to be endangered than here in Pereya's home. People leave him alone on both sides because he's got quality product. So he's like the armory in Switzerland. You come in, take out what you need, and leave. It's safer here than anywhere. You're safe with his arsenal."

She doesn't hear one word I've said. "You're leaving me behind," she repeats.

"I'm not. I'm taking a detour, and then I'll be back."

"All those things you said earlier, they were to pacify me, right? Tell the little victim what she wants to hear."

"No," I protest. I realize I've fucked up on so many different levels that it will take a land mine specialist to get me out of this mess.

"Take her down to Ipanema. It's safe there," Pereya not so helpfully offers from the top of the stairs.

At this, Regan presses her lips together and looks at me militantly.

"I've got a tip. A lead on something important. But it's in a real dangerous place, and I don't want to see you get hurt."

She's not buying it. There's no way I'm leaving her with Pereya. I can see it all over her face. With a sigh, I give in. I pack all the ammunition that I've bought from Pereya and drape my tactical vest around Regan's shoulders. Maybe if everyone sees she's armed, they'll think twice about pointing a gun in our direction. Maybe.

CHAPTER **THIRTEEN**

REGAN

This man is so full of shit. *I won't leave you behind, Regan. You can trust me, Regan.* All lies. All stupid lies. He's still trying to ditch me.

"It's not safe for you to go with me," he tells me, those blue eyes asking for me to understand.

I stare at him.

"I didn't come this far for you to be killed."

"And I didn't come this far to end back up in a whorehouse," I hiss at him, anger getting the best of me. I used to be such a nice girl. I never argued with anyone. Now I'm constantly screaming at Daniel. But it's his fault, damn it. If he wasn't so fired up to ditch me, I wouldn't lose my shit so often.

He glances over at Pereya, then back at me. "Not here." He calls over his shoulder, "We need our room again for a bit. See if you can find those jeans and boots for me." And with that, Daniel grabs me by the arm and hauls me back to the safe room where we'd spent the night.

I let him drag me. That's fine. His hand is pinching my arm, but if he's hauling me along, he's not leaving me behind. That's all that I ask.

We shuffle back to the safe room, and Daniel flings the door shut, then turns and glares at me. "Okay. We need to talk."

I adjust the heavy vest he draped over my shoulders. It's bulky and doesn't hang right over my boobs, but I'm not going to point that out. Fiddling with it gives me something to do without looking at Daniel. "So talk."

"This place I have to go today? It's a dangerous shithole."

"As opposed to all the other nice, safe playgrounds you've taken me to so far?"

"Damn it, Regan, I'm serious. I need to get a tip from a guy in a soccer field that's the favorite place of the local gangs for microwaving."

I look up at him, puzzled. "Microwaving?" Somehow I don't think he means Hot Pockets.

"Yeah. Someone fucks up, you take him out to the field, throw a few tires around him, douse him in gasoline, and set the whole thing on fire. Leaves a nice smoky skidmark to warn everyone else not to make the same mistake."

I swallow hard. That sounds worse than awful. And Daniel wants to go to this place? Alone? What if he never comes back? What if he leaves me here and I'm sitting with Pereya for weeks, wondering what happened? How long before Pereya decides to sell me to the highest bidder? "Sounds like a shitty place. I'm still going."

"No," Daniel says. "I'm in charge of keeping you safe. Taking you there won't keep you safe. We're in the middle of some primo gang territory around here."

"I don't care!"

"Well, if you don't give a shit about your life, I do."

I gasp. How can he say that to me? I've clawed and scrambled for every inch of freedom in the last two months. I've survived hell. In fact, I'm still trying to escape it. The fact that the one person I can trust is secretly trying to ditch me? It fills me with anger and fury and more than a little hurt. I slap his chest. "You think I don't care if I live or die? Really?"

Daniel closes his eyes and takes in a deep breath. "Regan, you know what I'm trying to say here . . ."

"No, you're saying shitty things to try to get rid of me. I know how you work. You lie and you try to piss people off so they'll go away. I'm not going away, though. Remember your promise? 'I'm not leaving you, Regan. I'm going to stay at your side and protect you, Regan.' What happened to that?"

"It didn't involve taking you to a killing ground when you can sit here quietly—"

"And what?" I cry, beating a fist on his chest. I've smacked him a few times as we argue, but he doesn't raise a hand to me. I know I shouldn't hit him; I'm just so fucking frustrated. "What happens if you don't come back? How long before someone sells the cute American pussy to the highest bidder again?"

His mouth flattens. "You have to trust me, Regan."

"Trust? Now who's crazy?" I laugh bitterly and throw my hands up in the air. "You said I was acting crazy when I jumped you, but I'm not so sure. I can guarantee that if you were getting your dick wet, you'd move heaven and Earth to make sure I stayed at your side, instead of trying to ditch me. So now who's crazy, huh?"

He reaches out and grabs the front of the flak jacket. I start to pull away, but he's only tying together two strings at the neck that will keep it closed. "So," he says flatly, "you want to talk about trust? How about you jumping all over me as soon as I close my eyes to try and manipulate me into keeping you around? How am I supposed to trust you after that?"

I'm shocked at his words, that he can turn the whole "trust" thing around on me and still make me wince after all this. It hits home. I have been manipulating him. "But . . . you like me," I protest. "You think I'm sexy."

"I do," he agrees, tying the cord into a bow and then reaching for another one under my arm so he can fit the flak jacket tighter to my body. "I think you're beautiful. I also think my appreciation of you is completely inappropriate, and I would never act on it. Have I done anything at all to make you uncomfortable? Acted inappropriately?"

Other than a few smacks on the ass and referring to me as baby doll? I want to point this out, but we both know it's to rile me up and distract me, and he's not serious about it. He's right. He's been nothing but good to me even when he doesn't have to be. If he snapped his fingers, I'd be on my knees sucking his dick out of gratitude because I'd feel like it would get me somewhere with him.

How fucked up is that? And how fucked up is it that Daniel's the Boy Scout in the situation and I'm the one throwing my body at him? Not that it matters. Sex is ruined for me. I don't think I could ever touch a man again without thinking of the brothel.

But then I look at Daniel's frowning mouth. He's been

straight-up appalled that I never had an orgasm. Curls his lip at Mike's name as if he's done me some sort of disservice. As if everyone else is the problem and not me. Not Work-Harder-to-Make-It-All-Better Regan who refuses to see problems in a relationship. Not Head-in-the-Sand Regan who tries to ignore the world so her little bubble isn't disturbed.

That Regan's dead now.

Daniel finishes tying one side of my jacket and then the other as I watch him move. He's got long eyelashes, and a strong jaw, and he's . . . really attractive.

I wonder briefly what it would be like to kiss him. Really kiss him. It might be Stockholm syndrome speaking, but that can't possibly be any worse than what I've already been through. And suddenly, I'm curious.

If I kiss Daniel, will it be like kissing men at the brothel? Will I want to vomit if his mouth touches mine? Or will it be . . . Daniel? The man with a pretty mouth who desperately wants me in his bed and won't touch me because he knows I have Issues, with a capital *I*.

I lick my lips, thinking.

"What?" Daniel asks, and I realize he's looking at me again.

I'm suddenly nervous. I step a little closer to him and put my hand to one of the buttons on his wrinkled shirt. "Can I . . . can I try something?"

"Shoot." He's watching me warily, but he doesn't move away.

I stand up on my tiptoes and press my mouth to his. He stiffens, and I part my lips, letting my tongue graze his mouth. I feel absolutely nothing. I might as well be kissing a stone for all that he participates, and after a moment, I pull away, frowning. "Why aren't you kissing me back?"

"I'm trying to figure out your angle."

For some reason, that hurts my feelings. I lower my heels and try not to feel stupid. "I wanted to kiss you and see if it was like kissing guys at the brothel. If it'd be different because it's you. Or if everything's totally ruined."

He groans and closes his eyes, then presses his forehead to mine. His hand cups the back of my head. "You're killing me, Regan. You know that, right?"

"I'm sorry," I say in a small voice.

"Shh. Nothin' to be sorry about, darlin'. If you want a kiss, I'll oblige you. You have some shit timing is all." He glances at the closed door behind us, then shrugs and turns back to me. "A kiss. Nothing more, though. You're not ready, and I can't afford a distraction. All right?"

"That works. I just want to see . . ." I trail off without finishing the sentence because it can't really end in a great way.

I just want to see if I'm broken.

I just want to see if I'm really fucked up in the head.

I just want to see if you taste good.

I just want to see if I'll puke.

"Okay. No pouncing, though. You ready?" His hand touches my cheek. "Feel free to push me away at any time if you freak out."

I nod.

Daniel leans in, and his nose brushes mine as his face angles in. I start to close my eyes because every kiss is usually better that way, but I worry that if I close them, I'll see the wrong faces. So I keep them open as his mouth carefully grazes mine. His lips move gently over mine, and then he's sucking at my lower lip, kissing me with careful presses of his lips against my mouth.

He's so tender that I'm surprised. I expected Daniel to be all talk and no finesse, but the man kissing me is infinitely gentle. His eyes are closed, as if kissing me right is the only thing that matters at the moment.

And . . . I'm not hating it. That's good.

He continues to press soft kisses to my mouth, and I let him, exploring my feelings. I'm not grossed out and I don't want to vomit. If anything, I wish he'd kiss me a little harder. Mike was never a big kisser; he only wanted to do it if it'd get him somewhere, and I'd accepted that. But Daniel . . . I suspect Daniel could kiss a girl for hours to watch how it affects her.

The thought sends a shiver through my body.

Daniel's mouth continues to nuzzle mine. "You okay?"

"I'm okay," I breathe against his lips.

"You want tongue?"

Oh God. For some reason, I find it arousing that he'd ask me. Like it's all totally my call. He's only giving me what I ask for, and that makes him safe. So I breathe out a quiet, "Yes," and wait for the kiss to change.

A moment later, Daniel's mouth opens wider against mine and his tongue brushes against my closed lips, seeking entrance. I part and let him in, tensing as I wait for the invasive feeling to return, for the sickness and revulsion.

But his tongue only gently laps against my own, coaxing me. It's as if he's asking me if I want to play. And I realize that I do. I bury my fingers in the front of his shirt. And I kiss him back.

And . . . it's pretty damn amazing.

Daniel's tongue strokes against mine, soothingly at first, then with little flicks that seem to pulse all the way through my body. He kisses like he has all the time in the world to savor me, and I melt under him. This isn't the hungry kiss of a man who's throwing me a bone so he can get his dick sucked. This isn't a man who wants to dominate me and show me who's boss. This is a connoisseur, and he wants to show me how good he can make it. It's kiss and invitation all at once.

I'm responding with lust, my own tongue meeting his, and I make a soft little noise in my throat that comes from sheer bliss. I hadn't realized until now how much I really, really like kissing and how much I've missed the intimacy of it. I've even closed my eyes to savor the caresses of Daniel's mouth, and I didn't even realize it. I feel like this is what I have always needed.

And it makes me confused. Shouldn't I be totally fucked up right now? Throwing up at Daniel's touch? But he's not touching me like everyone else. He's making love to me with his mouth.

I pull away, dazed, and notice that his eyes are narrowed with desire, his lids heavy. How have I never noticed before that Daniel is so sexy? So masculine? This *must* be Stockholm syndrome; I'm falling for Daniel because he's the only constant in my world.

That must be it.

I lick my lips—tasting him—and say, "We can't separate. Every time people separate in a horror movie, the girl always has a horrible death."

He looks surprised at my words, and then a slow smile spreads across his face. "Name one movie where that happens."

I begin to tick them off on my fingers. "*Cabin in the Woods, The Descent, Tremors—*"

"Okay, okay."

"*Ghostbusters—*"

He shoots me a look. "No one died in *Ghostbusters*."

"*Scooby-Doo—*"

Daniel throws his hands up. "All right. You can come with

me." He eyes my hair. "We need a baseball cap to stuff your hair in. Maybe we won't seem as out of place if no one can tell from a distance you're a woman."

I smile. "Quit trying to get rid of me, all right?"

"I'm trying to save your life. Excuse me for being cautious," he says, and there's a teasing note in his voice.

"I'd rather die next to you in a gunfight than be sent back to the brothel," I answer. And I'm a hundred percent honest about that. I'm not going back. Ever.

Daniel gives me a sobering look then shakes his head. "You know, you have Daisy fooled."

This strikes me as an odd thing to say. "Oh?"

"Yeah." His mouth quirks up on one side, and he begins to tuck knives into my flak vest and adjusts it again. "She told me you were sweet and agreeable and wouldn't give me any trouble."

I can't help it; I giggle at how rueful he sounds. Maybe I was sweet and agreeable before, but I'm not now. I'm tired of the world crapping on me, and I'm going to stand up for myself. "I guess she didn't know me very well."

"Guess not," he says with amusement. "Maybe we should get to know each other better if we're going to be glued to each other's sides for the next week." And his gaze slides back to my mouth, as if he's considering all the ways he'd like to get to know me better.

And for some reason, that makes me feel good. "Well for starters, I like horror movies. And I don't like to be left behind."

Daniel laughs. "Darlin', I already knew that."

CHAPTER **FOURTEEN**

DANIEL

Recalibration of plans then. It is obvious that Regan wouldn't stay with Pereya even if he were willing to keep her. Pereya finds some jeans and boots but no hat. Once outside the house, I take Regan's hand. "Stick close to me," I order unnecessarily. Her grip on my hand would have broken my fingers if I were any weaker or she were stronger. I make a mental note that we should eat before we get papers.

"There's a protein bar in the front pocket," I tell her. "Eat." She definitely does not have enough food in her belly. After this, I need to take her to get a good meal.

"Are you ordering me around because you're mad?" she asks but digs in and finds the protein bar. She breaks it in two and hands me half. While she nibbles on one end, I shove my entire part into my mouth and swallow before I respond. Regan's a liability, but her fear is overcoming any good sense. And after what happened inside Pereya's war room, I don't have the heart to tell her she's slowing me down. But I do want her to take some basic precautions. Tugging on her hand, I turn her so she can see I'm serious—but for a moment I'm lost looking down into those deep green eyes, more mysterious and beautiful than the waters of Rio. I'm so goddamn exhausted, mentally and emotionally and physically. I'd like to dive into those waters and not come up for days. It's this endless, wearying hunt for my sister and the fear that one day I'm going to find her in a body bag. It's knowing that scum out there like Freeze and Gomes and others seem to be winning.

But then there's Regan. She's evidence that things can go to hell and something good can still survive. It's my job, then, to not fuck this up. I need—no, want—to keep her safe.

"I'm not mad at you. Don't got time for that. What I am is worried. You need to follow my instructions at all times. If I say jump, you jump. If I tell you to eat, you eat something. If I say stick with me, that means there's no more than a paper's width between us. Our getting out of here depends on you listening. Got it?"

She nods, and a glimpse of the agreeable, sweet self that she referred to earlier peeks out. The whole situation is a clusterfuck, and I'm not even talking about taking Regan deeper into the slums. It's my stupid attraction to her and her need to see if she can wrangle some response out of me. I'm torn between wanting to tell her that if I were any more attracted to her that I wouldn't be able to get up and walk and not traumatizing her even more with my attention.

"Ouch," I hear Regan say, and I realize that this time I've squeezed her fingers too tight.

"Sorry." Letting her hand fall, I pick up the pace. The sooner we're out of here, the better.

The streets are narrow and curved here on Monkey Hill. There was no city planner to lay out roadways in strict geometric patterns. Instead, the people of the favelas have built this neighborhood by placing redbrick and rusted corrugated metal shacks on top of each other like a child stacking empty SPAM cans into a tower.

This high up you can see the Maracanã Stadium, where they are gearing up to host the World Cup and where Olympic soccer will be played in two years, at the base of the hill. Its gleaming new walls shine like a great false white hope.

Rio has tried to clean out the slums, raining down a barrage of bullets like a shield. The drug lords retreat but don't die. There's still an acrid smell that lingers here in the streets, the smell of spent bullets, burnt flesh, and grief. Down in Ipanema or Leblon, everyone has a smile for you. Up here, walking out your door is an act of courage. Smiling at a stranger signals your willingness to be shot down for being stupid.

Three-quarters of the way up, the community square becomes visible. At one time the large square compounds housed a daycare, swimming pool, and soccer field for the people on Monkey Hill. The drug lords won't allow the pool to be filled for no good reason. I'd think they'd like to bring people here to drown. The soccer field is devoid of grass except around the edges. Instead, it's one giant oval of dirt. This is where true footballers were once born. One thing that everyone up here agrees upon is that those that are Pelé-blessed shall pass through untouched. Drug lord or slum dweller, they all love their soccer gods. Edson Arantes do Nascimento and Manuel Francisco dos Santos, better known as Pelé and Garrincha, are more revered than the Virgin Mary.

A quick perusal of the field reveals no one. I lead Regan over to the brick half wall that's been tagged and retagged by small-time gangs trying to show their muscle to the ADA, the main gang that runs Monkey Hill. "Lean against the wall," I tell her, but I don't sit beside her. Instead I stay crouched, sweeping the grounds in a systematic pattern, ready for action. I've palmed my Ruger almost reflexively.

"Should I be holding my gun?" Regan asks.

"Your gun?" My attention is momentarily distracted as I swing toward her. Her blond hair has lost its luster and her face has dirt on it, some on the forehead and some around the edges of her cheek. She's dirty, kind of smelly, but I don't think I've seen anyone more appealing in my entire life. It's then that I realize my desire to leave Regan behind had little to do with the danger she presents to my body. I wanted to leave her with Pereya not because I'm really concerned that I couldn't protect her, but that the more time I spend with her, the less I want to let her go.

She pats the holster on the vest that holds the gun we took off our midnight visitor. "Yeah, I've decided this one is mine."

"Not yet, Annie Oakley, let's save that for when we're in real trouble. Right now the most I've got to be worried about is missing my informant." I return to my visual sweep.

"How will you know who it is? Are they wearing a red flower in their buttonhole?"

Smothering a laugh, I say, "I'll know." No one but snitches and patrols are up this early. "Pereya gave me the tip and described the informant. Five feet seven inches. Slim." *Probably going to try to shank us after delivering the tip.* I don't tell the last part to Regan.

"How come they don't fill the pool?" she asks.

"A sign of control. Filling the pool would be an act of defiance and a mark that the ADAs are losing their hold over the people here."

"ADAs?"

"Amigos dos Amigos. Each favela has its own gang overlord. Monkey Hill is run by the ADA. They move guns and drugs; not really into women, though."

Regan snorts. "Wow, so pious of them."

"Everyone has their hard limits." I shrug.

"Why don't the people revolt? You said everyone was armed here."

"The gangs provide structure and some sense of stability. The cops are crooked, so a gang with a lot of power and the right kind of leader can provide a better life for these people than the government. If your daughter is raped, the gang will enact justice on your behalf. Monkey Hill is one of the better places. The real danger to the people who live here is from the rival gangs who are pressing in on either side. Turf wars kill more people here than anything."

"Sounds like you approve of the gangs," she says.

"I was in the army before this, and I can tell you I killed a lot more people under the blessing of the U.S. government than I have on my own. I guess there's something about the ability to protect the people you care about without rules or regulations that I appreciate. On the other side, there's a favela called Tears of God, and it's been run for the last few years by a shadowy figure by the name of the Knife's Hand. There, the pools are filled and the soccer field is a deep green. They're experimenting with local crops and shoring up the existing structures and tearing down dangerous ones. The residents of the favela wear a medallion hammered out of local granite. They say that if you harm a member of the TG favela, you and your family and everyone else will be killed in retribution."

"That's harsh."

I think of what I'd like to do to the people who took my sister, the ones that have hurt Regan, and shake my head. Those fantasies might scare her off more than my sexual ones. "Maybe, but I've not heard of one turf war there, and the people don't walk around armed to the teeth, and the police aren't running through there with a tornado of bullets and hand grenades."

A lone figure appears on the opposite end of the soccer field, and I'm up and moving before Regan can respond. She's listened to me, though, because I can hear her footsteps close behind mine. And her hand rests lightly on the back of my shirt, not so tight that she'd hold me back or restrict my movements, but enough so that we aren't separated. I suspect her other hand rests on the butt of her gun.

The informant spots me and turns to walk down toward what looks like an old, abandoned grocery. The letters are mostly rubbed out, but at least one of the windows declares that there once were *frutas e legumes* inside. When we duck into the building, it's empty of even the metal shelves. Those are probably in several of the homes nearby serving as storage. The tile floors are chipped and there are dark stains, blood.

My informant walks toward a doorway in the back, and I hug close to the exterior wall. We don't trust each other, but we're strangers forced to do business. The killing won't start until after the transaction has taken place. The snitch is wearing a hoodie and baggy jeans, the universal attire of a teenage hoodlum, no matter the country. Except for maybe East Asia. Those guys tend toward skinnier jeans.

"Here." The informant's gloved hand holds out a micro SD card. The hand is shaking slightly, revealing the informant's nervousness. Nervous people tend to shoot first and then wonder about the correct avenue of action later. Everything about the informant screams novice, and I wonder if Regan and I are supposed to be an initiation kill. The gloves on the hands are too big, which will prevent the smooth extraction of a gun. The baggy pants look perilously close to falling down, and the hood is concealing his view. I move slightly to the left so that the fabric partially blocks his periphery.

Taking the SD card, I pull out an unactivated smartphone and slip in the card. Pulling up an app, I hand Regan the phone. "Read it. Out loud."

The informant protests. "Give me the rock."

"No." I shake my head. I hate—fucking hate—working with amateurs. "Look, woman, we're going to check your information, and then I'll give you the exchange."

Her head jerks up and the hood falls back, revealing a very beautiful Brazilian. High cheekbones, delicate nose, and dirty blond hair frame it all. "How . . ." she trails off.

"Voice," I say impatiently. "Plus, your hips." I gesture toward her waist. With a nod at Regan, I repeat my command. "Read it."

After a moment Regan begins reading.

Blond-haired, brown-eyed female.
Age 20 per admission.
Acquisition location: Cancun.
Date: 16 March.

Condition: Good health. Strange affect. Refuses to look people in the eye. Has strange convulsions. Possibility of self-harm. Claims extensive knowledge of computers and Internet systems. Offered to hack into Butterfield Bank, Caymans, and obtain rival bank account numbers. Challenge was accepted. Succeeded. Refused to do other work unless received own room and promise of no touching. Requests were granted. Suggested partnership with AB organization.

"And there's a couple of email exchanges. 'AB'?"

"Aryan Brotherhood," I explain. "They work with the cartels to move a lot of drugs. The U.S. has one of the highest consumption rates of illegal drugs in the world."

"Enough?" says the snitch.

It is. I can't explain the relief that surged through me when Regan read that. It's her. My high-functioning autistic sister. So brilliant. "Enough."

I pull out the velvet bag. Inside is a two carat musgravite, a stone that Petrovich had given me in payment for taking down his uncle. It's worth close to one hundred grand. I'd pay twice as much for this intel. The informant can barely pick it up with her gloved fingers. As she is looking down, I put the Ruger against her temple.

"Daniel," I hear Regan say in shocked tones, but I ignore her. I don't understand how she can be surprised by human behavior, but it's another sign of how she didn't let her imprisonment ruin her. She still cares enough not to want to see anyone else injured. Like I said, Regan's real danger is to that lump under my left breastbone. It's starting to beat again. I'll figure out if that's good or really fucking bad later.

"Here's how this is going to work. You're going to take your package and go back to your base. You can say you killed us. You can say you tortured us. Neither of us will be around to tell a different story. But you try anything, and I'll blow your brains out right here. I give two shits that you're a woman. Understand?"

She nods and my gun follows every movement, which she registers with widened eyes. "That's right. I've used this gun before many times. I'm not going to ask for your piece, because I suspect you're going to need it, but you'll be on the floor with a bullet through you before you can even get the weapon out of your front pocket. So be smart and you'll live at least ten more minutes."

"That's what you think," she sneers, and then I see a faint red dot on her forehead before everything goes to hell.

REGAN

It takes two seconds. One second, I'm watching the pretty woman's face, wondering why there's a dot from a red laser on her forehead. The next, there's a weird ripple effect, and her forehead explodes into a red tidal wave of shredded flesh, and my face is splattered with something wet and hot.

"Down!" Daniel shouts, his hand swatting my shoulders almost before I can even process that I'm wearing that girl's brains on my face.

I slam to the dirty, stained concrete floor, the air smacking out of my lungs. The guns and knives tucked into my vest jab my ribs, and I'm pretty sure I'll be bruised to hell, but I'm alive. For now. The girl's body has tumbled to the ground nearby, and blood is pooling close to my leg. Daniel's not pausing for a moment, though—he's snaking his body along the ground, heading for the wall. Once my initial shock wears off, I follow him. Close as paper, he told me.

We make it to the side of the building, and Daniel crouches behind a refrigerator that predates Nixon. Another shot rings out as I worm my way to Daniel's side, and something chips off of the nearby wall.

I give a frightened whimper even as Daniel takes my hand and hauls me up next to him. I plaster my body against his, trying to stay undercover as much as possible. He turns away from me, though, and I'm forced to cling to his back as he pushes the refrigerator door open to give us more cover.

Another shot rings out, and the refrigerator door bounces wildly. Daniel shoves it open again, and this time it stays open.

They know we're behind it, and they're watching for us.

"What . . . what . . ." I try to form a question that will encompass everything that's going on, but I'm failing.

Daniel shakes his head, gun in hand, his gaze scanning the front of the old grocery store like he'll be able to see something. "Don't know why anyone ever decides to snitch. Snitches always get plugged."

I turn and stare at the dead body of the girl then touch my fingers to my face. Still wet. I want to puke, but now's not the time. I swallow hard and mentally will the saliva pooling in my mouth to wait for a more appropriate moment. "She's a snitch?"

"Was," Daniel corrects.

I look at him and pull my own gun out of its holster. "You knew this would happen."

"Had an idea. Like I said, snitches get plugged. It's a dangerous job."

"I hope the information was worth her life," I say, still

appalled that the girl can be dead so quickly, so easily. Life is nothing here in the slums, and I'm reminded of how badly I want to go home.

"You have no idea," Daniel says, and there's a fervent note in his voice that makes me wonder. He's practically giddy with the information that we've found on this new blonde, and I'm surprised at the surge of jealousy that flares inside me. Is this the other woman who Daniel's been looking for the entire time? Is that why he agreed to come find me—because he's looking for another blonde? His girlfriend, maybe?

I'm a little ashamed at how jealous I am. Now's not the time. It might not be the time, ever. I'm a package to Daniel. A broken, slightly torn-up package that won't take itself back to the post office so it can be delivered.

All is quiet. No one's shooting anymore, but we're not moving, and at my side, Daniel is as tense and alert as ever.

"Is it safe to go?" I whisper.

"Hell no," Daniel tells me, and a small laugh escapes his throat. "They have snipers. Someone expected her to snitch, and they're pissed. We got a whole lot of valuable information in that phone, and when it goes up the food chain, they're not going to be happy about it." He still looks thrilled, though.

"So what do we do?" I ask.

"Haven't figured that out yet."

I think. "Can we wait them out?"

"Snipers can wait for a long fucking time," Daniel says. "And they have all the advantage since we're pinned down."

"So what do we do?" I ask again.

"We wait for them to make a mistake," he says and then glances back at me. A cocky grin flashes across his face, startling to see in such a grim situation. "And we calm the fuck down. Don't move from here, don't stick your head out to take a shot, and we'll be good."

Oh sure, easy for him to say. "You've been in shootouts before?"

He nods, and his attention goes back to scanning the rickety clapboard walls of the old grocery. Sunlight's pouring in through the cracks, and it's a beautiful day outside. Perfect day for a nice sniping, I suppose.

"Relax." He casually sticks his gun over the fridge door, fires, and almost immediately, there's return fire. "Yep, still out there."

"Relax. Right." I press my back against the wall, clutching my gun. Relax, the man says. Like people shooting guns and killing people in front of my face is nothing to worry about. But even so, I'm good at mentally "going away" in a bad situation. I've had lots of practice, and my thoughts turn to my favorite topic: horror movies. Guns are not uncommon, but most gunfights are one sided. Good guy shoots monster or cannibal of choice, film at eleven. Gunfights are things I associate with Westerns and action movies. "What's your favorite movie?"

Daniel brings his gun up, and immediately another bullet zips through the weathered boards. He lowers his gun as quickly, grimacing. It's a good thing we have the old refrigerator to protect us, or we'd be splattered on the concrete like the snitch. He glances over at me. "Are you really asking me this now?"

"Hey, you're the one that wanted us to become besties instead of screwing."

He snorts. "Okay. Okay." A moment passes, and then he glances back at me. "*Die Hard*."

I should have known. "Could you be more clichéd?"

"Maybe it's clichéd because it's fucking awesome. Seriously.

The guy invented 'yippee ki-yay, motherfucker.' We used to yell that in the army. Not too many movie lines making it into the army. Usually the other way around." His eyes narrow and he cocks his head, listening, then experimentally lifts his gun and shoots.

No return fire.

"It's quiet. Is that good?" I ask.

"Means they're on the move. Don't worry."

Oh sure. *Don't worry*, he says. *I'll never leave you, Regan*, he says. When is Daniel going to realize he's full of shit? "Riiiight."

"*Die Hard*," he says again, pulling his shoe off his foot as I watch him. "Defeated a platoon of bad guys in his bare feet. Even in the army, they let you wear boots." He wiggles his eyebrows at me, like a mischievous boy, then tosses his shoe over the top of the refrigerator and out toward the entryway of the old grocery.

It brings on a fresh round of shooting, and bullets fly hard and heavy. I duck and cringe against Daniel, my fingers going to his waistband for comfort. It's like if I'm holding on to him, I'm safer.

"Little more to the left, sweetheart. Though I have to say, your timing is terrible when it comes to foreplay."

Oh, come on. Like I'd blow him in a gunfight. "My timing's the only thing that's saving you from getting a fist in the dick right now. Exactly what purpose did throwing your shoe serve?"

"It tells me we've still got shooters at the back of the building. Though I don't think they're sniping anymore." He grunts. "Means they're moving up. So what about you?"

I release his belt and fumble for my gun. "What about me?"

"What's your favorite movie?"

Oh, are we still on that? I'd forgotten. Absently, I raise my gun and scan the room. I want to help if bad guys surge us. "*The Thing*, John Carpenter version, 1982."

"That's a weird-ass favorite."

"It's brilliant. Or would you have rather I'd said *The Princess Diaries* because I'm a girl?" I want to roll my eyes at him. "You're such a cliché, you know that? Your favorite color is camo, and you have a dozen sniper berets to match all the black turtlenecks in your closet."

He snorts and glances over at my trembling gun. I'm aiming it at the walls, waiting for a shadow to pass through the sunbeams. "Trying to remember your shooting lessons?"

"Now's a great time, don't you think?"

"Jesus Hermione Christ. Just don't shoot me in my goddamn balls, okay? I need those for the ladies."

A dozen irritated retorts spring from my lips, but I cut them off. Instead, I raise the gun, aim it, pull the trigger, and nothing happens.

"Safety," he warns me, peering around the refrigerator.

Right. I fumble with the gun, my fingers weirdly shaky. I figure out the safety, unlock it, and raise the gun again. This time, it goes off when I pull on the trigger, and my entire hand vibrates from the recoil.

There's no answering shot.

Daniel cocks his head and waits. He pulls off his other shoe and points at the far end of the room. "Shoot in that direction. I'm going to throw my other shoe in a moment and see if we get a response from either side."

I look at the far end of the room. There's a high window, and in the distance, I can see slums. What if I shoot and hit a passerby? "Can't I shoot at the ceiling?"

"Yeah, because it looks so sturdy," Daniel says sarcastically.

"The perfect thing to end a gunfight is the ceiling collapsing on top of you."

"All right, all right," I mutter. When he waves a hand for me to hurry it up, I shoot at the far wall. Daniel listens and a moment later tosses his other shoe at the door.

There's nothing but silence. It's so quiet I can practically hear the dead girl bleeding on the ground a short distance away.

"Sounds like they're gone," he tells me, but he doesn't move a muscle, so I don't, either. We listen to the eerie silence and hear nothing. Daniel looks over at me then nods at the open warehouse floor. "Either that, or they're trying to flank us. You stay here, and I'll check things out."

"No!"

"It's not a debate."

"I'm coming with you—"

"No, you're not," Daniel says, glaring at me. "It's not safe. Now stay here or I'm going to tear you a new fucking asshole when I get back, understand?"

I return his glare, equally furious. I watch as he slides around the side of the refrigerator and then slinks his way to the side of the building. He's entirely hidden in shadow, and if I blinked, I'd lose him entirely.

A low tremble starts through my body. I wonder if it's a trick. If he's going to turn and walk away and leave me behind for good. If he's ditching me, like everyone else has. A knot of anxiety locks my throat.

Fuck this. I'm going with him. I come out of cover and run after him.

The sigh of irritation he sends in my direction goes right over my head. I'm not being left behind ever again.

I watch him flatten his body and move along the wall, gun cocked and ready to shoot. Then, I follow his lead, moving to the other side of the door so we're both on a side, ready to shoot if anyone shoots back.

"So what's *The Thing* about?" he asks me casually. His gaze isn't on me, though. He's constantly scanning our surroundings, and I wonder if he's asking me to distract me.

"It's about Kurt Russell being a badass." I keep my answer short. I'm nervous, and my voice sounds too loud in the silence. It's making me anxious. "Doing what badasses do."

"Sounds like a great plot. How did I ever miss seeing it before?" Again, Daniel's all sarcasm and wit. It's like the more dangerous things get, the punchier his humor gets. He ducks low, which surprises me, and quietly gestures for me to do the same.

I nod, and it occurs to me that our conversation might be a cover to distract our shooters . . . which means they're closer than ever. Which makes me even more nervous. "It's full of blow jobs, too." I lie to see if he's paying attention. "Lots and lots of blow jobs."

"Sounds like my kind of movie now," he says idly. Then, whip fast, he rushes out the front door and confronts the men trying to kill us.

I hear a gunshot go off, something cracks like pottery smashing, and then I see Daniel turn and fire his gun at something out of my line of vision.

Once.

Twice.

A body slumps to the ground.

It's a blur of motion, it happens so fast. I stare at the dead man at Daniel's feet, his neck at an odd angle. Daniel fires one more shot, puts a hand to his side, and fires one more time. There's a thump nearby, and Daniel grunts, then holsters his gun. "We're good. You can come out now."

Come out? I haven't even had time to think about firing my gun. In a daze, I get to my feet, noticing that one of the bullets struck inches above my head. If I'd been standing, I'd be dead.

"Come on," Daniel says. "We don't want to be here in case their buddies come back."

He doesn't have to tell me twice. I rush to his side, stepping over the dead man at his feet as Daniel casually picks up one of his shoes and frowns at the bullet hole in the toe. He shoves them on as I look around for the other dead man. There, a short distance away, with a perfect bullet hole in the center of his forehead.

Jesus. Daniel moved so fast.

He takes me by the arm since I'm not moving fast enough, and we leave the grocery behind, heading back into the slums. Daniel looks over at me. "You okay?"

"Yeah." I'm still dazed, at his speed more than anything. I wanted to help, and I was useless. Less than useless. For the first time, I'm starting to realize what Daniel has been saying. Not only is my life in danger when I go with him, but I'm putting him in danger, too, because he has to watch for me. It's not a good feeling.

"You still got that grenade?" He reaches into one of the side pockets of my flak jacket and pulls it out, and my eyes widen. That explains what hurt my ribs, though I wouldn't have belly flopped if I'd have known I was belly flopping on top of a live grenade. Maybe that was why he didn't tell me.

"What's it for?" I ask him and glance around. "Are there more guys?"

"Nah. We're going to send a message to our buddies." He pulls the pin and pitches the grenade like a baseball into one of the windows of the old grocery.

"What's the message?" I ask as Daniel grabs my arm and we start walking away again.

Two seconds later, there's a loud boom and debris rains down. He looks over at me, boyish with glee. "Our message is, 'Yippee ki-yay, motherfuckers.'"

"Predictable," I tell him, but I grin until he winces and clutches his ribs again. Then I realize . . .

Daniel's been shot.

CHAPTER **FIFTEEN**

DANIEL

"Are you hurt?" she asks.

"You offering to play nurse?" I wiggle my eyebrows lasciviously. "I love that uniform. I think it's the white shoes."

"Would you be serious for one minute?" She tugs at my shirt, and I turn my head to hide a wince. So I got shot; since I'm upright and able to walk, it must've winged me. I'll need a little alcohol and superglue, and it'll be fine. The most urgent thing is to get Regan to a safe house.

"Come on, let's find a nice place where you can feel me up later. When we have more privacy. I'm not into public shows." Adrenaline's pumping hard throughout my body. If she'd been willing, I'd have taken her on the floor of the grocery.

She rolls her eyes but follows. "I don't think you're being funny right now."

"When do you ever think I'm being funny?" I press my hand against my waist to stanch the wound because I'm leaving a trail of blood behind me like bread crumbs. I hope this doesn't end in us getting shoved into an oven. "I'm curious. I want to analyze my jokes so I can get more laughs per words in the future." That sounded like something my sister would say, and I allow myself a small chuckle. Regan doesn't realize it, but I'd have suffered a lot more wounds than a slice through my side to get that information.

My laugh pisses her off, and she snaps back. "It's not like I have actual concern for your well-being for any reason other than you're my ticket out of here, so if you're injured I'm screwed."

I make a *tsk*ing sound. "If I thought that were true, I'd have to lie down from the wound in my heart. Thankfully for both of us, I know you're joking." She *hmph*s, which prompts a return wink. I can tell she's developing a soft spot for me. It might not be a sexual one, but she likes me. The smirk on my face dies off when we get close to Pereya's. Our bags are stacked outside, which means he's had someone watch for us and is now telling us to get the hell out of here.

"What's going on?" Regan asks as I grab both bags without stopping. The motion causes one of the bags to brush against my side, and the pain shoots outward, causing me to stumble and groan. "See, you are hurt." She tugs on my arm as if she thinks we can go back to Pereya's safe room.

Stopping, I cup her cheek and that intimate movement stills her actions. "We're not welcome there right now." She makes a distressed sound. "I'm not hurt. Really. I promise if I were, I'd tell you."

"Would you?" Her big, forest green eyes look up at me with trust and . . . is that longing there?

I give myself a mental head slap to dislodge a dozen unsuitable thoughts—such as her actually having feelings for me that arise out of something other than gratitude and wanting to kiss again. Hell if she needs more *practice*, I'm her man.

I content myself with rubbing my thumb along her dirt-streaked cheek. "Nothing's going to happen to you while I'm still breathing. Swear."

We stare at each other for what seems like an eternity, or at least two cycles of the moon, before she drops her gaze. "Okay," she says softly.

Her quiet acquiescence stirs a response in a place far above my belt line. If we weren't running for our lives, if I didn't have my sister to save, if everything were different, I'd sweep Regan into my arms and carry her off to the nearest horizontal surface to show her how sincere my words are. Not for the first time, I wish that I had met Regan when I was still in the army, full of cockiness and the belief nothing could ever harm those I truly loved. Those feelings are long gone, and the oppressive weight of guilt and fear that replaced them has become the new normal. My response to Regan staggers me, so to regain my equilibrium, I grab my junk and make a smart-ass comment.

"There's a part of me that is in real pain, baby doll, if you're feeling like you need to do something."

"Really, Daniel? Did you have to ruin it?"

Yeah, baby, I do, because neither of us has time for this strange pull between us. Giving her a strained smile, I head off down the hill. Like a good soldier, she follows. For all the shit I've thrown her way, Regan has done what I've told her without question. No one stops us on our way down Monkey Hill. Maybe word has spread of our shootout, or maybe we look dangerous. Dusty, dirty, and bloody, we look like two people who've walked out of a battle and aren't afraid to mow down anyone who tries to stop us. At least that's how I hope we look, because the truth is that Regan and I are weak as kittens right now. We need food, a shower, and sleep. In that order. At the base of the favela, I look around for some transportation because we need to put some distance between us and Monkey Hill. Ipanema, Luiz, and papers are about an hour away to the southeast. In between are more favelas, hills, and forests.

Glancing to my left I see an older-model Fiat and the *flanelinha* is nowhere to be seen. I tug on Regan's arm. "Let's go."

"You're not stealing this, are you?"

"No, I'm borrowing it." I take my gun and smash the driver's side window. Climbing in, I reach over and flick open the lock. "Get in."

Shaking her head, she climbs inside. "Someone really needs this car, I bet."

"Then they should've paid a *flanelinha* to watch it."

"A what?"

"Car attendant. Pay someone to watch your car so that some shitty criminal doesn't come along and steal it."

"Nice."

"Same thing happens in the certain parts of our great northern America. Some neighborhoods are entirely transactional." I fiddle with a few wires, and the car coughs to life. "Plus, are you up for walking forty kilometers or would you rather eat in an hour?"

"Drive, then."

Flashing her a big grin, I floor it. Throwing her my phone, I say, "Find the shittiest-rated hotel in Ipanema."

Fifty minutes later, we are checking into Real Aeroporto. Regan reads the reviews to me as I drive down the narrow, hilly streets. " 'Carpets are filthy. I was scared to even lie down on the sheets, so I slept in my clothes and when I woke up, I was covered in more sand than you could find on the beach.' "

"Sounds perfect."

"Not that I'm complaining because I'm not funding this, but why are we looking for something so awful?"

"Because we can't go into Copacabana Palace Hotel looking like we fought a drug gang in Monkey Hill. This place is going to be happy to accept our cash and not ask questions."

"I didn't think places this shitty existed," Regan says as we unlock our hotel room door. The hallway stinks like fish guts were spilled and never cleaned up. This room smells of stale smoke and too little air. I place our bags on the rickety desk and check out the bathroom. There are two towels that look as thin as tissue hanging on a towel bar and two extras on the bed. Flies are everywhere. "Maybe I should've asked you to look up the second-worst hotel down here."

"Thanks, genius."

I throw one of the towels onto the base of the shower floor. "Stand on those while you shower. I'll get you another dress so you can dry yourself off with it. It's cleaner than anything here."

Inside Regan's bag I find a swimsuit, toiletries, and a cover-up. The attendant at the shopping center had thought of everything.

Scooping it into my arms, I carry it into the bathroom and am rewarded with a yelp. "Jesus, Daniel," Regan harps. "A little privacy."

"Sorry," I mutter. Placing the clothes and toiletries on top of the toilet, I try to make it out of there without peeking. But a little scream halts my progress. Gun in hand, I whip back the shower curtain and there's Regan huddled away from the showerhead. Heart pumping, I look for the danger. Whisper-thin legs stretching out from a fat black body cling to the metal head. Shit, I don't like spiders, either. Glancing over my shoulder, I can see that Regan would be happy to have me shoot the insect with my Ruger. I shove the gun into the back of my jeans, grab a bunch of toilet paper, and remove the damn thing.

"I can't finish my shower," she says miserably.

"Sure you can."

"No, because I can't close my eyes now. I have to keep watching for spiders."

"You can shower with your eyes open."

"No, I can't. I haven't washed my hair. Will you . . . ?" She doesn't finish her question, but I can see it plainly in her eyes. "Please, Daniel."

And I find myself unable to turn her down even though I know this is going to be torture for me. I pull the gun out of my pants and rest it on the edge of the sink. With my other hand, I pull my shirt over my head, but I keep my pants on. I'm afraid if I don't, I'll not be able to keep my dick from attacking her.

"Scoot forward, baby doll."

She does, shivering and shaking even under the hot water. "I know I'm being unreasonable, and I don't even care."

I squeeze some of the shampoo from Regan's bag into my hand. "Lean your head against me," I order. She does and I'm acutely aware that my bare chest is about two steamy inches from her naked body. And even though I've tried to keep my eyes off of her, truth is her figure is stamped into the fibers of my neuro-system. Those images aren't ever coming out. And now I'm adding sensation and smell to the mix. I wonder if I'll ever fantasize about any other woman.

My fingers fork through her hair and press into her scalp. When she moans, I feel the vibration rip through my body and take hold of my cock. It springs to attention and tries to bust through my zipper to get to her. She doesn't stop making those sounds, and it's making me so horny I can barely stand still.

"You need to shut it, Regan," I bark more harshly than I intend, but goddamn, a man can only take so much suffering.

"I'm sorry," she says between moans, "but I can't. It feels too good."

I could ruin the moment, like I have so many before—with some stupid, sexist comment about how she could bend over and I'd give her a feel good that she'd never experienced before—but somehow I can't. I let her lean even more heavily against me, which causes my side to ache, but it's a sweet pain, one that I welcome because it means she's touching me. "Your shampoo is done, sweetheart," I tell her huskily. I turn her so that her pink-tipped breasts are thrust out in front of me, and it takes everything I've got to keep my hands in her hair and not drop them down the front of her body, following the path of the water droplets as the soap and water create erotic patterns on the surface of her skin.

She leans back, implicitly trusting that I'll keep her upright, and I do. With one hand at the nape of her neck to keep her steady, I smooth the clean water over her hair, making sure none of it spills onto her face. Over and over, I let the water wash us— uncaring that my wet jeans feel like a thousand pounds hanging on my hard cock or that the last of the soap streaks were gone five minutes ago. Maybe we would have stayed like this for hours more had the hot water not turned cold.

"All right, baby, out with you," I said gently. She swims to the surface of conscious thought, her eyes flicking open languorously. There is desire and need in them, and I want to pleasure her. *Give me a sign, baby.* But she stays silent, and finally I lift her out of the tub and wrap a towel around her and push her right out the door.

Closing the door, I strip out of my jeans and underwear and take hold of my throbbing cock. It really only wants Regan, I can tell, but my palm is the only relief it's going to get right now. I step into the cold shower and with one hand leaning against the tile, I take my cock in the other.

It doesn't take long. The cold water doesn't wash away the image of her body in front of me, the look of pleasure written large across her face as she tipped it backward into the stream of water. In my fantasy she drops lower and unzips my jeans and parts the sodden fabric of the denim. Her delicate hands reach in and pull out my cock. She makes a sound of pleasure—like a hum of want—and then tells me, "You're so big." Her eyes are large saucers of green, and her pink plush lips open and cover me.

She never stops looking at me, never stops telegraphing how much she loves this. I can hear the sounds of her moans around my cock, muffled by the thick flesh in her mouth but still audible. My balls draw up and a familiar tension sits low on my spine. Not the first time, I think. I pull away abruptly and lift her into my arms. Pressing her against the tile, I shove into her wet heat, and she screams in my ear that she loves it so much. I imagine that her cunt is tight and wet and hot. Her walls grip me as I slide out, as if she can't bear to lose even one inch.

Each thrust inside her body is like being hugged by a warm fist. It's been so goddamn long, and I let out a low moan of relief.

My head drops back, too heavy for my neck to support. All my energy is focused on the blood coursing through my cock as I imagine pounding into Regan over and over.

A porn reel wouldn't sound hotter than Regan's pants and cries. "You feel so good. You're so big. I want you so much. Come all over me." And so I do. I jet into her with long streams of ropy come that seem to be endless. Only it's my hand, and the cold water seeps into my nerves, and I finish cleaning off. As good as that felt, I know that it would be five thousand times better inside of her. But I also know that my hand is as close as I'm ever going to get to being inside Regan.

REGAN

It isn't fair.

I don't mind that Daniel shoved me out of the bathroom. I kind of expected it, actually. I was selfish enough to ask him to help me shower, knowing it'd drive him crazy and not caring that it did. Maybe in the back of my mind, it was a test to see how far I could push him. How insane with lust I could make him before he broke his word and started grabbing me. Then, maybe, I'd understand him. My brain would go, *Yep, he's like every other man*, and I could tuck him away into the same mental category that all men fell into now: users.

But Daniel never breaks his word. He never touches me sexually, and by the time he boots me out of the shower, I'm confused and a little sad to leave him behind in there.

I liked being touched by him. I liked that he touched me and I didn't have to worry. That no one was going to be forcing me to do anything, and that there was only caressing and tenderness. And God, I've missed tenderness so much.

I peel the towels off of my body, give my hair a quick rub to soak some of the water off, and then crawl back into bed and pull the sheets tight around my body. I should put clothes on, but I'm feeling weirdly vulnerable.

It's like I don't want to get dressed because part of me wants Daniel to come out of that shower and touch me. Show me what it's like to actually have great sex. Show me everything he can do. Hell, touch me a bit more without strings attached. I'd like all of that. But I can't ask. I'm the poster child for Stockholm syndrome, right? I should be loathing every man's touch at the moment, instead of lusting after a man that treats me with tenderness.

I should be thinking of my boyfriend.

The thought occurs to me, and I flush with guilt, huddling a little lower under the sheets. I haven't thought of Mike much at all, lately. Does he miss me? Mourn me like I'm dead? Shouldn't I be dying to get back to him instead of having all these mixed-up feelings about Daniel? Mike's a good-looking guy. We've been together since high school. Hell, I picked the college I went to because Mike wanted to go there.

But Mike never gives you orgasms, my traitorous brain whispers. *He never kisses you like Daniel did.*

Has to be Stockholm, I tell myself. I hear the water going in the other room and figure Daniel must be showering himself at this point. He won't be out for a few minutes. I can call Mike and . . . let him know I'm alive. That's what a good girlfriend would do.

I pick up Daniel's phone and dial the number to Mike's apartment. He won't answer his cell unless he knows who the caller is, so I'll try there first. After four rings, it goes to voice mail.

"Hi! You've reached Mike and Becca. Leave a message after the beep!"

I hang up, horrified but not entirely surprised. Mike and my best friend Becca? Mike and my oldest girlfriend? The one that was always telling me how lucky I am to have a guy as great as Mike?

How easy must it have been for them to get together if they're both mourning me? All it'd take would be a bottle of wine, some mutual sad commiseration, and then naturally, of course, they fucking move in together.

I shouldn't be hurt, but I am. Mike might have assumed I was dead . . . but it hasn't even been two months. And he never let me move in with him, even though we'd been dating for years. *I need space, babe*, he'd tell me. And I went along with it because that's what Regan Porter did. She was a nice girl that went along with things.

But Becca's moved in with my commitment-phobe boyfriend after less than two months.

I toss the phone aside. Then I lie down, my head on the pillow, staring at the wall. I don't know what I'm feeling right now. Can I feel betrayed by people who think I'm dead? Did they even look for me?

A low groan touches my ears, and I sit up. That was Daniel. I get up from the bed, sheets wrapped around my body, and tiptoe to the door of the bathroom. The water's still going, but I hear that low groan again.

He's jerking off in the shower.

I'm fascinated by that, and a little jealous. Sex hasn't been ruined for Daniel. He can still enjoy touching himself, I think enviously. I haven't wanted to masturbate since I was taken. I used to be a champion masturbator, since sex was never really

that great. I didn't blame Mike for that, though. I sort of . . .
went along with it. No orgasm? That's okay, really. Regan Porter
doesn't mind. Regan doesn't mind anything. She'll finish herself
off real quick while you take a nap.

Stupid Regan, I think to myself. Now it's too late and you're
scared of everything. Scared of spiders, scared of men, scared of
what happens if you let Daniel out of your sight.

I'm so tired of being scared. Of being unloved.

I suddenly feel heavy with unhappiness and return to the bed.
I tuck a pillow under my head and lie down and close my eyes,
curling up in the sheets. I wish the world would go away for a
few days. I wish I didn't care that Mike and Becca had paired up.
I wish . . .

I wish I was back in that shower with Daniel.

I picture him behind my eyelids, his strong arms flexing as he
lathers up his cock and jerks himself to fulfillment. I wish I could
see it. I'm not sure if I should want that, but I'm tired of being the
nice girl that does what she's supposed to. It's gotten me fuck all
in life so far.

The water stops, and two minutes later, the door to the bathroom opens. "Regan?" Daniel asks, clearly surprised to see me
tucked into bed. "Didn't you want to go get breakfast?"

I shrug, wallowing in self-pity. I don't open my eyes.

"You okay, baby doll?" He comes to the side of the bed, a
towel wrapped at his waist. A washcloth is pressed to the wound
at his side that he assures me isn't bad. You wouldn't even know
it was there from the way he acts, except there's pink seeping
through the white of the towel.

I know he's calling me that nickname I hate to rile me up, but
I don't have the energy to bite back at him at the moment. I'm a

tangled knot of emotions, and right now the only one that seems to rise to the surface is sadness. Regan Porter, the get-along girl, is totally broken. I hate that.

"What's bothering you?" he asks, and there's a hard edge of concern in his voice. I squeeze an eye open and see his eyes scanning the room, no doubt assessing a threat.

I feel guilty for making Daniel panic, so I sigh. "Is it weird if I say I think I need a hug?"

He looks down at me in surprise and then chuckles, that roguish grin stealing across his handsome face again. "You want me to slide into bed with you and cuddle?"

"Actually, that sounds amazing," I tell him and sit up, hugging the sheet to my breasts. "Is it weird if I want to cuddle?"

"Does it matter? Nobody's here to judge," he says, sliding a leg into bed and then pulling his big body down on the left side of the bed. He keeps a hand at the towel at his waist, and then he's lying in bed next to me and lifts an arm, gesturing that I should come tuck my body against his.

And I can't resist. It's been so long since someone's touched me with kindness and affection—not sleazy motives—that I move right over to him, tucking my face into the crook of his neck and wrapping an arm around his shoulders, even as he settles his arm against my back. He's warm and damp and he smells like fresh soap. So good. I love the feel of his skin pressing against mine, and the hand that tenderly strokes my shoulder. Not in a sexual way but to comfort.

I burrow against him. "Thank you."

"Anything you want," he says in a low voice.

I'm not freaked out by the touch of Daniel's skin against mine anymore. It doesn't make me want to puke. Instead, I relax and sigh as he continues to idly stroke my skin with one hand, my body pressed against his. We're both more or less naked underneath the sheets and towels, but it doesn't feel sexual. At least, not yet.

I can't really forget about him jacking off in the shower, though. It's there in my mind every time I close my eyes.

I open my eyes languidly, feeling warm and loved for the first time in forever. My stomach's growling, but I don't want to move. I am feeling too good. I see the washcloth is still on his side, and I slide my hand down his chest and peel it away from his wound. There's a bit of bruising, and it looks like there's a big slice down his side. It's still seeping blood. "You sure you're okay?"

"Nothing a bit of superglue won't fix," he tells me, and his hand brushes my wet hair off my shoulders.

It feels so good that I turn my face against his neck again and nuzzle him before I even realize what I'm doing. "Mmm."

Against me, Daniel stiffens. "Regan," he murmurs. "Baby doll—"

"I know," I tell him and let my tongue flick against the hot skin of his neck. Truth is, I'm relaxed and loose and I don't want to lose this moment. Nice, sweet, agreeable Regan Porter would be scandalized, apologize to Daniel, and retreat because that would be expected. But that's the last thing I want to do. He's warm and delicious and I'm feeling good in his arms.

I want to keep feeling good. So I slide a little closer to him and let the sheet drop from my breasts. "We're hugging, right, Daniel?" I say this even as I lean in and bite at his collarbone with my teeth. Ooh, he's hard and muscled everywhere, and so warm that it's like snuggling with a heating blanket. "You're not going to touch me, right?"

"Not unless you tell me to," he says.

I won't. I'm not ready for that yet. But I'm feeling a little . . . adventurous. I run my hand up his chest again, avoiding his wound and admiring the warmth of his skin under mine and how there's not an ounce of fat on him anywhere. He's pretty, this assassin. If I wasn't screwed up in the head, I'd be drooling over the sight of him every time I turned around. It's good that I'm all fucked up, or I'd jump him every chance I got.

My nipples are pressing against his skin now, and to my surprise, it feels good. There's a low, languid pulsing between my thighs that excites me. I'm aroused for what feels like the first time in forever, and Daniel's not doing anything but stroking my hair and my shoulders.

He's safe.

And that's even more arousing. I shift against him, letting my nipples brush against his skin again, and inhale sharply when it sends a jolt of delicious sensation through a body that I thought was dead to sexual feeling. I slide my hand off of his chest and push it between my thighs, curious.

I'm wet.

Just touching Daniel, snuggling with him, knowing that he's safe for me to play with is arousing me. "I'm wet, Daniel," I tell him in a soft voice, sliding my fingers against my pussy, delighting in the feel.

He groans and the sound is like the one in the shower, which makes my inner muscles clench all over again. I look down and the towel at his waist is tenting, his cock responding to my shameless rubbing against him. Or my words. Maybe both.

And he's not going to touch me. I could rub against him like a cat in heat, and he's not going to do anything but hug my shoulders because that's what I want.

I continue to stroke the slick flesh between my thighs, pressing my breasts against his side and licking at his neck. My hips are moving in little circles now, and I shift, sliding one of my fingers deep inside myself and whimpering at the sensation. Oh, masturbatory pleasure, my long-lost friend, how I've missed you.

I glide my tongue along Daniel's neck again and then nip at his ear, pleased to feel a tremor move through him. His hand hasn't moved from my shoulders, but he's gripping me a little harder than before, and I'm getting to him. I like that. My hand moves faster between my legs, and I rock down on it, enjoying the sensations moving through me. I look down at his lap, at the towel practically falling off his hips now. His cock is large under the towel. Guys like him that ooze confidence are always big-dicked, aren't they? You can tell in their swagger.

"You jerked off in the shower, didn't you?" I ask him, nuzzling my nose against his neck again.

"Hell, yeah. You're fucking sexy as hell," he says in a low, harsh voice.

"Mmm." I'm practically purring at the thought, and I rub my breasts against him again, sucking in a breath when my pussy clenches around the finger I'm working in and out of it. "Would you do it again for me?"

"You want me to jerk off again?"

"Mmmmhmm. Right here." I slide my nose along the tense cords of his neck, aroused by the scent of him. "So I can watch. I won't touch, though."

He mutters a ragged "Christ," and then his hand clamps on my shoulders, even as the other drags the towel away and he grips his cock in his hand. There's pre-come on the crown, and I admire the sight of him as he begins to work it in his hand. I've seen a lot of dicks in the last few weeks—more than I prefer—and Daniel has a nice one. Thick and meaty, with a nice, bulging crown. The kind that feels good deep inside a girl.

That gives me a shiver, and my finger works harder in my pussy.

I'm rocking my hips as I ride my fingers, and I watch him as he strokes his cock rapidly, hand working his length with an expert grip. I want to come, but I need more. I add my other hand between my legs and begin to play with my clit, my face pressing into his neck the only thing keeping me propped up as I work myself over. It's still not enough.

"Tell me," I say to him, "if I had sex with you, would you give me orgasms?"

"Goddamn." I feel the cords in his neck tense. "You want me to talk dirty to you?"

I nod then swipe my tongue against his neck again. I'm in my own little world right now, nothing but Daniel's skin and my own hands and the need to come.

"I'd give you the best fucking orgasms, Regan. I'd push my face between those creamy thighs of yours and lick your pussy for hours. I'd spread those sweet little lips of yours and bury my tongue inside you until you were wiggling on it, and then I'd make that little clit of yours pop out for a little attention of its own." His hands are moving faster on his cock, and I'm fascinated by the way he strokes the head, smoothing pre-come down his length with a quick, fluid motion, his pumping never ceasing. "I'd tease that clit of yours with the tip of my tongue until you were dripping hot and bathing my face with how much you want me."

I moan at his words, my fingers working faster in my pussy. My skin is making slick, wet noises with the force of my actions, but I don't care. I need to come, if only to prove to myself that I can.

"And I'd drink up every last drop," Daniel tells me. His voice is low and husky, and I feel it vibrating in his neck, against my face that's still buried in that safe spot at his throat. "And then I'd make you come all over again, to watch your face. And when you've come so many times you're screaming my goddamn name with every touch, I'd throw your legs over my shoulders and fuck the hell out of you."

The visual makes me shudder, and my fingers slide against my clit, faster and faster. "Yeah?" my voice softly whimpers.

"Oh yeah," Daniel says in a ragged voice, his hand working his cock even harder. "God, I'd love to see that. Touch your smooth skin all over and hear you screaming my name. See those sweet tits of yours bouncing as I fill you up."

I inhale sharply at his words.

"And when you're screaming my name, I'd lean in and kiss you," he says in a soft, delicious voice. "So you'd know what you taste like to me."

The thought of Daniel leaning in and kissing me as he's fucking me—that sweetness mixed with the rawness of sex—is enough to send me over the edge. A jolt shudders through me, and I realize I'm coming. I bite my lip as I do, which causes my breath to wheeze against his throat, but I don't care. It's glorious and wet and tense and wonderful and I'm coming and it's not ugly at all. It's safe and delicious and it's with Daniel.

As I come down, he's still stroking his cock, but his grip is so tense I know he's waiting for some signal from me to let himself go. I think if I told him to stop right now, he would. But I don't want that. I want to see. So I slide my fingers from my pussy and place them, wet, against his lips.

He groans hard, and then he's coming. His hips jerk as his

tongue brushes my fingers, tasting me, and I watch come erupt from his strokes, spattering on his stomach and groin.

And I sigh with pleasure, feeling languid and better than I have in days. "Thank you, Daniel," I murmur, cleaning him off with the sheet. His hand has never left my shoulders.

Daniel is totally, utterly safe. And I want him more than anything.

My stomach growls, reminding me that I haven't eaten a normal meal in forever. I ball up the sheet that I've used to mop his come, toss it off the bed, and then roll away. "We should get dressed. I'm starving." I'm actually feeling pretty pumped at the moment. My heart's still beating hard with the aftershocks of my orgasm, but I feel good and loose. The slickness between my legs is a nice feeling because it's mine and I wanted it there.

I'm not broken after all; I'm a little damaged. And the thought makes me feel alive.

Daniel, poor man, looks a little dazed at my rapidly changing mood. "Breakfast? Now?" He looks like he could take a nap.

I nod and drag my backpack onto my side of the bed, grabbing a T-shirt and bra and pulling them over my head, one at a time. "I'm starving. What's our schedule for today?"

When I finally pop my head out of the T-shirt, I see Daniel give his face a quick rub before swinging his legs over the side of the bed. "Breakfast. Then pharmacy. Then we meet Luiz for our papers. And then we see about getting a new room."

I bite my lip, thinking about how maybe we should get condoms. The thought doesn't make me want to puke like it would even a day ago. Because, in the near future, I think I want Daniel to touch me.

CHAPTER **SIXTEEN**

DANIEL

Regan is quiet as we order breakfast at the cleanest cafe I can find within walking distance. Maybe she's thinking about what the hell happened back in the dingy hotel room. It's all I can think about. Her smell is on my skin, and the sun is baking it into every pore in my body. I don't know if I will ever regret it, though. If this is all I carry with me when we part, isn't it enough? It'll have to be. "This is very, um, ordinary," she says, forking a bit of scrambled egg into her mouth.

"I thought something familiar might be appealing about now." I smothered my eggs with hot sauce, and I used to love the spiciness of chorizo sausages, but right now all I can taste is the tang of Regan's pussy as she pressed her fingers against my lips. The only thing I really want to eat right now is sitting across from me, her legs tucked primly to the side. Consuming food is reflexive at this point. My body knows it needs fuel, so I'm shoveling in the protein and carbs as fast as possible. But my head is back in the hotel room, and we aren't having a mutual masturbation scene. Oh no, I'm fucking her. I'm driving deep inside her cunt and feeling her slick juice lubricate every thrust.

"How do you know Daisy and Nick?" Regan's question shakes me out of my fantasy, and I drag my attention back to the table and her question. *Be a human being and make conversation*, I order myself.

"Ahhh, through friends," I say vaguely, wondering if I could avoid the topic of Vasily Petrovich forever. Russia is one of the leading exporters of flesh, although the home of the brave isn't so far behind. "You?"

"Daisy answered my ad for a roommate. She's fresh off the farm. I'm worried about her. You know she hadn't left her town in years because her dad was a big agoraphobic? She was running away from home at the age of twenty." Regan laughs a little self-consciously, tucking a lock of hair behind her delicate ear. If I were a soldier home for a couple of weeks of furlough and had run across her, I'd have been on her like gravy on biscuits. Hell, I'd have had to fight off some of my squad mates to get to her. And now I've had a taste of her. I'd heard her sexy noises as she got excited, the soft, wet sounds as her fingers worked her pussy, the moans of relief and satisfaction when she came. And I'm gone again.

"Daisy seems . . . trusting." Daisy and Nick were perfect for each other. He was a crazy psychopath, and she didn't know any better that he wasn't normal. I vaguely remember giving Nick dating advice at one time. He'd laugh—if he knew how—if he saw the state I was in.

"Yeah, too much so, I guess." Regan sighs and then pushes her eggs around on her plate a bit. "I called my boyfriend when you were in the shower."

Boyfriend? Oh right, the Mike dude who can't keep it up for more than five seconds. That's deflating. I'm cooking up fantasies about the fifty ways I could make Regan come, and she's worried about calling the guy who's never given her an orgasm. "That's fine. Phone's a burner." I wondered if she was worried that we were going to get tracked down. "You should call your parents."

"What can I say to them? I'm here in Brazil, but I'm on the run because some crazy guy with a blond-hair, green-eye fetish is preventing me from flying home? And by the way, Mike's already moved on to my girlfriend Becca."

"Sounds like she's not much of a girlfriend." I try to hide my satisfaction that Mike's not in the picture. I wonder if I should off him, though. Just for being a douchebag. I think the world can only sustain so many asswipes, and I'd be doing a favor making sure the scales were even.

"Yeah," she answers glumly.

I wonder if she's the most torn up about Mike or Becca or her parents. Girl has a lot on her plate. Guess she has the right to be upset about any and all things. I make what I hope is a sympathetic face and continue eating. It's either that or get on a plane and shoot Mike in the nuts.

"I'm in college, you know. I'm working on getting my CPP."

Taking the last bite of my chorizo, I look disapprovingly at Regan's nearly uneaten plate. I wonder if she doesn't like the food or the company. Too bad. She needs the fuel. "Start eating. We have places to go."

She frowns but mechanically starts eating again.

I lean back into my chair and stretch my legs out. Man, I'm tired. Regan and I need to get to Luiz, and then we need some serious sleep. Or I'm going to make a mistake—like touch her the next time she licks my neck. My fingers curl into my coffee cup as I think about that and her wet body and her pussy-slicked fingers pressed against my lips. That non-sex was just about the best sexual encounter I'd had in far too long.

"What about you?" She gestures toward me. "Did you always want to be a gun-toting maniac?"

"Nah. Thought I would go home after I got out of the army and help my dad out on the ranch."

"So why aren't you?"

"Because I was a hothead. I got into a fight my senior year with some guy, and I broke a few ribs. Jackass was making fun of my sister. Judge told me I could have a blot on my record or I could go enlist for four years. I chose enlistment. My dad was pretty pissed off, and we exchanged some angry words about me not being good enough to run the ranch and him being too much of a control freak. I ended up staying in the army and then . . ." I trail off. "Then something happened, and I haven't been able to go home. But once I right that problem I'm heading for the ranch, and I'm not leaving." I change the subject because I'm done talking about me. "What's a CPP?"

"Certified Payroll Processor. It's a pretty intensive certification program that you take so you can work in accounting and human resources. Once I'm certified, I have a standing job offer from a company that provides payroll services to Fortune 500 companies."

"And you are going to do what?"

She shrugs. "Nothing anymore. I'm not going to be able to

take the test in time, which means all my prep classes are wasted, which means I won't be able to start my job, which means . . . I don't even know anymore."

"This is a fucked-up world, darlin'. That you're still breathing oughta be counted as a win."

"It's . . . how do I go back to that?"

"To what? Your dick-for-brains boyfriend? Your job that you talk about with all the enthusiasm of a goat herder?" I'm getting angry, and I can't even pinpoint the real cause. Is it because I am pissed off that she still cared enough about her boyfriend to contact him? That she actually called him a boyfriend? That she didn't care enough about herself to be with a guy who could give her a real-life orgasm? That she is thinking about going back to Minneapolis, the coldest tit a witch ever froze, to take up a job that would turn her into a zombie in under three years? Or that she is so achingly goddamn beautiful, and that I want her so much my balls might fall off?

Even though my external word vomit doesn't match my internal bloviating, Regan still looks taken aback, but she rallies quickly.

"You know, I've gone through a lot and am still standing, so you can dial back on the Robin Williams *Die Hard* inspirational speeches. You suck at them."

"It's Bruce Willis, and I know." I grin at her because I've never been one to stay angry long, and her confusion between Bruce Willis and Robin Williams is funny as shit. "Let's go, fighter."

"Fighter. I like that. You can keep calling me that one."

"How about baby fighter? Or fighter doll?" I tease. I pay the bill and gesture for Regan to step out in front of me.

"You staring at my ass? Is that why you always want me to go first?" she sasses back, whatever hurt my incautious words may have caused apparently gone.

"You do have a fine ass, fighter baby." I whistle. "It's plump and bitable like a juicy piece of Brazilian fruit."

"Yet you haven't even attempted a taste. Maybe you don't like Brazilian fruit?" She sashays out in front of me, her ass swinging back and forth, looking like a true Rio native. All the ladies in Rio seem to have a special hitch in their step that makes people-watching down here almost mandatory. But right now my eyes are glued on this one Minnesotan's prime real estate, and my head's reeling from her very obvious come-on. I don't really know what to make of it.

"I love fruit," I say. "I never like to eat where I'm not invited."

"What kind of invitation is it that you need then? An engraved one with gold lettering?"

I want to pull her aside, maybe push her up against one of the concrete walls of the buildings lining the Rua Visconde de Pirajá and test out that invitation. She laughs and then snaps her fingers. "Better close your mouth, baby boy, or flies will land there."

Snapping my jaw shut, I hurry to catch up with her. Who said we needed sleep when we got done with Luiz? I'm thinking there are a dozen other things we could be doing in a soft, warm bed between some cool, clean sheets.

Whistling, I wink at Regan, and she gives me a big smile in return. Life is easy when you don't think about anything but the moment. We've got to get Regan papers, and then we're checking into a decent hotel room.

"This is a pretty nice place," she says as we walk down an avenue full of luxury brand stores. "I mean, I think these are nicer stores than we have in Minneapolis."

"Ipanema is the second-wealthiest neighborhood in Rio."

"And we're going to see a forger *here*?" she asks.

"Maybe it pays well?" I stop at the address that Pereya gave me. It's an art store—a high-end art store.

"This?" Skepticism drips from the word.

Opening the door, we step inside, the air-conditioning almost too cool for our skin. Regan shivers noticeably, and I wrap an arm around her instinctively. She leans into my embrace. For the warmth, I remind myself, but I find myself pretty damned pleased.

"*Tudo bem?*" A lithe, model-tall woman walks toward us, her dark hair caught up in a heavy braid that lies like a thick snake on her shoulder.

"Just awesome," I lie. "Look, I could give you a big song and dance complete with code words and shit like that, but I need to see Luiz. Pereya sent me."

A speculative glint appears in her eyes, and she says, "Wait here."

"Is this the place?" Regan whispers after the leggy brunette disappears into the back room.

"Hope so." I force myself not to follow the brunette into the back. Shifting our heavy bags over one shoulder, I try to relax. The artwork on the wall is stunning, but clearly directed toward tourist tastes with iconic shots of Sugarloaf Mountain and the Christ the Redeemer statue. In the middle of the room on a pedestal is a crystal sculpture that looks like a futuristic piece of kryptonite, only it's not green, just clear glass. After a moment, the attendant waves us in the back.

Luiz is a small man, barely coming up to my chest. Or maybe he was once taller, but he's spent so much time bent over a table, his natural height reduced about four inches by the forward roll of his shoulders.

"What do you need?"

"Credit cards, passport."

"For who?"

"Two blondes."

"This one?" He points to Regan.

"Yeah, and one more."

"Do you have a picture?"

I do. "It's twenty months old, though," I caution. Pulling out my wallet, I lift out the picture I've kept in a vellum envelope in an interior pocket. I've had this picture with me for a long time, just for this purpose. When I first started out in mercenary work, I hadn't realized how important false identities were—being able to change your name and move throughout countries with ease is something of a necessity in my line of work. I have dozens of identities but none for Regan. I have a couple of stolen identities I carry around for my sister, but I might as well have something made up for her while I'm at it.

Luiz nods and takes the photo with tweezers. I can tell by his meticulousness that our papers will be flawless.

"It will be two weeks."

Regan, silent the whole exchange, finally speaks up. "Two weeks?"

"Tomorrow," I say implacably and pull out a wad of cash to sweeten my demand.

Luiz shakes his head. "Detailed work takes time."

Regan makes a distressed sound, and I shove the cash at Luiz. "Tomorrow." At his hesitation, I draw a gun and everyone ducks, but I aim it toward the crystal sculpture of Sugar Loaf Mountain sitting in the middle of the showroom. "Tomorrow," I repeat.

Luiz looks at me, the heavy bags at my back, and then the

cash. "Tomorrow then." He gestures for Regan to stand against one empty space of white wall and takes her picture.

I holster my gun and shove the cash in his hand. Gesturing toward the door with my head, I urge Regan out.

"Why not now?" She looks like she doesn't want to leave without the papers, but I don't want to piss off Luiz any more. I drag her out of the forger's office and into the street. She looks unhappy, and I miss her sunshine-like smile from earlier this morning.

"Let's go get our stuff and then check into a better hotel. I feel like I need another shower after lying in those sheets."

"Who's the girl?" she says.

"The girl?" I'm not sure I follow her. What girl? She's the only girl I'm with.

"The other girl. The one with her picture in your wallet? Who is it?"

"My sister."

CHAPTER **SEVENTEEN**

REGAN

His sister.

A few things click into place, my brain suddenly making sense of things. He's got a sister—a young, pretty blonde who was sold into slavery, like me. That's why he's hunting blondes. That's why he's in and out of brothels in the slums and knows people like Luiz and Pereya.

That's why he was so giddy when we got the information from the snitch.

I want to laugh with relief. I've been trying not to think about the other mysterious blonde he's so excited at the thought of finding. I've been having flares of jealousy, quickly tamped down again. What right do I have to be jealous of anyone or anything Daniel does? He's not mine. He's my rescuer that I'm forcing to stick with me.

But . . . I'm still glad it's his sister and not a rival for his attention.

We leave Luiz's art gallery and head onto the streets of Ipanema, mingling with the crowd. I look over at Daniel and he's full of barely leashed energy. If an assassin could be giddy, that would be Daniel. I wonder if it's because he's close to getting his sister . . . or close to getting rid of me? Or both?

I'm not sure how that makes me feel. The conversation at breakfast has left me a bit at odds with myself. I don't know how I'm going to slide back into my old life and pretend like nothing has happened. I'm a scholarship student, and the company I'm slated to go work for has paid for a large chunk of my schooling. It's one of the reasons I went into accounting as a major: a guaranteed job at the end of college and someone was willing to pay for most of the classes, provided I keep my GPA up. Of course, it's midsemester right now, and I've missed two months, which means I've now flunked out of all my courses unless I drop them. Either way, I'm screwed.

But I'm alive, as Daniel has pointed out. I should be grateful instead of anticipating problems.

As we head back into the rougher part of the city, the streets clear out a bit. There's not as many people strolling the shopping districts, and there are a few people loitering in doorways of nearby run-down shops. We're walking the streets of Ipanema, heading back to the hotel, when Daniel grabs my ass. "Damn, baby doll. I can't get over how fine this is." His voice is loud, his Texas drawl thick.

I'm startled, and I jump at his touch, scurrying away a few feet. What the hell? "What are you doing?" His touch, so callous and out of the blue, has made me jittery, and bad memories start creeping up in my mind.

"I don't think I can wait to tap that again," he says, and his arms go around me again. Before I can protest, he drags me over a few feet into the alley and pushes me up against the wall. His mouth presses down over mine.

A deluge of bad memories sweeps over me as his tongue presses into my mouth. This aggressiveness isn't like Daniel. He's always let me take the lead before, and the difference in his touch is like night and day. I've craved more of his touch and wanted to explore . . . until now. Now, I want him to get off of me before I suffocate under the thoughts crowding my mind. Memories of men with guns and sweaty bodies, forcing my mouth open, pushing me down on a dirty mattress . . .

I whimper and push vainly at Daniel's chest, but he's got me pressed against the wall of the building. I'm trapped against his body as he grabs my leg and pulls it to his hip, practically wrapping me around him even as I struggle.

"We're being watched," he murmurs against my mouth. "Quit fighting." And then he goes back to kissing me.

My fists stop beating him on the chest as I realize this is all an act. My eyes open, and I look at Daniel's hard face. His eyes are slits, and he's watching a nearby doorway even as his mouth crushes against mine again.

I'm not responding. I can't. This is too much like the times in the brothel. There's no delicate lead for me to take. I need to sit quietly and accept. I need to trust Daniel.

But I can't stop the tears from welling up in my eyes and spilling down my cheeks—or the saliva from pooling in my mouth. I'm going to throw up if this continues for too much longer. Wait it out, I tell myself. It's not like before. It's not. But even as I tell myself this, I remember the gun pressed to my head and the awful feeling of futility as I dropped to my knees in front of the man who'd bought me.

"Shit," Daniel says against my mouth. "So fucking sorry, fighter. Just hang on for me." He hitches my leg against his hip again and grinds his pelvis against mine. Even as he does, I feel something jostle, and I realize he's pulled a gun free of its holster and holds it against my leg.

When I think I can't bear this any longer, he lifts his mouth from mine and scans the street, tilting his head. I swallow hard and wipe the back of my hand against my mouth surreptitiously, trying to scrub away the feelings.

"I don't see the gunman anymore, but I don't want to take chances," Daniel says. He gives me a quick, apologetic kiss on the forehead. "Come on. We're going this way." He drops my leg and gestures that I should head down the alley.

Shivering, I do so, trotting a few steps ahead of him as he watches carefully behind us. My earlier buoyancy has been entirely deflated. I was feeling so good this morning, so normal. And now, poof, it's gone again.

I want to curl up and cry, my go-to after I've been violated, but we don't have time for that. We're in danger—I can tell from the tense set of Daniel's shoulders and the way his mouth is in a firm, angry line—so I choke back the feelings and let Daniel lead me on.

Eventually, he points ahead and leads me through an alley door. We're back at the hotel, but the back entrance, where fresh laundry is delivered and food trucks bring in packages.

We head through the back halls of the hotel, up the fire escape stairs, and eventually make it back to our room. The hallways are empty, but Daniel presses himself against the wall next to the door, carefully pushing me behind him. It's clear from his raised-gun stance that he expects trouble in our room, so I wait for his signal, pulling out the gun I now carry with me at all times. It makes me feel a little better to hold it, knowing there's an option if a man other than Daniel tries to shove me down against another dirty mattress in the future.

I can always shoot someone, right? *Or yourself,* my brain reminds me, but that's not an option. Then again, neither is whoring.

"Wait here," Daniel says in a low whisper. "I'm going in. Shoot anyone that comes out of this doorway. Even me. If it's clear, I'll call you 'fighter baby.' Got it?"

"Got it," I choke out in a low voice, even as he heads through the door, gun at the ready.

There's an incredibly long moment of silence, and I scarcely breathe, waiting to hear something, anything.

A moment later, Daniel says, "All clear, fighter baby. Come on in."

I release the breath I've been holding and enter the room. Immediately, it's clear to me that the room's been ransacked. My clothes have been torn apart and strewn across the room, and the bed has been overturned. Thank God Daniel took the bag of guns with us. He refused to let them out of his sight, and I see now he was right to do so.

I swallow hard at the sight. "Good thing we went out for breakfast, huh?" I try not to think what would have happened if they'd have found me in bed with Daniel, rubbing up against him. Both of us could have been killed.

"Looks like your friend hasn't given up on you yet." Daniel's mouth is set into the hard, angry line I'm becoming all too familiar with. "Goddamn it. Least we have most of our ammo still on us, but it looks like you're going to be wearing that outfit for a while."

"At least there's that," I agree faintly.

"You okay?" he asks me.

My lower lip feels like it's on the verge of trembling, but I nod. "I'm fine." I'm not, but there's no point in going into how fucked-up my head is at the moment, because it doesn't matter.

"Let's go," Daniel says. "Pack your things again, and we'll head to a new hotel. Change of plans. We're heading for the best hotel money can buy. Figure since they're going to know where we are anyhow, we might as well hide in plain sight. They're going to have to work a lot harder to try to steal your ass on Main Street."

"Okay," I say in a small voice again.

"You sure you don't know why Freeze is so hot for you? You great with pony play or something?"

"I don't even know what that is."

"Never mind. I'm being a jackass. This shit's not making sense and I'm getting riled trying to figure it out." He rakes a hand through his short hair and blows out a heavy breath. "Fuck. Let's go."

I pack my things quickly, tuck my gun back into my belt, and try to remain calm while Daniel texts something into his burner. When I'm ready, I nod at him and we leave the room behind. As soon as we get back out into the streets, Daniel hails a cab and puts an arm around my shoulders, like we're a couple. I don't shrug him off even though I'm feeling so weird right now. I don't want to be touched, not at the moment, but I don't tell Daniel to take his hands off of me.

We get in the cab. Daniel tells the driver an address in Portuguese and then puts his arm over my shoulders again. "Can't believe we're finally Mr. and Mrs. Parker," he says in that drawling fake Texas accent I'm starting to learn is his "let's pretend" voice.

"That's right, baby," I say quickly and press a kiss to his cheek, even though my voice sounds a bit more wobbly than I'd like.

I tune out as Daniel keeps up a steady stream of chatter with both me and the cabdriver. He's playing the role of a young newlywed tourist with great aplomb, occasionally giving me affectionate little touches that keep reminding me of the surprise kiss I reacted so badly to a short time ago. I do my part to keep up the pretense, but I'm sure it's clear to both Daniel and the cabbie that I'm miles away mentally.

We get to the hotel, check in, and head up to our room—all the while Daniel is yakking in my ear about sightseeing tours and the nude beaches of Brazil, hand at my waist. It rests close to my gun, a reminder that despite the smiling people and pristine appearance of this hotel, we're no safer than we were before.

The room is gorgeous, though. It has a king-sized bed with fresh linens, a stack of fluffy towels waiting on the corner of the bed, and a lovely view of the city from the balcony. The bathroom's bigger than my old apartment.

As we enter the room, Daniel locks and chains the door behind us, moves a dresser in front of the door, and then pulls the curtains closed. Then, he turns to look at me.

"So," he says. "You want to talk about what's bothering you?"

DANIEL

Regan turns away, her face flushing with . . . embarrassment? Shame? I'm not sure. She doesn't need to feel either. I'm damn confused. "Sorry," she mumbles.

"You don't have to be sorry. I'm trying to understand so I don't make the same mistake again." I watch as she wanders around the room, opening doors and drawers to look for something. Or at least not to look at me. I dump our packs on the floor and head to the minibar. Inside I find a bottle of vodka. Perfect. Picking up the bag with the superglue from the pharmacy that we stopped at before hitting the hotel, I set up shop in the bathroom.

"What're you doing?"

"Making a mess," I joke, pouring the bottle of alcohol over the open wound that is now bleeding again. "Fuck that hurts."

"Here let me help you." She pushes my hand away. Handing her the bottle of vodka, I pull off my shirt and lean against the sink, watching her in the mirror. Her lower lip is caught between her teeth as she pulls slightly at the skin to open the wound. "Looks bad," she comments.

"Looks worse than it actually is." I gesture toward the bottle. "Pour that on and then glue me up."

"Is this really safe?"

"Yup. Did it all the time in combat." Truthfully we had Dermabond, a medical-grade glue, over there, but the only real difference is that the Dermabond burned less and was stronger. Superglue will do fine.

"Okay." She grits her teeth as if she's the one getting burning alcohol poured all over her open wound, but I've suffered worse, so I tip my head back and bite the inside of my cheek as she sets my side on fire. Then cool air hits my side, causing me to glance down. Regan's kneeling beside me blowing little puffs of cool relief onto my wound. The sight of her down so close to my groin is setting something else afire. I grab for some tissue and start dabbing at the wound so we can glue it up and she can get off her knees before I make an inappropriate suggestion.

She leans back on her haunches while I dry myself off. "Want to glue me shut?" I waggle the bottle at her. Nodding, she pulls the cap off. "Dab a thin line on both sides of the wound, and we'll be good to go."

Carefully, she spreads the glue in place and then I squeeze the flesh together, hissing a little as glue stings. I slap a gauze strip over it and hand her the tape. As she winds the tape around my waist, her breasts touch my back and that—combined with the touch of her soft hands—is enough to give me a semi. Worse, on the third pass, her arm brushes a little too close to my crotch, and the semi grows into full wood.

"Sorry," I say through gritted teeth. "Delayed adrenaline." A total lie but given that Regan freaked out before in the alleyway, I'm working extra hard not to provide more fodder for her nightmares. "Let me finish up." I hold out my hand to take the tape from her.

"No, I've got it," she says, but on the next two passes she makes sure she's well away from my lower region. It doesn't matter. Just her nearness is making me dizzy with arousal and want. "How's that?" she asks finally.

"Good," I say and then nearly run to get out of the bathroom. I flop down on the sofa, wishing I had at least a couple of those bottles of vodka down my throat instead of on my side. I'm going to need something so I don't think about having sex with Regan every five seconds.

She follows behind, and suddenly the big bedroom that I booked for us is way too small. I would've gotten two rooms if that had been safe, but I couldn't protect her if she wasn't within eye sight. Maybe she's worried that we have to sleep in the same bed. "Don't worry," I assure her. "This sofa has a pullout. You can have the bed."

Absently she nods and then sits on the side of the bed, bouncing a little as if she's not sure if she wants to sit or pace. Rather than worry about that, I close my eyes and let the exhaustion of the past few days roll over me.

"Tell me about your sister," she says.

I'd rather make puppets with my socks, because Naomi's story will give Regan a legitimate reason to hate me but she probably deserves to hear all of it. "She's seven years younger than me and a fucking genius. Like, when she was in elementary school, she could think circles around me. I went to her for math help, not the other way around. She skipped all kinds of grades. Graduated high school when she was fourteen and then started taking college classes. Not sure if she's really autistic or whether her lack of socialization with kids her age hurt her, but she's really socially awkward. Has a hard time relating to people, but she's so damn sweet, Regan." My voice grows pained as I think of what happened next. "I wanted her to have some fun, you know?"

"You can't feel like what happened to her is your fault," Regan protests.

"Really? Maybe you should reserve judgment until I finish the story," I say shortly. Surging to my feet, I lunge at the minibar. I need some alcohol to finish this story. There are six more bottles of liquor inside. I take out the Jack Daniel's and swallow the bottle in one gulp. In my absence, Regan has moved to the sofa and is patting the cushion. With a sigh, I head back and crack open the bottle of rum. Rolling the small bottle between my hands, I finish the story. "So I'm telling her to get out and do some normal stuff. She's studying at MIT, some kind of string theory shit that is more complicated than how the F-16 is constructed. During one of our Skype calls, she tells me that some classmates of hers are going on spring break to Cancun, and I encourage her to go. No." I stop and drink down the bottle, tossing the empty container on the coffee table. There's not ever going to be enough alcohol to make the pain of this memory go away. "I force her to go. I tell her that she's wasting her life in school, that the real world is passing her by— she's gotta get out and live it." Those last words come out with so much bitterness and self-hatred that even Regan leans away.

"She goes and on the second day is kidnapped. I get a Red Cross call—the line family members can use to inform you of an emergency—and fly twenty hours home. When I get to the ranch, my momma looks like she's aged fifty years and can barely rise from the chair to greet me. My dad doesn't want me to even step foot on the porch of our house. He tells me to find her and not come home until I do."

"Oh, Daniel." Regan leans over and starts rubbing my upper shoulders, which feels far better than I deserve at the moment. "Have you been saving girls for the last eighteen months?"

That and killing people.

"Every time I walked into one of those houses or pulled over a truck carrying fucking kidnapped girls, I didn't know whether I felt relief or disappointment at not seeing her face. Until a few hours ago, I believed she was dead." I hunch over my knees, using my hands to cradle my head. "And now I'm feeling so much fucking relief, I can't even tell you, Regan."

"Do you need to cry it out?" she murmurs.

"What?" I crank my head around.

"Cry it out? You know, let it go. That's how my, I guess, ex–best friend Becca and I used to deal with things."

"I hope you know I'm not Becca."

She smiles, a bit sadly. "I hate that you found me in that house. I hate that I'm a fucked-up victim."

Turning swiftly, I grab her by both arms. "You are not a victim. You are a fucking survivor. You have more life in you than half the people walking around living their normal lives." I shake her a little so she gets this. "You are not a victim."

I don't think this penetrates, because she continues. "Earlier, in the alley,"—she gestures in some vague direction behind her—"I freaked out because you were pressed up against me. I felt like I was back in that room." Her breath catches as if she's holding back some tears, but I don't encourage her to cry it out, because I don't know if I can deal with her tears at this moment. "What if I can't have sex like a normal person? What if all I can do is mutual masturbation?"

Her words are conjuring up wild, erotic images, which I'm sure she wouldn't appreciate. Swallowing hard, I push my lust away and attempt to speak normally. "I think you'll move past that."

"I wanted you this morning," she admits. "I mean, you saw me. I really wanted you. I was fantasizing about you touching me, you rubbing me, your dick inside me."

Oh Christ. This sex talk is making my dick stand up. But what if . . . ? A thought occurs to me. A really selfish thought. One generated by my dick, but I can't help myself. Standing up, I say, "Then take me."

"What do you mean?" She sounds bewildered but intrigued.

I unbuckle my pants and then lie on the bed. "Why not come over and use me? Do what you like to me. Tell me what you want me to do, and I'll do it. If all you want me to do is lie here while you feel me up, then that's what we do. If you want to climb on top of me and ride me, that's cool. Shit, you can even tie my hands up." I shiver at the thought. "Use me."

"But what if I get upset and leave you hanging?" She's up off

her feet and standing right at the edge of the bed, fiddling with
the bottom of her shirt like she wants to whip it off. *Do it, baby.*

"So I have to jerk it myself. You're okay with that, right?"

She nods.

"Then it's all good." I spread out my arms. "I won't move
unless you tell me to."

"But what if I get on top of you and then I'm like, on you but
have to, um, disengage?" She's placed a knee on the side of the bed.

"So you're saying you're riding me, and your wet pussy juice
is coating my dick, and then you decide, nope, this train ride's
too rough or I'm feeling queasy?"

Her head bobs and her breathing is a little more rapid, a little
louder. "Then I guess you climb off and I take myself in hand,
and I either jerk off with your hot little eyes watching every move
or I go to the bathroom."

"But that seems so unfair to you." This time she's fully on the
bed, kneeling right beside me. My dick is so hard I could hang a
fifty-pound weight off of it.

"Making you feel good is a privilege, not a chore. You hear
me? No matter what happens, you tell yourself that getting close
to your pussy is a goddamn fucking privilege. Got that?"

I only get a nod, but this is important shit so I make her repeat
it. "Say it. Say 'making me feel good is a motherfucking privilege.'"

She giggles but repeats my words. "Making me feel good is a
privilege."

"No, 'a motherfucking' one. Say it again."

She screams it. "Making me feel good is a motherfucking
privilege." Then she collapses on the bed beside me and we both
laugh. It's stress relief or maybe actual humor, but I can tell we
both feel better.

"Wouldn't it be hard not to want to keep going?" she asks, rolling onto her side. Her head rests on one of my outstretched arms. I'm careful not to move like I promised.

"I've gone without for a long time, baby. I can last a few more days," I say wryly, knowing her next question is going to be how long. Because that's Regan: always asking the follow-up. She should've been a reporter or investigator or something instead of an accountant.

"How long?"

I grin. "Couldn't help yourself, could you?"

She smiles back and shakes her head. "If you knew I was going to ask, why didn't you offer it up?"

Shrugging, I sink into the bed a little more. She draws closer to me, her head now resting on my shoulder and her left hand absently stroking my chest. "It's been . . ." I squint into the distance. "A couple of years? My last leave I was in a bar in San Antonio. Some cougar propositioned me, and I took her up on her offer to teach me some moves. And yes, before you ask, she did teach me a couple of things."

"I don't know what to ask you first. Like, why has it been that long, and what is it that she taught you?"

"She taught me to listen to my partner and that making her happy was going to end in good times for me. As for the other . . ." I scrub my free hand across my mouth. "After my sister was taken and I started learning more about what happens to these lost girls, I kinda lost my appetite for it."

"But with me, it seems like . . ." She trails off.

"That I'm always hard?"

"Yeah, kind of."

"Don't know how to explain it. You turn me on like no one else has ever cranked my chain."

"Would you really let me tie you up?"

All I hear is genuine curiosity, and I want to feed it until it turns into desire, want, and unrestrained need that she fills at the fount of Daniel.

"Yeah, but I'm going to be honest: I'd be able to get out of any restraint you could think of, so tying me up will be illusory. You trust me?" I hold my breath because none of this is going to work unless she's fully on board. Regan's got to be able to embrace her own reactions—but even more, she has to believe that she is safe with me.

Her gaze is downward, and she's silent. All I can hear is my own heavy breathing that sounds like harsh static on a radio airwave.

"I don't know if I can trust you," she says finally. "That's the issue for me. I don't know what I'll be able to take or not until I'm there."

It dawns on me that Regan doesn't need to trust me; she needs to know that I not only trust her but I'm okay with everything that she does. I need to give myself over to her fully and let her do what I asked—which was use me, take me. I force my breathing to calm. "Here's my promise: I'm not ever going to get angry for anything you do or don't do in the bedroom."

She bites her lip and then passes a hand over the surface of my body, and it's more erotic than if she had performed a lap dance.

"I'm not sure what I should do. Like, should I take my clothes off?"

Yes please. But this is her show. "Whatever you want."

She fingers the bottom of her shirt again and then casts a glance upward behind a veil of lashes, looking mysterious and coy, but I know it's her lack of surety. I give her my reckless smile, as if what she does is of no importance. As if I can take it or leave it. As if I'm not going to die if she doesn't put a hand on me.

I offer up some suggestions. "You could kiss me. You could let me lick your sweet pussy. Or you could rub against me." Or all of the above.

"I'm a little wet," she admits.

Me too.

"Climb on up then, and let me kiss you between your legs and get you good and wet. You'd like that, right? Wouldn't you like my tongue lapping up all that juice?" The invisible restraints against my arms are chafing hard. I want to flip her over and bury my fingers and tongue in that hot, wet cunt, but I promised her that I wouldn't move until she told me I could.

But I'm still going to talk.

"I thought I was in charge?" she mock complains, but I can tell she's more comfortable.

"You are, baby. I'm throwing out ideas."

Regan tugs off her shirt and then throws a leg over me so that she's straddling my abdomen. Her damp panties are rubbing against my bare skin. My hands dig into the mattress as I fight the urge to grab her ass. This is so much harder than anything I've ever done before. My only outlet right now is my mouth, so I let it fly.

"Oh yeah. I can feel you, sweetheart. I can feel that you are turned on. If you were a little higher you could place one of those teacup breasts into my mouth. I'd love to suck one of your tits until each one is good and hard. Do you think you'd feel that between your legs? I can't wait until my mouth is all over you and I've licked and sucked on every inch of your skin at least twice."

She runs her hands over my chest, smoothing her palms along the planes of my pectorals and then down to my abdomen. I've never been a gym rat. I've worked out because it helped me survive on missions, but now I'm very glad that my body is cut, because I can tell by the worshipful way Regan caresses every ridge, how she shifts on top of me, that my body turns her on.

"Tell me what you want," I beg. "You are killing me."

"Will you watch me again?"

I nod eagerly. She places three fingers against my lips and I suck them inside my mouth, coating each finger with my tongue. With a pop, she pulls her fingers away, and I'm reluctant to let even that contact go.

My eyes track those glistening fingers until they disappear into her panties. "Take your panties off, sugar. Let me really see you work your pussy."

Her chest heaving, Regan does as I tell her. She slides backward between my legs and pushes her panties off her ass, lifting a little, and I catch a glimpse of her soft hair and the pretty dark pink flesh of her cunt. I lick my lips, and saliva pools as I remember how good she tastes. I need more of that. I need to *feast* on her.

Then she's back on my chest, a little higher now. "Am I too heavy for you?" she gasps as she rubs herself, the three fingers I sucked on now getting wet from her own juice.

"Not at all." Her slight weight isn't what's killing me right now. It's my inability to touch her. "But if you come up a little higher, I can help you out. I can suck on your clit and lap your come as you finger yourself."

Her fingers stutter as she responds to my words. Biting her lip, she peers down at me indecisively and then gives me a small nod. I refrain from a double fist pump, but this is better than a hole in one. Rising on her knees, she inches forward and I move downward.

"Grab hold of the headboard with your one hand, for stability," I tell her. She does but her pussy is still about an inch too high. I think she's afraid she's going to break my face or something, but if anything is breaking off it's my dick, because it is so goddamn hard right now a stiff wind could shatter it. "Lower baby. Sit on me."

"Won't I suffocate you?" she worries but lowers until that juicy pussy is resting right on top of my mouth.

"Oh, baby, if only." I give her one long lick—from her fingers rubbing the top of her pubic bone all the way to her tiny rear rosette.

"Ohhhhh," she breathes out.

"This pussy is so gorgeous. It's shaped like one of those white flowers, and every time I push away a fold with my tongue, I find a more tasty delicacy." I'd tell her more but I'm too busy running my tongue inside her, scooping out her arousal, sucking on each cunt lip and then her clit. I can hear her panting above me, each quickened breath telling me how much she wants this, but even if I couldn't hear her, I can see the visible evidence of her arousal in how wet she is and how engorged her flesh is. I spear her with my tongue and then lash her clit until she's thrashing above me and her thighs are clenched against my cheeks. She's given up fingering herself to grip my hair, alternatingly pulling on my hair and pushing my face closer to her pussy. I love it. I love her fierce touch and her physical exertions. She's so into this, into me, that she has lost control of her senses and completely let go.

I would rend anyone limb from limb who tried to come between Regan and me. From now on, the only one who will hear her scream when she comes is me. The only man who will get to taste the nectar between her legs is me. The only cock that will ever pleasure her, from this moment until I never draw another breath, is *mine*.

I eat at her, lapping at her arousal and listening to the sounds of her pleasure as she comes and comes. My arms feel heavy with the desire to touch her, and my dick is pulsing with need, but the promise I made to her is just as effective as bonds. I'd never hurt her, never break my promise to her. Not in this lifetime or the next.

When the last of her orgasm leaves her weak, she collapses against the wall and headboard and then slowly slides down until she's prostrate on top of me. "Can I hold you?" I whisper against her ear.

"Please," she says. And my arms band around her so tightly she squeaks.

"Sorry." I force myself to loosen my hold, but I don't let go.

CHAPTER **EIGHTEEN**

REGAN

Daniel's hand strokes up and down my back in slow, soothing motions. I'm lying on top of him, my legs spread over his hips, my breasts mashed to his chest, and he's quietly stroking my back and ignoring the raging hard-on I feel pressed against my pussy. We're both ignoring it. I suppose sooner or later, it needs to be addressed. Just . . . not right now. I'm feeling too good to think about anything but what we did.

His fingers dance along my spine in a light touch. "Did I break you?" he asks, and I hear a teasing note in his voice.

I laugh a little, but the truth is, I'm feeling a little stunned. That's the first time I've ever been on the receiving end of oral, and it was every bit as good as it had been made out to be. I'd sat on Daniel's face, and he'd acted like I was giving him a present. I think of Mike and how I'd blown him countless times and how he'd never reciprocated. "I'm not a big fan of pussy," he'd tell me and complain about the smell, as if I was something diseased instead of his girlfriend. The few times I'd begged him to do more, he'd told me that guys who said they liked eating pussy were liars, and made tuna jokes.

I sit up, a frown on my face as I stare down at Daniel.

"What?" he asks.

"Did you enjoy that?"

His eyes narrow and now he's frowning, like he's not entirely sure he understands the question. "Did I enjoy eating your pussy? Wasn't it obvious?"

"Just answer the question."

"I could eat that pussy for hours and never get tired of the way you taste," Daniel tells me, and his fingers skim up my spine again. "Love your honey on my tongue and the way you shiver when I touch your clit. So, yeah, I fucking loved it."

I tremble a little at the intensity of his gaze. "Sorry. I guess that was a silly question."

"Not silly," he says to me.

"Mike didn't . . . he . . ."

"Can we not talk about Mike when you're spread on top of me?" His hand stops moving along my spine, and the closed look on his face makes me realize I've hurt his feelings.

I need to make this better. So I lie back down on him and curl up against his hard chest, my cheek pressed against his heart. "I'm sorry. Mike's my only real experience . . . before. And I'm starting to realize now that it wasn't very good."

He pats my back. "S'okay."

"You ever have bad sex?" I ask him. My head feels deliciously comfy on his chest, and his nipple is a mere inch or two away from my face. I lift my fingers and begin to trace circles around it. Daniel's got a dusting of chest hair all across his pectorals, but I like it. It feels warm and a little fuzzy against my cheek.

"Shit yeah. Who hasn't?" His fingers move along my spine again, and after a moment he says, "I once banged a girl—a base bunny—who called me my sergeant's name the entire time. We were both too drunk to care but, I admit, it kinda shriveled my dick when I sobered up. Never touched that ass again."

"Because your feelings were hurt?" Poor Daniel.

"No, because Sarge was fucking disgusting. Man was seventy if he was a day, bowlegged, dentures, and the worst damn breath. Kinda insulted that she mistook us."

I giggle at that, because I picture a girl mistaking this breathtakingly gorgeous man for that and it seems absurd. "Maybe she was really, really drunk."

"Shit, I sure hope so. He had these bizarre caterpillar eyebrows that looked like they were ready to crawl off his face."

I'm laughing now, all tension gone. He sounds so very disgruntled.

He chuckles underneath me, clearly pleased by my response. "Damn, Regan, but you have the prettiest laugh. I think I need to hear that more often." And his fingers caress my cheek.

Just like that, my laughter dries up and I'm feeling relaxed and good . . . and even more blatantly aware of Daniel's cock pressing against me. He's ignoring it, but it's obvious he wants me. And suddenly, I want him, too. I want to see if I can have sex with this man without freaking out. Oral sex with him had been amazing, but now I'm greedy and I want more. How good would flat-on-your-back, sweaty, pounding sex be? My wavering courage tells me that if I ride Daniel, it'll be safer to get up, easier to run away.

But . . . I also wonder what it'd be like if Daniel were in charge. Would I lose my cool the moment he covers me? Or would I be too busy having the best orgasms of my life to even care?

Do I want to try? My fingers slide away from his nipple and move up to his mouth, and I trace his lips with my fingertips.

He inhales sharply, and his tongue reaches out to flick against my fingers. A low groan escapes him. "I can still taste you on your fingers."

"Do you like it?" I ask softly.

"Makes my dick harder than a rock."

I give my hips a little shift, rocking them against his erection. "I can tell." My voice is becoming breathless with excitement. "Do you have condoms?"

"Yep." No pretty words, no questioning if I'm sure or not. Just a solid affirmation. It's handled. For some reason, that makes me smile. Everything's always handled with Daniel. When I'm with him, it's harder to spin out of control. He's got me. I like that.

So I sit up a little and shift forward until my lips can reach his. I kiss him, because I like kissing this man. My mouth plays over his, the kiss light, gentle, and totally controlled by me. His lips brush over mine, his tongue flicking against my own, and it feels incredibly good. So good that I want to try and go a little further.

I roll off of him, and my hands drag at his shoulders, trying to pull him over me. But Daniel sits up and gives me a wary look. "Regan, you sure—"

I nod. "Keep kissing me, okay? I'll let you know if I freak out."

"All right." He shifts his weight, and then his chest is pressing against mine and his mouth covers mine again.

I can feel the old fear flickering in the back of my mind, and the urge to start counting off horror movies rises. But then Daniel's tongue brushes against my own, and pleasure returns. I make a small noise of protest when his mouth pulls away from mine, but he's only pressing light kisses along my jaw, tickling me with their touch. And that's all right, too. It's tender and loving and nothing like the horrible experiences I've had in the past.

"You're so beautiful, Regan. So fucking beautiful it drives me crazy." His hands slide over my body, caressing me, and his leg moves between mine. His movements are slow and easy, clearly designed not to startle me, and I appreciate his thoughtfulness. It's like he knows this is a huge moment for me and that I could go either way: either scared of sex forever or move on past my trauma.

I want to move on. More than that, I want to move on with him. I tilt my head back, exposing my neck for his mouth to move over, and it feels so good as he scrapes his teeth along my sensitive skin. I gasp when his mouth latches onto my earlobe, and he tongues it then lightly sucks on it. A moan rises from my throat, and my nipples ache; my ears are really sensitive.

"You like that?" he murmurs into my ear as I cling to him. "You want my tongue sliding all over that sweet little ear of yours like I did your pussy?"

Daniel's a dirty talker, and it's a little crazy at how erotic I find it. For some reason, his describing what he wants to do to me is as effective as his touches on my body. I cling to him, burying my fingers in his short hair as he gives my earlobe the same treatment he gave my clit a short time ago—and it's making me as crazy as that did.

"Can I touch your breasts, Regan?" One hand skims my side even as his mouth continues to make love to my earlobe. "I won't if you don't want me to."

But I do want him to. It's enough that he asked, and it's

enough that his mouth keeps nibbling and sucking on my earlobe to remind me that this is about making me feel good, not about taking from me. I press my hand to his free one and move it to my breast, giving him silent encouragement.

His groan of pleasure is in my ear. "You've got the sweetest little tits, Regan. I bet they'd fill up my mouth nicely. I bet those nipples are as juicy as your pussy. Are they?"

I gasp and nod, whimpering some sort of answer in my throat. Daniel's relentless make-out assault is reminding me of the old days back before Mike and I started sleeping together, back when foreplay was fun and not thirty seconds of squeezing before Mike decided he wanted sex. Back when it was about me.

And I like it. I like it so much that when Daniel's head slides down and he tongues my nipple, I moan his name aloud. "Oh God, Daniel."

"That's right, fighter baby," he murmurs against the tip of my breast. "It's all Daniel. And Daniel loves your body. I want to put my mouth all over it." And he nips at the peak in his mouth, as if teasing me with what he wants to do. "Do you want that?"

"Yes," I moan, clinging to him. When Daniel moves his attentions from my neck and ear down to my breasts, it's as good as when he was tonguing my pussy. He lavishes attention on each one, brushing his fingers over my skin and teasing me, then devouring my nipples with hot, needy kisses and nips of his teeth. Just when I think I can't stand it any longer, he moves over to my other breast and gives it the same attention, his fingers toying with the aching nipple he's left behind.

By the time he comes up to kiss me again, I'm wild with need, panting his name, and my hips are rocking against him. I need to have sex with him. "Condom," I whisper.

"Be right back." He kisses me again for so long and so hard that it's on the tip of my tongue to tell him to forget the condom and to get inside me, but then he rolls off the bed and jogs across the room to his pants. I rise up on my elbows, watching as he pulls out his wallet, removes a condom, and then carefully checks the expiration date. "Whew. Just in time."

For some reason, this strikes me as funny. That a man as sexy and dangerous as Daniel would have a condom in his wallet for so long that it's close to expiring. I stifle my giggles, but he hears them anyhow.

"Not what a guy wants to hear when he's rolling on a sock, sweetheart," Daniel tells me, ripping open the package.

"Sorry," I say, trying to smother my laughter, but I can't seem to help it. Daniel's the last person in the world who would have a deflated ego.

He smooths the condom down his length and returns to the bed, careful to approach me in slow, steady motions. He eases his body down onto the bed next to me again, leans over, and cups the back of my neck as he begins to kiss me once more.

I respond to his kiss with a hungry one of my own, and soon we're making out all over again and I've nearly forgotten about sex—except for the feel of his cock pressing against my hip and the aching need deep inside me.

A moment later, Daniel moves back on top of me and I part my legs, welcoming him between them. His weight settles there and he kisses me for a moment longer, then hitches one thigh up around his hips, moving me into position. Still, he kisses me, and still, it's all right.

"You can back out, fighter baby," he murmurs against my lips.

"It's okay, I promise." I want this.

He gives me a light kiss, and then his cock presses at the opening of my sex. Daniel pushes in, and I suck in a breath as a crowd of memories—and unpleasant faces—surges to the forefront. Oh shit. Oh shit.

But then he leans down and kisses me again, his hands smoothing my hair. He whispers soft, dirty things in my ear, and I remember it's Daniel. My tense body relaxes under him, and I begin to return his kiss, slowly, hesitantly.

I can feel his body trembling with exerted control, his muscles tense as he hovers over me, not moving a muscle except to kiss my mouth. He's not going to do anything until it's clear I'm fine with this, and I stroke my fingers over his cheek, his shoulder, his arm, trying to let him know that it's okay. That I'm okay.

"It's fine, Daniel," I whisper when he still doesn't move.

But he only moves to my neck and begins to kiss and suck on my earlobe again, his tongue doing delicious things to that sensitive little area, and I begin to moan and wriggle underneath him again. His skin is slick with sweat, and my nostrils are filled with his warm, delicious scent. It's Daniel. All Daniel.

He gives my earlobe a gentle bite and I moan, feeling a pulse of desire deep in my core again. He shifts a little and his cock moves inside me a bit, and it feels good, too. I raise my hips against him, indicating that I want more.

He gives me more, then. His hips move in a slow, steady rocking motion that feels good, and I wrap my arms around his neck and hold on to him as he continues to lick and suck at my earlobe. Before long, I'm moaning under the onslaught, and my clinging to Daniel has a desperate clench to it. My pulse is throbbing all through my body, and my breasts ache with need, but Daniel's thrusts are like clockwork—slow, steady, even. I know if he sped up, I'd move that much closer to an orgasm.

But he doesn't—even when I beg—and I begin to thrash under him, becoming wilder as the need grows within me. And still he continues that slow, steady motion, pushing deep inside me, dragging out ever so slowly, and then pushing deep again. All the while, he's tonguing my earlobe and pressing kisses to it and murmuring all the filthy things he wants to do to me.

"You ever have an orgasm with a guy inside you, Regan? Make you come so hard that you're practically sucking his dick inside you because you've clamped down on him?" he whispers in my ear and outlines my earlobe with the tip of his tongue.

I'm shivering with need, and my response to him is only a low moan of his name.

"I think that's a no," he murmurs. "And I think that's a real fucking shame. Because I want you to squeeze down on me so hard that you're seeing goddamn stars, fighter baby."

Is he ready to come? Is this a hint for me to hurry up and have an orgasm? I've gotten pretty good at predicting Mike, but Daniel is an unknown to me. Still, I dutifully hitch my breath and squeeze my internal muscles around him, beginning my fake-out so he can finish up.

"Uh-uh," he says to me. "I want the real thing."

My pleasure is suddenly ebbing away. "Daniel, I don't know—"

"I do," he says, and he shifts his hips, reaching between us. His fingers find my clit and he puts his thumb over it, even as he pulls back and thrusts deep inside me again.

My entire body clenches hard, and I'm startled at the pleasure that rolls through me. I gasp, my eyes going wide. The sensations he's sending through me now are so intense they're almost frightening. "Daniel—"

"Shhh, I've got you, fighter baby," he murmurs, and he begins that slow, steady hammering again, his thumb bouncing against my clit with each movement. And I'm not able to sit back and enjoy the ride anymore. I'm going crazy underneath him, my hips moving to buck against his every thrust, pushing that thumb harder against my clit, our bodies slapping with the force of each thrust.

I'm frantic, soft little whimpering sounds escaping my throat as I move higher and higher toward fulfillment. It feels like too much, but I don't want it to stop, and I cling to Daniel, gasping his name, my nails digging in to his shoulders.

"That's right, Regan, sweetheart. Sweet fucking fighter baby doll. Come for me." His voice is a growl of need, and his thrusts are growing rougher despite his slow, measured hammering.

I try to push his hand away from my clit because it's getting to be too much, but he won't let me. He knows I'm almost there, and when I come, it's going to be brutal. And I'm a little scared of it. My whimpers take on a frightened edge.

"Shhh, Regan, I've got you," he tells me even as he sinks deep. "I'm here, and I've got you."

With a sob, I'm there. I orgasm so hard that I do, in fact, see stars. My body seems like every muscle has squeezed itself into a taut line, and I feel as if I'm folding up and exploding into nothing all at once. My breath escapes in a little scream, and I can feel my pussy clenching around Daniel in hard little squeezes, echoing the contractions of my muscles as I come and come and come. Daniel's saying something in my ear, and his movements are rough, and I realize he's coming, too.

He's coming, and he's still got me.

When I can breathe again, Daniel collapses on top of me, and then jerks away as if burned. A second later, he rolls me on top of him, dragging my limp body over his as he begins to stroke my back once more. "Sorry. I wasn't trying to scare you."

"I'm . . . I'm okay," I say, and I'm horrified to see that I'm crying. But I am. I don't know if it's the intensity of my release or being with Daniel or what it is, but I'm crying and it feels good. "Really. I don't know why I'm crying."

He pats my shoulder. "Because it was that bad? You can give it to me straight. I know I'm rusty."

For some reason, that makes me giggle through my tears. "No, it was g-good," I say through my tears. "Thank you. I think I'm . . . letting everything out." And I shudder a breath into my lungs.

I know why I'm crying.

I'm crying because I'm in love with Daniel and I absolutely, positively should not be.

CHAPTER **NINETEEN**

DANIEL

Regan crying after sex feels about as good as a stick up the ass. I pat her awkwardly with one hand as I pull off the condom with the other. With a twist, I knot it and toss it into the trash. Meanwhile I rifle through the video memory I'd captured, trying to see if there was a point at which I'd forced her to continue. It seemed like she loved it. Her pussy was squeezing me so tight I thought my dick would snap off—but I'd be a happy dickless man. For the sake of my own sanity, I accept that her tears are as she said—letting it all out. I rub her back, enjoying the feel of her soft body spread out all over mine. Lust still licked around the base of my spine. One time really wasn't enough. I needed her to ride me until there wasn't any emotion, fluid, or feeling left in our bodies. Until we'd fucked each other so hard and so long that all we could do was melt into the bed, two formless beings drained by sex. The outside world could go to hell so long as I could lie here inside of her.

I'd been running for months, looking in every hideaway and whorehouse between Europe, Asia, and the Americas. All I wanted to do now was hold Regan. Okay, hold her and fuck her—but with a lot of meaning. I'm going to have a hard time letting her go, because in the short time that we've known each other I realize she fits me better than anyone else I know. She's unperturbed by my smart-ass mouth and, in fact, gives back in equal measure. She's stronger than anyone and hasn't slowed me down an iota. Plus, she's hotter than the sun in the desert.

"You should come to Texas," I blurt out because my mouth is still being run by the little head that is growing harder with each passing moment. Suddenly I want to shed a few tears. How did I not think to buy condoms at the *farmácia*? Shit, could I glue my dick shut? No, I'd end up busting a nut—literally—by the unpurged sperm.

"Yeah?" she asks, wiping away the moisture on her cheeks.

"Yeah." Now that I've voiced the idea, I'm warming to it. I can totally see Regan on my ranch, wearing one of my old work shirts with the flaps tied under her boobs like a Dallas Cowboys cheerleader. Her smooth belly would be bared to the sun, and her tight jeans would sit low on her hips. We'd ride out into the pasture and watch the sun sink below the last visible strip of land, until only the stars and the deep midnight of the night sky blanketed us. I'd lay her down on a magically produced blanket, and we'd make sweet love among the silver sage that grows wild on the fields. "You could learn to ride. My mom makes a mean sweet tea and pot roast. After dinner, we'd walk down to the pond and listen to the crickets tell each other secrets about the day. Later that night, I'd take you to the old foreman's cabin and pleasure you until the sun came up the next day."

"Sounds lovely." She tucks her head under my chin and I pull the covers up so she's not chilled by the air-conditioning. "Maybe you could come to Minneapolis. It's as cold as the arctic and without the cute penguins."

"It sounds irresistible." *But it has you*, I think; and sappy as that may be, it's all I need.

"Your dick is trying to push its way into the wrong place." She wiggles her ass a little, like she's not all that averse to the feeling.

"Can't be helped. You're naked, lying on top of me. We got done having atom-rattling sex and my cock's not a dummy. He knows there's a hot, tight, wet little place for him." I shift her slightly and rub my cock along her ever-increasingly-wet slit. We both groan. "Just ignore it." But I palm her ass with both hands, allowing my fingers to pull her cunt lips apart so that more of her juicy pussy slides along the hard ridge of my cock.

"Ignore what?" she gasps, and there aren't any tears in her eyes, just a growing haze of lust.

"Nothing, fighter. That's not my cock rubbing your cunt right now. You aren't getting wetter by the minute. I'm not holding your apple-plump ass cheeks in my palms." Digging my heels into the mattress, I angle my hips up, and the head of my cock tip slides right into her bare pussy. My eyes roll back. "Oh darlin'," I groan. My fingertips press into her flesh, opening her even more. Knowing this is wrong but not being able to stop, I pump into her shallowly. Each time, my cock dives a little deeper into her slick, hot channel. "You play 'I never?'" I ask. "Because I've never felt anything so good as riding bareback in your tight little pussy."

She's panting now. "It feels incredible. I swear I can feel every vein and ridge on your cock. You feel enormous."

Her words make me swell longer and harder than I've ever been. "I don't have a motherfucking condom," I curse, but she doesn't climb off and I can't bring myself to pull out. Worse, she squeezes me tight and I feel like shooting a truckload of spunk into her right then. "I know this sounds stupid, but I swear I'm clean. We got checked regularly in the army for everything." And we both knew she was clean from the post-rescue clinic visit.

She nods and then clenches around me again. "Yes." It comes out on a breathy, sexual sigh.

With one surge, I'm seated to the hilt, and Regan lets out a low, keening cry. Her forehead drops down to mine and I take her mouth, fucking her with my tongue and cock. She responds with a matching hunger. This time it's a frenzied, crazy fuck— our bodies slapping against each other like we're in a race to see who can drive the other mad first. The palms of her hands are digging into my shoulders, but the pain is a welcome sign of how needy she is for me.

I'm pistoning inside her with long, hard strokes. Lifting her slightly and then pulling her back down. "Harder, fuck me harder, Daniel," she moans into my mouth. The taunt, the plea, whatever it was, bursts through my fogged brain and I flip her over onto her back and fold her legs so that her ass is tilted upward. In the next motion, I've sheathed myself inside her again, pounding into her as she digs her heels into my shoulders and her nails bite into the sides of my thighs. *She's marking me,* my hindbrain chortles, and I love it.

"You're so hot, so beautiful right now," I tell her. "Your cunt is swallowing me up, like a hungry flower." The tension of my orgasm has gathered at the base of my spine, and I'm ready to spend all over her. "You coming with me, Regan?" I growl at her. "Come with me."

I lift one leg over my shoulder and reach around so that I can roll her clit between my fingers. I need her to share this moment with me. My fingers catch and tease and pinch her clit as I stroke her with fast, hard thrusts. She's crying now, but it's clearly from pleasure. Her head is thrashing back and forth on the bed until her orgasm overtakes her, tensing her whole body as she bows up off the bed. Her climax causes her pussy to clamp down on me, and it takes superhuman strength to wrench out of her. I palm my throbbing cock, and come jets out of me and all over her stomach and tits. I feel like I come for hours, and when the red-hot fog of lust evaporates, I see that she's covered in me. The streaks of milky-white semen look like abstract art on her flushed flesh, and I feel more amazing than fucking Picasso.

I can't stop myself from spreading it around, rubbing it into her pelvis and her stomach and up the underside of her breasts. "You look good in my come."

She barely has the energy to stick her tongue out at me but manages a small snort. Her face is turned to the side of the mattress, and she's trying to catch her breath. Me too. I fall down beside her, still rubbing my come into her skin.

"You're an animal," she whispers, but it's not an insult. It's a simple observation and a true one at that.

"No doubt, fighter." I draw her close to me, and this time our kiss is languid and exploratory instead of a frenzied meeting of mouth and teeth and tongue. Her lips are petal soft, and she tastes like home, better than my mom's sweet tea and pot roast. I could live on her taste and nothing else.

A pounding on the door interrupts our postcoital make-out session. "Ignore it," I say, more interested in having Regan's tongue in my mouth than food in my belly. I figure it is room service—although I don't remember ordering any. The thought penetrates, and I sit up abruptly. No one should know we are here. Jumping out of bed, I grab my Ruger from the nightstand. "Get under the bed," I order in a hushed voice. She nods and slides off the bed, but not before she grabs the other gun.

"Don't shoot me," I say with a grin, trying to alleviate some of her fear. Standing next to the doorframe, my back against the wall, I tell the persistent knocker to go away. "We don't need any assistance."

"Open the door," a deep voice commands in Russian.

Oh fuck me. Vasily Petrovich. Just what I don't need. "Hold your horses." I have no idea if that Western idiom translates, but I figure he'll get the message.

Crossing the room, I crouch down beside Regan, who is kneeling beside the bed, the gun clutched between both hands. I reach over and push the safety back on.

"What language were you speaking?" She looks at me with suspicion. Cradling her cheek in my hand, I search for the right words to say but before I can get anything out, the door is kicked in.

Regan lifts her gun, disengages the safety, and shoots twice.

"Motherfucker!" yells Petrovich, who dives to the side.

I knock Regan's hands upward and wrestle the gun away. It's then I realize we are both nude and she's probably sticky from my attentions.

"Fuck." I pick a struggling Regan up in my arms and hustle her into the bathroom. Reaching into the shower, I flick the hot

water on and then sit down on the toilet. Her body is shaking—
with fear, not desire—but she's not crying.

"That man out there . . ." She points a trembling arm toward
Petrovich, whose moans of pain have stopped.

"You must have winged him, fighter."

I try to lift her into the shower, but she's all limbs right now.
It's like trying to handle an octopus. I get her inside the stall, but
she fights the whole way. "We don't have time to shower," she
screams at me. "We've got to get out right now." And then understanding dawns on her as she stares at me under the spray of the
water. I can't tell if there are tears mixing with the shower water,
but the expression on her face is killing me.

"You know him." Her voice is dead. Zero inflection.

"Let me explain."

She retreats until her back hits the tile wall. Her head is shaking back and forth, as if by sheer force of will she can make this
knowledge go away. "No. No, you are one of them."

Her body is taut, and she looks like she's about to retch. "I let
you touch me. I trusted you." Her last words are screamed at me,
but it's not the volume that makes me wince, it's the shredded
pain underlying each sound.

"Regan, please." I drop to my knees, uncaring that water is
flooding out onto the bathroom door. "I know him only because
he had a lead for me. He sent me to you. To rescue you. I promise."

"How do I know you're not part of a whole ring? Are you
going to sell me, too?"

"No!" I shuffle closer, but she holds out her hands as if I'm the
devil come to steal her soul. "I'm Daniel Hays. I'm a former soldier
from Texas. My sister was stolen. I haven't lied to you. Not once, I
swear it." I raise my hands in the air. Her next words kill me.

"He sold me."

And my heart breaks. I lean down and kiss her feet.

"I'm sorry, fighter. I'm so sorry." With my face on the cold tile and my hands on either side of her feet, I wait for her to forgive me. I *need* for her to forgive me.

"Where's the other guy?" She's shaking so hard with fury that she can't stand, and she slides down the wall until she's seated. Her voice is low and harsh. "He raped me before he handed me over to them."

"I killed him. Broke his neck and left him behind a gas station. I should have made it more painful, now that I know that." I climb in beside her. The hot water from the showerhead is almost cool by the time it hits our feet. When she hears that Yury is dead, she relaxes slightly and that awful, brittle look washes down the drain with the water. But my heart is breaking for her.

Gesturing toward the outer room, she asks with incredulity, "Are you really friends with him?"

"Who? Nick?"

"No, the slave trader."

"I know him. Met him a few months ago. Knew of him longer, though." I tell her everything. "I've been searching for my sister, so I got involved with some guys who make money killing bad guys."

"Hit men?"

"Mercenaries. Hit men. I needed a way in to find Naomi. I started watching people, reaching out if I thought that they had some personal code, because I felt I might be able to trust them. Nick was one of those guys. He was very careful with the jobs he took on. He researched them, and he was very good at what he did, so I reached out to him. When you and Daisy were kidnapped,

I knew it was my opportunity to do him a solid, so he'd owe me."
She's listening to me, which I take as a good sign.

"The Petrovich *Bratva* is a powerful Mafia, but the head of it
was running the organization into the ground. Vasily Petrovich
approached me. Said that he would help us if we killed the head
of it and made sure it can't be traced back to him. Nick, Daisy,
and I took care of Sergei Petrovich. Vasily gave me your information and then hinted that there's been a long funnel of blondes
from Russia to Rio. I think maybe Naomi is here, also. You know
the rest of it." I scrub my hand across my head.

"What's he doing here, then?"

"There's something here he wants, too." I have my fear about
what that is, but I think Regan's had enough revelations at the
time.

"I don't want to be near him." Defiance has replaced fear as
her current emotion.

"That's fine. I'll take him down to the beach and figure out
what he wants."

She nods.

"Are we okay?" I ask.

There's nothing but silence, and then her hand slips over
mine. "I can't go back."

I rise up on my knees. "I swear on my sister's life no more
harm will come to you. Not if I have to lay waste to the entire
southern seaboard to keep you safe. You will never go back."

Regan's lower lip trembles, but she bites back her emotion
and then mirrors my pose. Her small hands creep up around my
neck. "I believe you then, Daniel."

I want to kiss her but know that would be very foolish of me
to do at this moment. Instead, I squeeze one of her arms. Rising

to my feet, I tell her to shower. "I'll get you some clothes." I tuck a towel around my waist and leave Regan to clean up.

Outside I find Vasily sitting on the sofa, a white cloth wrapped around his left hand.

"Is she okay?" He jerks his chin toward the shower. I stomp over to the packs and pull out some clothing for us.

"No thanks to you." I hadn't realized that Vasily was directly involved in her sale, even though I knew he had kidnapped her. He'd had to in order to sell the scheme thing to his uncle, but his *ends justifies the means* attitude makes me want to take the butt end of my gun and rearrange his face. Shaking it off, I head back for the bathroom. Regan is drying off, and I try hard not to watch her, but even the bathroom is too small to avoid seeing a few glimpses of her fine body. My own body reacts predictably, and the towel around my waist lifts up.

"Sorry," I mumble.

"I'm going to take it as a compliment," she sighs. "My outrage meter is worn out. I'm worn out."

We dress hastily, and I ignore my growing hard-on.

Regan leads us out of the bathroom but stops short with a gasp. Vasily has stripped off his shirt and laid a belt on the bed. He's kneeling with his hands laced behind his head.

"What are you doing?" she demands.

"Recompense." Vasily does not turn around. He barely moves.

"He wants you to hit him with the belt," I offer helpfully.

"He thinks that me hitting him is going to make up for selling me?" she shrieks.

"I guess?"

Regan goes over to the bed and picks up the belt. We wait.

She runs the belt through her fingers and then juggles the buckle end in her hand, perhaps testing its bite.

"Wrap the small end around your hand and strike with your whole arm," Vasily instructs. This is surreal. Vasily is giving Regan directions on how to best beat him. Looking around, I spy the sofa and head toward it. This whole scene seems like something out of a bad art house drama. Regan does as he instructs, winding the soft end around her hand. She whips the belt up and down a couple of times. I think I'm flinching, but Vasily is not. Her arm pulls back, and she whips it forward. We all hear the whistle as the belt flies through the air. Vasily doesn't move an inch, and the buckle falls harmlessly. Regan tosses the belt onto the bed.

"Live with the guilt," she spits out. "I don't absolve you."

"You were not to go on sale," Vasily says. "You were to sit in a safe house until Daniel could come for you, but . . ." He pauses. "Something went wrong. Someone I trusted betrayed me."

This is too much for Regan to hear. She collapses onto the sofa next to me.

CHAPTER **TWENTY**

REGAN

I've gone from pure happiness to pure misery all over again. Daniel—wonderful, amazing Daniel, who I've fallen hard for, my savior from the brothel—is working with one of the men who sold me.

Daniel says to trust him. I do. But it's hard. Every time I see the new man, I see my apartment and remember being tied up and duct-taped so I can't scream. I see Yury's face as he grunts and sweats over me.

But Daniel killed Yury. At least there's that.

And now this one is backtracking.

I look at the big blond man's face. He's waiting, still kneeling on the floor and staring straight ahead. It's like he expects me to change my mind and say, *Oh yes, actually, I do feel like beating you.* Like he expects me to pick up the belt and go to town on him suddenly.

Like he expects me to sink to their level.

I won't.

"So I wasn't supposed to go on sale?" My voice is dull, even to my own ears. "That's a big fucking mistake to happen, don't you think?"

Daniel's hand brushes my cheek. "You okay?"

Instinct tells me to push him away, to protect myself, but for the first time in a long time, I ignore it and lean into his touch. If I can't trust Daniel, I have nothing. "I'm okay."

"You must have restitution," the blond man says, interrupting us.

I look over at him, and he hasn't moved. His face—harder and somehow crueler than Daniel's ever could be—is impassive. He's still waiting.

"What's your name?" I ask.

"I am Vasily Petrovich of the Petrovich *Bratva*," he rattles off. His voice is one of the deepest I have ever heard, his accent slight but familiar—and hated.

"Well, Vasily . . ." I think for a moment. I look over at Daniel, and he looks as uncomfortable as I do at Vasily's display. "I forgive you."

The big Russian stiffens. "You cannot forgive me without recompense."

"Nope," I say, denying him what he wants. "I forgive you. Let's move on." I don't mean it, of course, but I know that it'll be a bigger mindfuck to him than my taking the belt and whipping him. I'm guessing pain makes more sense to him than mercy, but it's not mercy I'm offering, not really. I'm dicking with his mind. I don't even feel guilty about it.

Vasily doesn't move.

I get up from my seat and stand in front of the big, frightening Russian, who is still kneeling on the ground, waiting for a beating that's never going to arrive. Instead, I stick my hand into his face. "Shake on it? We can start fresh from here."

He recoils from my hand, which surprises me.

Daniel moves forward then, tugging me away. Maybe he's guessed my game and doesn't approve. I don't blame him—it's a bit like teasing a wounded bear. "Vasily's not a handshaker," he says to me. "Doesn't like to be touched."

"Oh." Oh, the ammunition this gives me. "All right," I say sweetly. I won't forget this little nugget of information.

Daniel moves to the far side of the bed and picks up his gun, checking the clip and beginning to arm himself all over again. He casts a quick glance at Vasily, who hasn't moved, and exasperation crosses his face.

"Get up, man," he tells Vasily. "You're weirding me the fuck out. Regan doesn't want to beat you."

Vasily looks rather disgruntled, which makes me happy. Slowly, he gets to his feet and returns to his full height. Daniel is tall, but this man is a giant. I'd forgotten he was so big and scary. And he wanted me to whip him? Strange man. I edge a little closer to Daniel, heading for my own gun, but Daniel pulls it out of my reach before I can grab it. He only raises an eyebrow at me, as if asking who I intend to shoot.

I roll my eyes and drag on his arm so I can pull the gun from his hands. "I'm not going to shoot anymore," I mutter, making sure the safety is on before I stuff it into my belt. The silencer attached to the barrel feels like it's sticking into my hip, but I don't care.

Vasily looks over at me one more time and then picks up his

belt. He considers it then slowly begins to thread it through his pant loops.

"Fuckin' freak," Daniel says to him, but his voice is easy, almost affectionate. "Put your damn shirt on, and tell me how you found us."

"I put a tail on you once I found out you did not dump the girl at the embassy," Vasily says. As he pulls it through the loops, his shoulders twist, and I realize what I should have realized all along—Vasily's back is one massive length of scars.

Mine would not be the first beating, and—judging by his attitude—it wouldn't be the last. Okay then.

"A tail? Thanks a fucking lot for all the trust."

"I trust no one right now," Vasily says in thickly accented English. "My own *Bratva* is rotten from the inside. The best hit man I know has defected to go live in the States with a woman. I had my uncle murdered because he could not be trusted. *Nyet*, comrade, I do not trust anyone at the moment."

Daniel snorts and swaps a clip out on one of his guns. "Figures. You had to show up now, though?" He sounds disgruntled. "Regan and I were busy."

"That is obvious," Vasily says in that cold, deep voice. Then he barks something in Russian that I don't understand.

"Fuck off," Daniel says, and he tenses under my arms. "And speak in English. It's damn rude."

Vasily's eyes are cold. His gaze flicks over me, then dismisses me as if I am nothing and returns to Daniel. "You were supposed to send her back to Nick."

"I didn't."

"My plans do not involve dragging along a woman."

"Change them."

Vasily's glare is so ominous that it makes me anxious.

"You would put her in danger simply because you wish an easy fuck, comrade?"

Now that's hitting below the belt. Daniel's practically vibrating with tension, and I am guessing that Vasily's deliberately being a jackass to try to get his way. Or he's really that much of a jackass. Either way, it's a sore spot with Daniel. I wait for him to point out that I wouldn't go to the embassy on my own, to place the blame on me.

"She stays, so figure something out." And he sits down on the edge of the bed and drags me against him.

I lean in and press my breasts to the side of Daniel's face as I cling to him, feeling smug and powerful and not a little bit turned on. He's on my side. He could sell me out to Vasily, who he apparently knows and has worked with for a while, but he's protecting my secrets.

And that makes me want to throw him down and fuck him all over again. Funny how someone loyal who protects me is such an aphrodisiac.

Vasily is watching me with such an expression of distaste that I suddenly feel dirty again. What, does he think I'm not good enough for Daniel anymore? Because I'm a dirty whore?

I wait for him to say something, but he only pulls an undershirt over his head. Enormous muscles flex as he does so. Then he takes his dress shirt off of the bed and begins to button it with slow, careful fingers.

"What is so important that this couldn't wait a few more hours?" Daniel wants to know.

"I asked someone to come to Rio and get Hudson's hacker. He says to me, 'Yes, I will get hacker and do favor for Nick.' Now, I see Nick's favor has been done and my hacker is nowhere to be found." Vasily's face looks like stone. "And you wonder why I do not trust."

"Fuck off, man. I was getting to it. We've sort of been busy for the last few days getting our asses shot at. There's more going on with Regan than we planned for. She's got some shitbag hot on her trail, and someone killed my snitch right in front of me. We're doing all we can to keep our asses alive."

"It looks to my eyes as if you are doing all you can to fuck her ass," Vasily says. He looks over at me again, then at Daniel. "Are you certain you wish for her to know of all our plans? She could be a decoy."

"She's not a decoy."

"A honey trap then. Sent to seduce you and bring down everything from inside."

"I'm right here, you know," I point out. "I can hear everything you're saying."

Daniel's stiff in my arms again, and I can tell that he's irritated at Vasily's words. "She's not a goddamn honey trap."

"You'd better hope not, comrade, because you have clearly fallen for her wiles."

Now I wish I'd shot something more than his hand. Vasily is a dick with a capital *D*.

Vasily adjusts the cuffs of his dress shirt and looks over at Daniel. "Are you done fucking at the moment?"

"Yeah, having you show up has effectively killed any sort of hard-on I might have had," Daniel says in a dry voice. "And Regan can be trusted. I won't have you saying shit about her, okay? She's a fighter, and she's with me. She's not leaving my side."

God, I love hearing him say those things. For that, he's totally getting a blow job as soon as I get him alone.

"So you want to take her to Hudson's compound?" Vasily snorts. "It is, as the Americans say, your funeral."

"You know where Hudson is?" Daniel looks a little surprised. "How'd you manage that?"

"While you were fucking, I pull strings and grease palms." Vasily's expression is utterly cold, and he shoots another look of blame at me. "It is not hard to find people to notice a snow-pale man with a fetish for blond women from North America who arms himself with dozens of mercenaries."

I frown at his words. "Did . . . did you say snow pale?"

Vasily's gaze moves to me, his eyes slits. "*Da.*"

My heart begins to thump erratically in my chest, and I feel my skin prickle with an all-too-familiar fear. I lick my lips and then gesture, asking, "Short, white-blond hair? Pale eyes and pale skin? About this tall?" I gesture a few inches above my head. "Wears light-colored suits and sunglasses indoors?"

"You know this man?"

"That's Mr. Freeze," I whisper through numb lips. "The one who wants me back once I've been 'broken in.' He's the one watching the embassy, waiting for someone to drop me off."

Daniel's arm tightens around my waist, noticing my fright. "He's not going to get you. I promise that."

"So," Vasily says, "we leave her here, and you and I pay Hudson a visit. We retrieve this hacker and we find out more information about your sister. Everyone is happy."

"Wait, no," I cry out and cling to Daniel. This time, I'm smashing his face against my breasts, but I don't care. "You can't leave me here. You have to take me with you."

Daniel's voice is muffled against my breasts. "Fighter baby, you know I wouldn't ask you to stay behind if it wasn't safe, but—"

"No! You're not abandoning me."

"Regan—"

"I'm going with you." Vasily being here has made me all edgy again, and I have a feeling I'm going to be clinging to Daniel harder than normal. Even the thought of Daniel leaving the room for five minutes and being here alone with Vasily is enough to make my skin prickle with gooseflesh. "You can't leave me behind. You can't. You promised."

Daniel sighs. "I know. I know. We'll think of something. It's . . . fuck. It's not safe, okay?"

"When has any of this been safe?" I ask him.

Vasily snorts.

"I'm going," I say stubbornly.

"You are not invited," Vasily says to me.

"If you leave me here, I'll follow you," I say, fighting the panic that's rising. He can't leave me behind. Not after all this. He can't. If he does, I know I'm going to turn a corner and see Mr. Freeze lurking there, waiting for me.

"You heard the lady," Daniel says. "She goes."

Vasily spits out another phrase in Russian, and Daniel flips him the bird. They look ready to come to blows, staring down each other. After a tense moment though, Vasily throws his hands up, conceding.

Daniel peers down the scope of his rifle, scanning the compound far below. "That's thirty-one," he says. "Which means there will be more inside."

The three of us are perched inside one of the hovels in Monkey Hill. We stopped by Luiz's place, picked up our papers, and then headed back to the slums. Or at least, we did after both men tried to talk me out of going again.

I refused. I'm not leaving Daniel's side. I won't feel safe until he delivers me back to my doorstep in Minneapolis, so why does it matter that we're heading to someplace dangerous? Everywhere is dangerous.

Once in the slums, Daniel paid someone to let us make use of his place for a few hours. Vasily guards the door, an enormous handgun held high as he scans the hallway. I'm crouching next to Daniel by the window, a piece of scratch paper in hand as I mark an X onto my sketch of Hudson's compound. I have an X every place that Daniel has found a soldier.

My paper is littered with Xs.

"Thirty-two," Daniel murmurs. "One hiding in the stairwell. Fuck, the man has an army with him. Paranoid son of a bitch."

I make a mark on my paper and look over at Daniel. He's still squinting down the scope of his rifle, monitoring things. "So what does this mean?"

"It means we're not going anywhere near him."

I frown and peek out the window, gazing down at the walls of the place. It's not exactly pretty—nor is it inconspicuous. The walls are made of enormous concrete blocks, and the double doors open only to allow the occasional truck in. The tops of the walls are curling with barbed wire, and Daniel has said they even have a sniper on the rooftop, like us.

"So why don't we start shooting? Take as many out as we can and then charge in once we've picked off a bunch of their guys?"

Vasily mutters something derisive in Russian behind me, and I'm pretty sure he's calling me stupid.

"No can do, fighter," Daniel says, finally putting down his

rifle and looking over at me. "I could pick off one or two before they notice, but then they'd figure out where we're coming from and swarm up this hill. It's too dangerous."

"Why don't we sneak in at night, then? We could get a few blankets and some ladders, toss a blanket over the barbed wire and climb our way over. I saw that in a movie once."

"If he has thirty men outside, he will have thirty more inside," Vasily bites out. "He is expecting us. He is ready. We need a new plan."

Daniel rubs a hand down his face, looking as frustrated as I feel. I want us to go in there, guns blazing, and shoot Mr. Freeze in his ugly, pale face until he can't come after me ever again. But if two assassins are saying it's too dangerous, then maybe it is.

"So what do we do?" I ask.

"Tears of God," Vasily says.

"Fuck. No way," Daniel retorts. "I'm not taking Regan there."

"What's Tears of God?" I ask, my gaze moving between Vasily and Daniel. "What?"

"Remember I told you about the favela that's controlled by the mercenaries? The one that no one fucks with?"

"That's Tears of God?"

"They owe me favor," Vasily says curtly. "This can be the favor."

"Goddamn it, no, Vasily."

"Why?" I ask again.

Daniel shoots me a dark look, and he seems rather upset. "No one goes into Tears of God without being checked over first. They take your guns, they take your clothes, and they search you. All of you. I'm not putting you through that. Fuck that. We'll figure something else out."

Vasily barks something harsh to Daniel.

I swallow, trying to imagine being patted down by a bunch of mercenaries. Walking into a place like the one below, naked and vulnerable. But there are two people being held in that compound—Daniel's sister and the hacker. Daniel's told me that wherever we find the hacker, we'll find Naomi. I can't stop thinking about that. Maybe she's suffering the same things I went through. Hudson likes them broken. I try to picture a girl like Daniel but broken, and I shudder internally then force a calm look on my face. "I can do it."

"No, fighter—"

"No, Daniel. I said I'd go with you. I have to take the good with the bad. I can stand to be patted down by a few guys, I promise."

His jaw clenches, and I can tell that he doesn't like it. That it's vulnerable, and we'll be naked and at their mercy if they try anything. If they decide to get rid of us, we're fucked.

But I trust Daniel. So I force a wobbling smile to my face. "Let's go."

CHAPTER **TWENTY-ONE**

DANIEL

"There's no way in." Regan's dismay echoes my own internal frustration. It's a sign. If you believed in signs, warnings, or symbols, the lack of an obvious entrance to Tears of God clearly said *fuck off.* I run my hand along the concrete walls and corrugated metal barriers that stand where the paved road indicates the entrance should be.

"What do you even know about this group?" I turn to Petrovich, who is standing slightly apart, hands on his hips, looking upward as if Touchdown Jesus will bend down from his place on the hill and part the metal seas for us.

"They are loyal, men of their word," he answers and then points to the inscription written in Portuguese above the gate.

"What's it say?" Regan asks.

"Revelation 21:4." It's a scripture. I read it out loud. "And

God shall wipe away all tears from their eyes; and there shall be no more death, neither sorrow, nor crying, neither shall there be any more pain."

"That sounds nice. Maybe it would be more comforting if there wasn't a dagger punctuating the end," Regan observes wryly. I flash her a quick grin. That's my girl.

I pull out my gun and point it at the dagger. "What are you doing?" Regan hisses.

"Gotta get their attention somehow."

Before I can squeeze off a shot, a door appears in the wall to my left, and a large hulking figure steps out. His heritage is indeterminate, which likely makes him a true Brazilian. Native Brazilians are almost a greater melting pot of heritages than the U.S. African, Asian, and American mix in fantastic harmony. The only real important thing about this stranger is his size—extra large—and weaponry. He's got machine gun belts draped over his chest like suspenders. On his arms are leather wrist guards that double as knife sheaths. He's got an AK strapped on his back and an armory belt with guns, knives, and more ammunition.

Utopia is clearly enforced by martial law.

But all that show only means one thing: this guy must be a bad shot. I holster my gun, casually try to hide Regan behind me, and place my hands up in the air.

"We're here to see the Knife's Edge."

"State your business." He folds his massive arms across his chest, the movement pushing the hilts of the wrist knives out toward me. With a quick mental calculation, I figure I can pull out one of the knives and pin his hand to his chest in about ten seconds—that is, if the blade is long enough. Behind me I feel Regan's slight form creep closer.

"We're here to do a trade."

"We don't trade in flesh," he growls.

Enlightenment dawns. He thinks we're here to trade Regan for . . . something. I pull her to the side. "Nope, she's with me. My Russian buddy is going to pull out some money so you can see that we're interested in information and some services in exchange for cash." I didn't want the guard to get trigger-happy when Petrovich reached inside his suit pocket.

Petrovich hands a wad of cash to the guard, who doesn't even count it, just flips it in his hand as if he can measure us merely through the weight of the cash. Maybe we should have brought gold. Without a word, he disappears inside and closes the door.

"Nice friends you have, Petrovich," I mock.

"I associate with you, do I not?" he retorts. Regan stifles a semi-hysterical giggle.

A minute passes. Maybe five. I cross the street and sit on the curb. We aren't leaving until we speak to the person in charge. Petrovich stands by the door, like he's a soldier awaiting orders.

"He's super-strange," Regan observes.

"Yup."

"Like, I think he really wanted me to beat him."

"Yup."

"Are all your friends that fucked up?"

"Yup."

She's silent for a minute. "I guess I see why you like me."

This brings a grin to my face. "Fighter, you're the least fucked up of all the people I know. You're like the normal control in a sample full of crazy."

"You weren't always part of this world, though." She gestures toward the favela.

Leaning back on my elbows, I raise my face up to the sky. The sun is warmer here, more intense. Its rays touch you with a close hand. If not for the kidnapping, my missing sister, and the surly Russian standing five feet away, I could pretend I was lying on the beach sipping a fruity drink with an umbrella with Regan in a barely there bikini, her body glistening with the oil I'd spread over every square inch of her. "You know why bad guys win?"

"No." She sounds as despondent as I felt staring into Hudson's compound.

"Because they live in these fucking compounds. When I'm done here, I'm going to buy my own fucking island and you and my sister and I are going to live there and drink fruity drinks with little umbrellas. I'll grill some steaks, and after we've gorged ourselves, you and I will go inside and make sweet love while Marvin Gaye serenades us."

"I like that you've put a lot of thought into that."

Before I decide to get my gun out and start shooting holes into the walls in front of me, the guard comes out and gestures us inside. The door opens into a small room with one table. There are no windows here, and the space is dark and cool, lit only by a couple of bare bulbs. There are two other guards standing in front of the only exit. Nice. My gun hand twitches. The first guard hands the wad of cash back to Petrovich. "Strip." I raise an eyebrow at Regan, and she gives me a wan smile.

When her hands fly to her blouse, the guard barks out, "Stop." We freeze.

"Not you." He waves a hand toward Regan. "Stand over there," he orders, but Regan doesn't move. Her fingers creep out and loop into the waistband of my pants.

"I'm not leaving Daniel," she says.

"Sorry." I shrug my shoulders. "We're a package deal."

He snaps his fingers, and one of the men standing in front of the rear exit leaves. A few minutes later a woman appears with a folded cloth in her hands. She approaches. "If you'll come with me, you can change into this. I promise to return you."

Regan looks reluctant, but stripping down to nothing in front of these three seems like it would be more traumatic than being separated.

"I won't leave without you. I promise," I tell her, and she releases me with reluctance.

With Regan gone, Petrovich and I undress swiftly. The guard who left to get the woman comes over and pats us between our legs. I'm not sure how many people can hide a weapon up their asshole—and I don't think I even want to know—but the guards here are more invasive than a TSA agent. I hope Regan isn't suffering the same kind of inspection.

"Kind of overkill, don't you think?" Petrovich is a good shot, and there are a lot of weapons in the room even if we are naked. The guy on his knees in front of me could have his windpipe crushed by my leg.

I hope it doesn't come to that. We're handed loose shifts made out of coarse cloth. It's kind of like wearing the metaphorical burlap sack. With our hands secured behind our backs with modern zip ties that look suspiciously like the ones we used in the army, we're escorted out of the little room and onto the street. I can see now that the main road into the favela has been blocked off with a row of three houses. They serve as guard gates. Whoever is in charge here is paranoid and kitting out this patch of land like it's a fortress ready for an epically long siege. Regan is waiting for us, wearing a similar loose-fitting sack that extends down beyond her knees. The length of the sack is fairly ingenious because it doesn't allow for much movement. You'd have to lift the material to run or topple over from the restraint.

As we climb up the steep winding road, people peek out of windows and doorways. We're a pale imitation of the *Carnaval* parade. No floats, only nearly naked foreigners with armed guards in the front and to the rear. I resist the urge to wave. At the top of the hill, the houses fall away and there is a large gravel expanse interrupted by burn marks on the ground. A huge granite slab sits like a sacrificial altar in between burn marks. There is lumber to the right, stacked in precise piles of varying lengths. There were rumors about this favela—that they burned their enemies at the stake. Right now I'd like to drop-kick Petrovich in the balls for bringing us up here and placing Regan in danger.

A man comes out, simply dressed in a cotton button-down camp shirt, the sleeves rolled up to show tattoos on both arms. He's wearing loose-fitting cotton pants and is entirely weaponless. The sun's rays blot out his face until he comes closer.

"Jesus Christ. Rafe Mendoza? What the fuck?" I'm stunned to see one of the members of my old Delta unit standing in front of me. Mendoza's apparently just as dumbstruck, because he says nothing for a moment and then reaches out to grab my hand. When he realizes that I'm trussed up like a Thanksgiving turkey, he awkwardly thumps me on the back.

"Hays, what the hell are you doing in my little fiefdom?"

I jerk a shoulder toward Petrovich, who is silently watching the whole exchange. "I'm with the freak show there. He says you owe him a favor."

Mendoza studies the Russian. "Don't know him."

"Not you, a lieutenant. I rendered him aid during a melee over in Dubai six months ago," Petrovich explains.

He nods and then turns to a boy, barely out of puberty based on his size. "Confirm with Fetler." The young boy runs off, and Mendoza turns back to me.

"And the girl?" Mendoza asks.

"She's with me," I answer.

"Merry band, you have," he jokes.

"Every gang needs at least one Russian and one hellcat." I stretch to ease the tension in my back. We aren't going to die today. There's no need to make more small talk, because the young boy returns and whispers something to Mendoza.

"Fetler vouches for you," he says to Petrovich, "which means I castrate him if you do harm to anyone who belongs to me."

Petrovich nods stiffly. "There will be no harm to your people from my hands."

We follow Mendoza past the burn marks and an open field, up to the last building on the hill before a wild bramble of trees and jungle foliage takes over. From the exterior, it looks squat but inside I see that it is much larger than I assumed. There are a dozen people in here. In one room it appears that they are folding and stuffing envelopes. In another is a bank of computers.

Mendoza leads us to a back room that appears to be some sort of office. There are several wooden chairs around a rectangular table and a desk at the very end. "Cut them loose," he orders the guard who has followed us from the front gate all the way up. The ties around our wrists are sliced open, and Mendoza gestures for us to sit.

"What brings you to our beautiful city?" he asks. I tell him the entire story. When I get to the part where Regan is at the brothel of Gomes, Mendoza stops me.

"Silva, go and bring Gomes here."

He waves for me to continue.

"There isn't much more. Gomes works for Hudson, who must have sixty men guarding him at all times. Petrovich's hacker is in there." I don't say what I know must be true, what I haven't been willing to acknowledge since I stood on Monkey Hill hearing Regan read the email from the snitch's phone. Naomi must be the Emperor—the hacker that Petrovich is desperate to get his hands on, and she's likely the same one controlled by Hudson. I don't want Petrovich to know that his hacker is a woman and my sister. That fight will be for later. I just need her out of there.

"We do not have the manpower to have a shootout with a U.S. government contractor who provides security services to the embassy," Mendoza admits grimly. "I've lost one of my own to him. We've sent men in to find our lost dove, but they've come up empty. Where the girls are stored, I do not know. We've not acted because of his military ties but . . ."

"It's time to take him down," I declare, and Mendoza gives me a short nod. Mendoza's power is in question here. Hudson must go.

"Perhaps we do not need the manpower," Petrovich suggests. "We simply need to get inside, Daniel and I. From there, we can extricate one woman and one man."

"Vasily is right. Finding Naomi in is our biggest challenge. We can fight our way out."

"What do you know of Hudson, then?" Mendoza asks.

"He is a wealthy U.S. military contractor with a thing for North American blondes. Likely has control over the Emperor."

At this Mendoza starts. "The Emperor? Of the Emperor's Palace?"

Petrovich nods stiffly. "He is mine."

I try not to hit him. Naomi belongs to herself. To the Hays family. Not to some Russian madman.

Mendoza whistles. "He must be making a fortune with all the illegal money he's moving through that network."

"I am not interested in the money," Petrovich says. "I need the expertise."

"We need more information," I interject. I'm not a fan of hearing Naomi being referred to as a man, especially one that Petrovich wants. "We don't have the time."

Mendoza nods and then reaches for the phone on his desk. He is too far away for us to hear even though I'm straining. We all are.

"What's he saying?" Regan asks. The Portuguese is too faint and rapid for me to make out.

"Not sure, but he mentioned the consulate."

When Mendoza returns to us, he says, "I'm having someone come who may be able to provide some insight. Until then, let's have something to eat."

A spread of fresh fruits, meats, and cheeses is set out buffet-style in another room, one that faces the large gravel area and the burn marks.

"What have you got going on here?" I ask Mendoza as we stand in front of the large windows.

"Security, Daniel."

"I've heard that you were doing freelance work after you separated from the army."

"I've heard the same about you."

"My sister was kidnapped. I had to find her. Making money

killing bad guys while trying to gather information seemed like a bonus," I reply.

"And for me, I need money to build my army here." He taps the window. A throng of young kids have come to the top of the hill, and they move down the gravel expanse toward a grassy field I didn't see initially. "These people are my family. Did you know that the Roman Empire was so powerful that the citizens could walk throughout the land unmolested? It was known that even the least of the citizens was so important to the empire that if even one was maimed, the entire beast would fall upon the violator's head. I want that for my people. I want for them to walk through any street in Brazil or Africa or the United States and for people to know that if one of mine is hurt, the entire hand of God will rain vengeance upon them and their family. Hudson is a blot on our record, and this is a perfect opportunity for me to make a show of power. So I'll help you, and then some-day you can return the favor."

"No problem." Madmen and their compounds. I need to get me one of those.

A scuffle outside draws my attention to the front doors. The soccer game has stopped, and the children stand in a loose line as a man is brought to the field. He is strapped down onto the granite slab. Many of the children disperse but a few older ones remain.

"Regan," Mendoza calls out. "We need an identification."

We troop out into the sun toward the granite altar. When we reach it, the man is securely tied spread-eagle on the slab. He is completely naked, and there is a leash around his dick, pulling it downward between his legs.

"It's Gomes," Regan says in a gasp.

Mendoza nods at one of his soldiers who holds a whiplike

object in his hand. "Positive ID confirmed." At the nod, the whip sails out and lands with a snap right between Gomes's legs. Petrovich and I grimace while everyone else stands there like this is any other Saturday. Gomes's screams ring out in the courtyard, scaring up birds and other small animals in the foliage. With a backward glance, I note that the five or so kids left on the soccer field are still motionless, as if they are in class learning exactly how to run a mercenary empire.

"Ask your questions," Mendoza orders. Regan and Petrovich look to me. Scratching my head, I lean over—not too close, because I don't want the whip to accidentally strike me in the balls.

"Gomes, you look really uncomfortable."

He's sniveling; tears and snot are running down his face. It's an ugly look for him. "Let me go," he pleads. "I know nothing."

"The thing is, we kind of know that's a lie." I give a nod to Mendoza, who relays the silent order to his whip man. The leather sails out, and now that I'm closer I see there is a granite ball at the end. It makes another thud as granite strikes granite, the small column of flesh doing little to cushion the impact. Even though I'm expecting the blow, I still cringe—but maybe that's due to the high-pitched scream coming out of Gomes's mouth.

As sadistic as this is, though, it's the right punishment if you believe in the eye-for-an-eye concept, which Mendoza clearly ascribes to. Gomes is slobbering now. "Why Regan?" I ask.

He turns slightly, his eyes unfocused with pain. "Hudson likes blondes. They remind him of his wife. But this one, so mouthy. Hudson sends her to me for training."

"Then what?"

He opens his mouth and then closes it.

"Bad choice," I counsel, and look up to Mendoza. The ball

falls again, and this time I'm prepared. I don't think Gomes is, though. We wait until the pain and screams subside, and I ask him again. "What happens when the girls are trained?"

"They go back into his compound. They serve as his companion until . . ." Gomes trails off, but we can all finish his sentence for him.

Mendoza waves his hand and the men disappear and the kids go back to kicking their soccer ball.

"There's your way in," he says with a pointed look toward Regan.

"No." I shake my head. "Not happening. We'll think of something else."

"There is no other way," Petrovich argues.

I look at Regan because right now she's the only one who matters. I don't want to leave my sister in the hands of Hudson, but I can't send Regan back to be raped again. I won't. There's another way. I have to figure it out.

CHAPTER **TWENTY-TWO**

REGAN

Daniel's got an awful look on his face. It's the look of despair, of a man who's backed into a corner and has no way out.

He can either send me in to Hudson's hell in the hopes of getting his sister or he can forget about her. Either way, he's miserable. He shakes his head again at Mendoza. "Fucking forget it, man. I just got Regan out of there. No way in hell am I sending her back to that sadist."

The big Russian, Vasily, only looks over at me, as if waiting for me to interject. To him, I'm another playing piece, one that is obviously only useful on my back. He's not wrong, though. I'm the one mucking up all the works here. I'm the one who slowed Daniel down. If it wasn't for me, would he already have his sister back?

"How long?" I ask.

"Regan, no." Daniel's voice is furious. "I'm not sending you back in to be raped—"

I move to his side and pat his arm, trying to soothe him. He's practically bristling at my suggestion, and I know he hates it. "We didn't come this far to turn around, Daniel. I can do this."

After all, what's one more rape in my logbook? I don't say that out loud because I know if I do, Daniel will shut down entirely. I want to do this for him. For him and for his faceless sister who's stuck in the same hell I was in for so long. I can't let her stay there, just like I can't let Daniel give up.

"Fighter, no," Daniel's telling me in a soft voice. He touches my cheek, oblivious to the eye roll Vasily is sending our way. "You don't have to—"

"I know," I say softly and bite the tip of the thumb he strokes across my lip. "But you're going to come get me, right?"

"I'd fucking die before I left you in there," Daniel says, and the intensity in his eyes tells me it's the truth.

"Then we do this," I say. I turn back to Mendoza. I'm still surprised to see that the man running this weird military compound full of families and children is young and handsome, and he could be on the cover of *GQ*. Well, maybe more like *Guns & Ammo*, but he's still pretty. He's thick with muscles and deeply tanned, his hair a dark buzz against his scalp. His eyes are this fascinating shade of amber I've only seen on models.

My friend Becca would eat him up.

Then again, *fuck* Becca.

Mendoza regards me for a long moment, waiting to see if I'm going to lose my shit. When I return his gaze, calm and easy, he nods. "A day at the most."

"A day?" Daniel explodes. "A full day? No. Absolutely not—"

"What is plan?" Petrovich interrupts, his accent thick and calm. "Send her in with poison?"

I swallow hard. I'm supposed to kill someone? "I don't know that I could do that."

Mendoza cuts him off with a wave of his hand. "We can put a GPS on her. Send her in. Even if she's immobilized, she'll be placed in a location that hasn't been discovered through my sweeps. I've sent in caterers, repair techs, pool people, but we can't locate the safe rooms. I'm guessing they're downstairs, but we haven't been able to get down there. We've got the technology to make a map based off Regan's movements." Mendoza grins at me, and I return a weak smile. "I've wanted to shut it down for a while but have been waiting for the right moment. We will go in, fetch the women and the man you want to retrieve, come out, and destroy everything in our wake."

I nod. "So I go in and try to get to as many places as I'm allowed, look for an American blonde named Naomi, look for a hacker, and sit pretty. I can do this." I glance over at Daniel, but his face is like ice. He's not happy, but he knows we're stuck. "But if you send me in with Gomes, how do we know he's not going to warn the others that it's a trap?"

"He has a car, does he not?" Mendoza says. "We send you in his car with a note. Gomes said it's Hudson's birthday tomorrow. We send you in as a present."

I shudder at the thought. "All right."

"When do we do this?" Vasily asks. "Every hour we waste is another hour he can find out what we're up to and slip away."

"We start in the morning," Daniel says. "The sooner we get this done, the sooner I get Regan out of there."

I nod, concealing the trembling in my hands. I'm terrified, but it's a risk we have to take. "Let's do this."

DANIEL

The plan is simple but so flawed. There are so many things that can go wrong, but if we don't let her go . . . There has to be another way, but if Mendoza's men have been in more than once and can't find the hideaway, then sending Regan in with a GPS tracker might be our only chance.

I try not to make love to her that night like it's our last time together. As I move my hand over the curve of her waist, down over the hill of her ass, to the hidden crease between her legs, I'm memorizing the path only because it's beautiful and erotic and every man should have a physical memory like this. When I dip my head to her chest and suckle and bite the tender flesh as she grips my hair and breathes out my name like a benediction, I close my eyes and try to imprint this moment in my mind because the soundtrack of my life should only be the soft cries of arousal followed by screams of completion.

"Daniel. Daniel. Daniel," she chants as I move lower between her legs. I take my time here, licking her in long slow movements. So good. Her taste on my tongue is an aphrodisiac. My cock becomes harder, swells bigger as each droplet of excitement hits my mouth.

I bury my nose into her cunt and breathe deep. This is the only scent I ever want in my head. Inside her channel there's more of her essence, and I spear my tongue inside, trying to devour her. My fingers stretch her opening wide so that every inch of the delicate flesh is exposed to my ravenous appetite. My tongue and lips and teeth work every inch of her pussy and clit until she is drenching them with her arousal.

"Come all over my tongue," I growl. Her thighs quiver with the force of her orgasm as she obeys, and I lap every bit of her liquid up. My cock is wet from my own small release. I spread my pre-come down the sides and then hold up my palm to her face. "Lick it."

She does more than lick it. She mouths each finger and then laves my palm with the flat of her tongue. I'm groaning and panting at how her fucking tongue on my palm makes me want to come all over her. With enormous effort, I pull away so I can slide two fingers inside her, where I scoop out her moisture and lather it on my straining organ.

"I want you all over me," I whisper. With one hand I rub my cockhead against her opening, flicking her little clit until her hot little body is shaking all over with want. I glide in slowly, my teeth gritted, enjoying each pulse of her cunt walls against my dick. The tendons of her neck stand out in sharp relief as she tips her head back in answer to my first thrust inside her. I pull almost fully out of her and then shallowly pump so that she hugs just the head. It's a tease for both of us, but I want this night to last forever.

"God, Daniel," she half sobs, half laughs and then rises on her elbows to pin me with a glare. "Stop tormenting me, damn it."

I lay a hard palm on the top of her pelvis and drive into her with one swift motion until I'm fully seated. She falls back with a scream.

"Is this how you want it?" My voice is so hard and rough that I barely recognize it.

"Yes," she snarls back. "I want it harder, faster. I want *more*." My hips move with such force that she's sliding across the mattress. Her hands and feet are scrambling for purchase as she seeks some way to push back. I grab her around the hips and pull her toward me. I may have started out with gentleness, but my self-control has left me and there's only one way out of this maelstrom. Her hands latch on to my wrists. As if there's a jackhammer driving through my spine, I thrust inside of her relentlessly. My fingers are leaving bruises on her skin, but the way that she's clawing at my arms tells me she is with me all the way.

"I'm close. Soooo close," she cries. I maintain my rhythm, hard, fast, and steady until she's exploding. Then I lean over, one hand braced by her head, both her legs over my shoulders, and I hammer furiously into her wet tight glove until my orgasm comes.

"I've got you," I shout. "Let go."

When I'm spent, I collapse by her side, pulling her into my arms. We rub each other's backs and arms and spread soft, drugged kisses over the skin available to us.

"I love you," she whispers in between caresses. No matter what happens tomorrow, we'll have this. I clutch her body closer so I can feel her heartbeat against mine.

REGAN

I'm pretty good at lying to myself, it seems.

I told myself that after I left the brothel, I never wanted another man to touch me. Lies.

I told myself that I'd never be vulnerable again. Lies. I'm vulnerable every time Daniel looks at me with that wicked grin on his face and my heart jumps in response.

I told myself I'd never go back to the brothel. But here I am, volunteering to go to Freeze's house because that's where Naomi is, and I'm what we need to get her out. I know Daniel wouldn't judge me if I chickened out. He doesn't want me to go. But I need to go. If not just for Naomi, for all the other girls that have been stolen and disappeared behind those walls, never to appear again. It's not just for Daniel.

But . . . there I go again, lying to myself.

I smooth my hands down his spine, enjoying the feel of his sweat-slicked skin against my own. In Daniel's arms, I'm whole. In Daniel's arms, the world is safe.

And I'm leaving his arms for the enemy tomorrow. I shiver and burrow my face into his neck, breathing in his sweaty scent.

"You okay?" Daniel asks, running a hand down my arm.

"If things go bad tomorrow," I ask in a soft voice, "you'll come and find me, right? No matter what it takes?"

He props his body up on his elbows and gazes down at me, all relaxation gone from his body. He's practically vibrating with tension now. "Nothing's going to go wrong, Regan."

"It's just . . ." I swallow hard. "Hudson's not right in the head. I don't think I could deal with two months with him. I lived through two months in the brothel, but I don't think I could do it with him. If you can't come get me, I'll figure out a way—"

"A way to what?" Daniel's voice is harsh.

"To make them shoot me," I say. But my voice is very small in the face of his anger.

"No," he growls, and he grabs my chin in his hand and forces me to look at him when I avert my eyes. "You think I won't come after you? You think I'd let that fucker touch one hair on your head while I've still got breath in my body? You don't do anything but what we outlined in the plan, Regan, because I swear I will fucking come and rescue you like some goddamn knight in shining armor. And you don't believe otherwise until they roll my dead body at your feet, all right? Because the thought of you killing yourself because you don't have any hope left eats at my fucking gut, and I'm not going to be able to let you go in there if that's even on the table."

"All right," I tell him softly. "All right."

"It's not all right." There's a fierce possessiveness in his eyes as he pulls me close and begins to press feverish kisses to my skin. "You're mine, Regan Porter. You don't get to decide if you die or not. Because if you do, you're destroying me, too."

"It was just a suggestion," I say and drag my fingers through his messy hair. "I didn't mean anything by it."

But there I go, lying to myself again.

CHAPTER TWENTY-THREE

REGAN

In the morning I've been trussed up like the present I'm supposed to be. One of the ladies in the favela took me aside and gave me a white shift to wear that's practically see-through. Underneath, I'm wearing a white lacy panty and bra set. I don't know how they managed to get these things in such a short period of time, but Mendoza's people are incredibly efficient. Once I'm dressed, the woman curls my hair, fixes my makeup, and then works a GPS tracker the size of a pearl into the seam of my bra cup. It's utterly invisible, but I can feel it there, and it makes me anxious. I wish I had my gun, but I'm not allowed that. I'm not even allowed shoes.

When I head out to the car, Mendoza, several of his men, and Vasily Petrovich are waiting. They're all armed to the teeth. Daniel is crouching on the ground, raking a hand through his hair over and over again, and he gets to his feet at the sight of me. He approaches, a dark expression on his face.

"How do I look?" I keep my voice light so he doesn't know how scared I am.

"Like a fighter," Daniel tells me grimly. His hand brushes down my arm, and he keeps looking me over, as if making sure that I'm still okay.

I force a smile to my face. "That's not the object here, Daniel. I'm supposed to look sexy."

"Regan," he tells me and grabs the back of my neck, dragging me against him. My breasts mash against his tactical vest that is studded with weapons. While I've been getting ready, he has, too. "Look, just because we're sending you in there doesn't mean that you have to do whatever that sadistic bastard wants, okay? You fight him if he touches you."

I shake my head. "Daniel, you know that I can't. I was sent to Gomes because he wanted me obedient. If I'm not obedient, he's not going to keep me around."

"I don't care," Daniel grits out, and his voice is hoarse with barely contained rage. He presses his forehead to mine. "I'm not sending you in to get hurt. I can't take that—"

I silence him with a kiss that's going to ruin my lip gloss. It's a quick one, but I love the feel of Daniel's mouth on mine. "I know," I breathe against his mouth when I pull away. "Daniel, I love you. I trust you. You'll come and get me. I know you will."

The look he gives me is tormented. "Regan—"

"And when you do," I murmur against his mouth, wishing I had time to kiss him properly, "we're going to go find that private island of yours, and you can spend all the time you want oiling me up. I promise."

"Damn it, fighter. Don't give me a boner right now."

I giggle.

"Time to go," Vasily says in a flat voice behind us. For a moment, my laughing, cocky, devil-may-care Daniel looks murderous. But he releases me with another quick kiss pressed to my brow.

Gomes's car is out front, and it's a flashy lowrider with a cherry red paint job. Yeah, we'll be noticed. Gomes is sitting behind the front wheel, and he's sweating with terror. "We can trust him?"

Mendoza opens his hand, revealing a small vial. "He's poisoned, and I am the only one with the antidote. He'll be watched. Any sign of betrayal and this goes down the drain."

"Creative," I murmur. Another bead of sweat rolls down Gomes's nose while I watch.

Vasily hands me something. It's a birthday card. I snort and tuck the envelope against me. "Should I, you know, do anything if it's all going to hell? Do I need a backup plan?"

"No," Daniel says flatly. "It doesn't matter because I'm coming after you either way."

I smile at that. "Deal."

We test the tracker to make sure it's working, and then there's no more time to stall. I take in a deep breath, get into the back of the car, and Gomes turns out of the compound.

I clutch the envelope in trembling fingers, watching the streets and alternately watching Gomes as we make our way through the favela. He's sweating like crazy, and I'm worried it's going to give something away. This has to work, though. It has to.

All too soon, I see the familiar compound rising in the distance. I quell the panic rising inside me. I can do this. I can do this. Naomi, I think. Naomi and a hacker. I need both of them. Actually, all I care about is Naomi, but if Hudson is holding someone else against his will, I want to save that man, too.

Gomes pulls up to the gate sideways, my door facing the massive gate. Two soldiers approach, guns in hand. "Time for you to get out," Gomes says to me in a trembling voice.

"I'm going," I say quietly and open the door.

One man trains his gun on me while the other approaches, and my heart stops. My hand is shaking as I hold out the birthday card. I say nothing.

The man takes the birthday card and looks over at Gomes. Then, he nods and eyes me. He says something to me in Portuguese—a question.

I panic. "I . . . I don't know," I say, my voice small, and I cringe when he repeats it again. It's not hard to act scared in front of these men. I'm terrified.

He says something again and then begins to pat me down roughly, taking his time squeezing my ass and breasts. I cringe and endure his touch, my eyes closed, horrible memories flashing through my mind again. I can do this. I can do this.

Naomi, I repeat to myself. I must save Naomi.

The man slaps my ass and laughs when I jump, then hands the card back to me. He gestures me forward, and the gate opens. Only then do I realize I hear party music.

Of course. It's his birthday party.

The guard leads me in, and I stare in amazement as people swirl around us. There are balloons and people in suits and girls in bikinis everywhere. And guns. Everywhere, there are guns and armed men. It's a weird contrast to see someone holding an assault rifle and standing next to the punch bowl, but there it is.

And at a table under an umbrella near the pool, sits Mr. Freeze. He's a sliver of ice among the sea of color, and I feel my stomach churn in fright at the sight of him.

The guard leads me right to him, and all eyes turn in our direction.

Oh God, I feel so utterly conspicuous. Do they know I've got the tracker? Oh God. Oh God.

Hudson gets to his feet, his pale hair gleaming in the afternoon sunlight. His suit is a pale, pale blue that almost seems white, and his tie the same color. His sunglasses are the only splash of color anywhere. He says something to his guard that I don't understand, and then both look at me.

With a shaking hand, I hold out the birthday card, my head bent.

Hudson takes the card, flips it open and reads it, then tosses it aside. He steps closer, and his hand brushes my cheek. Even his fingers are cold. It takes everything I have not to flinch away, but I keep my gaze downcast.

"So, little biter," he says to me. "Are you ready to be mine now?"

"Yes, master," I say. I hate the words. Hate them. He's not my master.

He tucks a finger under my chin and tilts my head back, examining my face. My eyelashes flutter and I keep my gaze down and let a shiver or two in so he knows that I'm afraid.

After a moment, he grunts approval. "And have you learned the games I like?"

Games?

Panic flashes through me. Games? What games? Gomes was supposed to teach me games? What kind of sick games does this man like?

My response must show on my face. He *tsk*s and turns to his table, saying something in a pleasant voice. Then, he gestures at his guard. "Take her to my room. Make her ready."

The guard grabs me by the elbow, and before I can ask what he means, I'm dragged inside the house. I get a glimpse of a mansion filled with potted plants and pretty tiled floors as I'm dragged through, and then I'm heading up a set of stairs and down a hall. Passing several more doors, I'm brought into a bedroom.

The guard heads right on in through the bedroom and to a door at the back of the room.

"Where are we going?" I stammer. "Hello?"

The guard doesn't answer me. Instead, he flings the door to the closet open.

Except, it's not a closet. It's another room. A guard is sitting there, smoking a cigarette and flipping through a magazine. He stands at the sight of me, and the two guards begin a conversation. The new one eyes me lasciviously, and then I'm passed over to him.

We head through another door, and I'm taken down a narrow, cold set of stairs. Hudson's house is a maze, and it almost feels like I'm being taken through a secret tunnel or something. I hope Daniel will know where to find me, but I'm getting more frightened with every moment.

The new guard takes me a few doors down and then opens one marked *privado*.

This room . . . is a sex room. There's a cross with cuffs on it at the back of the room, a wooden horse, and all kinds of various paraphernalia in this room. It's horrible. My frightened gasp makes the guard laugh, and he pushes me in. "Strip."

"I . . . what?" I cling to the shift I'm wearing.

"You strip," he tells me, pointing his gun in my direction.

Oh God, the GPS. Will Daniel know where I'm going? "Strip?" I repeat, stalling for time.

"You. Strip."

When the man starts to head forward to do it himself, I wave him off and begin to remove my clothing. I peek at the guard, but he's not paying attention to me. Instead, he's heading to the far side of the room as I undress.

I remove everything and ball the clothes together, tucking the panties and bra into the shift so he won't find the GPS. I look at the door. I might be able to escape before he shoots me . . . but then what? Then Naomi is lost. I suck in a breath and clutch the ball of clothing to my chest.

The guard returns a moment later with handcuffs. He takes the clothes from my hands, clasps one handcuff around my wrist, and drags me toward a metal pole in the center of the room. There are a few iron circles at the top of the pole and he clasps the other end of the handcuff through it, locking me there.

"Stay," he tells me. "Good dog." And he laughs in my face.

He's still laughing as he leaves me in this horrible room. I'm naked, handcuffed to a bar, and surrounded by deviant toys that are clearly meant for the enjoyment of one party, and it's not me. There are spikes and whips and things I can't even begin to imagine their use, but it doesn't look good.

I'm naked, and I'm trapped, and I don't even have my GPS

tracker anymore. There's no sign of Naomi. There's no sign of anyone. I'm stuck in this torture room all alone.

My bravery deserts me, and I begin to sob.

Time passes, and I keep crying until I'm hoarse, until the sobs that rack my chest are ugly and painful. I can't seem to stop. It's like all the pressure that's been building up has exploded with nowhere left to go except tears. I've messed everything up. I'm supposed to be finding Daniel's sister and the hacker, and handling things. Instead, I'm naked and handcuffed in a sadist's sex basement.

So I cry. And cry.

And cry.

There's a knock at the door, which startles me out of my tears and sends me back into terror. I back up as much as the bar will let me, my now-raw wrist slamming against the handcuff above my head.

The door opens a moment later, and a woman in a beaten-up baseball cap peers in. She scowls in my direction, shuts the door, and walks toward me. "There must be silence if I'm to work. Those are the rules."

I blink my tears back, startled. "W-what?"

"Silence. I told Hudson that if he wants me to be his Emperor, I have to have silence. Silence makes the atoms happy. If the atoms are happy, my brain functions at a higher level." She crosses her arms and looks down at me. "You're making my atoms very unhappy."

"I . . . I'm sorry?" I twist in the handcuff. This girl is odd. She's odd, but she's also about my age, and I have a hunch. "Are you . . . are you Naomi?"

"I've told him," she says as her hands smooth along the brim of her beaten-up cap, over and over again, "if he wants the Emperor to work, there must be silence and all foods must be brown or green, but not both together. Those are the rules, and he said that was fine. And now you're here, making all this noise—" Her fingers flutter on the brim of the cap, agitated. She's not meeting my curious gaze. "And I can't think!"

I sniffle hard. "I'll stop crying if you get me down from here."

"Really?" Her gaze flicks to my face and then just as quickly skids away again.

"Yes, really."

She considers the bar I'm handcuffed to, and her fingers slide along the brim of the hat, over and over again as she thinks. Then, she says, "I'll have to tie you up somewhere else. Those are the rules."

"That's okay," I say quickly. Anything has to be better than being handcuffed here. "If you tie me somewhere else and get me something to wear, I promise I'll stop crying."

"Good. Good." She nods, and her fingers flutter on the edge of her hat again. "I'll be back."

"No, wait," I say, but she's gone as quickly as she came. I fight the urge to start screaming again, my terror over being alone returning like a tidal wave. I choke on sobs for what feels like eternity.

But then she returns, and she's got a sleep shirt with her. "Here," she says and holds it out.

I jangle the handcuff over my head. "Can we get rid of this?"

"Yes, of course." She gives me the shirt and heads to the far wall, plucking a key from a hook with an expertise that makes me wonder how many other women she's seen in this room. She returns, grabs one of the weird sex stools, climbs it, and undoes the latch on the handcuffs for me. "Now you'll be quiet so I can work?"

I clutch my wrist to my chest once it's free. I feel like crying again, but it won't serve any purpose. "I'll be quiet. You're Naomi?"

She blinks at me, steps down off the stool, and then shrugs. "Most of the time. Sometimes I'm the Emperor."

I tug the sleep shirt over my head. It's a Mickey Mouse shirt, and I'm trying not to be weirded out by something so clean and childish in this bizarre place. It feels good to be wearing something. "The Emperor? That's not another hacker? *You're* the hacker?"

"I'm the hacker," she agrees, and her gaze skids to the door again, as if she doesn't like to look at me. "But I can't hack anything if it's not quiet."

"Sorry," I say and wring my hands. I'm feeling shaky and fragile, but excited all at once. "Daniel sent me," I murmur in a low voice. "He's here to come get you."

"Oh no," she says. Anxiety flickers across her face. Her hands go back to the brim of her cap. "Oh no. That's not good. He can't be here."

"Wait, why can't he be here? You want to stay?" I'm shocked.

Naomi looks at me then shakes her head, gaze skidding away again. "Don't be ridiculous. Of course I want to leave. But he can't be here. It's dangerous."

I bite my lip. "I don't have any way of telling him not to come. I had a GPS tracker, but they took it with my clothes."

She nods absently and pulls at my sleeve. "We'll figure something out. Come with me."

CHAPTER **TWENTY-FOUR**

DANIEL

Letting Regan go back to Hudson is about the worst thing I have ever done. Petrovich and Mendoza literally sit on me to keep me from dragging Gomes out and punching him until his face is raw, tenderized meat. Kind of like what's between his legs right now.

"It's time." Petrovich hands me a cheap pair of black pants, a white shirt, and a vest. These are our uniforms. The GPS Regan has will alert us to her location and hopefully that will reveal my sister. Petrovich is still working out where his hacker will be. He thinks basement. I don't really give two shits.

"Do I tape my gun to the bottom of the tray?"

"No weapons," Mendoza reminds me. Only Hudson's carefully vetted guards are allowed weapons. Even those in the kitchen are screened due to their placement near knives and heavy objects, but I guess the waitstaff is not. At some point,

Petrovich and I will have to disarm two guards, take their weapons, and find Regan.

Getting inside Hudson's compound is ridiculously easy if you have no weapons and are dressed like staff. Mendoza has done it before; at the time he was unwilling to level the place to find his lost girl. But I guess it ate at him, and now we've tipped him over the edge. That and we're the ones taking all the risks.

"You eat this shit?" Petrovich asks, sniffing at the squares of raw tuna speared by a toothpick.

"We can't all live on borscht," I mock, picking up my own tray. "Let's do one circle, meet back here and then decide on our targets."

He nods and—with one more disgusted sniff—walks out.

Petrovich and I as waiters is a foolish disguise. I can already see the Hudson men eyeing us with suspicion. If it were just me, perhaps it wouldn't be an issue, but Petrovich is a bear of a man with a dour expression—like Nick. Humorless.

Inside, I count eight Hudson men stationed at the corners of the room and two at each entrance. Their weapons aren't visible, but their watchful eyes and careful poses set them apart from the party guests. The guards at the back of the room are being the least attentive; their eyes are wandering all over the barely clad bodies of the female party favors. Hudson's idea of party is a two-to-one ratio of prostitutes to men. My guess is that several of the "guests" are actually businessmen, although I see the familiar haircuts of military folk as well. Money, booze, and lack of control over one's dick are the downfall of many careers.

"The men at the back," I inform Petrovich when we meet in the expediting room, where all the trays of food are delivered from the kitchen.

He nods. "There are four outside. First take out the two by the French doors. I will provide the distraction."

I pick up my tray and head toward the back of the main party room. The French doors are open, and there is a near-constant stream of people moving toward the back where the pool is. Women are getting naked and drawing the crowd out. It's easy enough to come up behind the guard on the right. Even easier to jab the discarded cocktail fork I've appropriated from a nearby table into his neck. He falls backward, but his descent goes unnoticed when Petrovich's loud voice yells, "Bomb. There's a pipe bomb."

The guests start screaming and running in different directions as no one is sure where the bomb is located. I twist the neck of the guard and let him collapse on the floor. Moments later, his jacket is around my shoulders and the familiar weight of a semiautomatic is in my hand. I take out the guard in the corner with an elbow to the nose. Two down, a million more to go. Over the melee, I see Petrovich disabling the guard across the way. I've got the ammunition and weapons of two. That's enough. With a jerk of my head, I indicate I'm headed into the private rooms of the Hudson compound. I pull out the phone from my pocket and engage the GPS tracker. It's good within five feet, Mendoza informed me.

The signal indicates that it's northwest of my position, but as I look to the northwest, I see only a well-manicured lawn. The house doesn't extend to the northwest from my position near the terrace and the French doors leading to the pool. Basement then. Damn it. I wish I had a blueprint of this fucking place. The tracker doesn't map depth, only location. Regan was led north and then backtracked, but the private area of the house is too closed off. I'm going to have to find another way in. In the kitchen

I find chaos. People are screaming and running several directions. I grab a worker by the collar as he sprints past me.

"*Onde fica a adega?*"

He shrugs and wiggles like a worm on a hook. Worthless. "Where's the fucking basement?" I scream, but no one answers the crazy Texan.

Methodically, I start throwing open doors. Closet, pantry, stairs to a cellar. *Bingo.* I run down the stairs, past wooden boxes and shelves of cheese and casks of wine. It smells cool and fresh, as if there is regular circulation of air down here. The thick brick walls mask the upstairs disarray, and I can hear the trickle of water and the hum of electricity and not much more.

I move through the cellar as soundlessly as possible, noting that its size outpaces the house that sits atop of it. About thirty feet in, the room stops and there is nothing but stacks of foodstuffs and wine bottles against the wall.

But the freshness of the air quality down here doesn't fit with the room ending at thirty feet. Above me I see the air ducts and an electrical conduit that don't terminate at the brick wall but actually continue beyond. I start tapping to find the opening. Between two barrels of wine and crates of something, I find a vertical seam in the brick. To the left, on the floor is a depression. I fit my foot into the depression and press downward. Holding my breath, I lean against the bricks and am rewarded with the sound of a lock mechanism disengaging. A slight push and the hidden door swings inward on well-oiled hinges. The hum of electricity is louder now, and I wonder if the hacker lair is positioned down here. It would explain the conduit, the well-circulated air, and the noise.

I have a gun in either hand as I creep down the hall, my one shoulder glued to the brick wall on my right.

"I'm hungry," I hear a female say. The voice is muffled, but it doesn't sound like Regan.

"What do you want?"

"Root beer float. For me and my new friend. I think she looks like she needs a root beer float."

"Hudson isn't going to like that you brought her in here."

"The crying was bothering me. Wasn't it bothering you? How am I supposed to work if there's all this crying?"

God, that voice. I know that voice.

"You'll be the one crying if he puts you in the locker. Last time he did that you wouldn't stop sniveling for days," the male voice sneers back.

"And he lost several hundreds of millions of dollars, so I think that I won't be going back into the locker anytime soon. That wouldn't make sense." Oh Jesus. I slide down onto my butt. It's Naomi. The relief I feel at hearing her voice is sapping all my energy. I want to lie down on the concrete and cry like a baby.

"Saying that Hudson makes rational decisions is your first mistake. Eh, your problem." There's a pause, then I hear him speak. "The Emperor wants a root beer float. Make that two." Another pause. "What the fuck is going on up there?" I creep closer until I'm right outside the door. The voices are crystal clear now. I place the guns back in my pocket. My sister is in that room. Maybe even Regan. I can't take the risk that I'm going to shoot either of them. "All right." He sounds annoyed. "I'm coming right up." There's a rustling sound. "Something is going on upstairs. Stay put."

"Where am I supposed to go?" There's no sarcasm in the question. No, Naomi truly doesn't know.

"Don't go wandering around again, no matter who's crying."

The voice is coming closer to me and so are the footsteps. I don't know who else is in the room, so I stay crouched down. The door opens, and the feet exit. Exploding upward, I drive the heel of my palm into the man's nose. The sound of the cartilage crunching into his skull is extremely satisfying. He stumbles back, and I push him down, crouching on top of him with one hand on his windpipe and my left knee in his balls. My gun is out now, and I take a quick look about the room. In a chair, trussed at the mouth and feet and wrists is Regan, looking wide-eyed, scared, and a little pissed off. Make that a lot pissed off. Behind a bank of computers is my sister, Naomi, looking only slightly older than she was eighteen months ago, pale-eyed and pale-skinned like she never ever sees the light of day.

There's no one else in here.

"Look away," I order the girls but neither do. "Fuck it," I say. I drive my elbow into the windpipe of the downed guard twice, and he passes out from lack of oxygen. But I'm not leaving this to chance. I drag him out into the hallway and shoot him once in the head and then another time in the chest.

"He was from Massachusetts," my sister says behind me.

"I don't even know why that's important." I don't wait for her to answer but drag her into my arms. "And I don't want to hear how you don't like to be touched. That's not going to fly with me today."

She stands stiffly in my arms, but I don't care. Relief, grief, joy all wash over me in an uncomfortable shower of emotions, but I endure it and make her suffer it as well because I'm so grateful to see her alive. I squeeze her tight and then head over to Regan. Her eyes are gleaming, and maybe if my sister wasn't there and a dead body wasn't lying ten feet away, I'd do something more than bury my head in the crook of her neck, thanking all the deities above for showing me some fucking mercy.

"Will this work?" There's a tap on my shoulder, and I turn to see Naomi holding a long knife. I presume she's taken this from the dead man. With a short nod, I get to work on Regan's bonds. The minute that she's free, she's back in my arms and the tears are falling. I'm pretty sure some of them are mine.

REGAN

It was Naomi's idea to tie me up but keep me at her side. I guess the guards were used to her weird behaviors. She simply waltzed into her workroom with me, sat me down, and began to tie me up in a complex set of knots, checking each one over and over again and muttering to herself. But she didn't tie me up tightly, and the looks she kept sending my way told me that this was all an act.

But then the door busts open, and Daniel is there. I barely notice that he effortlessly executes a man in seconds. All I care is that he's here, and he's come to get me. To my shame, I start crying again. I told myself I'd be strong, that I could do this and be the fighter Daniel thinks I am.

But I keep weeping. I've been so utterly terrified, and seeing him brings it all to the forefront again.

I twist in my bonds, anxious as Daniel hugs his sister, and I see the relief and happiness in his face as he pulls her close. I know that look—he's accomplished his goal now. He's found his long-missing sister. He can go home now.

Strange how that scares me. If Daniel's done here, what does it mean for me? Is he going to send me home with a pat on the back and a few memories?

Now's not the time to think about it, though. Just as quickly as he hugged his sister, he heads over to me, and his knife rips apart Naomi's careful knots in a matter of seconds. Then he drags me into his arms and buries his face in my neck. I feel a tremble rush through him, and I realize with wonder that he was as scared for me as he was for his sister.

And my tears start all over again.

"I'm sorry," I say, huddling against Daniel. "I was trying to be a fighter, but they took my clothes and chained me in that room, and I-I couldn't—" A broken sob escapes my throat.

"Shhh." He strokes my hair. "You're the bravest girl I know. There's nothing to apologize for."

I cling to him and then begin to press frantic kisses to his face, his throat, anywhere I can find skin. I'm so relieved to see him. I knew he'd come back for me, but knowing and seeing are two different things—and in the long minutes when I was trapped, naked, in Hudson's sex prison, I worried that my luck had run out. That there would be no happy ever after for me.

Naomi makes a disgruntled noise at our hugging, so Daniel reluctantly pulls away, dragging me to my feet after him. His hand clutches mine tight, and I'm so glad. Then he releases it and offers me a gun, which makes me almost as happy.

He goes back to Naomi and looks his sister over. She cringes, wrinkling her nose as he hugs her close again and touches her, looking for bruises. "You're okay, Naomi? You're not hurt?"

She holds up a finger. "I have a paper cut."

He laughs, and for a moment he looks so relieved that I want to laugh, too. "No, I mean, did these assholes hurt you? Did they touch you?"

"I don't know why you're discounting my paper cut," Naomi says, disgruntled. "It's quite deep."

Daniel leans in and gives her a rough kiss on the cheek. "I love you, you nut. You know that, right?"

"I'm fine," she says in a softer voice. "If that's what you're asking. No one has hurt me." She puts her hands out and begins to straighten Daniel's clothing, adjusting his collar and smoothing a wrinkle out of his sleeve.

"Thank God." He seems to visibly deflate for a moment, and then he looks over at me. "Come on," he says. "We need to get out of here. We've got one more guy to find, and then we're busting out of this turkey farm."

"This is not a turkey farm," Naomi says, a furrow of concern on her brow. Her fingers dance along the brim of her cap again, apparently a nervous reaction. "This is an extremist compound. And if they find out I've escaped, they will kill Mom and Dad. I can't leave."

"They're not going to kill anyone, Naomi. I promise." Daniel's words are so confident, even I believe them. "Now, come on. We have to get out of here."

But Naomi hesitates, then shakes her head. She turns back to her desk and begins to straighten things, as if a tidy room will stop the anxiety she's feeling. "I can't leave. I can't. Everyone gets hurt if I leave."

Daniel casts his sister an exasperated look when she sits back down again and then moves to my side. "You okay, fighter?"

I nod, unable to do much more than that.

"Good. Okay. Stay here and shoot anyone that comes through that door unless it's me or Petrovich. Hell, shoot Petrovich. I don't give a damn. Keep yourself and Naomi safe and don't worry about Petrovich. All he cares about is finding the hacker."

"Here," Naomi calls from her desk. She raises her hand as if we're in class.

Before Daniel can say anything in response, a massive form fills the doorway, and we all turn, pointing our guns there.

It's Petrovich, and for a moment, my finger itches on the trigger. He's got blood splattered on his face, and he's wearing the same ridiculous waiter uniform that Daniel is. Except on his enormous body, it's tight over the arms and looks as if he's been stuffed into it. Not much of a disguise. He's got a gun held aloft, and there's a wild look in his eyes.

"We need to leave right now," he says in that ominous, deep voice.

"Good-bye," Naomi says from her workstation, and her voice is sad.

"Did you find the hacker?" Vasily asks.

"Here," Naomi says again and raises her hand. She doesn't look at either man, just goes back to typing.

"Naomi's the Emperor," I whisper to Daniel, moving closer to him as Petrovich pushes his way into the room. "She's the hacker. They're the same person."

"I know." He sighs.

"Then she is mine," Vasily says in a satisfied voice. To Naomi, he says, "You come with me."

"Now wait a goddamn minute," Daniel begins.

Naomi stands up, eyes Petrovich in that weird, not-quite-looking-into-your-face way of hers, then reaches out and straightens his collar. "I'm not going with you."

DANIEL

"Can we fucking talk about this later?" There's no way my little sister is going with that fuckhead Petrovich. I'll kill him myself if I have to, but I need his muscle to get out.

"There is a caterer's truck that is stalled, and they have abandoned it. Come now," Petrovich orders.

"Go." I gesture toward the women who, after a stalled pause, scamper after Petrovich as he barrels down the hall. We race toward the cellar space beneath the kitchen. Petrovich is first up the stairs. He fires two shots and then curses. When his magazine tumbles down the steps, I realize he's out of bullets.

"Give him your gun," I order Regan.

"What?" she clutches the black stock tighter between both hands. "No!"

"Give me the fucking gun, you stupid woman." Petrovich grabs for the gun, but Regan resists.

"Don't call her stupid, you asswipe." I barrel up the stairs past Naomi and pull Regan away. "Here, take my gun. You're the stupid fuck who ran of bullets." Regan scrunches her nose and reluctantly hands me the Ruger. "Thanks, fighter." I give her quick kiss on her lips and push Petrovich in front of us, using him as a shield. What do I care if his bear of a body gets riddled with bullets? I only want to get my girls out of this fucked-up place.

Two of Hudson's men are barricaded behind the center

kitchen island and fire off a series of rounds when Petrovich's head peeks out.

"*Ebanatyi pidaraz*," he roars and then dives out, shooting five bullets quickly. I hear return fire and hold Regan back. Behind me I hear the harsh breaths of Naomi as her anxiety ratchets up.

"Fucking motherfucker," she translates unnecessarily or maybe for Regan's benefit, and then she begins rocking on her heels. "Too loud," she's saying repeatedly, her hands over her ears. Fuck. Fuck. Fuck.

I yell the last profanity out loud. I have to get them out. Regan's crying but places a comforting arm around Naomi's shoulders. I don't have time to tell Regan that Naomi isn't a fan of touching before Naomi lets out a piercing scream.

"Oh shit. I'm sorry, Naomi," Regan says, releasing Naomi immediately. My sister is rocking back and forth on her feet, her hands over her ears.

Petrovich is looking at us like we are a circus troupe. A really bad one that he'd like to shoot to put out of our misery.

Fuck this shit.

"Stay here," I order, and then I dive out toward Petrovich. More rounds are fired off, and I feel a fire in my side. Fuck. I've torn open the glued wound. Army crawling toward the back of the island, I can feel tile chunks and plaster pieces raining down on us. "What I wouldn't give for some C-4 right now," I joke to Petrovich, who merely grunts. "You got a plan?" I ask.

"Shoot. Kill. Leave," Petrovich answers.

"Nice plan. On two?" I point upward.

He nods in understanding.

"One. Two." We both spring upward and over the counter. Hudson's men are still looking to the sides, and it is too late for them because by the time I'm over the counter, I've shot both in the head. Petrovich shoots another man at the entrance. For a moment, there is silence. Only the echoes of the bullets remain.

"Now," I gesture toward the girls with my gun, but Naomi isn't moving and Regan seems uncertain about following my command and leaving Naomi behind. If I didn't love her before, my heart about seizes now as I see the care that Regan's showing toward Naomi. Yeah, Regan's never getting rid of me.

My side is aching like crazy, but I run toward Naomi—only Petrovich beats me there. He picks her up and slings her over his shoulder as if she's a sack of rice. "Let's go."

I don't wait for another invitation. Grabbing Regan's hand, we run outside. The caterer's van is still there, doors completely open and the metal siding riddled with bullets. I throw Regan inside and Petrovich does the same with Naomi. We slap the doors shut, and then Petrovich heads for the hood. He fiddles with something before coming around the driver's side.

"Distributor cap?" I ask.

He nods, puts the van in reverse, and floors it. The girls fly backward against their seats. "Get down," I bark. Regan pulls Naomi down as I lean out the door to shoot at the guards by the front gate that is closing. "Don't fucking stop this vehicle."

Petrovich grunts but doesn't slow. I have six bullets left. There are three guards. The van is swaying like a drunk trying to walk on the train tracks. Lifting the gun, I sight the first guard, the one almost squatting. I shoot his kneecap off, and he topples over. The van lists to the side as Petrovich runs him over.

The guard by the gate is next. He gets two shots. One in the forehead. Poof. One in the chest. For surety. The third guard is on Petrovich's side, which requires me to haul my ass out of the van and sit in the window so I can shoot him over the top of the van. A lucky return shot wings me in the shoulder and makes my first shot go wide, but I correct and the next two take him down as Petrovich slams into the now-closed gates. The force wrenches me forward, and I would have fallen out of the van window if not for Petrovich and Regan dragging me back inside.

"Thanks, fighter."

Regan gives me a wan smile. Turning around, I see Naomi curled in a ball on the floor. The only thing that matters is she's alive. Holy hell. We're all okay. Petrovich drives like a madman for the Tears of God favela, and it still seems like it takes too long. "I think I ripped the glue on my side," I tell Regan.

She looks worriedly at me. "Let me see."

"Nah, it's nothing." Although I do feel light-headed. It's the result of being whipped around outside of the van. Maybe I knocked my head and can't remember it. "I want you to know that you were fucking amazing back there."

"Rrrright," she snorts. "I ran. I screamed. I wouldn't give the gun to Petrovich."

"You were trying to take care of my sister in all that bullshit. Thank you," I tell her. "Now come over here and kiss me like the hero I am."

This puts a smile on her face, and she clambers onto my lap. I ignore the fierce burn on my side and the one in my shoulder, because who cares about that? I've got a warm armful of Regan Porter in my lap. Fighter. Survivor. Kickass human being. "I tell you I love you?"

"Not yet."

"Love you, babe," I croak out. Pulling her down, I part her lips with my own, and her tongue slides along mine, sending happy bolts of electricity down to my groin. She arches against me, and I revel in the feel of her slight breasts rubbing against my chest. The memories of our heated night together run in a loop behind my closed eyes. My hands drop down to cup her ass cheeks and pull her closer to me.

"Ow," I grunt when her hand presses against my shoulder. She starts to move away, but I draw her back down. I can't get enough of her. I want to lift her shirt and cover the tip of her breast with my tongue, suck her whole tit inside my mouth until I'm stuffed full of her. "Uhh," I grunt again, the pain in my shoulder more acute. Shifting her to the side, I manage to dislodge her hand, and the relief is immediate. But I can't stop kissing her. I don't care that Petrovich is two feet away from me. My only thought is getting her closer to me. Her soft hands are cupping my face, and I've got sweet ass in my palms. I try to open my eyes to stare at her, to watch her lust-filled gaze as she grinds down on me, but there's a fog that's obscuring my vision. The pressure of her lips is decreasing, and she's calling my name. I struggle to respond. My mouth is open, but there's no sound coming out of it. Regan. I call to her. Regan. Regan. Regan. But there's no response. No sound. Only a roaring in my ears and then . . . nothing.

CHAPTER **TWENTY-FIVE**

REGAN

There's no worse feeling in the world than kissing a man and realizing he's going completely limp under you.

I don't understand what's happening to Daniel at first. We're kissing and all over each other, the adrenaline of escaping Hudson's compound racing through his body like it's racing through mine. But then his lips part and fall slack, and I'm confused. I sit up and realize the spark in his eyes has gone glassy. "Daniel?"

When his eyes roll back, I scream. "Daniel?" I repeat his name over and over, tapping his cheek. "Daniel? Daniel!"

There's no response. I slide off of him and gasp to see blood soaking the side of his shirt and a similar spot on his shoulder. "Oh my God, how fucking hurt is he?"

"Too loud, too loud," Naomi cries behind us in the van. Her

hands are pressed over her ears, and she huddles in a small ball on the floorboards. "Too loud!"

"Everyone fucking shut up," Vasily growls at us. "I am driving!"

I want to comfort Naomi, but I'm scared for Daniel. His face is so pale. I rip at his shirt, now stained with blood, to see what the damage is. There's a spot on his shoulder that's leaking blood, but his side is worse. It looks like he's been hit a second time, and there's blood everywhere. I choke back a sob and begin tearing his shirt up, pressing the fabric against the wounds to stop the blood. I'm covered in it. I'd rip the nightgown I'm wearing off of my body, but it's all I've got.

Then, I think, *Fuck that*, and tear it off anyhow. I don't care if I'm naked. Dozens of men have seen and touched my body. All that matters is that Daniel lives.

"Too loud," Naomi whimpers again.

Vasily mutters a curse and stares in the rearview mirror as another gunshot rings out. "We are followed."

"Of course we're being followed," I cry, my hands slippery with Daniel's blood as I try to stem the bleeding. It's everywhere, and my own panic is rising. "You stole the fucking Emperor out from under his nose. He's not going to throw his hands up and say 'Oh well!'"

The big Russian shoots me a dirty look. "Wake him up. We need him to shoot."

"Fuck you," I say. "He's hurt."

"We will all be hurt unless someone takes care of them," he growls at me.

I look over at Naomi, but she's a mess. I don't know what to do. Let go of Daniel and hope he doesn't bleed out? Or hold on to

Daniel and hope we don't get shot first? "Can we make it back to Tears of God?"

"If we do not return fire, they will shoot out our tires. Then we will not go anywhere," Vasily yells. He holds a gun out at me.

"Okay! Okay, goddamn it!" I snatch the gun from him. "Naomi!" I bellow, though internally I'm wincing at my voice. "Come put your hands on Daniel's wounds right now."

"Dirty," she whimpers, hands over her ears.

"The sooner you do this, the sooner we get someplace safe and quiet," I tell her, taking the safety off the gun and making my way to the back of the van as they shoot at us again.

I duck as the back window shatters. Vasily curses again, and Naomi shrieks, but she's heading to Daniel's side.

Good enough. I ignore the glass on the floorboards and crawl forward. I'll pick it out of my wounds later. My sticky, bloody hands make it hard to hold the gun, but I raise it, even as the van swerves, and shoot. Two shots.

They don't hit anything, but I'm pleased to see Hudson's car swerve in reaction. If I can keep him off balance, I can buy us time.

"Drive fucking faster," I yell at Vasily, and when he pumps on the gas, my body slams against the side of the van. Well, I got my wish at least. I wince as more glass digs into my feet, but I raise the gun again. If I can hit the windshield . . .

I bite my lip, use both hands to steady the gun, and start shooting. It kicks wildly with every shot, and I miss every time. Every damn time. Then, to my shock, a lucky hit pings a side mirror on the car and the mirror goes flying, and Hudson's car swerves wildly again.

"Keep shooting," Vasily tells me. Like I didn't know.

I fire once more, aiming down instead of at eye level. All my shots have been going wide, so I try a different tactic.

Blam! This time his windshield shatters, and I watch his car skid.

"Yes!" I scream.

"Loud!" Naomi yells back at me.

"Sorry," I murmur and raise the gun again. They're still following us, but not as close now, and they're weaving all over the narrow road.

The trigger clicks in my hand. Shit. "I'm out," I yell at Vasily.

"We are almost there," he calls back at me. "Hold on. We go in hot!"

I don't even have time to ask what that means before we turn a corner so sharply that my entire body is flung against the opposite wall of the van, and I slam into a storage cabinet that rattles like it holds a million pieces of silverware. It gives me an idea, and I throw down the gun, jerk open the latched cabinet, and begin pulling out cutlery and tossing it out the window. Maybe that will buy us a bit of time or distance if it manages to hit Hudson's car.

They shoot again, but they're swerving madly . . . and so are we. I slam into the wall again and see stars when my face slams against the door. That's going to hurt in the morning, but adrenaline is pumping hard, and I don't even pause. Each handful of forks makes Hudson's car swing wildly to the side.

Then I hear Vasily slam on the brakes, and I careen into the side of the van again. Jesus. I'm going to be black and blue from the getaway trip.

"We are here," Vasily calls.

I stare in horror as the van comes to a stop; Hudson is still following us. "He's still behind us," I scream. "Vasily!"

"Good," he says in the most brutal voice I have ever heard.

Hudson pulls right up behind us, and before I can demand that Vasily start the van again, shots ring out. The remaining windows in Hudson's car shatter, and someone yells something in Portuguese. I see hands go up in the air.

Hudson is surrendering.

An explosive sob of relief escapes me, and I crawl back to the front of the van, to Daniel. Naomi is at his side, her hands pressing against his wounds. He's still breathing, but he looks so pale.

"We need a doctor, Vasily," I tell him, but he's not getting out of the driver's seat. As I look around, there are men, armed men, swarming Hudson's car. It's Mendoza and his men.

Oh, thank God. I push the passenger door open and practically spill out onto the concrete, all naked, bloody, and snot-faced from crying. "Mendoza," I cry out. "Daniel needs a doctor! He's been shot!"

He rushes to me, barking orders at his men. Someone hands me a shirt, and I try to get to my feet, but pain stabs me. I collapse on the ground and stare at the red soles of my feet that are gleaming with shards of glass. I can't stand. "Daniel," I say as someone tries to help me up. "Get Daniel!"

Then, there are men dragging him out of the van, gesturing another man—hopefully a doctor—forward. Mendoza is draping the shirt over my naked body as I hug one of my glass-embedded feet.

"Come," Mendoza tells me. "Put the shirt on. I want both you and Daniel in the infirmary."

I nod and slip my arms into the shirt, hugging it closed. Mendoza picks me up in his arms, and I want to yell for him not to touch me, but I can't walk, and I want Daniel more than anything. I crane my neck and see that they've brought him inside, and that's where I want to be. In the distance, Hudson is surrounded by dozens of armed men, his hands behind his head. Good.

As soon as we step through the doorway of the compound, I hear an engine start. Startled, I turn at the same time Mendoza does, and we watch the catering van drive out of the compound, despite the number of people in the courtyard.

I look around. Naomi is nowhere to be seen.

Neither is Vasily.

Daniel's friend has re-stolen Daniel's sister. Oh no. My heart sinks.

"We need a blood transfusion," someone yells up ahead, and I forget about everything but Daniel. Clutching at Mendoza's shoulders, I don't relax until I'm in the clinic with Daniel.

And then I can do nothing but watch as Mendoza's doctor goes to work on the man I love.

CHAPTER **TWENTY-SIX**

DANIEL

"Sergeant Hays, you have a Red Cross call."

I look up from the picnic table where I've got a ten and a five. Rubens, one of the direct assault troops in my squad, has a face card and a four. *Do I hit or stay?*

"Wait," I say. "Did you say Red Cross?"

The lance corporal delivering the news nods his head stiffly. A Red Cross call is an emergency call, a special number that connects families of troops with deployed soldiers no matter where they are. I've never had one in the eight years I've been in—not even when I was in theater and my old man had a heart attack. It was a minor one, but I learned about it an email four days after I'd come back from a mission in Beirut assisting the Lebanese in ferreting out a leading member of Al Qaeda. The U.S. military is enjoying using its Middle East staging ground from Afghanistan to launch all kinds of Special Forces missions. "Hit me," I tell the other recon sniper assigned to my squad. He lays out an eight. "Fuck."

"Busted," Rubens crows and drags in the cigarettes we're using as currency. Three of them break, and the tobacco leaves a trail on the scarred and cracked wooden surface. "Sergeant?"

I jerk my head around. Nothing good comes from a Red Cross call, but I go and lift the phone up like it weighs more than a .50-cal machine gun.

"Your sister's been kidnapped. You need to come home and find her." My dad's voice is hoarse, as if he spent the whole night crying or, more likely, shouting at people. I stagger on my feet, looking for a chair and can't find one. I slide to the ground.

"When?" I ask. I need details, but there's silence on the other end. Finally, my dad sighs.

"Two days ago."

"Two fucking days ago and you're calling me now?" I scream down the line. My heart is pounding so hard and fast now I fear it will jump out of my chest. This is my fault. All my fucking fault. I was the one who encouraged her to take this spring break trip. I had almost bullied her into going, telling her she needed to spend time with people her own age.

"You need to come home, Daniel." It's my mom's voice, so quiet I can barely hear her. She's crying, and her tears remind me of Naomi. "Daniel, come home." More tears. Lots of tears.

"*Save me, Daniel.*"

I see those words in a thousand faces. The hunt for Naomi started in Cancun, but it has taken me everywhere. From the Philippines to Dubai to Russia to London. Girls are being sold everywhere. Their red mouths and tiny hands reach out to me, but before I can reach them they are shot, one by one. I turn around to stop the shooter, but no one's there. A heavy weight drags down my arm, and I see a smoking gun. I throw it away with a scream.

There's a fire in my shoulder and another in my waist. I'm burning up. It's the fires of hell, I think. I'm in hell and being burned for my failure. For my sins.

"Daniel. Stop." It's Regan.

"Fighter. Wait for me," I tell her. "I'm coming for you."

Wetness falls on my face. "You promised not to leave me," she screams. Her screams are so loud. I see Hudson above her, his whip hand reaching back to strike again. Grabbing it, I pull him away, but there's another man and another and I can't reach her. "Regan," I scream. "I'm coming. Hang on."

Arms try to hold me down, but I have to get to her. I'm not leaving her behind. I've got to keep my promise.

"Don't come home until you find her." The stern face of my father appears next to me. My mother lies in pieces at his feet. Someone's shaking my arm.

"I'm coming, Regan, wait for me." They've immobilized me, but I'm not being held back. "I won't leave without you!" I roar. And then a blow across my face renders everything black.

CHAPTER **TWENTY-SEVEN**

REGAN

I clutch Daniel's hand in mine for hours. He's asleep, due to the heavy-duty drugs they've given him, and isn't aware that I haven't left his side. I still hold his hand anyhow. They've pumped blood into him, and his color is better, his wounds are stitched up, and they assure me he'll be fine. But I won't believe that he's going to be all right until he wakes up and smiles at me and calls me "fighter." Then, I'll know he's okay.

Then, I can tell him that his sister's gone again.

Vasily has disappeared. Mendoza sent some men to hunt him and try to stop him, but both he and Naomi have vanished without a trace. Mendoza thinks that Daniel will know where Vasily has taken Naomi, and I hope so.

I worry he's going to be furious at me because I didn't do enough to stop Vasily from taking her again. And I worry that

Daniel will look at me with loathing because I'm still here and Naomi's gone again.

Mostly, though, I sit and worry.

One of the favela doctors swings in and checks on Daniel. Daniel has a new bruise on his face from when Mendoza came in and clocked him in the jaw to get him to stop yelling. The doctor smiles at me; I think he's impressed that I never leave. He checks Daniel's vitals, switches an IV bag, and starts to leave again.

"Is he going to wake up soon?" I ask softly.

The doctor doesn't look concerned. "Soon. How are your feet?"

"They're fine," I say flatly. I have bruises all over, and my feet are torn up from all the glass I had to have extracted from them, but it's unimportant. Daniel's all that matters. "How soon is 'soon'?"

The doctor shrugs and turns to leave. He looks so unconcerned. Maybe he's used to patching up bullet holes far too often. He nods at me. "Soon."

And then he leaves again.

I press my mouth to the back of Daniel's hand. He's so still in bed, so lacking that vibrancy that I'm used to seeing. I never realized until now how very alive Daniel is and how much I ache to see that devilish smile of his again.

Instead, I'm here, listening to every breath he takes and hoping it's not his last.

"You promised you wouldn't leave me," I murmur against his hand. "You promised, Daniel."

He doesn't respond. Of course not. I press another kiss to the back of his hand, thinking. Then, I smile. "If this were a horror movie, you and I would both be dead, you know." I pause, as if imagining his outraged response, then nod. "It's true. Horror movies follow basic stereotypes, and those stereotypes always get picked off. One of the first ones to go is always the slutty blonde. Bad guys love a good, slutty blonde." I imagine his laugh and smooth my fingers along his skin. "They usually die screaming and running through the woods, only to trip because they wore some ridiculous high-heeled shoes. And you, of course, would be the cocky, arrogant asshole stereotype. Those die pretty fast, too. You're far too competent, too good at what you do, too good-looking. I think the movie writers make it their mission to take down guys like you." I nip at his fingers idly. "Which is ironic because we both know you'd toast anyone or anything that tried to get past you, and you'd do it with a smile."

"Who lives?"

My head jerks up at the softly worded question, my heart hammering in my chest.

Daniel's eyes are mere slits in his face, but he's smiling at me, and the hand in mine squeezes briefly. "Hey, fighter."

"Hi," I say, and my vision blurs and more tears stream down my cheeks. I'm so relieved. The doctors said he would be fine, but I don't trust anyone's words anymore. All I trust is Daniel.

He's all I trust, and all I need.

"Hey, hey." His voice is soft, and he tries to reach for my wet cheeks. "Why you crying, fighter?"

I shake my head, excusing my tears. "Just kinda emotional."

He looks around the room, dazed. "Naomi?"

I freeze for a moment. I don't want to tell him what happened. Not right now, not when I know he'd climb out of this bed, unhook his IVs, and go after her. He needs to rest. "She's out," I hear myself saying and hope he's not too angry about the lie later.

He nods and relaxes back in bed again, those sleepy eyes gazing at me. "You look tired, fighter."

I shrug. I'm tired because I haven't slept a wink since Daniel got shot. But that sounds needy, so I hold it back. "I'll be fine."

"How badly was I shot?"

"Once in the shoulder and once in the side. They say that you were lucky it didn't pierce any organs." I shudder, my breath catching on the words. "You should be fine in a few days. You lost a lot of blood."

"Mmm." His eyes are sliding shut again, and he looks exhausted.

I kiss the back of his hand again. "Sleep, Daniel. I'm not going anywhere."

He slides his hand out of mine and pats the side of the bed. "Come curl up next to me. I'll sleep better with your body against me."

I shouldn't. There are tubes and IVs and he's fucking hurt, but I can't resist. I crawl into the bed on his good side and hope he doesn't notice that my feet are covered from the calf down in puffy bandages with big, white, fluffy socks over them. But his eyes are closed, and when I slide in next to him, my butt leaning off the edge of the bed, he puts an arm around me and nuzzles against my neck.

"Mmm, you smell good," he tells me.

"And you're going to sleep, you horn dog," I tell him in a prim voice.

He chuckles, but goes silent again. I snuggle close and listen to the sound of his breathing for long, sweet seconds of peace.

Then, after a moment, he says sleepily, "Who lives?"

"Hm?"

"In a horror movie. Who lives?"

"Oh." I think for a moment. "The innocent girl. The virgin."

He snorts as if this is ridiculous. "I'd take you over Daisy in a horror movie any day."

I smile and slide in even closer. "Sleep."

He does, and I sleep next to him.

DANIEL

I'm pretty much out of it the first day, but by the second, the drugs that Mendoza's doc has pumped into me are masking my pain, at least the pain in my shoulder—Regan's sweet kisses and honeyed fingers are driving me crazy.

"Fighter, I need you to climb on top of me, right now." The pain in my pants is going to kill me if I don't get relief.

"Shut up, we're not having sex."

"How can you say that?" I whine. "I'm a wounded man. You need to render aid and suck on me."

"Pretty sure that's succor," she says, but there's a small smile running around the edges of her mouth. I'm thinking she could be talked into this.

"My dick is so hard right now that if you don't cover it with your pussy, it's going to break off. I don't think you want to be responsible for that kind of damage." My right arm is undamaged, so I use it to palm her sweet breast. The nipple firms up under my fingers, and Regan bites her lip. Yup, she's convincible. I slip my hand around to her back and pull her down. She resists at first, but with a firm tug I have her mouth right against mine. "Pretend I'm Sleeping Beauty," I whisper against her lips, and she's laughing until I slide my tongue into her mouth.

She whimpers sweetly in response. I plunge my tongue inside

her mouth like how I want to be fucking her hot little pussy. "Climb on top of me, fighter." My one good hand grips her ass and pulls her on top of me, but her clothes are in the way of our feeling good.

Fortunately, she's wearing a loose-fitting skirt, which I wrench out the way. There's a tearing sound, but I couldn't care less. The thin blanket covering my lower half is kicked off, and then her hot cunt is sliding against my rock-hard dick. The wetness slicks her path, and my body is engulfed in flames. I'm burning up with want for her. "Jesus, I need you on my dick right now." Taking my aching cock in hand, I center it at her entrance, and she slides down slow.

I can't take my eyes off our joined flesh.

When her hot, wet heat envelops me, I drop my head back, and both her hands crash down on either side of my head. Her hips rise, and she pulls off me almost completely before gliding back down in slow, small torturous increments. It's like she wants to kill me—but if this is how I go out, then glory fucking hallelujah.

My one hand grips her hip as I try to hurry her along, but she's having none of it. "Sleeping Beauty," she whispers, "if you want me to save you from villain Blue Balls, then you need to let me run this show."

"Yes, ma'am," I say, because what else are you going to do when the love of your life is basically telling you that she'll fuck you to death and then bring you to life again? "I fucking love you."

"I love you, too," she answers and tightens her pussy to punctuate her words.

I'm panting because she's doing a number on my body. Her slick walls against the sensitized bare skin of my cock is killing me. I feel every little vein and ridge inside her cunt, and it's fucking glorious. Heaven won't be this good. Shit, this *is* heaven. Being inside the tight cunt of the girl you love more than life itself is something close to it at least. Nothing has ever felt this good, and I suspect nothing else will. I'll always be chasing her down, trying to get inside that pussy even when I'm eighty.

I brace my foot against the thin mattress to push up a little, and I'm rewarded with a breathy moan.

"Right there," she whimpers. I wish I could flip her over and pound into her, but I can't. Not in my sorry condition. Instead I reach between us and find her little nub of delight. I pinch it lightly and thrust up at the same time. "Oh my God, Daniel," she screams.

I roll her clit between my fingers and piston my hips upward. If I could hold on to the feeling forever, I would, but we're both chasing down the hurricane of pleasure. Ignoring the pain, I use my left hand to pull her head down to mine so that we can fuck each other with our mouths at the same time my cock is spearing her sex.

We're slamming against each other when her orgasm hits. Her walls close around me like an undulating wave, clenching and releasing. Her cunt is a hot glove of power, and I'm completely under her control. The pulsating grip pulls my own orgasm from the base of my back.

"I'm coming inside you in three seconds. Pull off if you don't want a bunch of my swimmers attacking your eggs." It's the only warning I can get out, but Regan bites down on her lower lip and looks me straight in the eye.

"I want it." And I explode on her command. My hot seed jets into her, and she throws back her head and clamps down again, a second climax chasing my own. We finally stop pumping against each other, and she collapses on her elbows, still careful to avoid my injured shoulder.

"You're so fine, Regan Porter," I murmur, running my hand

through her cloud of blond hair. "You're a motherfucking rock star at this."

She giggles against my neck.

"No, seriously, you are." I turn my head and awkwardly kiss her cheek. "Best ever."

"Really?" she asks, and I sense the question isn't really rhetorical.

"No shit." I draw her down flush against me because having her body next to mine is worth any amount of pain. The bullet wound in my shoulder isn't keeping us apart. Nothing ever is again. "I'm going to need a daily dose of this in order for me to fully recuperate. Maybe two doses a day."

Even though I don't mind that she's resting on top of me, Regan wriggles over to my side, avoiding both wounds. "What's going to happen?" she asks.

"We're going to go home. You, me, and Naomi."

She doesn't respond, which worries me. "Or I can come to Minnesota with you." I'm not letting her go. "I hate to tell you this, but you're stuck with me now. I'm going to follow you around, and if you don't let me into your house, I'll sit outside on the porch."

"Nah, I'll let you crawl in through the doggy door."

"That's good enough for me," I tell her, giving her a one-armed hug. We fall asleep like that, or at least I do. When I wake up, Mendoza's standing over me. Quickly I look down to make sure Regan's body is covered up. It is, thank Christ. I don't think she'd be at all comfortable with even Mendoza seeing her bare.

"What's up?" I whisper, trying not to wake her.

"Judgment," he answers somberly.

I nod and ease out from under Regan. She mumbles softly but

doesn't wake up. Mendoza throws me pants and a button-down shirt. "You need help dressing?"

"No, I got it."

He gives me a chin nod and heads out. It takes some effort, but I get the pants on. They have an elastic waist, which makes it a heck of a lot easier. The buttons on the shirt present a greater obstacle, but given I'm not able to lift my left arm, there was no way I was pulling a shirt over my head. I decide to forgo fastening it. It's not like I'm going to dinner down at the beach. I'm off to see an execution. At the doorway, I pause and look back at Regan. Her hands are folded under her cheek like a schoolgirl's, but Regan's no schoolgirl. Her innocence was robbed from her. I'm not sure if I'm making the right call, but I know it's not a decision I can make for her.

"Regan." I shake her shoulder slightly. Her sleepy eyes flicker open, and she gives me the sweetest smile this side of the equator. And everything in me rebels at what I'm about to do.

"Hey, honey," she says, reaching her hand up to cup my jaw. I turn and press a kiss into her hand. My somber expression alerts her that there's something happening she might not like. "What's wrong?"

I drop my hand to her forehead, smoothing out the frown lines that have appeared, but I can't linger. Mendoza's waiting.

"Fighter, outside Mendoza is ready to administer some justice to Hudson. You can stay in here and it'll all be over soon or you can come outside and watch. It's up to you."

Her hand falls, and she turns her face away. Outside I can hear hammering as the cross is prepared. Soon they'll be hammering into flesh and bone. "If you stay inside, you're gonna want these." I place two foam ear cushions in her palm. "It'll muffle some but not all of the noise. You can go down to the base of the hill, too. Inside the second-to-last house, there'll be a place where they'll be playing music pretty loud." Not everyone in Mendoza's paradise agrees with his methods, or maybe they agree but don't want to be a party to it. But I made this call. Mendoza gave me the option of shooting Hudson or subjecting him to what Mendoza calls judgment. For the torture of Regan, the kidnapping of my sister, and for my own sanity, I chose judgment. Maybe this is a decision that Regan should have made, but Mendoza came to me and I made the call.

She picks up the foam cushions and closes her hand around them. "Will it be bad?"

"Yeah." I don't sugarcoat it. "You may have nightmares."

She gives me a sad smile. "I'm already going to have those. Maybe this won't be a nightmare. Maybe this will kill some of my fear."

I shake my head. "I'm no psychologist. I'm a soldier. I don't know if this will lessen your fear or make a mark that you can't shake off. Some things . . ." I pause and think back to my time outside the wire in Afghanistan, some of the secret operator missions I've been on, and all the haunted eyes I've seen in the girls I've rescued. "Some things can't be unseen."

"But you're going out there?"

I nod. "I've got nightmares, too. He's one of them. I'm not sorry to see him die."

"Me neither." She puts her hand in mine, and I feel the foam between us. "Let's go."

CHAPTER TWENTY-EIGHT

REGAN

Daniel warned me that it would be bad. But I should have guessed that if he was trying to shield me from it—after all we'd been through together—it would be really, really bad.

I see a cross in the center of the compound's courtyard, and that's enough for me to flinch. "Are they going to—"

"Yup," Daniel answers flatly.

"Oh." My stomach feels a little weak at the thought and at the kindling I see people stacking at the bottom of the cross. There are people gathered, people everywhere. It's like the entire favela has turned out to see this. Mendoza's men are armed and grim-faced as they make a protective ring on the outskirts that no one will cross.

Hudson is standing nearby, stiff as a board, gazing off into the distance. There are two armed men standing next to him, but he's calm. He's calm even when they begin to lead him forward. There's another man kneeling near the base of the cross. His hands are bound behind his back, and his head is bowed. I think he must be crying, because his shoulders are shaking.

Mendoza stands over him, a fire behind him illuminating the whole macabre scene. "Recite his crimes," he instructs the man on the ground.

"Carl Hudson has committed acts . . ." the man half speaks, half whispers. The words dribble out between heaving sobs.

"Louder," Mendoza commands.

The bound man starts again. "Carl Hudson has committed acts of depravity for which he will be punished. He has stolen thirty-four women, raped them, and passed them around to his helpers until they were dead. Two of those women belonged to Tears of God. Those people belonged to Rafael Mendoza and had his protection. Touching any of Mendoza's people means death. But for the other thirty-two women, we require more than an execution. Mendoza and the Tears of God require judgment."

Mendoza raises his arms to his people. "Do we agree that Carl Hudson should die for his sins and be judged by *Cristo Redentor* of his final destination?"

"We do!" the crowd shouts back.

I hate the man, but I'm not sure I can see him nailed to a cross and burned. I swallow hard, and my hand sneaks back into Daniel's.

He pulls me against him. He drags me against his body and tucks my face against his neck, holding me there. In my ear, he murmurs, "You don't always have to be strong, fighter."

I nod, inhaling his scent and clinging to him, my arms around his neck. I stay there, because I don't want to be anywhere else.

I'm there when the sound of a hammer strikes and Hudson

starts screaming. I'm there as the hammer falls over and over again, and then the screaming gets louder and the crackle of a fire starts. Smoke fills the air. I inhale Daniel's scent, trying to drown out the smell of burnt flesh, and hide my face against him, letting him be the tough one here.

After a while the screaming dies down, and Daniel touches my cheek. "It's over. Let's go inside, fighter."

I don't look back. I don't need to see—it's going to be in my nightmares plenty.

We go in and return to Daniel's room back in the infirmary. Daniel sits on the edge of the bed, and Mendoza follows us in. I sit in a chair close to Daniel's bed, but I don't want to hover. The last thing he wants is a clingy girlfriend all over him while he talks to his old army buddy. But I want to be clingy. I want to burrow into Daniel's side and have him hold me while I try to process what happened.

Hudson won't be bothering us anymore. He won't be coming after me or wanting to check my teeth. He won't be waiting for me to be broken. No more girls will disappear into his dungeon and never reappear. By doing this, we've saved so many, and gotten justice for that many more.

And I should feel relieved about all of this, but all I can think of are his screams as he was nailed to the cross. And I don't feel good about it. I can try to be tough and be a fighter, but I don't know that I'll ever be as tough as Daniel needs me to be if we're going to stick together.

This thought worries me as Mendoza adjusts his belt loaded with guns. It's nothing to him to walk around armed to the teeth, to live in a favela where people don't bat an eye when an enemy is nailed to a cross and burned alive.

To them, it says safety. To me, it says torture porn.

"How are the bullet holes?" Mendoza asks as Daniel pats his side, grimacing.

"Well, they're not magically better yet," Daniel retorts.

"Maybe it's because you're a little too vigorous in your sickbed, eh?" He grins at Daniel and my face flushes. "She was kissing my boo-boos," Daniel says easily. "Don't be a hater because one side of your bed is cold."

"Hell, yeah," Mendoza says, and I get embarrassed all over again. I curl my legs under me in the chair and try to pretend that Mendoza and all his men haven't seen me naked recently. They're not safe, like Daniel, and they still make me anxious, even if they're nice.

"So," Daniel says casually, glancing at Mendoza and then at me. "When's someone going to tell me what happened to my sister?"

I freeze in my seat, anxiety rising to the forefront. Daniel's voice is calm and even, but he's been looking for his sister for two years. How is he going to feel once he knows I let Vasily take her? I don't know what I'll do if he looks at me with cold indifference. I need Daniel. I need him the way I need air, and I know that's not healthy and I don't care.

My hands drag through my hair anxiously. I've been hiding the secret of where Naomi has gone for the past few days, and every time Daniel starts to look around his sickroom, or ask questions, I distract him with kisses. It's not that I hate the kisses—God, I love the kisses so much—but I know I've fallen back on my old bag of tricks that Daniel hates.

Don't want him to ditch you? Get his cock's attention.

It's needy and wrong and stupid of me and I can't help it. I'm terrified because I don't know what's going to happen now. I was with Daniel until we got papers and got Naomi. Then, we added "take down Hudson" to that list.

Now, I have papers.

Now, Naomi's gone again, and Hudson is handled.

There's no reason for Daniel to keep me at his side unless there's sex involved. It doesn't matter how much I love him and desperately want to be with him. I'm still messed up in the head, deep inside, and I know if he sends me back home, I'll shatter into a million tiny broken pieces.

And Daniel tells me he loves me, and he gives me sweet words, but at the end of the day, am I just pussy to him? What happens when he has to track his sister down again and it becomes dangerous? He's a sniper, an assassin. He works with dangerous men. There's no place in that for a girl like me, because I'm a liability.

But if I'm a good fuck, maybe he'll keep me. Maybe.

Still, I look at Daniel's hard face as he waits for me or Mendoza to answer, and I crumble. Weeping, gasping sobs escape my throat, and I lose my shit all over again. I'm not the fighter Daniel wants me to be.

I'm terrified he'll abandon me now, and I love him so much.

DANIEL

Mendoza looks as scared as any man can be when confronted by the terror that is a crying woman. He books it out of there like God himself is about to loose a lightning bolt on us. Me? I'll take Regan snarky or sobbing. At least I have her. We're both alive. My sister is safe, and we're going home.

"I have to tell you," I confess in low tones, trying to make her laugh. "I get the most inappropriate boners when you're crying. I don't really know what that's all about, but I'm going with it."

I'm guessing this is stress relief. Chicks cry for no reason at all. At age twelve I made my mom a janky homemade Valentine's Day card that I threw together between my morning masturbation session and breakfast. She sobbed all over me when I gave it to her, and I had to pat her back awkwardly until my dad rescued me. He took me out to the barn and tried to explain a little about women. Or at least my mom.

"Be happy she's crying," he said. "That's when you know they still feel something for you. The time when they look at you with dry eyes is when you've lost them."

When her crying continues unabated, I pull her onto my lap and try to kiss the tears. I wasn't lying about the hard-on. It sprung up almost immediately when her ass landed on my thighs. Maybe it was the proximity of her pussy to my dick. Or maybe it was because I was a dirty sonofabitch. Could be both.

I shifted her back a little so she didn't feel the press of my erection against her ass while she sobbed. Then I hugged her to me, marveling that we'd made it. When her hiccups signal the end of the storm, I tip her head back and cover her mouth with my own, giving her the comfort that I don't know how to put into words. After a halfhearted attempt to kiss me back, Regan wrenches her mouth away from me.

"I have to tell you something," she whispers.

"Shoot, baby doll, can't imagine you telling me anything that is more important than us kissing." I joke, but a thread of fear winds its way up my spine because something is really bothering Regan.

"I don't want us to be separated." She scoots higher up on my lap until her ass crack is cradling my semi-hard. On contact it grows harder, but she pays it no attention, which has me all sad and worried.

"We're not going to be," I assure her. "My cock would fall off if I had to spend more than a few hours away from you, so trust me, I'm sticking to you closer than flies on shit."

At her crestfallen expression, I tamp down my urge to roll off one awful joke after another in hopes that one of them hits her funny bone. "Sugar tits, nothing you can say is going to upset me unless it's that you're leaving me—which I'd ignore and follow you around like a stray dog you fed once that expects you'll feed it again."

"Sugar tits?" She rears back and offense is written all over her face.

Finally a non-teary response. "I was trying for *that's not good* instead of *slap your face* insulting. How'd I do?"

"Yeah, don't ever call me sugar tits again." And for a moment I think we're on our way to happy town, but then her face crumples again.

Impatiently, I jostle her on my legs. "Regan, let's go find Naomi and get the hell out of here. I'm ready to eat some barbecue and drink some Shiner Bock. You think they have Shiner Bock up there in Minneapolis? Because if they don't, then you're going to have to hold me while I cry."

At the mention of Naomi's name, the tears start up again and that thread of fear I felt before has transformed into a heavy cloak of dread. "Naomi's okay, right?"

"I didn't see what happened," she sobs. "I was so worried about you, and the next thing I know both Naomi and that asshole Petrovich are gone. Mendoza says he looked everywhere, but between the gunfight outside the gate and then you at death's doorstep and them crucifying Hudson, I lost track." Her noisy sobs make some of her words kind of hard to understand, and for a moment I'm distracted by the sheer amount of salt water she's leaking out of her body. She's going to be dehydrated before long. Then her words sink in. That dirty fucking freak show has my sister. With a roar, I yell for Mendoza. I stand up but Regan still clings to me, so I swing her into my arms and stride for the door.

Mendoza meets me at the entrance of the sickroom but won't step in any farther.

"Sorry." He raises his hands. "I suck with crying women. Pretty good at killing people and striking fear into the hearts of many. Not so good with the comforting thing."

"Shit, man, where's my sister?" I snap.

He shakes his head. "No idea. Like your girl said, it was chaotic, and I was more interested in killing Hudson's men and capturing him than I was making sure that the Russian didn't run off with your sister."

With a snap of his fingers he calls the attention of a young kid draped in a crisscrossed ammunition belt. I roll my eyes, and Mendoza shrugs. "Kids," he says. "What can you do?" The kid hands him a tray of food, which Mendoza brings into the room. "Eat. I've got a cargo plane that will take you to Costa Rica. From there you should be able to get home. You got your papers?"

I nod. "Thanks."

"Sorry about your sister." At the doorway, he pauses and says with not a little longing in his voice, "You got a good one. Hold her tight."

So the king wants a queen to keep him company in bed. Interesting. I don't give any more thought to Mendoza's lack of romantic prospects because I've got other concerns to worry about. On the tray there's a pitcher of water along with two bowls of hearty gumbo and a few cheese rolls. Regan is silent through this whole exchange, and her tears have tapered off.

Setting her on the bed, I pull the table in front of her.

"*Pão de queijo.*" I offer her a roll. "They're cheese and bread. Trust me, this is one of the best things that has ever been made. Like *Cristo Redentor* himself must have delivered the recipe to the original settlers of Rio."

She gives me a sad, watery smile and takes the cheese roll. Because these rolls are so damn good, even tragic Regan can't stop her moan of pleasure. "Right?" I say, eating half of my own roll. "Crispy crust on the outside and fucking heavenly delight on the inside." I wait until she's swallowed down one whole roll before I hand her a glass of water. "Fighter, we are in this together. It's not your fault that Vasily ran off with my sister. Plus, I know where he lives. Like, literally. So we're going to eat up and then head off to Costa Rica."

"I want to come with you," she says, mouth halfway around another *pão de queijo.*

"Sure." I lean over and give her a quick kiss. "I wouldn't want to go back to Minneapolis and mess with payroll systems, either."

This finally gets a tiny grunt of a laugh from her. "You're really not upset with me?"

"Christ, no." I set down my food and stare at her in surprise. "Is that what the torrent of tears was all about? That I'd be mad because of Naomi?" She gives me a small nod. "Look, Naomi was not your responsibility. If anything, it's on me because I got myself shot. Vasily's not going to hurt her." I hope not at least. My initial fear was that Naomi had gotten separated and was out wandering the streets of Rio, which would not be good. She's not good with new places, bright lights, disorder, or crowds—which is kind of what Rio is.

"I feel terrible and thought you'd be done with me."

Setting down the bowl of gumbo, I cup Regan's face with one hand and push the table away with the other. "I'm not ever going to be done with you, fighter. What'd I tell you before? You're going to have to kill me first before you can scrape me off." I stop and then say, "It sounded a lot less creepy in my head."

Laughing, she draws one finger along the ridge of my prominent erection. Thin linen pants do very little to hide what's going on, particularly when I'm free balling it. "Your creepy thoughts make me feel safe." Her voice takes on a teasing quality, and a damp spot appears close to the tip of her finger.

"I have lots more where that came from." I tumble her down on top of me, and as I lick inside of her mouth, I know that nothing will ever taste as good as her. She trembles under my hands and moans against my mouth.

"Can you always wear skirts?" I ask, shoving up the fabric so I can find the true heaven on Earth. My hand delves between her legs, and I swell even harder, bigger, thicker, when I find that she's soaking wet and completely naked.

"It gets cold in Minnesota," she gasps. "There'll be times I can't wear them."

"Then we're gonna have to live somewhere warmer." Pulling my own pants down far enough to spring my cock free, I roll her over and position it at her wet, hot entrance. The first push is always so amazing, as her cunt welcomes me with a silky, tight embrace.

I wish I could kiss with her less ferocity, and in the back of my mind, I wince at the marks I'm leaving. Then I grow even harder at the idea of Regan wearing signs of my possession. I hope she makes some of her own on my body. Kneading her ass cheek in one hand, I impale her completely. "I'm never leaving you," I tell her, desire making my voice harsh. "Not for a day or an hour or a minute. I'm always going to be with you."

She winds her arms and legs around me. "I'm always going to fight to be at your side."

"That's more than any man can ever ask for." Then I'm done talking. Crushing her mouth to mine, I ravage her. I fuck her hard with my tongue and my cock, until I feel the spasms of her arousal hug me tight. My whisper-thin control breaks and my body starts pounding into hers, but the cries of *"oh my God, Daniel, yes,"* and *"harder, harder"* tell me that she's right there with me. I pull out at the last minute and come into the folds of her skirt that are bunched between us at her waist.

"Goddamn." I whistle, flopping onto my back. "One of these days we gotta either get a rubber or get you on the pill."

She rubs her cheek against my chest. "Maybe neither someday?"

I clutch her tight to me. A baby with Regan? After my sister was taken, there wasn't life in me anymore. I had only one goal, and having a family and settling down wasn't part of my future. I wasn't even sure I deserved a future, and now I have Regan. She's got me by the balls, and if she wants to lead me by the dick, then I'm happy to follow. Wherever. If it's babies she wants, then hell yes. I want to have a family with her. Life's getting better and better. "Yeah, I'd like that."

Finally I heave to my feet because we've got to get going. "Eat your food," I tell her, and then I drag myself toward my bag. Inside there are clothes I can travel in. A pair of cotton pants, underwear, a button-down shirt. At the bottom are a bunch of guns, ammunition, knives, and a burner phone—all of which I'll leave for Mendoza. The notification light on the flip phone blinks, and I notice there's a message for me.

Picking up the phone, I enter the code to retrieve the message. It's Naomi and because it's her, there's no greeting. Greetings are superfluous in her estimation.

Vasily has given me a ride to Russia. He says that there are places in Russia where it is white and there are very few people. I like that. Also, he wants me to do something for him, but he says that it will help people. By people, I think he means it will help him, but he also says that this can—what does he call it?—provide me recompense for the bad things I've done for Hudson. My balance sheet is uneven, so I'm going with him. Vasily says I have to call you or you will follow me to Russia. Don't. I won't like that. I do like that Vasily is quiet. He grunts most of the time, but I'm learning what they mean.

She draws a breath and pauses.

I love you, Daniel. And I stole all the digital currency people had placed in the fake bank I created in the Emperor's Palace and converted it into francs and then funneled it into five different accounts in the U.S. It was too big for one account. I emailed you the details. I had to give some of it to Vasily or he wouldn't allow me Internet access. But I was able to save some for you and Regan. And Mom and Dad if they need it. It's from bad people, so don't be angry. You can't really steal money from bad people. This is like a redistribution. Like recompense.

That was it. Naomi doesn't say good-bye.

"Was it Naomi?" Regan's voice is so hopeful that I'm glad I can say yes.

"She says hi and that she converted fake drug money into real money and that she thinks she's going to like it in Russia." I feel a little dazed. The phone is going to have to come with me. "Hold on," I tell Regan. "I need to call Petrovich."

The phone rings only once. It's as if Petrovich is expecting my call, and I light into him before he can utter a word. "So you kidnapped my sister. Give me one reason I shouldn't come and hunt you down like a dog. Or better yet, reveal to your *Bratva* how you were involved in the assassination of your uncle."

Petrovich is silent, perhaps not expecting me to throw this back into his face. But fuck honor. My family is on the line.

"I swear on my mother's grave that no harm will come to your sister. I will protect her as if she were my own sister from the womb of my dear mother. Every hurt she suffers, I will bear twice in payment. She will want for nothing, and I will return her hale to the bosom of your family."

Beyond him there is a murmur of sound and then a swift argument.

"Yes, Naomi, I will return you." Then he's back online with me and in a stiff voice says, "I will return Naomi only when she desires it. I have promised her this."

Before I can say anything else, he hangs up.

"Is she going to be okay?" Regan asks.

I nod and take a few deep breaths. "Yeah, he promises on his dead mother, so you know it's all good."

"Then why is the phone crumpled in your hand?"

I look down and see the burner's plastic face and back are cracked, the edges of it drawing blood from my palm. Tossing it aside, I wrap my arms around Regan because she's become *my* safe harbor. Her neck smells warm and comforting, and the angry pounding in my head over the knowledge of my sweet sister in Petrovich's hands subsides a bit.

"I guess I have to trust him. I've got a pretty big weapon to hold over his head, so unless we're up for a battle with one of the most powerful Russian crime families, I'll just have to believe in his promises. Petrovich took control of his *Bratva* by helping us kill Sergei and Sergei's lieutenants. If the rest of his organization knew that he did this, he'd be killed. Plus"—I rub my forehead—"he really believes in honor and family, which is why he had Sergei killed. Sergei was bringing the Petrovich family to ruin, and Vasily needed to stop him."

"I'll go to Russia with you," Regan offers.

"Know what, fighter? Huge Dicked Daniel is tired. He needs some R and R." The thought of going to Russia and dealing with Petrovich all over again mentally exhausts me. I know Naomi is safe. And I know she's got some bug up her ass about a new project, which means I'd be fighting both of them to bring her home. And for now, I'm just fucking tired of it all. I want to pull Regan into my arms and fuck her for days on end and not have to worry about anything other than running out of condoms.

"R and R is fine," Regan says, smoothing a lock of hair from my forehead in a possessive gesture. "I just want you to know I'm with you. We're a team now, right?"

I squeeze her tight and drop a kiss on the top of her forehead. "We're a team."

"So . . . what does this team do now?"

With effort, I stand up and grab my pack. Holding out my hand, I say, "We go home."

CHAPTER **TWENTY-NINE**

REGAN

I'm holding Daniel's hand as we get out of the taxi and approach the run-down apartment building. It's . . . kind of a dump. "Are you sure this is the right place?"

"It's the address Nick sent me, yeah." He checks his phone again, then shrugs. "He's Ukrainian. Maybe he thinks this is high on the hog."

I wrinkle my nose, but in reality, it's not that bad. It's clean, the roof is all one piece, and there's no trash in the streets. That automatically makes it better than most favelas. "I thought it would be . . . I don't know. I can't imagine Daisy in here." Sweet, adorable little Daisy with the innocent blue eyes that went so wide every time something broke down in our old, beat-up apartment.

"He said it was a fixer-upper," Daniel says and releases my clinging hand to sling both of our bags over his shoulder. Then, he takes it again because he knows I need him. His touch grounds me.

We've been out of Rio for about two days now. Two days of travel, staying in hotel rooms, and more travel. I'm not entirely sure where we've flown; all I know is that it wasn't a straight line. Something about not being obvious and avoiding the wrong people. I don't question. Daniel knows the slippery side of the law better than anyone, and I trust him to keep me safe. I'm still having nightmares, though. It's like now that I know Hudson is dead, he's haunting my dreams. Daniel holds me close and tells me it's normal after what I've been through. He never lets me go.

He's exactly what I need to make me feel whole again.

We head inside and no sooner do I step into the foyer of the apartment building than Daisy's barreling down the stairs and running for me, arms outstretched.

"Regan!" she squeals in a high-pitched, happy tone, and she's on me and hugging me close before I can tell her that I don't like to be touched by anyone but Daniel.

"Daisy," Daniel begins, "Don't . . ."

But it's okay. It's just Daisy, fragile little Daisy with her big, cornflower blue eyes and dark hair and round, innocent face. Daisy, who looks like she should sing in a church choir and says sweet little prayers before bedtime. Daisy, who fell for a hit man and got me into this mess. I shove the bitterness down and hug her back. It's not Daisy's fault that any of this happened. And while I'm not glad I was sold into slavery, I have Daniel now. And Daniel's all that matters.

He's giving me faintly concerned looks as I hug Daisy for a long time, checking to see if I'm okay. I nod at him and hug Daisy back. She smells clean and fresh and as wholesome as ever; and I feel a little better knowing that through all of this, Daisy has remained as innocent and as lovely a person as she ever was. I'm glad, and I mean it.

"It's good to see you," I tell her softly.

She pulls away, tears brimming in her big eyes. "I was so worried about you. But Nick said we sent Daniel, and Daniel's the best there is, so . . ."

"Daniel *is* the best there is," I agree and swat Daniel when I see him begin to make a lascivious face out of the corner of my eye.

"Come upstairs," Daisy tells me, so excited she's practically bouncing like a puppy. "Nick's making dinner."

"Oh shit," Daniel says with a grin. "Now this, I've got to see."

We head up the main stairs of the apartment building. Daisy says that the elevator's busted at the moment. Apparently Nick was trying to fix the wiring, got pissed when it shocked him, and took a sledgehammer to it in retaliation. Daisy looks a little disgruntled at the situation, and I see Daniel smothering a laugh behind her. "He's not very good at being domestic," she tells me, her cheeks glowing.

"And you're letting him make dinner?" I ask, trying not to giggle, myself. It feels so good to have Daniel behind me, his hand on my back to let me know that he's here, and Daisy chattering away in front of me. The stain Rio left on me is falling away like it never existed.

"He insists that he wants to help out," Daisy says with a helpless shrug. "It's so cute. One day, I came home from class and he was making Hamburger Helper. 'I do not understand what it is helping the hamburger to do,' he tells me. I lost it." She giggles even now, thinking about it.

Daisy gives us a quick tour of the apartment building as we

walk. There was water damage on the top floor, so most of those apartments are still being worked on. They're redoing the tile on the bottom floor, and she and Nick are on the second floor, along with an apartment for her father if he ever wants to visit. He doesn't leave his farm much, Daisy tells me, but the fact that he leaves it at all makes her happy.

"And there's an apartment for you," she says, pulling a key off of the key ring and holding it out to me.

"Me?" I'm surprised. "Why?"

"We lost the other apartment," she says in an embarrassed voice. "By the time I got back, there was an eviction notice. All I could do was grab everything, and so we moved here."

"Oh," I say, and my voice is smaller than I'd like. Of course we lost our apartment. I'd been scraping by with scholarship funds before Daisy moved in to pay her share. But for some reason, I thought my apartment would always be there, waiting for me to come back to it when I was ready.

The fact that it's not there kind of rattles me. The world went on while I was gone. Like I never existed. I think of Mike and Becca, and I swallow hard.

"You doing all right, sugar tits?" Daniel says in my ear, his breath warm as he leans in.

Daisy turns and gives us both a horrified look. "What did you call her?"

For some reason, I erupt into giggles. Maybe it's Daisy's aghast expression or the fact that Daniel's so naughty to call me that in front of her, but I lose it. Hysterical, silly laughter bubbles up, and I have to hold my sides, I'm laughing so hard. Daniel chuckles and his fingers brush my cheek affectionately while Daisy looks at me like I'm crazed.

I finally get control and wipe tears from my eyes, still giggling. "It's an inside joke," I tell her since she looks ready to wag a shaming finger in Daniel's face.

"I'm . . . going to go check on Nick and dinner," she tells me and reaches out to wrap my fingers around the key she gave me. "Why don't you check out your apartment? Take your time. We'll keep dinner warm for you." The look on her face is kind and sweet and so totally Daisy that I want to hug her all over again.

I don't, but I think she'd understand why. "Thanks, Daisy."

"We're in 2A," she tells me. "Come by when you're ready."

Then Daisy heads down the hall, and I'm alone with Daniel and my new apartment key. I stare down at the key for a moment, then look over at Daniel. "Sugar tits again, huh?" My lips twitch with laughter.

"Great conversation starter, ain't it?" he drawls.

"I need a conversation starter of my own," I mutter as I put the key in the door. "Like 'sweet dick' or 'pork and beans.'"

"Do I get a vote?" he asks. "Because I'm partial to 'big Johnson' or 'Goddamn Daniel Your Dick's So Huge.'"

I snort and push the door open, trying not to giggle again.

Then I grow silent as I stare at the new apartment.

Daisy's thoughtful, I'll give her that. The new apartment, despite a slightly different layout and a higher ceiling, is set up like my old one. She must have unpacked everything and put it down how it was, right down to my beat-up cookie jar on the counter and my B-grade horror movie posters on the walls. There's even the crappy futon that I had in place of a sofa, and my DVDs are lined up on their familiar shelf.

It's like walking into a dream. "It's my stuff. All of it." Tears brim from my eyes as I walk inside.

"That was nice of Daisy," Daniel says in a careful voice behind me. He sets our bags down on the futon and tucks his gun into his pants, then proceeds to go through the entire apartment, checking it out, while I stand, numb, in the doorway. It's a process of ours, and one that I normally don't mind—especially not after Rio—but it feels weird in this new place with my old stuff. "All clear," he tells me a moment later and then moves past me to shut the door and lock it.

I step inside, still in a daze. There, on my coffee table, there's my old picture of me and Mike from a friend's wedding. I pick it up, staring at his face. I don't feel anything for him, oddly enough. Maybe an irritated twinge that he moved right on to Becca, but there's no love lost, no sadness.

Daniel's arms move around my waist, and he peers over my shoulder. "Is it bad form if I say the guy looks like a lousy fuck?"

I giggle again. "You sound jealous."

"I am jealous," he admits, his arms tightening around my waist. "He should have fucked your brains out and given you a jillion screaming orgasms, but all he did was think of himself." Daniel sounds totally disgruntled.

I put the picture aside and turn in Daniel's arms, wrapping mine around his shoulders. "No need to be jealous. He never gave me one orgasm. You gave me more orgasms last night than he did in all the years we were together."

"I am pretty awesome," he teases, pretending to consider this.

"Pretty awesome," I agree, and suddenly I'm feeling frisky. To think that a guy as gorgeous, sexy, and dangerous as Daniel is jealous of my old boyfriend is kind of . . . sweet. Daniel is a thousand times better to me than Mike ever was. There's no comparison. And I want to show him how sexy I find him. "Have you ever had a blow job on a futon while sitting underneath a poster of *Attack of the Killer Tomatoes*?"

"*Attack of the Killer Tomatoes*? That's a real movie?"

"Oh, it's real. I have it on DVD. That and the sequel."

"You're shitting me. They made a sequel of that?"

"They made a few," I tell him, pushing him backward toward the futon. "Would you rather watch it than get a blow job?"

"Christ, no," he tells me. "But don't you want to go see Daisy and Nick?"

"Soon," I tell him, putting a sultry note in my voice. "But right now I want your cock between my lips and in my mouth."

He groans, and I know I've won this round. I'm delighted as he flops back on the futon, takes the gun out of his pants and tosses it onto the old, beat-up coffee table that I rescued out of a rummage sale. He watches me with hot, avid eyes.

"I love you," I tell him as I sink to my knees in front of him, pushing his legs apart.

"I love you more than anything," he tells me, and he's so serious for a moment, so intense, that I feel a shiver go through my body. Then, I give him another naughty look and unzip his pants.

"This loves me, too, obviously."

"Shit yeah it does," he tells me. "Fucker can't get enough of you."

"Mmm." He's already hard, and I wrap my hands around his length, admiring him. "I think I might have to spoil my dinner with this."

His eyes gleam as he watches me lean in. His hand goes to my hair, stroking it back from my face. "This is the perfect angle for me to watch you suck me."

Even though we talk dirty in bed to each other all the time, with those words, my mind flashes to the brothel. The gun pushed to my forehead. I close my eyes and swallow hard. Those memories aren't gone. I don't know if they'll ever be gone.

But then Daniel's hand is caressing my cheek, the touch loving. "God, you're beautiful."

And just like that, I'm okay again. I open my eyes and it's Daniel's handsome face I see before me, Daniel's skin warm underneath my hands. And when I lean down to drag my tongue over the crown of his cock, it's Daniel's taste on my tongue.

I can make new memories, starting now. I lick the head with a quick swipe and look up at him when his hand fists in my hair. "You trying to distract me, baby boy?"

"Fuck no," he rasps. He lifts his hands in the air as if to show me that he won't touch. "That's the last thing I want."

I take the head in my mouth again and giggle, and I feel him shudder as the vibrations from my laughter move against his skin. My hand grips the thick base of his cock, and I tease and stroke the head with my tongue while my other hand toys with his sac.

I'm pleased when his head falls back on the couch, his entire body tense, and his cock seems to visibly swell in my hands. He's extremely hard, the head leaking pre-come faster than I can lick it up. He loves this, and I love doing it to him. I love the pleasure on his face.

"I want to put my hands all over you right now," Daniel says as I lean in and suck his length into my mouth, careful of my teeth. "Just drag those pretty tits out of your shirt and play with them while you suck my cock."

He's not touching me, though. He's just lying back and watching me work on him. Maybe he realizes that if he grabs me, it'd be too much for me to handle with memories pushing at the back of my mind. This makes me love him all the more, and I show my love by taking him deep and sucking so hard that my cheeks hollow.

His groan of pleasure is delicious to hear, and it makes me redouble my efforts. I practice all the skills that I know, working him with my mouth and now both hands at the base of his cock, pumping him in time with my motions.

"Christ, you're good at that," he rasps when his cock prods at the back of my throat again and I loosen my jaw so my gag reflex doesn't kick in.

I don't respond—my mouth is full. My mouth is full, and my senses are full of Daniel: his salty taste, the feel of his warm skin, the tickle of his groin hairs on my hands as I work him, the pleasure on his face with every pump of my mouth. There's nothing but pleasure here for me.

I'm disappointed when he grabs me and tosses me down on the futon.

Well, almost.

But when he plunges into me, I give a shriek of pleasure and cling to him like a wild woman. His strokes pound me against the futon, and we're slamming it against the wall, and it doesn't matter one bit because we're both coming hard and fast and I'm so happy I might burst.

We don't make it back to Daisy's apartment for well over an hour. And that's okay, too. Somehow, I think Daisy was expecting that.

DANIEL

Making love to Regan in a place where we don't have to keep one eye on the door and one foot on the floor is both weird and amazing. I can't wait to actually go to bed with her and then be able to wake up and have morning sex. Then we can go back to sleep and wake up and have midmorning sex. When I suggested that we stay in the small futon bed and pretend we fell asleep, she shakes her head. Daisy is expecting us. *Well, fuck Daisy*, I think, but I pull on my trousers and join the surly Ukrainian and his farm girl for dinner. At least they have food. In the kitchen, the girls are making drinks that contain candy canes. I don't mind a fruity drink now and then, but I draw the line at candy canes in my booze.

Nick, in a rare fit of insightfulness, invites me to the rooftop. In theory it's a good idea. Go outside and get a fresh perspective. The reality involves standing out in subzero temperatures, which sends my balls inside my body for warmth. I hope the boys come out when we see Regan again. Nick is Ukrainian, so apparently he's impervious to the cold because he's standing in a thin cotton shirt looking like he's enjoying the Arctic breeze. I'm drinking my Shiner Bock as fast as possible to get some heat into my veins.

Nick doesn't speak, merely stares out impassively into the distance. I wonder if he misses Russia or how he feels about the current situation in the Ukraine, but we don't have that kind of relationship, so instead I admire the night landscape. The night is cloudless and the slice of moon brightens up the sky enough so that you can make out the dark blues and black in the atmosphere. It's strange to see Nick without a gun, though. He was an exacting, methodical, and successful hit man. If he took your job, your mark was dead. The only project he didn't complete was his last one, because he had to run off to rescue Daisy in Russia. Now he's an art student and a landlord. The world has turned upside down.

"You are to meet the parents?" Nick asks pensively, as if he is worried for me.

"Tomorrow, first thing," I answer and then frown. No mid-morning sex, then. Maybe we'll have sex first thing when we wake up, and I can eat her out in the shower. That might hold me over until I can have her again around lunchtime. "Why? Did you have issues with Daddy Miller?"

Nick nods. "He does not like people."

"You two should be besties then, because you aren't a people person, either," I point out.

"*Da*, this is true." Of course Nick takes me seriously. While I appreciate his concern, I have no worries about meeting Regan's parents. My biggest issue is what I'm going to do with myself now that I'm not focused on running down my next lead in search of my sister. Fortunately, I don't have to decide that today or tomorrow or even next week. I drain my bottle and reach for another. One positive thing about the frigid temps is sticking your bottles in the snow keeps the beer nice and chill. About four minutes of silence later, after I've completely forgotten about the subject, Nick asks, "Besties?"

"Best friends," I explain. It never fails to surprise me how inept Nick is at social interaction—but given that he spent most of his time killing people, I suppose it made sense to erect emotional barriers. The army is full of people who kill, but it's a family of some sort. A sniper is never without his spotter, and even the recon teams are made up of four to five members. Suddenly I realize that part of the emotional toll the last eighteen months had taken on me is due to the fact that I was alone for most of the time. During my stint as a mercenary, I tried to create connections with others like Nick because I'd missed my team so much, and now I am missing my family. Regan talks about how I can never leave her, but it's me that can't live without Regan. If she were to leave me, I'd be nothing. Might as well shoot me in the head, because her walking away from me would mean I was already dead from heart failure.

"Vasily Petrovich has your sister," Nick muses.

"Yup. I threatened to rat him out to the *Bratva* if he harms her."

"Or we could go kill him," Nick offers as nonchalantly as if he's asking if I want a cigarette. But I guess if you're raised to kill before you can feed yourself, then that's how you act. Who was I to talk? I killed Nick's last mark—the trauma surgeon in Seattle who was harvesting diseased organs and selling them on the black market—so Nick could get out of the business. It was a wedding gift for him and Daisy, although they haven't gotten married yet.

"For some reason I actually trust him. Besides, you aren't allowed to go back to Eastern Europe, remember?"

Nick shrugs. "To kill Petrovich, may be worth it."

I sit, kick out my legs, and drain my second beer, but I don't pop open another. I have plans for Regan tonight that require sobriety. "I'm tired of it, Nick. Tired of killing people, falling asleep with my gun on my chest, not sure if I'll have to wake up shooting. I'm tired of closing my eyes and seeing blood splatter. I want to go to sleep in the same bed every night and wake up in the morning. I want to make love to Regan on a real mattress with soft sheets." Up on the roof I can see the skyline of Minneapolis to the north and the outlines of planes taking off from the airport to the south. I get why Nick has picked this place. Subtle signs of gentrification are everywhere. In a couple of years this place will be worth a fortune, but living in the city, responding to a hundred daily complaints or painting pictures, even ones with a lot of black and red paint, doesn't interest me. I want to go home, show Regan the land that my great-great-grandfather settled. Have her watch the foals being born and the bluebonnets poke their heads out of the earth. Turning to look at Nick to see if he gets it, I say, "I'm done with death."

"*Da*, I am too." He lifts a bottle of vodka. "But what will you do now?"

"Don't know, man. Have any advice for me?" It's a joke, a reference to when Nick asked me dating advice when he was stalking Daisy. But Nick doesn't know how to joke, so he gives it some serious thought—which he washes down with a quarter of the vodka.

"It is easier to decide whether to pull the trigger or use a garrote to take down a mark than know what will bring happiness in the future," Nick finally declares.

"I know Regan makes me happy. I'm going to stick with that. For now, though, why don't you let me take a look at some of your honey-do list."

CHAPTER **THIRTY**

REGAN

Now that we're back in Minneapolis, I have a laundry list of things to do. I go to the doctor and get a birth control shot so Daniel and I can continue to have gloriously, deliciously intense sex. I also get checked for diseases again, because I'm paranoid. I turn up clean of everything, including pregnancy. I'm actually a little sad about that, but now's not the time to start a family.

I also sign up for counseling because I still have panic attacks when Daniel leaves the room for any length of time, and I still have nightmares. I know I'm not totally right in the head. The psychologist understands, though, and she's supportive. Daniel goes with me to counseling, and it's good. It's a step in the right direction.

I want to go back to college and jump right back into my career path, but the psychologist doesn't think it's a good idea, and I'm surprised when Daniel agrees. They want me to take time off and get used to normal again. Normal without so many people, that is, since people still make me anxious. It's weird to think about, but I try to submerge myself back into "normal." I watch a lot of horror movies with Daniel, and we paint our apartment for something to do.

I visit my parents, and it's as tear-filled and awkward as I thought it would be.

I don't tell them that I've spent two months on my back in a brothel. I think that would break them almost as much as it came close to breaking me. We come up with a lame cover story instead. I took an impromptu vacation with my roomie Daisy to Cancun, hit my head while cliff diving, and Daisy thought I'd drowned. I woke up in a hospital with amnesia and just now got better. And Daniel was in the bed next to me with a tropical disease, and we fell in love.

It's all very *Days of Our Lives*, and I'm not entirely sure they buy it, but it's a nicer story than the truth.

Nevertheless, they're concerned for my health now. They want me to come home for good. I can't, though. I'm not their little girl anymore. We stay with them for a few days, but it makes me restless. It's clear that they don't understand, nor do they understand why Daniel needs to clear a room before I go in because it makes me feel safer.

Daisy's my new best friend and always at my side. When Daniel and Nick are busy working on the apartment building, Daisy goes shopping with me or runs errands with me or whatever needs to be done. I'm not alone for a second, and it makes me feel safer. I don't know if Daniel's asked her to be my shadow or if she senses that I'm scared of being abandoned, but I appreciate it either way. Her attentiveness has gone a long way to resolving the festering resentment I've been harboring against her.

And one day, I get a wild hair up my ass to go and visit Mike and Becca. I don't bring Daniel; I'm half afraid that he would shoot Mike because he can't stand him for being, well, Mike. For being selfish and self-absorbed and hooking up with my best friend. I don't think it's Mike's fault as much as it is mine, though. I went along with everything before. That's not me anymore.

I do take Daisy with me, though, because I don't like to go anywhere alone. We pull up to Mike's apartment building, and it's one I'm intimately familiar with. How many times did I drive over after a football game for a quick fuck and cuddle because Mike wanted to get laid? How was I ever okay with that?

"You sure you want to do this?" Daisy asks me for the hundredth time as we walk into the building and head for the elevator.

"I'm sure," I tell her. "Mike deserves closure, too, don't you think?"

"I suppose," Daisy says, and she looks troubled. She's a good friend. I squeeze her hand to let her know it's okay, and we head up to the fifth floor, where Mike has lived for the past few years.

And we knock on his door, even though I have a key back in the apartment. It's taped to the bottom of my cookie jar. It was only for emergencies, after all. In case Mike needed something taken care of when he was out of town with buddies. It wasn't so I could let myself in whenever.

Man, I really was a doormat before. I smirk to myself at the thought. Wonder what Mike's going to think of me now.

He answers the door. I'm a little disappointed it's not Becca, because wouldn't that be a great conversation starter. But Mike looks utterly stunned to see me. "Oh my God. Regan."

And he bursts into tears and reaches out to hug me close.

I have to admit, this is not the way I pictured our reunion. I pat his back awkwardly and give Daisy a helpless glance as Mike hugs me and blubbers on my shoulder. He's so thankful to see me alive again, he says between gulping sobs. He thought I was dead.

And then he pulls back and tries to kiss me, and I recoil.

"Don't," I say. I don't want to be kissed by him, ever again.

He looks shocked that I pull away from him. "What's wrong? Baby, are you okay?"

"What's wrong? Mike, I know you're with Becca." I can see her shit on his kitchen counter from where I'm standing.

He shakes his head, and his face is a little paler. I notice that he starts to close the door to his apartment behind him, blocking our view, and I fight the urge to giggle when sweet little Daisy rolls her eyes at this move. "No, baby. That was, you know, a thing. We were comforting each other."

"Uh-huh," I say flatly. "How fast did you two start comforting each other? I'm curious. Was it a day or two after I was kidnapped or did you wait a whole week?"

Judging from the ugly flush that crosses his cheeks, I'm not hitting far off the mark. He's embarrassed. "It's not like that, Regan. I was . . . so upset when you disappeared." He squeezes my shoulder and gets choked up again. "I kept drinking, and Becca came over to talk some sense into me. And she . . . kinda never left."

"You make it sound like Becca hopped onto your dick."

He shakes his head again and tries to rub my arm, but I bat his hand away. "Baby, you know I love you and only you." He smiles at me through his tears. "Are you . . . are you okay?"

"Better than you," I say, and I'm surprised to find that it's the truth. He's got snot running down his face, and he's a mess. His shirt's filthy, stained with breakfast. It looks like he hasn't shaved in a week or two, and his hair is greasy. He does look like he's gone through hell.

Which is ironic since I'm the one that went through hell, not him. But when his eyes tear up again, I find myself patting him on the shoulder. "I don't think you meant badly by it, Mike," I say. "I'm sure you were hurting and lonely. And it's always been all about you."

"What?" he says, as if he didn't hear me right.

"Did you even look for me, Mike? Or did you hear I was missing, throw your hands up, and start fucking my old BFF?"

His eyes dart back and forth from my impassive face to Daisy's, looking for sympathy. He won't find any here. "Why are you blaming me?" he says in a sad voice. "I did everything I could. The police said they would handle it."

"I'm sure they did," I say. And maybe in his mind, Mike thinks that he did do everything. Maybe he can go to sleep at night knowing he placed a few phone calls and was appropriately sad that his girlfriend disappeared. Maybe that's all that's required for Mike.

But I think of Daniel. I think of him searching through the hellish streets and digging through brothels for a year and a half, looking for Naomi. I think of all we went through together. And I know if I went missing, he'd tear the world apart to try to find me.

He'd never stop.

And . . . I smile. I'm with the right man. I may have had to go through hell to get to his side, but I'm where I need to be now.

Mike returns my smile tentatively, but he's clearly confused. "You want to come in, honey?"

"No," I tell him. "And I'm not your honey anymore. Becca is now." I clasp his hand. "I hope you two are very happy together."

"But . . . no," Mike begins. "Regan, I want you—"

I shake my head. "I'm here to give you closure, Mike." I give his hand a little squeeze. "You and I are done. I've moved on, and you did, too."

He starts to cry again, and Daisy's expressive face has gone from scowling to horrified all over again, which I'll laugh about later when I tell Daniel all about this. "But, Regan, I love you, not Becca."

"Then I suggest you give her some closure, too," I say lightly and give him an impulsive hug. I pull away before he can entangle me in his arms again. "Good-bye, Mike."

I hear his blubbering good-bye as Daisy and I walk down the hall. He doesn't come after me. Mike's not the type. And before, I wasn't the type of girl that thought she needed that kind of guy.

Guess we've both changed.

DANIEL

Regan tells me that she has visited Mike and that he's happy she's moved on. I give two shits about Mike's mental state and still think that I'd be doing the world a favor by putting him down like the diseased, worthless dog he is, but I figure Regan would not be okay with that. All that really matters is that she's happy.

We had a good time visiting her parents again. They still treat me like I'm a god—as if falling in love while she has amnesia is some great accomplishment. The one good thing about visiting her parents is that they give us a ton of food that Regan and I eat for a couple of days after. Maybe I should look into a cooking class. Regan's not the best cook, and neither am I. One of us is going to have to learn to operate the stove for something other than heating up soup.

I did make a mistake of complaining about the cold, which prompted her dad to produce an old jacket that made me look like I was the Stay Puft Marshmallow Man. Later that night she had us watch *Ghostbusters*, which was, she said, sort of a horror movie. Regan asked me to put on the jacket, and she stuck two pieces of paper on my head to mimic the creature's hat. I did so because she was laughing so hard that there were happy tears in her eyes. I would act out mime sketches in the park if it would keep that jaw-dropping smile on her face. But she agreed I needed warmer clothes, so the next day we went to one of the banks where Naomi had deposited the money she stole from the drug dealers. Regan was stunned by the amount. I kind of expected it. Naomi had been treated well primarily because she was so valuable.

"You can be a lady of leisure," I joke as we leave the bank. I'd just wanted enough cash to buy my own jacket, one that didn't feel like I was walking around wearing two pillows stitched together, but the amount in this one account leaves me thinking I could buy that island compound.

"That sounds terrible," she says. "I'd go crazy sitting around doing nothing."

"On the bright side, it's a good thing you know about accounting."

"I don't think my calculator goes up that high," she answers with disgruntlement.

Kissing her forehead, I place an arm around her shoulder as

we walk to the bus stop. "Just think, you can put a sticker on your backpack that says 'My other bag is Hermès.'"

She punches me in the gut, but the padding of the coat completely shields me. Huh, maybe this is good for something.

I keep myself busy doing handyman work for Nick. For a guy who could watch a mark for hours without moving, he's showing surprisingly little patience with the mundane things around the apartment building.

"You really think that being a landlord is the right occupation for you?" I call after Nick's retreating back as he stomps out of the first-floor apartment to turn the water off. We are attempting to hook up the sink, but apparently we've done something wrong. I'm pretty good at breaking shit, shooting guns, and running cattle—but wiring and plumbing? That's like trying to figure out the inner workings of a female mind. It takes time and patience, neither of which Nick is displaying nor am I interested in exerting.

Regan is off at the university trying to argue that she should be allowed to take her tests and get her degree, rather than go through an entire semester's worth of classes again. One thing about living in a world with rules, you can't hold a gun to someone's head and force them to do your will. Or I guess I could, but Regan wouldn't allow that. I flip the wrench in my hand. It's heavy, and the ratchet end would do a lot of damage. I could kill a man with a well-placed blow to the temple. Definitely incapacitate someone by a strike to the knee or the elbow. I swing out my arm to test the air resistance against the heavy steel tool.

"What are you doing?"

Jerking up, I see Regan at the door left ajar by Nick. "Ah, nothing?" I prevaricate, moving from my lunge position where I was kneecapping an imaginary foe with my new weapon. Guiltily, I set the wrench behind me on the counter and stride toward her.

"Looks like you were practicing some kind of assassin moves." Skepticism is clear in her face and voice.

Pulling Regan into my arms, I place wet kisses along the column of her throat. "You never know when I'll need to protect you from a spider or cockroach. I can't allow my skills to get rusty."

Tilting her head to the side, she allows me greater access to the sensitive skin on her neck. She shudders when I reach the hidden spot behind her ear. Her arms slide around me, and thoughts of home repair drop out of my head to be replaced by the feel of her lush body against mine. Regan's been eating regularly since we've left Brazil, and it looks good on her—not to mention how much I enjoy the feel of her roundness in my palms.

"God, you are so fucking hot. Let's go upstairs." Without waiting for a response, I lift her over my shoulder and squeeze one delectable ass cheek.

"I'm losing all the blood in my head," she complains.

"Not to worry. Soon it will be between your legs." This is a good position, because she can't see my smug expression.

"That's you, baby boy."

"I thought we'd agreed you'd call me Huge Dicked Daniel."

My reward is a few more pummels to my back, but those little punches turn to caresses once we are inside the bedroom and my head is between her legs. Her hands knead my shoulders as I concentrate on the taste and smell of her fantastic pussy.

When I finally do enter her, she rewards me with a dreamy smile and a breathy observation. "You do have a huge cock, Daniel."

"It's getting bigger with every compliment," I grunt, clutching the flesh at her hips and driving hard into her sweet warmth.

"It's humongous. Bigger than an elephant."

My quakes are from laughter, and I allow her to flip me over and ride me like I'm a wild mustang. Sex with Regan is glorious— fun, intense, passionate.

After a sweaty bout of bed play, Regan swirls her index finger in the whorls of my chest hair. If I had any sensation left in my body this might have been ticklish, but she has worn me out.

"You seem restless lately."

"I think we need a bigger bed. Not enough room in here to really do everything that I've been fantasizing about."

She tugs on a few hairs. "I'm serious. I'm worried about you. I don't think general handyman is what you want to do for the rest of your life."

I roll her over and pin her arms above her head. "If the rest of my life is spent with you, then it's all good. That's the only thing I have going on of any importance."

"Then you should stick your cock inside me again." Her voice is playful, but her eyes contain a worry I don't really know how to dispel. "Do you want to go home?"

"I am home." I'm not deliberately misunderstanding Regan. It's the truth. My home is with her. "As long as you love me, I'm complete." She looks like she wants to protest or argue some more, but I've got other ideas. Swinging her up in my arms, I carry her to the shower, where I show her how good home feels. It doesn't matter that I can't go home until Naomi is done with her thing in Russia, because I wouldn't leave Regan anyway. Not for all the ranch land in Texas.

The next day, I'm back working on the sink. Nick's at art class, and I'm getting a lot done without him around to curse in Ukrainian and kick the pipes. The bathroom sinks are connected, and I have to add a U trap and connect the garbage disposal and I'll be done. Regan is wrong. I'm getting the hang of the fix-it stuff, and I don't mind it. I'm so caught up in my work that I don't hear the door open or the footsteps that trample into the apartment. I don't even realize I'm not alone until I crawl out from underneath the sink to see my old man standing next to Regan, looking like he's about thirty years older than his actual age.

"Dad," I say warily, pulling off the leather work gloves and tossing them into the sink. "You're a long way from the ranch." I can't remember the last time my old man left Texas. I blink a few times to make sure I'm not hallucinating.

"It was a direct flight from Dallas," he says shortly and looks around the room at everything but me. I take the opportunity to look quizzically at Regan, but she just smiles mysteriously. "Nice place."

"Not mine." I can match him word for short word if that's what it comes to. Regan throws up her hands like she can't believe me and turns a brilliant smile on my dad. Given that Regan is hotter than a dozen Dallas Cowboys cheerleaders, that smile works on my dad better than bacon grease on a skillet. He blinks a couple of times in stunned appreciative silence, and then she takes mercy on him by walking over to me and slaying me with the same look.

Fortunately I'm building up immunity to it, so I'm only out of it for half the time. "So, Dad, it's good to see you. Mom with you?"

He shakes his head. "Your sister . . ." He stops and clears his throat. The mention of Naomi makes me stiff as a board. "Your sister called and said she's working on a project and that she can't come home yet."

"She emailed and said she was doing good," I tell him. Part of my deal with Vasily is regular contact; sometimes he has to interrupt her to get her to conduct her daily check-in. Naomi gets lost in her own world a lot of the time.

Dad nods. "Yes."

And then there's nothing else we say to each other until Regan throws up her hands and cries, "For God's sake. You two are impossible. Naomi called me and asked why we hadn't gone to the ranch, and I said you couldn't go home until she got back. She then told me she didn't know when she was coming back, so we called your parents together. Daniel, your parents want you to go back."

A rush of emotion rolls over me, and I stagger a step, grateful that Regan is right beside me. "Is that true?"

Dad nods, looking down at the floor at first, and then raises his wet eyes to meet mine. "We miss you, son. Your momma, she needs her boy."

It's hard to speak because I've got a big old frog in my throat, but after a minute I'm able to turn to Regan. "You wanna come see my home?"

She gives me that heart-slaying smile and says, "I'm with you until my last breath."

CHAPTER **THIRTY-ONE**

REGAN

We drive down from Minnesota to Texas so I can take my boxes of DVDs, my clothes, and my tiny hatchback car with us. Daisy weeps the entire time we say good-bye, promising to come visit. Nick looks as stoic and Ukrainian as ever, though he and Daniel exchange a quick, one-armed bro-hug before we depart.

It's strange, but I'm not sad to be leaving Minnesota behind. It's a clean break. I'm transferring my college hours to a local university. I don't have much left in Minnesota that I can't take a weekend and visit. And if Daniel is going to Texas, then that's where I want to be.

We take a few days and drive down, stopping at rest stops and taking pictures next to WELCOME TO— state signs for fun. We hit up a few tourist traps, eat at greasy spoon diners, and park the car and make love in the cramped backseat when we can't stand it any longer. It's the most fun I've ever had on a road trip. Every day that I wake up and see Daniel's face next to mine in the bed, I am so thankful that he's all for me, that he never gives up on me, even when I'm at my most needy and demanding. Not every guy would take up with a damaged girl fresh out of a whorehouse. But Daniel has never made me feel dirty or used or anything but incredibly beautiful.

So if he wants to go to Texas and help his parents on the farm? We are heading to Texas. There's not a question in my mind.

Texas is definitely not what I expect. I guess I have nonstop cowboys and longhorns on my mind, so it's surprising to me when I notice that the biggest thing about Texas is that . . . it's flat. It's flat for miles and miles around. There are some stumpy trees, but overall, there's endless rolling grass. Daniel tells me that West Texas, which is where we are headed, is different from East Texas, which is nothing but trees. I think he's pulling my leg, but whatever.

The Hays ranch is right smack-dab in the middle of nowhere. I'm surprised when we turn off a road and see a big metal gate with a sideways *H* bisected by a *D*. "That's our brand," Daniel tells me, and there's a hint of pride in his voice. It's fascinating.

"And what is it exactly that you brand?" I ask him as we drive through the gate.

"You know. Steer, calves, blondes that don't behave." He gives me a waggle of his eyebrows that makes me snort.

"Guess I'd better behave, then," I tell him in a sultry voice, and I love the fact that he groans and clutches at my knee.

"You'd better," he tells me. "Because I can't have wood in my pants when I hug my mom."

I'm giggling as we roll down the long driveway and park in

front of the ranch house. It's a monstrosity of wood and stone and has a long, wraparound porch. In any other state, it'd be called a mansion. Here, it's called home.

As soon as we get out of the car, two people come out of the house. It's Daniel's dad and a woman with a cap of gray hair who must be his mother. She's weeping and has her arms outstretched even before she makes it off the porch. Then she's hugging Daniel and crying and his dad piles on, and they're lost in their own little world for a few minutes.

Then, Daniel's mother breaks away, wiping at her cheeks, and heads for me with her arms outstretched. "Oh my. This must be Regan. She's so beautiful, Daniel." And she envelops me in a warm hug before I can sidle away.

Her touch makes me stiffen for a moment, but then Daniel's hand goes to my shoulders, and I'm okay. "Mom, I told you—"

"Oh," she gasps, her hands flying away. "I'm so sorry—"

"It's okay," I say quickly, before anyone can get offended. "I'm fine."

She gives me a sweet smile. "I was so excited to see my new daughter."

New daughter? Is there something I don't know about? I give Daniel a suspicious look, but he only pulls me in for a kiss. "I told her we were a package deal. I think she took that as we're getting married."

"Oh," I say, startled. "Like . . . right now?"

Daniel laughs. "Maybe not right now, but . . . soon?" There's a question in his eyes, and I'm surprised and pleased all at once.

"Maybe when I get a real proposal," I tease him, sass in my voice.

"Demanding little fighter," he says, a grin on his face.

And then his mother is chattering up a storm, and his father has this patient look on his face that reminds me so much of Daniel in his quieter moments, and, like that, we're home.

Hours later, I'm crawling into bed with Daniel. The ranch house has a split-house plan, which I've never seen before. Daniel and I are in what feels like a separate little house, connected to the main house by a covered walkway in the back. There's a bedroom, a luxurious bathroom, and even a tiny kitchen. Across from our little house is the pool, and in the distance are the stables. Daniel tells me the house was built as a mother-in-law cabin, but was never used until now. It's perfect, really. We're private enough from his family but close enough to spend lots of time with them.

The day has been a busy one. I've been given the grand tour of the ranch, complete with hundreds of longhorns, a trip through the barn, and a ride around the perimeter. It's like they own their own little island of land.

I like that. It's like a minifortress, but instead of gunmen, there are cattle. Either way, it makes me feel safe.

Daniel seems to be happy, too. There's a light in his eyes that I never saw in Rio, and when he looks at me, he can't stop smiling. I know what it is—his picture is complete. He's found Naomi, and even though she won't come home, she's safe. He's home with his family. He's got me.

"Tomorrow," he tells me as he drags my body against his and begins to press kisses on my neck. "Tomorrow, we ride horses, and I'll show you the newborn baby goats. You'll like those. Cute little buggers." His hand slides to my breast and cups it.

"Mmm." I drag my fingers through his hair. "Are you planning on turning me into a farm girl? Because I'm warning you, the moment something poops, I'm out of there. You might be disappointed."

He chuckles and rolls my nipple between his fingers, distracting me. "Fighter, I am never disappointed with you."

For some reason, this brings tears to my eyes. "No?" It comes out a little softer and more tear-warbled than I wanted it to be. Daniel thinks I'm strong, but I seem to be weepy.

"Never," he tells me fervently and rolls on top of me. Then, he gazes down at me, his fingers grazing my jaw. "How could I ever be disappointed in you, Regan? You're a little damaged. So am I. Maybe we're both a little more fucked up than normal, but we'll be nice and fucked up together. And someday, we're going to have a family, and Naomi will be home, and we'll all manage the land together."

I nod, because it sounds beautiful. "Together."

"Until my last breath," Daniel murmurs again. "I'll never leave your side. Ever."

And I know it's true.

If you wish to receive an email when the next book in the Hitman series is released, text BOOKNEWS to 66866. By texting BOOKNEWS from your mobile number, you agree to receive text messages requesting your email address and confirming your wish to receive an email about the next book. Your consent is not a condition of purchase. Standard messaging and data costs may apply.

ACKNOWLEDGMENTS

Special thanks to Lisa and Milasy from the Rock Stars of Romance for their unflagging support and encouragement. We've had such a great time working together.

To our early readers: Daphne, Heather, and Katy. Your insight was invaluable.

To Veronica Mesquita, who so kindly helped us out with the Portuguese words.

Thank you to all of the bloggers who participated in our blog tour and/or reviewed our books. We know that your help is invaluable.

To all the reviewers who've left reviews and readers who've read our book, we will never be able to give enough thanks.

Read on for an excerpt from

LAST **HIT**

The love story of Nick and Daisy.
Available now from Berkley Books
And watch for Vasily and Naomi's story
to be published in May 2015!

CHAPTER **ONE**

DAISY

I have planned for this day in secret for six long years, I think as I wake up and stretch, a giddy burn in my stomach that might be nerves.

Today, I will escape.

The day starts as any other. It's like the world can't see how excited I am inside, but I'm practically vibrating with anticipation. Freedom is so close I can taste it. I get out of bed and dress in a dark, floor-length skirt and matching blouse. I throw a sweater on over it, so every inch of my body is covered. Then I go to my mattress and pull out the disposable cell phone and the small wad of cash I have saved up.

Seven hundred dollars from six years of saving. It has to be enough. I tuck them both into my bra to hide them.

I go to the bathroom and pull my dark hair into a ponytail and then splash water on my face to cleanse it. I stare at my reflection. My face is bleach pale, but there's a flush on my cheeks that betrays me. I don't like it, and I wet a cloth and press it to my cheeks, hoping the color will fade. When I can't delay any longer, I leave the safety of my bathroom.

My father is seated in the living room. The room is a dark cave. No light comes in. There's a chair and a sofa, and a TV. The TV is off, and I know it's only programmed to broadcast happy, chaste channels like religious TV or children's shows. If I'm lucky, I get to watch PBS. I long for something edgier, but my father has removed everything else from the channel list, and I'm not allowed the remote.

As usual, the only light in the room is a small lamp beside his chair. It halos his recliner, and my father is seated in an island of light in the oppressive darkness. He reads a thick hardback— Dickens—and closes it when I enter the room. He's dressed in a button-up shirt and slacks, his hair neatly combed. It is ironic that my father dresses so well, considering he doesn't leave the house and no one will see him but me. If I ask, he will simply say that appearances are important.

Our entire house is like the living room: dark, oppressive, thick with shadow. It's sucking the life out of me, day by day, which is why I must do what I can to escape.

"Sir." I greet my father, and wait. My hands are clasped behind my back, and I'm the picture of a dutiful daughter.

He eyes my clothing, my sweater. "Are you going out today?"

"If the weather is nice today." I don't look at the windows in the living room. Not a shred of light comes through them. It's not possible. Despite my father's pristine appearance, the house looks like a construction zone. The arching windows that once filled the living room with light are boarded up with plywood, the edges smoothed down with yards of duct tape. Father has made the living room into a fortress to protect himself, but I have grown to hate the oppressive feel of it. I feel like a bat trapped in a cave, never to see sunlight.

I can't wait to escape.

He grunts at my words and hands over a small key. I take it from him with a whispered thank-you and go to the computer desk. It has a roll-down top that my father locks every night. He doesn't trust the Internet, of course. It's full of bad things that can corrupt young minds. He has a filter set up on the browsers so I can't browse explicit websites, not that I would. Not when the only computer in the house is ten feet from his chair.

I calmly go to the computer and type in the address for the weather website. Today's forecast? Perfect. Of course it is. "The weather looks good."

"Then you will run errands today." He pulls on a pair of glasses and picks up a notepad, flipping through it. After a moment, he rips off a piece of paper and hands it to me. "This is the grocery list. Go to the post office and get stamps as well."

I take the list with trembling fingers. Two places today. "Can I go to the library, too?"

He frowns at my request.

I hold my breath. I need to go to the library. But I can't look too anxious.

"I'm already sending you to two places, Daisy."

"I know," I tell him. "But I'd like a new book to read."

"What topic?"

"Astronomy," I blurt. I'm only allowed to read nonfiction

around my father. It's a harmless topic, outer space. And if he presses, I can say I'm continuing my education despite finishing my homeschooling years ago. Father won't relax his grip enough for me to go to college, so I have to continue my learning as best I can.

He stares at me for a long moment, and I worry he can see right through me, into my plans. "Fine," he says after an eternity. He checks his watch. "It's eight thirty now. You'll be back by ten thirty?"

It's not much time to go to the grocery store, the post office, and the library. I frown. "Can I have until eleven?"

His eyes narrow. "You can have until ten thirty, Daisy. You are to go to those places and nowhere else. It's not safe. Do you understand me?"

"Yes, sir." I close the computer, lock the desk, and hand the key back to him.

As I do, he grabs my arm and frowns. "Daisy, look at me."

Oh no. I force my guilty eyes to his gaze. He knows what I'm doing, doesn't he? Even though I've been so careful, he's figured it out.

"Are you wearing makeup?"

Is that all? "No, Father—"

His hand slaps my cheek in reproach.

We both stare at each other in shock. He's never hit me before. Never.

My father recovers first. "No, *sir*," he says, to correct me. I stare at him for so long that my eyes feel dry with the need to blink. Resentment burns inside of me, and for a long moment, I wonder what my father would do if I slapped back. Or if I marched down to the basement and shot off a few rounds into the wall of phonebooks that acted as the backstop for father's makeshift (and probably illegal) indoor shooting range.

But I can't think like that. Not right now. I'm not yet strong enough. So I swallow my anger.

"No, *sir*," I echo. Calling him "sir" is a new rule. Now that I'm twenty-one, I'm not allowed to call him "Father" anymore. Just "sir." My heart aches at how much he's changed—as if every year the terror in him grows stronger and if I stay here, it will overtake me, too.

He grabs my face with his other hand and examines it closely, though I know it's dark enough that he can't see me all that well. The festering resentment continues to bubble in my stomach, but I permit this. It won't be much longer. After today, I won't have to deal with this ever again.

After a moment, he licks his thumb and rubs it on my flushed cheek, inspecting it under the light. No makeup. He makes a *hmmph* sound. "Fine. You can go."

"Thank you, sir," I tell him. I take the list he hands me, and the cash, and rush to the front door.

There are six locks and four deadbolts on the door, and it takes a moment for my trembling fingers to undo all of them. I get to go out.

I get to leave.

I'm never entering this house again.

Once the door is unbolted, I carefully shut it again and then wait a moment. The sound of my father locking and turning all the bolts again reaches my ears. Good. I stand on the covered porch for a moment and stare out at our yard. Our small house has a rickety fence in the front that is falling down, but we don't repair it. The grass is knee high because Father won't let me mow it but once a month. Surrounding our house are acres and acres of farmland that we let out to neighboring farmers. We don't grow anything ourselves, since that would entail being outside.

And the Millers don't go outside unless they can't help it. I know that when I was eight, he witnessed my mother's murder while shopping. I was too young to remember much about her, just a smiling, happy face with warm brown hair and even warmer eyes that disappeared one day. And I know that my father reported her murder to the police but that the killer was underage. A fluke, a random shooting at a grocery store, and my mother had been the victim. Two years later, the murderer was back out on the streets, and he'd commented in court that he was coming after my father for locking him away.

I think it was bravado, nothing but the bragging of a young boy full of rage. My father took it to heart. He refuses to go outside, believing himself safe and protected in his home.

I can't hate him for it. I want to, but I can't. I know what it's like to live every day in fear.

I head down the road, practically running to the bus stop so I'll have time to do everything. The bus arrives a few minutes later, and I go to the local grocery store. I get my cart as if it's just another day. I shop for the items on the list, taking great care with my selections. When I get to the checkout, they frown at me. They recognize my face. They hate me at this grocery store, but I don't care.

As soon as I have my purchases bagged, I immediately head to the customer service counter. I place two of the items I've bought—vitamins and ibuprofen—on the counter. "I need to exchange these."

The clerk there knows my routine. I'm sure she thinks I'm

crazy, but she simply waves a hand. "Get what you need and bring it back."

I do, and five minutes later I have exchanged the expensive, pricey brands for two cheap generics. After years of receipt scanning, I know which ones don't print brand names on the receipt and I always, always switch them out and pocket the change. It's the only way I can save money and not have Father notice it missing.

Now I have seven hundred and fifteen dollars.

I take the groceries with me to the post office, get the stamps, and then head to the library. I should have gone to the library first so the groceries would stay colder, but today, I don't care.

I head to the romance shelf, looking for the book I was reading. It's there, tucked safely behind other books so no one will borrow it until I'm done reading it. I fish it out and read chapter seven while standing up. I wish I could take the book home with me, but Father would never let me keep it. I'm only allowed to read classics. So I come to the library as often as I can and read a chapter at a time.

I close my book with a dreamy sigh a few minutes later. The hero has just kissed the heroine and is sliding his hand into her panties. I want to read on, but I mustn't. There's still so much to do. I will dream about how he touches her, I'm sure. I want to be touched, too.

I want a hero. A big, strong, handsome prince to come rescue me from my miserable life. But since one has not arrived, I must rescue myself.

I soar through the nonfiction and grab a book on astronomy. Then I pause, and I put the book back. I don't know why I'm keeping up the pretense. I'm not going home to Father. Not today. I head back to the romance section and grab my novel.

Then, I move to the computers and pull up the Gmail address I have created for myself. If Father only knew that the library had computers to use that could access the Internet, he'd never let me come here.

There's a response in my email. I dance in my chair, so excited I can barely stand it.

Daisy,

I'm so glad you found my ad! You sure you don't want to see the place before you come here? It's not the greatest, but it's a roof over the head, and the rent is cheap enough. Come by and say hello before you decide anything. We'll have lunch.

XOXO
Regan

There's a phone number at the bottom of the email. I print it out, along with the original Craigslist listing for the apartment in Minneapolis. Will she get upset if I meet her for lunch and then just never leave? I hope not.

There is a second email as well. This one is a confirmation of an appointment. Today, at ten thirty. The timing is perfect.

I also print out the bus schedule. I check out my book and head home. The bus drops me off on the road fifteen minutes before the person I've scheduled will arrive. Nerves begin to gnaw at me. I walk exceedingly slowly, watching for a car to pull up in front of my father's boarded-up farmhouse.

It shows up right on time, and I rush to meet the man that emerges from the car. He's big, middle-aged, balding. No-nonsense looking. He wears dark scrubs and frowns when I come running out of the bushes, grocery bags in hand.

"I'm Daisy Miller," I say breathlessly and extend my hand to him.

"John Eton," he says, and glances at our house, taking in the boarded-up windows, the overgrown lawn. "Someone lives here?"

"My father." At his skeptical look, I say, "He's agoraphobic. He won't leave the house. That's why the windows are boarded up." I want to tell him so much more about my father's craziness and his controlling nature, which has gotten worse over the years, but I can't. I need to leave.

A look of sympathy crosses the man's face. "I see."

"He's going to need an assistant twice a week," I tell him. "That's why I've hired the service—you." I sound so calm, even though I'm dancing inside. "I need you to come by and see what errands he needs to be completed. Check in on him when he needs it. He doesn't use email and won't answer his phone unless you ring once, hang up, and then ring again. That's how he knows who is calling."

John Eton stares at me like I'm the crazy one. "I see."

"When you knock at the door, you have to knock four times," I tell him. "Same reason."

"All right," he says. "Shall we go in and say hello?"

I hold the two grocery bags out to him. "I'm not going in."

"I'm sorry?"

"I'm leaving," I say, and I offer him the grocery bags again. To my relief, he takes them. "Father . . . wants me to stay. And I can't. I can't stay any longer." Tears well up in my eyes, but I blink them away. I love my father, I do. I just can't live with him for one more moment. The entire world is out here, waiting. "I hired you to take care of him. His disability check is direct deposited on the first. I've set up the service to be auto-debited on the fifth of every month. I just need someone to come out and take care of him, since he won't leave the house."

"I see." John doesn't look happy, but he glances at the house and then back to me. "Are you running away?"

I'm twenty-one. Can adults truly run away? But I nod. "I can't take it any longer."

Sympathy crosses his face again. "I understand. Is there a number I can reach you at in case there are any questions? Or if something goes wrong?"

I'm startled at his words, guilt coursing through me. Something . . . goes wrong? I'm leaving my father in the care of this man. A stranger. A service I've hired that won't care that he has a panic attack if he hears a car backfire, who won't care that my father weeps when he goes to bed every night, who won't care that even a hint of sunlight in the living room will send him into hysterics.

But I can't think about that, because if I do, I'll end up staying. I give him the number of my disposable phone, knowing I won't answer it. There's too much guilt involved. My father will be heartbroken and angry that I have left without so much as a good-bye. But I know my father. I know that if I go in and confront him, he'll overpower me. Not physically, but with guilt.

And I have to leave. I just have to.

So when John steps toward the house, I clutch my wallet close and then run. Tears stream down my face as I go, but they're not tears of sadness.

They're joy.

The sun is bearing down on me, the birds are singing in the trees, and for the first time, the world is wide open.

I'm free.

Clutching the printout close, I head up the dirty stairs to the fifth floor of the apartment building.

I have just gotten off of a six-hour bus ride to Minneapolis, and it feels good to stretch my legs. I should be tired, but I feel invigorated instead. I'm free. I'm free. I'm free.

Earlier, I texted Regan to let her know I was on my way. We set up a meet up at the apartment, and then we're going to go to dinner afterward to hang out and get to know each other and see if we mesh and I want to move in. I don't care if she's the most obnoxious person in the world. I've lived with a difficult, demanding person for twenty-one years. Nothing she says or does can be that bad. I will still want to move in.

The building is dirty, but it's buzzing with life. There are people hanging out in the hallways, chatting, and people out on the streets. I smile at everyone. I can't stop smiling. I'm so excited to be out living a real life. A normal life, like everyone else my age.

I find Regan's apartment—224. It's at the end of the hall. I knock, and a moment later it's answered.

A cheerful blonde opens the door. She's tall, statuesque, and gorgeous. She's wearing tight-fitting clothing and her hair is curled into loose waves. Regan is beautiful. She lights up at the sight of me. "Are you Daisy Miller?"

I smooth a stray lock of brown hair into my ponytail, feeling very plain next to her. "That's me. You must be Regan Porter."

"You're so cute! Not what I imagined at all." She examines

me with an excited look on her face. "But . . . I hate to ask. You sure you're not pulling my leg about how old you are?"

"I'm twenty-one," I say, pulling out my identification card. It's not a driver's license; that would have involved Father letting me leave the house for longer than an hour at a time. I make a mental note that I need to learn how to drive in this new life.

She takes the card from me and nods. "Sorry. I just had to ask. You have this . . . I don't know. You look younger than I thought." She squints at me. "Or just sweeter, I guess. Anyhow, how's it going?" Her enthusiasm is back, and she waves a hand at me. "Don't just stand there. Come on in!"

I enter the apartment, clutching my wallet to my chest, and look around. It's a tiny apartment, easily a quarter the size of my father's house. The walls are grimy and there are cracks in the corners, but the back wall has three enormous windows that give a view of the city, and I'm pleased to see that they're wide open. Sunlight pours in, shining on scuffed wooden floors. There are posters of horror movies up on the walls, and a futon for a couch. There's a folding chair off to one side and an ugly coffee table.

I love it.

"I know it's not much to look at, but I'm slowly furnishing by hitting estate sales," Regan says to me with a grin. "It'll get there."

"It's just fine," I say enthusiastically. "I love it."

She laughs. "Well, you're not hard to convince. So Pollyanna of you. I like that. Come on. I'll show you the rest of the place."

The bathroom is little more than a closet with an ancient tub and a toilet. My room isn't much bigger, but there is a bed, an old dresser—courtesy of Regan's last roomie who'd moved out—and a nightstand with a lamp on it. There is also a window. I move to the window and glance out. It faces the street and a building across the way. I don't care what the view is as long as it has one.

"So, what do you think? Like I said, your share of the rent is four hundred, due on the first, and that includes all utilities paid. It's not a great place, but it's pretty central to everything, which is good if you don't have a car. Do you?"

I shake my head. "I don't."

"Like I said in the ad, my boyfriend stays here a lot. If that bothers you, this might not be the apartment for you. My last roomie couldn't handle it, so she left." She shrugs her shoulders, unapologetic. "Just putting that out there up front so there's no misunderstandings."

"I don't mind." I don't care if she has three boyfriends.

"There's a laundry room down in the basement if you want to wash clothes." She eyes me curiously. "If you don't mind me asking, where *are* your clothes?"

I don't have any bags with me. "I . . . left them at the farm." I know I must seem weird to her.

"Fresh start, huh?" She pats me on the shoulder and then rubs my arm. "I know how that goes."

I nod, feeling a lump in my throat. Fresh start, indeed.